SHE MADE ME DO IT

BOOKS BY ANNA-LOU WEATHERLEY

DETECTIVE DAN RILEY SERIES
Black Heart
The Couple on Cedar Close
The Stranger's Wife
The Woman Inside
The Night of the Party
The Lie in Our Marriage
The Housewife's Secret
What Kind of Mother

Wicked Wives
Vengeful Wives
Pleasure Island

Chelsea Wives

SHE MADE ME DO IT

ANNA-LOU WEATHERLEY

bookouture

Published by Bookouture in 2026

An imprint of Storyfire Ltd.
Carmelite House
50 Victoria Embankment
London EC4Y 0DZ

www.bookouture.com

The authorised representative in the EEA is Hachette Ireland
8 Castlecourt Centre
Dublin 15 D15 XTP3
Ireland
(email: info@hbgi.ie)

Copyright © Anna-Lou Weatherley, 2026

Anna-Lou Weatherley has asserted her right to be identified as the author of this work.

All rights reserved. No part of this publication may be reproduced, stored in any retrieval system, or transmitted, in any form or by any means, electronic, mechanical, photocopying, recording or otherwise, without the prior written permission of the publishers.

ISBN: 978-1-80550-099-5
eBook ISBN: 978-1-80550-098-8

This book is a work of fiction. Names, characters, businesses, organizations, places and events other than those clearly in the public domain, are either the product of the author's imagination or are used fictitiously. Any resemblance to actual persons, living or dead, events or locales is entirely coincidental.

For MPW

Love grows where trust is laid, and love dies where trust is betrayed.

UNKNOWN

ONE

ERIN

Seven years ago

The sound of sirens screaming in the distance causes me to drop the kitchen knife I'm holding in my shaking hands. *Thank God*, they're on their way.

I glance down at him on the ground. I'm fairly certain he's dead. He's silent and still and a thick pool of dark red blood is collecting next to his body.

Not quite so brave now, huh?

I feel a momentary sense of relief, which makes me feel bad because I think I've just killed someone. The police are surely going to arrest me, and I'm terrified, but no one ever tells you that bravery feels a lot like fear, and so I just have to hold my nerve. They will understand once I explain it was self-defence and that I did it to protect Samantha.

'Step back!' The sudden shrill command of the female officer's voice causes me to spin round.

'Thank God you're here… I—'

'Erin? Erin Santos?'

'Yes.'

'OK, Erin, I want you to stay where you are. Place both your hands behind your head, where I can see them. Now, slowly step towards me...'

I do as I'm told. I've no need to object. We're on the same side.

I glance at the discarded knife on the ground, hear the slamming of car doors and heavy, purposeful footsteps as more officers approach.

Where is Samantha? Moments earlier she'd been right here, next to me, but now I can't see her. She must've gone to get help.

I don't resist or object as they snap the cuffs on me, though they feel tight around my wrists and the cold metal bites into my skin.

'I'm the one who called you,' I say as they pull me towards the patrol car and bundle me into the back seat. I've never been inside a police car before.

It smells funny.

'Is he dead?'

The officer doesn't answer me.

'Erin Santos, I'm arresting you on suspicion of murder. You do not have to say anything. But it may harm your defence if you do not mention when questioned something which you later rely on in court. Anything you do say may be given in evidence. Do you understand?'

'But I didn't mean to kill him...' The words sound shrill as they sputter from my lips. 'He came at her, *at us,* with a knife!'

'OK, Erin, keep calm now,' the officer says, gently but firmly. 'I want you to take a deep breath in, OK? In and out, OK, Erin? *In and out.*'

'At least now she is safe and he can't hurt her anymore.'

The female officer glances at me in the rear-view mirror.

'Hurt who, Erin?'

What does she mean, hurt *who?*

'There's no one else here. Officers have checked and there's no other female present at the scene, it's just you and the victim.'

'My friend!' I shriek. 'She was just here... the blonde woman, Ari's fiancée, she'll need to come to the station too, she can tell you everything! Her name's Samantha Valentine, and if I hadn't done what I did then she'd be dead by now – we both would.'

The officer narrows her eyes at me in the mirror.

'Who's Samantha Valentine, Erin?'

TWO

It's a night of firsts for me as I'm escorted inside the police station. Even during the darkest periods of my life, I've never found myself on the wrong side of the law. I'm just not that type of person. Fundamentally, I'm a people pleaser by nature. You know, the sort who apologises to someone else for stepping on my foot?

I don't kill people.

It's Thursday night and the custody suite is loud and harshly lit. I feel the emotional charge, tangible around me, as I answer the jovial sergeant's questions on autopilot: name, address, date of birth...

'Do you suffer from any mental health problems, Erin? Are you feeling suicidal, taking any medication?'

'No,' I reply honestly to his questions, 'not anymore.'

Next I'm ushered into a small, sterile room where another female proceeds to take my fingerprints and photographs me from various angles.

I don't like my photograph being taken. In some cultures they believe it steals your soul.

After asking me to remove my clothes, she hands me a grey

melange tracksuit to wear. It's ugly and swamps my small frame as I silently dress, but it's warm and at least it isn't covered in Ari's blood. *Ari.* I see a moment of brief recognition, followed by surprise on his face as I had plunged the knife into him. It made me feel nauseous, but what else could I have done?

Another police worker takes samples of my hair. She scrapes the inside of my fingernails and cheeks with a long cotton bud and uses another to swab the congealed blood on my hands. It's sunk into the lines and grooves on my palms, and I can smell it, meaty and metallic on my skin. I'm desperate to wash it off, but I'm reluctant to ask in case it makes me look like I'm trying to tamper with evidence or something. I really don't know how any of this works.

'When can I speak to my friend, Samantha?' I muster up the courage to ask. 'Is she here, at the police station? Is she OK?' But the expressionless woman simply shrugs her shoulders unhelpfully, saying, 'They'll be down to talk to you soon.'

Anguish and despair are stuck to the walls inside the small holding cell as they lock me inside it. It's claustrophobic and airless and my guts begin to churn with anxiety. I'm desperate to pee in the metal toilet, but I spot a camera on the ceiling. I'll never be able to go now.

The blue plastic pillow, similar to the ones you get in hospitals, is flat as a pancake and reeks of the sweat of a thousand men and women before me as I lay my head down on it and pull the thin, scratchy blanket up over me. I think about asking for another – it's chilly and I'm shivering – but I don't want to sound like a diva.

Somehow, incredibly, I must fall asleep because when I wake up I instinctively sense that it's dark outside. A few moments pass before I hear the clunking noise of the iron door as it opens. I hold my breath as a male face I haven't seen before peers around it.

'Erin Santos? They're ready to see you now.'

THREE

The stout, short, dark-haired woman introduces herself as Detective Sergeant Amanda Pritchard. They've sent a female to interview me. This is good. I figure she'll be more inclined to listen to what I have to say than any man might. After all, it's because of one that I find myself here. *Women don't start wars.*

The duty solicitor sitting to my right has just introduced himself as William – 'call me Bill' – Roberts, with a lacklustre handshake. His limp effort does little to instil confidence in me. I'm sure that once they've heard my story, then this horrible mess will all be sorted out. Maybe they'll even let me go?

Bill advises me to reply 'no comment' to the questions the police are about to put to me, advice I have absolutely no intention of following.

DS Pritchard switches the tape recorder on.

'Start by taking me through the events of today if you can, Erin,' she says. 'Whatever you can remember.'

I nod, take a deep breath. I'm genuinely keen to talk.

'I got a Snapchat message from my friend, Sam – Samantha Valentine – around 4 p.m. today, while I was at work. She was begging for my help.'

I realise Snapchat is generally more popular with teenagers than it is with thirty-somethings like myself, and I find the chirrupy notifications beyond irritating, but it's that or nothing if I want to communicate with Sam.

'We have to message in secret, you see, and Snapchat deletes them once you've read them. They're end-to-end encrypted, so there's no trace. Anyway, *that's* how much of a control freak Ari was. He wouldn't even let her speak to her friends and checked her phone constantly. He was *obsessed*.'

I've always taken the ability to talk and breathe at the same time for granted, but now I'm struggling.

'I knew it was all going to come to a head sooner or later.' I fidget in the hard plastic police seat, legs pulsing with adrenalin. 'I could feel something terrible was about to happen, but this time, *this time,* thankfully, I was prepared.'

The detective cocks her head at me.

'Prepared for what? In what way were you prepared, Erin?'

'I'd been expecting it. Ari was a ticking time bomb.'

'What did the message say exactly, this message you received from your friend Samantha?'

Instinctively, I reach for my phone in my pocket to show her, forgetting for a moment that they took it from me – and my clothes – when they booked me in.

'It said something like: "He's got a knife, he's going to kill me! Come quick!" She sounded terrified!' My voice is a little pitchy and I sip some water from the plastic cup on the table.

'Did you try calling her?'

I shake my head.

'Too dangerous – if he saw my name or number come up on her phone it could've set him off even more. Ari doesn't like me, you see.' I hear the contempt in my own voice. I cough a little, try to mask it. 'He thinks I've been trying to talk Sam into leaving him, which I have been, so he's really got it in for me. Ari's a liar and a cheat and a bully who has to control through fear.' I fold my arms across my heaving chest. 'Abusive relationships are the hardest relationships to leave, you know? They say it takes a woman an average of seven attempts to leave an abusive partner. *Seven!*' I shake my head, blow air through my lips. 'If they're not dead already by then!'

Detective Pritchard watches me carefully.

'Did you take anything with you, when you went to help Sam at her apartment? You said you were "prepared"?'

'Take anything with me? Like what?'

'Erin...' Bill the solicitor leans into my ear. I can smell the coffee and cigarettes on his breath and the oily, unpleasant scent of his scalp beneath his thinning hair. 'We can prepare to submit a statement if you like, but at this stage, I'm seriously advising you go "no comment".'

'I've got nothing to hide,' I hiss back. 'I want to tell the truth.'

'You didn't think to contact us?' Detective Pritchard continues. 'Why didn't you dial 999 if you thought your friend, Samantha, was in serious danger?'

I pull back from her into the seat.

'Are you kidding? After what you lot have done, or, should I say, *haven't* done? You've been called to her apartment on numerous occasions now and nothing's ever come of it! No arrests, no charges, not even a warning!' I feel my cheeks flush hot with anger again. I've been here before. I don't mean *actually* here, in the police station, but in a similar situation whereby the authorities have failed to protect someone I love from serious harm. The police are the ones with previous form. *They're the bloody criminals!*

'Samantha could've been killed tonight if I hadn't been there to stop him. He could've killed me too!'

She stares at me blankly before scribbling something down on the notepad in front of her.

'Erin, does the name Bojan Radulovic mean anything to you?'

'No. Why, should it? And can someone, anyone, *please* tell me where Samantha is, or if she's even OK?' Irritation and stress prickles hot on my skin.

Detective Pritchard tucks a piece of her black, bobbed hair behind her ear. She has good hair, thick and shiny, and I randomly wonder what type of shampoo she uses to get such an impressive sheen, or if it's simply down to good genes.

'Bojan Radulovic is the name of the man you killed, Erin, the man you stabbed to death outside of Pengally Court at around 6.05 p.m. this evening. This man here.' She slides a piece of paper towards me, taps a short, neat fingernail on it. 'Do you want to tell us what happened, Erin?'

Who?

I look down at what appears to be Ari's passport picture and wait to feel something, but in truth, I don't feel much at all save for relief. I'm *glad* he's dead, though I'm wise enough to keep this thought to myself.

'No, that's Ari,' I say. 'It's Ari Hussain, Sam's boyfriend. And I didn't mean to kill him. I never set out to. It was self-defence, like I've told you.'

She taps the picture again.

'Can you read the name for me there, Erin, the name that's printed on the passport, next to the photo?'

I lean in for a closer look.

'Yes, it says...'

Wait! What?

I glance up at her, confused.

'Is this some kind of trick?'

'His name is Bojan Radulovic, Erin.' She repeats herself. 'A thirty-three-year-old *single* man, originally from Montenegro. He'd been living alone in apartment 22a at Pengally Court, the address you gave us when you called dispatch, for a little over eighteen months. He worked for an exclusive chauffeur business in West London as a driver after emigrating to the UK in the early 2000s.'

'No!' I say, shaking my head. 'You've got it wrong.'

I have no idea what or who she's talking about.

Clearly, there's been a terrible mistake.

FOUR

'*This* man is Ari Hussain.'

It's my turn to tap the face on the photo as I look directly at Detective Pritchard. She's got it wrong, but that's no real surprise judging by past experience.

'He's been in a relationship with my friend, Samantha Valentine, for the past year or so,' I explain. 'He works in the city, for some big tech company. I can't remember the name of it now, but she did tell me. Anyway, Sam will tell you herself! Where is she?'

Panic spikes in my voice. I don't think I much like where the detective is going with this – it sounds like she doesn't believe what I'm telling her. 'She can corroborate everything I say. This man, this Bojan whatever his name is... it must be a false name!'

I'm shrieking now though, and Bill the solicitor is staring at me, unblinking – both of them are.

'How many times have you met Bojan Radulovic, Erin?'

'Never! I've never met anyone by that name! The man in this picture is Ari Hussain. I'm telling you!' Only I'm fast getting the unsettling feeling that she *really* actually *doesn't* believe me, and it's beginning to make me feel pretty unsafe.

'Am I going to go to prison for this?' I tuck my chin into my chest, not wanting to even entertain such a terrifying thought. 'For tackling a crazy abuser with a knife who was about to stab my best friend, *stab me* to death?' I take in a deep lungful of the stale air around me. My stress levels are on red. This isn't going how I thought it would. She's treating me like a criminal when in fact I'm more of a hero than anything. I protected my friend. I've done her job for her.

'OK, Erin.' Detective Pritchard's tone softens a fraction. 'I'll rephrase the question. How many times have you met Ari Hussain?'

'Never,' I repeat, 'well, not actually in person, not until today.' Suddenly, I realise how this sounds. 'But I know exactly who he is,' I quickly add. 'He's Sam's boyfriend, well, fiancé, actually. I've seen them together...'

Now I think of it though, that's not entirely true either. I've never actually seen them together *in person*. But I've seen photos, I've watched her go up into the apartment they shared many times. *And I'd seen the bruises.*

'We can't find anyone by the name Samantha Valentine registered to that address, Erin.' Detective Pritchard's tone is direct. 'The only person registered to 22a Pengally Court is Bojan Radulovic, the man you admit to killing. Samantha Valentine doesn't live at that address and there's no record of her ever having done so.'

'That's incorrect.'

I can't stop shaking my head. Seriously, I'm beginning to think that the police must've all graduated from the same school for idiots. They can't seem to get anything right. 'That's *definitely* her address.' But panic is beginning to cut through my confusion and disbelief.

Detective Pritchard pauses again.

'When did you meet Samantha Valentine, Erin?'

'Sixteen weeks ago, almost to the day.'

'That's very specific.' Her eyebrows gently rise. 'So she's a relatively new friend, this Samantha?'

'I suppose so, but we feel as if we've known each other forever.' I look into her eyes; they're small and brown and a bit piggy, if I'm honest. 'We're kindred spirits, soul sisters. Honestly, we were destined to become friends.'

'I see. How did you meet her?'

'At a job interview, for Austin Marz Productions, the production company in town where I work as a receptionist. Or did.'

I feel a jab of despair in my ribs. I liked my job, and generally I got on well with my boss. They were definitely going to sack me now though.

'We've checked your phone, Erin. But we can't seem to find evidence of any communication between yourself and anyone named Samantha Valentine on it. There's no one by that name in any of your contact lists either, no messages, no record of any calls between you, nothing on your social media. Can you explain that?'

I feel slightly sick in my stomach, like suddenly I'm free-falling out of a plane without a parachute and plunging to earth at 300 miles an hour. *That can't be possible.* I take a breath, try to compose myself. I have nothing to fear if I just tell the truth, right?

'Look, I have no idea who this Bojan Ludovic is. Ari must've been using a fake identity or something, unless that's his actual name and he's been lying to Samantha about who he *really* is.'

'Was,' Detective Pritchard corrects me, 'who he *was*. And it's Radulovic,' she says, 'Bojan Radulovic. We recovered his passport from the possessions we found inside his apartment, along with some other formal means of identification.' She leans in a little closer across the table towards me, starts shaking her head slowly. 'The man you killed, Erin, was not Ari Hussain. His name is Bojan Radulovic.'

I wish she'd stop saying his name.

'You've got this *so* wrong. Samantha will identify him! Is that where she is now, down at the morgue, identifying his body?' I glance at Detective Pritchard expectantly, my nerves jangling like wind chimes in a hurricane. The look she's giving me suggests that she knows something I don't.

'Erin, police officers conducted an area search; they've made door-to-door enquiries and spoken to Bojan's neighbours. Every one of them has confirmed who Mr Radulovic was, and that he lived alone, in his apartment, by himself. No one has ever seen him with a woman – any woman, in fact – who matches the description you've given us of your friend, Samantha.' She reads from her notes, 'Slim build, long blonde hair, green eyes, around five feet four. You described her to one officer as,' she pauses, '*unforgettable...*'

My brow has been locked in confusion for so long that it's started to ache.

'The neighbours definitely knew what was going on because they'd called the police on a few occasions, when they heard her screams through the walls.' I glance at her, then back at Bill the solicitor. 'Not that the police ever *did* anything.'

Detective Pritchard links her fingers together on the table.

'Is that what Samantha told you, Erin? Because we have no record of ever being called to any domestic incident at that address. In fact,' she says, 'we have no record of ever being called to that address at all.'

I open my mouth to speak, but a series of stunned exhalations comes out instead. There's been some kind of bizarre, inexplicable mistake. *Mistakes plural.* I turn, confused, to Bill again and he mouths the words 'no comment' with an ominous shake of his head.

'But you *must* have it on record? She told me! Why are you saying all of this?'

I rub my temples again in sheer frustration and outrage. Is it even possible for the police to be this inept? I'm going to make an official complaint once this is over. They're a disgrace.

'Erin, you were admitted to Ashdean Psychiatric Hospital in March of 2024 after you were found acting erratically in a public place. Is that correct?'

'I'd like to speak to my client in private,' Bill the solicitor cuts in.

'No need.' I turn sharply to him. 'Yes, I was.' I raise my chin. 'Only I don't know what that has to do with any of this.' I'm affronted she's even brought it up.

'You were detained by the Mental Health Act 1983 and placed in the care of Ashdean hospital in Leeds where you were treated for severe depression, including acute paranoia, delusions and drug-induced psychosis. The notes we have obtained state that you were considered a danger to yourself, and potentially to the public, and that's why you were detained under Section 136 and subsequently held against your will.'

I shake my head in disbelief, though I'm clinging on to the idea that Detective Pritchard is still willing to hear me out and all of this will be easily resolved.

'I wasn't kept at Ashdean against my will!' I protest. She's got her facts wrong! 'I was there perfectly willingly of my own volition!' My incredulity is charting. 'Hang on, so you think because I suffered a mental health episode in the past then that means I must be lying now? Isn't that discrimination?' My jaw swings open as I look at Bill. 'They can't be serious, can they? This is *ridiculous*...'

His eyes are trained on me.

'Please, Erin, you need to think about taking my advice.'

But it's too late for that. I'm incensed that the police should bring up my historical mental health blip like I'm some kind of nutcase not to be trusted. What are they trying to say?

'A neighbour of Mr Radulovic told us that he had mentioned to him that he was being stalked by someone, a female he'd allegedly had a recent sexual encounter with. He didn't have a name, or a description to give us, only what Mr Radulovic had told him in passing. Do you have any idea who he may have been referring to?'

'No. No idea,' I answer abruptly. 'Sam never mentioned anything about any stalker... Though it wouldn't surprise me if he'd been cheating on her. He was forever accusing *her* of cheating on *him*. Typical narcissistic mind-games. Always accusing the other person of the exact behaviour they're guilty of themselves!'

'You said Mr Radulovic came at you with a knife outside Pengally Court?'

'Yes!' I want to jump up out of my seat. 'No! Not Radulovic... You're trying to put words in my mouth!' This is starting to feel like an attack. 'It was *Ari*, Ari Hussain. How many times have I got to explain it? He charged at me, at me and Sam, with it in his hand, so instinctively I took the knife from her, the one she had taken from the kitchen and... what was I supposed to do? It was kill or be killed!' Anger suddenly rises up into my chest. *What is this bullshit?*

'There was no knife, Erin.' Detective Pritchard looks directly at me. 'Mr Radulovic was not armed.' She's shaking her head again. 'The only knife we found at the scene was the knife you used to fatally stab him with. We found no other weapon on his person, or at the crime scene. Mr Radulovic was holding his phone in his right hand when he died, a silver Samsung. Do you think you could've been mistaken about the knife?'

'Mistaken? About someone coming at me with a knife?' I actually can't comprehend what I'm hearing, I really can't! I try and replay the moment that Ari came at me in my head. I'm sure he had a knife because Sam screamed at me, *He's got a knife, Erin! He's got a knife!* But – *oh my God* – now that I'm thinking about it, *did* I actually see it? I'm pretty sure I saw *something* in his hand, something shiny... I must've done, but it all happened so fast.

'Look, why aren't you speaking to Sam? She can resolve all of this. Where the hell is she?'

'There's no record of her existence, Erin.' Detective Pritchard's tone drops down to an ominous octave as she fixes me with a hard stare. 'No current or previous addresses for her, nothing from the electoral register.' She's shaking her head again. 'We can't find a birth certificate for her, an NI number, any medical records, or employment history... and there's nothing on social media, not one photo of her anywhere.' She leans in towards me once more. 'We can find *nothing* to prove that this Samantha Valentine friend of yours is a real, living person, Erin.'

I'm sweating beads of pure terror now, the itchy grey tracksuit top is sticking to me like fire. I sip some more water but my hands are shaking so much that I spill some of it onto my bottoms, watch as it seeps into the cheap, nasty grey fabric. 'No-no-no. This *can't* be right... I *know* she exists! You need to find her! She'll tell you who Ari is and what he's been doing to her. She'll tell you exactly what happened and that I acted purely in self-defence! You *have* to speak to Samantha Valentine. She'll explain everything.'

FIVE

DAN

Present day

I can smell it in the air, fresh, like an abattoir, the moment I walk through the front door – blood.

My heart plummets. I'm not especially superstitious, but it's as if the cosmos somehow knows whenever I've got a night off. It's when all the killers seem to come out to play.

'Fatality, gov. Single stab wound to the chest, the body's in the kitchen.'

DS Lucy Davis, my revered number two and trusted 'work wife', had moments earlier greeted me outside the apartment complex on Stockwell Gardens.

She was wearing full PPE and an apologetic look. I was on my way home, you see, looking forward to spending some time with my *actual* wife, and our three kids – not to mention enjoying the pad thai dinner that was waiting for me – when the call came through, forcing me to do a quick U-turn.

'Looks like a domestic, gov. Victim is a Mr Milo Harrison, thirty-four, a banker in the city, apparently,' Davis informs me as I step into a protective suit. 'He was pronounced dead at the scene by paramedics. Dr Leyton is on her way.'

This cheers me up a bit at least. I've got a soft spot for my favourite pathologist, Victoria Leyton, even if she is a bit too keen on a cadaver for my taste.

'Who called it in?'

'Tilly Ward, a friend of the victim's partner, placed the 999 call at 6.31 p.m., gov. Local woman, thirty-six years old. She claims that the victim came at her and her friend with a knife, and that she stabbed him in self-defence. She requested police assistance and an ambulance.'

'Who's the friend?'

'Someone called Samantha Valentine, the deceased's girlfriend apparently, also living at the address according to Ward.'

'And where's Tilly Ward now?'

'Inside the apartment, gov. She's pretty traumatised.'

'I would imagine so if she's just stabbed someone to death.'

'She's saying that she got a message from this friend, Samantha Valentine, earlier today around 5 p.m., asking her to come to the apartment because the deceased had become violent and was threatening her with a knife. Tilly says she left work immediately – she's a sales assistant at a local bookstore – and drove over to the apartment. She claims she walked straight into a bad situation and that while the three of them were in the kitchen, Milo Harrison came at them with a kitchen knife. She then says she picked up a knife, or Samantha gave her a knife, she can't remember exactly, and she defended herself, stabbing him once in the chest.'

'What about Milo Harrison? Does he have any previous, any DV on record?'

She shakes her head.

'He's clean as a whistle, boss – nothing.'

'And where's the friend now, this Samantha Valentine, can she corroborate all of this?'

If she can then we might be looking at a Section 76 – lawful use of force used in an act of self-defence – and I might be home in time for microwave pad thai after all.

'Yeah, well, that's just it, gov, we can't find her.'

'Can't *find* her?'

'Apparently, she wasn't at the scene when the first attending officers arrived. She may've got scared and run off, gone to a friend's? We're trying to trace her now, gov. Tilly says she was on foot, so she can't have gone far.'

'Do we have a phone number for this Samantha?' I glance up at the apartment complex. It's a posh building, newly built with a glass façade, the kind that looks more like a swanky hotel. It's no doubt got a communal gym and swimming pool, but it stands out like a clown at a funeral against the backdrop of the other poor-relation high rises that surround it.

'If we haven't, get one. And let's start door-to-door and make sure the whole area is sealed off. No one else in or out – and Davis,' I turn to her, 'let's find this missing Samantha Valentine quickly, yes? Clearly, she's a vital witness.'

I zip my suit and glove-up as I make my way through the short hallway into the kitchen where the body is, noting a small pair of women's boots neatly placed by the front door. SOCO has arrived now. I hear the pops of the cameras and the rustle of their protective green suits as they invade the property like a swarm of giant locusts. Like me, any of them could have dinner going cold for them at home tonight, but this is the job; it's what we all signed up for.

A pair of uniformed officers step aside the body as I enter the sparse-looking kitchen. It's a modern room – lots of white and exposed brick – and there's not much in the way of furnishings. The walls are almost bare – there's a large mirror on one and a clock on the other, opposite – and the shiny chrome appliances appear almost untouched, like the occupant rarely uses them. I think my wife refers to this type of aesthetic as 'minimalistic, industrial chic', something I imagine, as a man with three kids, only exists in glossy magazines and on social media. There's no obvious signs of any altercation having taken place; there's nothing smashed or broken, nothing upended.

'Sir.'

I take in a long, deep breath as I brace myself to look at the body. The day I stop doing this little ritual is the day I should give the job up. It never gets any easier.

He's lying on his back, his arms lightly outstretched either side of his body, and he's bare-chested. There's a large, dark, teardrop-shaped puncture wound above his heart. You can see it's deep – it's practically a hole – and the blood is still glistening fresh and oozing from it.

The rest of him looks untouched at a cursory glance though; no clear injuries, no bruising or defensive wounds. I crouch down with a sigh beside him and whisper his name aloud.

'Milo... Milo Harrison...'

His eyes are open, fixed in a look of surprised confusion, like he wasn't expecting what happened to him to have happened at all. A chill tickles my spine. It's never pleasant viewing a dead body, not least one with their eyes wide open, grimacing in a death mask. Like I say, I'm not particularly superstitious, but it has been said that the dead capture their final moment in their eyes like a snapshot, and that if you look deep enough into them, you can see it. The only thing I see, however, when I fix mine upon his, is my own convex reflection from the fancy hanging light above.

I think it's a fair observation to note that Milo Harrison was a good-looking guy. He's got that dark five o'clock shadow thing going on, and judging by his defined torso, he wasn't shy around a gym either. I don't know his story yet. Is he a domestic abuser who got a taste of his own medicine? I stare at the deep black hole in his chest, at the blood that is only now just beginning to coagulate. It doesn't look like a frenzied attack. There's only one stab wound, albeit a fatal one. Tilly Ward's initial account could be plausible. She hasn't fled the scene, and she called for help promptly, though a post-mortem will give us more insight.

I let out a long breath.

Whatever has happened here reeks of tragedy already. Every domestic always does. Statistically though, the body I'm staring at would be more likely to be Milly than Milo.

'Ah! The famous DCI Riley!' Vic Leyton appears behind me. She's holding up a copy of a newspaper in her hand. I groan. Archer – Superintendent Gwen Archer – my boss, had recently talked me into doing an in-depth profile piece on 'a week in the life of a homicide detective in the capital' for the *Standard Life* newspaper, and it was published this week. I was a reluctant interviewee – I'm much more comfortable asking questions than I am answering them – but I knew by Archer's tone that I wasn't going to get out of it.

'It'll be good for PR, Dan,' she'd said. 'And you're the best looking out of a bad bunch.'

Flattery got her everywhere. And it got my mugshot plastered all over social media.

'Great photo, Dan.' Vic arches an eyebrow from beneath her PPE. 'You look...' she pauses, thoughtfully, '... *distinguished!*'

'I'll take that.' I smile at her, try to disguise my discomfort about it all.

As always, it's a pleasure to see Dr Victoria Leyton, and yet every time I do, we're united by the worst kind of circumstance, which makes it a strange and unique relationship in that respect.

She casts her eyes at the body on the kitchen floor with a sigh of her own.

'A domestic?'

'Looks that way,' I say, adding the caveat, 'on the surface at least.'

'Well, if it is, then I hope he deserved it.'

I look down at Mr Harrison, at his young, fit and healthy-looking body surrounded by a large dark red pool of his own blood, and wonder if anyone really does.

'Well, it looks as if he was standing when he was struck by the knife. I can tell by the position of the body, how he's fallen.' She crouches down next to him on the kitchen floor, and I watch with a certain awe as her eyes scan him in detail. After a moment she looks up at me.

'I suspect the assailant is left-handed, or that they held the weapon in their left hand when they struck the blow.'

'How can you tell?'

'You see the direction of the dots of blood, how the splatter appears to get bigger at the top of the wound?'

I crouch down next to her again and she points to the hole in his chest.

'Yes,' I say. 'I think so.'

'Well, for each hand, the starting point of entry wound is different.'

'Is that so?'

Every day is a school day with Vic. I've learned more about the human body from her than I ever did in any biology lesson. If she'd been one of the teachers at my school, I would definitely have had a crush on her.

'Right-handed wounds start right and end left, but in this handsome chap's case, it's the reverse, which suggests the assailant held the weapon in their left hand. It's not conclusive, of course, but in my experience...'

Davis appears in the doorway.

'Lucy...'

'Yeah, well, it's all a bit strange, boss, but it appears that the friend and girlfriend, this Samantha Valentine, isn't officially registered at this address.'

'OK. So where is she registered?'

'That's just it, gov, it seems she isn't registered *anywhere*. The neighbours are saying that Milo Harrison lived here alone and that they have never seen him with a girlfriend, or anyone who fits the description that Tilly gave us.' She raises an eyebrow.

'We're running checks now and a number of Samantha Valentines come up in the UK – but no one who matches the description, demographic or geographic – no one local.' She shrugs. 'And just take a look around the apartment, gov, there's no trace of her, of any female at all; no possessions, no toiletries, clothes, photos – nothing to suggest a woman lives here. I dunno, gov, what do you reckon? You think it could be a ruse of some sort?'

As if on cue, I hear the sound of a distressed female's cries coming from the next room.

'Well, Davis. Let's find out, shall we?'

SIX
DAN

'Have you found her yet?' She jumps up from the sofa the second I enter the living room. 'Have you found Samantha?'

She has blood on her, dark splashes of the stuff splattered all over her baggy cardigan and jeans.

'Tilly Ward? I'm DCI Dan Riley...'

'*Please—*' Her fingernails dig into my flesh as she grips my arm. 'You *have* to help me! You have to help us!'

Her voice is urgent and anguished, but I detect something else, something in the tone, or lack of, perhaps?

'OK, it's OK, Tilly.' I approach her gingerly. She looks out of her skin with distress. 'Let's sit down, shall we?'

Hyperventilating, she grips me like a frightened child as I help lower her, shaking, down onto the sofa. I notice a couple of empty, discarded chocolate bar wrappers on the seat, incongruous to the rest of the pristine apartment.

The TV is on and it's playing the 70s musical *Grease*, though the sound is muted. My eyes are drawn to it for a brief moment as John Travolta effortlessly leaps from the bonnet of a 1949 Ford De Luxe, wearing tight black trousers with a slicked-back quiff, before I switch it off. *Show-off*.

Diminutive and waifish, Tilly Ward appears more like an adolescent teenager than a grown woman; even the thick black-framed glasses she's wearing seem a little oversized for her doll-like face.

'Are you OK, Tilly? Have you been checked over?' I glance at the two uniformed officers standing to the left of the room and they both nod. 'You're not hurt or injured in any way?'

She looks down at herself, at her vibrating, bloodstained hands, and shakes her head.

'OK, take a deep breath… in and out… *innnn* and *ouuuuut*, that's it.'

I demonstrate with her, try to help her regulate her breathing.

'Do you want to tell me what's happened here today, Tilly?' I keep my tone calm and reassuring.

'Is he dead?' she sputters, wiping mucus from her nose and mouth with the back of her cardigan sleeve. 'I've killed him, haven't I?' She drops her head into her lap, causing her mouse-brown hair to sweep in front of her face like a curtain. That's when I glimpse it, behind her left ear, a hearing aid.

My stomach tightens.

'Are you registered deaf, or hard of hearing, Tilly?' It makes sense now, the slight, flat monotone in her voice.

Some months ago, Jude, my now one-year-old son, was confirmed deaf. The news hit me and my wife, Fiona, hard. After all, it's not something you would wish for your child, is it? I suppose we're still struggling to come to terms with it, but the difference between hope and despair is a different way of telling a story with the same facts, and so we're learning sign language in case the cochlear implant device we're hoping he'll eventually be fitted with doesn't work for him. Learning to sign is harder than I'd imagined it would be, though the wife seems to have taken to it like the proverbial duck to water, and Jude's protective big sister, our three-year-old daughter, Juno, or 'Pip' as I call her, has almost mastered the basics already.

'Yes, I'm hard of hearing.'

I glance down at her bare feet and feel a rush of protection towards her.

'Where's Samantha? Is she OK?' She grips my arm again. 'Please tell me she's OK.'

'We don't know yet, Tilly. We're hoping you might be able to help us with that. You told my colleague that Samantha lives here, at this address...'

'Yes,' she nods. 'They live here together, her and Milo. He's attacked her before, you know, this isn't the first time... but I never thought it would come to this! I never thought... *Oh God...*' She starts to rock back and forth on the sofa, hugging herself. 'He came at me... I was in fear for my life... it all happened so quickly...'

'OK... it's OK.' I touch her forearm gently. It's hard to imagine someone of her stature attacking anyone. Overall, her demeanour smacks of a victim's, though I know that at this stage keeping an open mind is essential.

'Have you any idea where Samantha might be now? Could she have gone to a friend's house perhaps, or a family member?'

'She doesn't have any family, or none that I know of anyway. I'm her best friend, her *only* friend. Milo, he didn't like her having friends, you see. He was trying to isolate her. He was so controlling...'

'Does Samantha have a job?'

She shakes her head.

'She wanted to work, but he wouldn't let her. He wouldn't let her do *anything*. She was practically a prisoner in her own home.'

She looks up at me then, and I notice that beneath the large black frames, her eyes are a bright emerald green.

'I got a message from her earlier today, on Snapchat. She

said he'd really flipped out this time and that he was going to kill her!'

'Why didn't you call the police, Tilly? That would've been the sensible thing to do, wouldn't it?' I keep my voice soft, mindful not to sound like I'm chiding her. I can tell she's teetering dangerously on the edge as it is and I don't want to push her over it.

'I know!' she wails. 'But she begged me not to! She just wanted me to come and get her, take her away somewhere safe… I know I should've called you, but she said it would only make it worse for her. She wouldn't listen… and… and now look! Oh my God, I've killed him! I'll go to prison!'

She starts bawling again, stringy mucus streaming from her nostrils and mouth as she sobs. I take a pack of tissues from my inside jacket pocket and pass them to her.

'I've always got some to hand.' I smile, trying to bring the emotionally charged atmosphere down a notch. 'I'm a dad of three.'

'I can tell.' She manages a thin smile in return as she wipes the snot bubble from her nose.

'Listen, we're going to get you down to the station soon, Tilly, get you cleaned up and checked over by a doctor, take some samples for forensic purposes, and then we can talk all of this through properly.'

I squeeze her arm in reassurance.

'The officer here will need to caution you, OK?'

She gives me a terrified nod without looking up.

'Try not to worry.' I realise the ridiculousness of this statement given the gravity of the situation, but it's the best I can do in the circumstances.

'Are you going to cuff me?'

My stomach lurches again.

'It's standard practice, Tilly, given the nature of the incident, but it'll be OK, OK?' She grips onto my arm once more.

'Will you be there, at the station? Will you come with me?'

'One of the officers here will be with you the whole time, OK? You need anything, then you speak to one of them, anything at all.'

She drops her eyes back down into her lap. She's shivering, and I suspect she's going into shock. I need to get a grip on exactly what's taken place here, but realise she's in no fit state to give a coherent statement at this point.

'Tilly, I need to ask you, could your friend Samantha be using a different name for any reason?'

'A different name?' Her brow crinkles with confusion. 'No, I don't think so... Why?'

'Well, we've run some checks on her and that name doesn't come up as being registered to this address.'

She looks at me blankly.

'I don't understand.'

'Do you have a phone number for Samantha? A photo of her? We'll need to take your phone, Tilly.'

'Of course.' She retrieves it from the pocket of her cardigan and hands it to me.

DS Davis is once again standing, pensive, in the doorway, and I momentarily leave Tilly's side and go to her, half closing the door behind me.

'What you got, Lucy?'

She's shaking her head in a slow motion that instantly unsettles me.

'This really doesn't look right, boss. Reports are coming in from door-to-door. As it stands, it seems Milo Harrison lived alone. No one has seen him with a woman, any woman, since he's lived here. And the guy next door claims to have heard a commotion around the time of the incident today. He says he heard raised voices, a male and female shouting.'

'One male voice, one female?'

'So he says,' she nods. 'There's something odd about this set-up, gov. Take a look around you. There's nothing to suggest anyone else but Milo Harrison lives here. Do you think she's lying? I mean, she sounds genuine enough, but...'

I pause.

'Let's get her down the station, Davis. Get her looked over by medics. We'll need a psychiatric assessment as well, make sure she's fit for interview.'

'Yes, gov.'

'And just so you're aware, Lucy, she's hard of hearing – she's wearing a hearing aid.'

'Oh.' Her voice drops in tandem with her expression. It's a delicate subject.

'I want her carefully looked after, everything by the book, OK?'

'Yes, boss, of course.'

I drag my hands down my face.

Something tells me I won't be getting to sample that pad thai this side of midnight after all. I suppose it's just as well. Like our witness, it seems my appetite has completely vanished.

SEVEN

ERIN

Eight weeks ago

My name is Erin Santos. And here are a few honest, random and hopefully fun facts about me!

- I'm forty years old, 5 feet 4 inches tall and my weight fluctuates somewhere between 110 and 120 lbs.
- I was born in York, in the north of England, where I subsequently spent most of my youth, and where, to my knowledge, I still hold the record for winning the hundred metres hurdle race five years in succession while attending St Swythen's Comprehensive School.
- My hair is black and my eyes – inherited from my Venezuelan father – are a striking jade green in colour, and have even been remarked upon by total strangers!
- I have arthritis in my left ring finger, brought upon by a historic fracture that I sustained during a

netball accident as a teenager. I think it's a sign I should never marry.
- I am terrible at crosswords yet proficient at Scrabble – during my seven years here at Larksmere Hospital I have never been defeated.
- I am a convicted killer who was coerced into stabbing a man to death by a sick psychopathic con artist who pretended to be my friend.

OK, so I don't include the last line on this frankly ridiculous list, though I would've liked to just to see the look on Dr Wainwright's face. Plus it is also a fact, though perhaps not so much of a 'fun' one.

Dr Wainwright thinks that this list could act as 'useful conversation starters' as I embark upon the process of integrating myself back into society, if they decide I am no longer a danger to it, that is. *And they say I'm the mad one.*

'So, Erin,' Dr Wainwright addresses me with his usual condescending sageness. 'We all know why we're here today, don't we? We've been working towards this for some time now, since you were transferred to the low security section of Larksmere last year.'

I nod with a polite smile and remember to maintain eye contact. I need to demonstrate my sincerity today as well as verbalise it. I need him – and the rest of the tribunal – to believe it, to *believe me,* which is something that hasn't happened in over six years of my life, and is ostensibly the reason why I am still here, stuck in Dante's Ninth Circle of Hell. That and a woman they tell me isn't, and never was, real anyway.

'Today is really more about ticking the right boxes, Erin, crossing the i's and dotting the t's,' Nurse Ledbury says, instantly flushing red as she realises her verbal slip-up. I've noticed how she often appears a little flustered in Dr Wainwright's company and gets her words all in a muddle. I reckon she's got the hots for him. Maybe she's really a secret slut underneath all those roll-neck sweaters and sensible shoes.

Nurse Ledbury is my favourite of all the nurses at Larksmere Hospital, and I don't even like her all that much. I imagine she probably has some amusing sticker on the inside of her locker that says something like, *You don't have to be mad to work here, but it helps!* It sounded promising though, when she said, 'crossing the i's and dotting the t's'. They've allowed me out on day release for five weeks running now without incident. If they approve my final release, then I could be out of here in a matter of days. And that really would be something to celebrate.

'What do you think of now, Erin, when I say the name Samantha Valentine to you?' Dr Wainwright cocks his head at me, like a dog waiting for a treat. 'How does it make you *feel*?'

I can't tell him the truth of course. That really *would* be madness. I can't tell him that I despise that name with the burning white-hot fire of ten thousand suns, or that it triggers such acute rage and injustice at the years – at the life and future – I have been robbed of that I want to scream until my larynx collapses. I can't tell him that it is *her* who should've been here instead of me, slowly decaying, year by year, day by day, hour by hour, or that *she* is really the dangerous one. They won't believe me. No one ever has. In my darkest moments, I have even struggled to believe myself.

'It makes me feel ashamed,' I reply, mimicking his sageness back at him. 'Remorseful, but hopeful too, I suppose.'

'Hopeful?' He raises a bushy ginger eyebrow. Dr Wainwright has the wildest eyebrows I've ever seen, thick and wiry with rogue grey hairs sticking out at random.

'For the future, a future in which I can, and intend to, repay my debt to society and become part of humanity again.' *Tick those boxes*.

'Do you still believe that Samantha Valentine exists, or that she ever did?' Dr Jameson, a cold woman with a pinched face that she deserves, looks up at me from behind the crescent-shaped desk. I'd anticipated the question of course – not least from her – and had rehearsed my answer, parrot fashion, until the words no longer stuck in my throat.

'During my time here in Larksmere, in this hospital, throughout the years of different treatments and multiple therapies, the one-to-one sessions and group discussions I've engaged in and with, I have gradually come to realise that I was quite ill at the time I committed my crime.'

Dr Wainwright looks at me almost like a proud father. Sally the Social Worker is nodding her head in agreement, and Nurse Ledbury is looking at me in that way she always does, like I am a pitiful lost cause she feels begrudgingly obliged to be kind to lest I may decide to stab *her* to death.

Old Face-Ache Jameson doesn't even bother to look up. Miserable cow.

'I understand now that it was the illness,' I press on. 'Although for a long time I struggled to accept that there was a possibility that she never really existed, and that she was just a symptom of my psychosis. But with all the help and support I've received here, from you, from everyone at Larksmere, I now understand and have come to terms with this truth.'

My captors watch me silently, intensely. It feels good to have an audience hanging on my every word for a moment, even if it is only because I'm saying what they want to hear.

'Why now?' Jameson pipes up again. 'You have always been so consistent and *in*sistent in your belief that she was a real person. Throughout most of your sentence you have never deviated from this narrative. So what's different, Erin?'

The clock on the wall of the sterile office ticks loudly and is a little off per second. It's distracting.

'For a long time I hid behind self-denial because it was too painful to face up to the realisation that I had committed, or was even capable of committing, such a heinous crime. Creating a fictitious character enabled me to minimise my actions to myself and stay stuck in that denial.' I scan their faces to check if they are buying it. I can't call it.

'The chaplain has helped me enormously in arriving at this point,' I add, as though it were an afterthought to mention it. I'm mindful that if I tell them outright that 'I have found God', then it might sound contrived, like a cynical and tactical move on my part to bolster my chances of securing my liberty, which is exactly what it is.

'I pray every day now and ask God for his forgiveness, his guidance and help in coming to terms with my crime, and understanding the illness that led me to commit it. "If we confess our sins, he is faithful and just and will forgive us our sins and purify us from all unrighteousness." 1 John 1:9,' I add.

'So it is God who has helped you to finally accept the truth?' Dr Wainwright sounds pleased. He is, after all, a good Christian man himself. I know this because he wears a small silver crucifix around his neck and sometimes quotes the psalms, though not fanatically. Despite our weekly therapy sessions together throughout the past six years, I actually know very little about Dr Wainwright, and yet he knows everything about me – everything except the truth anyway.

'Very much so,' I agree enthusiastically. 'Without my Bible studies and sessions with the chaplain, I think it would've taken me longer to arrive at the place I find myself at today, or even arrived at all.'

'And where is this place that you find yourself at today?' Jameson chimes in again, her pen poised as she scribbles something down onto a notepad in front of her. She looks a bit bored.

'"A false witness will not go unpunished, and whoever pours out lies will perish." Proverbs 19:9. And so, put simply, I am no longer prepared to lie anymore, not to others or myself, and especially not to God.'

Jameson is right though. Refusing to confess that Samantha

Valentine was – is – a creation of my own damaged mind had, for the most part of my sentence, never been an option. Accepting it would've meant succumbing to the madness they have spent years trying to gaslight me into believing I am suffering from. And while I am undeniably a killer by default, I still have principles and my integrity. *Thou shalt not lie.*

But I *have* to get out of here, and the only conceivable way to do this is by lying about the truth. How's *that* for a twisted irony?

I have never once denied my crime, or the fact that I committed it. When I was arrested at the scene, I went without incident and co-operated with the police as fully and best I could. I gave them a full and frank confession. *I told them the truth.* Only they didn't believe me. They decided I was delusional the moment they ran a background medical check on me and discovered I'd spent a stint in a psychiatric ward. From thereon in they stuck to their narrative and didn't bother investigating my account in any real detail. On the surface it seemed as though Samantha Valentine was simply a manifestation of my psychosis – they could find no trace of her anywhere in existence – despite my endless protestations to the contrary. Lazy, discriminatory policing at its finest, it suited them to write me off as a just another headcase who needed taking off the streets.

If only they had dug deeper, or even bothered to dig at all – but they had their story that wrapped everything up nicely and nothing I said or did could stop them from sticking to it. I suppose, to give the police their due if I must, it really was, *is*, a crazy story, the kind of story a crazy person would tell. Only that doesn't make it untrue, and neither does it make me mad. The truth is often stranger than fiction, and in my case, stranger still.

I had wanted to plead not guilty to the charge of second-degree murder and go before a judge and jury to give them my side of events, tell the truth of what had *really* transpired. But my brief – who I suspected didn't believe me either – had strongly advised against it.

'If you lose – and you will lose, Erin – you'll go to prison, possibly for the rest of your life. But if you plead guilty to the lesser charge of manslaughter on the grounds of diminished responsibility, then I'm hopeful the judge will be lenient and send you to a psychiatric hospital.'

'But I don't need to go to a psychiatric hospital,' I said. 'I'm not mad, and I'm not lying!'

I learned then, however, that sometimes the facts have little to do with the truth, or maybe it's the other way round. Either way, it meant I was facing a potential lifetime behind bars or the supposedly cushier option of a secure mental asylum. And so I chose what I was led to believe to be the lesser of two evils, which now, with the benefit of hindsight, was simply yet another example of me putting my faith and trust in the wrong people. I really *must* stop doing that.

After I was sent to Larksmere Hospital, I knew that either one of two things was probably going to kill me: the guilt that tormented me daily for what I had done, or the hatred for the person who had coerced and tricked me into doing it.

I should say at this point that killers aren't born, *they're made*, and I'm really not a violent person by nature. I'm a pacifist who has always detested aggression of any kind. Ironically, this is partially the reason why she was so easily able to manipulate me like she did. Though *why* she did remains the biggest mystery still. Did she choose her victims at random? Were Bojan and I singled out for a reason? If so, what? The police never even followed up on the neighbour's statement about a potential stalker; those bozos never followed up on *anything*.

The judge in my case was sympathetic, citing my childhood trauma as a mitigating factor that 'No doubt would've significantly impacted upon your mental health into adulthood', and gave me six years for manslaughter on the grounds of diminished responsibility. My brief was ecstatic at least. It was lenient, a more than fair sentence, I suppose, which is perhaps the only thing in all of this mad, bad and sad story that is – because mine was a crime that should never have happened, orchestrated by someone who didn't exist. *Work that one out if you will.*

I knew her as Samantha Valentine – though I know that wasn't, *isn't* her real name – and according to the police and the doctors and the nurses and the social workers and the judges, she was, *is* simply a creation of my damaged and psychotic mind.

Only, they're wrong. And once I am out of here, I'm going to prove it.

EIGHT

DAN

Present day

I observe her closely from behind the video screen as she sits, motionless, on the orange plastic chair in Interview Room 1. Her hands are folded neatly in her lap, and she glances nervously towards the door like she's expecting someone to walk through it at any moment.

Hidden behind those large bifocal frames, her face looks pale and drawn and afraid. I doubt she's slept much. I'd managed only a couple of hours myself last night on a makeshift camp bed in my office. We have just twenty-four hours to hold Tilly Ward without charge – no time to go home – so I washed and shaved in the bathroom at the station before hastily dressing in yesterday's old clothes. Tom Ford, eat your heart out.

As I was brushing my teeth and rubbing my stiff neck, I noticed that some joker had stuck my photograph from the newspaper article up on the bathroom wall using crime scene tape. In thick black marker pen, they'd adorned my face with a pair of glasses and a comedy beard with a speech bubble coming from my mouth that said: 'The name's Riley... *Dan* Riley...'

Yeah, very funny, I laugh. I'm really no 007 though, so the hapless photographer with the *Standard Life* had his work cut out for him. To be fair, I think he did his best to make a silk purse out of a sow's ear. Anyway, my wife, Fiona, had liked it at least.

'Ooh, I think you look all sexy and rugged,' she gushed, proudly, but then again, she does need to wear glasses, and what was that word Vic Leyton had used yesterday to describe me? *Distinguished*, that was it. I spat the toothpaste into the sink.

'Sexy, rugged and distinguished, eh?' I muttered as I pulled at the crepey skin underneath my tired eyes and stuck my tongue out in the mirror. 'And they say the camera never lies.'

'So, listen up, people.' The incident room falls to a hush as I enter. Like me, the team has been at it through the night and everyone looks a little frayed around the edges. 'We've got the green light to interview Tilly Ward this morning following both the medic's and psych's assessments. Lucy, DC Parker, you fit for the job?'

'Yes, gov,' they nod in unison.

'We're not sure of all the facts yet, so let's see what she has to say, but don't go in too hard. Tilly Ward is partially deaf and she wears a hearing aid, which makes her vulnerable, so speak slowly, clearly and concisely and try and maintain eye contact with her so that she can follow your dialogue. Forensics will start coming back soon, so whatever we get from them we'll drip-feed straight back into you. We've only got ten hours or so left to hold her without charge, so we may need to apply for an extension, though I'm hoping to avoid this if we can,' I add. 'And I'm sure Tilly Ward is too.'

Parker is looking at me tentatively, like he wants to say something.

'What's your take on this, gov...? Do you think she's trying to create a false witness?' He adjusts his glasses a little awkwardly. 'I don't know, boss, but I think there's something more to all of this than at first glance.'

Ah, Parker, my most promising protégé; he senses it too.

'Well, if it is just a concocted story, Parker, then it won't be too difficult to dismantle it. If this Samantha Valentine is a ruse, then the evidence will prove that and we're looking at a murder charge,' I say. 'And so is Tilly Ward.'

'But why would she do that?' Parker presses me. 'What reason could she have to make up some cock and bull story about a fictitious friend and witness, knowing that we'd quickly pick it apart? And if she has made it all up, then what's her motive for killing Milo Harrison in the first place – we can't establish any physical link between her and the victim, or not yet – and we can't find Samantha Valentine either?'

Motive is secondary to the facts – the law states that you don't need to prove motive in a murder trial, though it can be extremely compelling. But as my dear old departed pops used to say, 'There's a reason for everything, son, and everything for a reason.'

Currently though, I can't attribute any of the usual customary themes – sex, money, jealousy or power – to explain why Tilly Ward might want to 'unalive' Milo Harrison – or to explain Samantha Valentine's absence.

'She could be time-wasting, Parker. Giving us the runaround, using our resources to locate a fictitious person while redirecting the spotlight away from her.'

It's difficult to imagine someone like Tilly Ward coming up with such an elaborate story though, and not least because – why? Creating a false witness isn't unheard of, of course – some criminals will do and say *anything* to get you chasing your tail, and get themselves off the hook – only this type of diversion trick is almost instantly quashed with basic intel. You see, the moment we're born, we begin to leave a paper trail of who we are and where we've been – birth certificates, bank accounts, driver's licences, NI numbers, electoral registers, mortgages, medical notes, qualifications, marriage certificates... it's an inexhaustible list. Add to this that almost everyone now has some kind of social media, an electronic footprint, and we are all, more or less, traceable. So far however, we have found nothing concrete to corroborate Samantha Valentine's existence, or to confirm that she is who Tilly Ward says she is.

I cast my mind back to last night, when I had met Tilly at the crime scene. From my observations, both her actions and reactions were indicative of someone who is telling the truth, or at least the truth as they know it to be. And there's the caveat right there: *as they know it to be*, because in my experience, no two truths are ever the same. It all depends on the lens you're looking through.

I pick up the psychiatrist's report on Tilly Ward and silently skim-read it once more.

'... Anxious and distressed though not hysterical... coping skills present... lucid and aware of situation... appears articulate, coherent, intelligent and helpful... refused offer of an appropriate adult present during interview... no previous mental health issues, history of depression or signs of paranoia or personality disorder... deemed fit for police interview.' As far as initial mental health assessments go, it's practically glowing.

I turn to the rest of the team.

'Well, we had, at first, thought that this might be a straightforward case of a domestic manslaughter, self-defence – our suspect has admitted to fatally stabbing Milo Harrison, and has offered an explanation as to why – but the fact that we have a vital missing witness is beginning to throw some shade onto Tilly Ward's account.'

Adding weight to my long-standing theory that she's a mind-reader, Davis hands me a flat white and a paper bag containing something greasy. I look at her like she's just fallen from heaven as I mouth the words, 'Thank you.'

'Tilly Ward's account seems plausible on the surface.' I take a sip of coffee, lick hot froth from my top lip. 'But we need evidence to support it. We need CCTV and witnesses who can corroborate what she's telling us – one witness in particular – Samantha Valentine, who apparently left the scene at some point after Tilly had inflicted the fatal stab wound, and hasn't yet been located, or identified.'

I stop. I've just had a thought. The boots that I had seen by the front door in Milo Harrison's apartment, the ones that looked like they belonged to a female and had been placed there, neatly. In such a critical, potentially life or death situation as Tilly had described it, would you think of removing your shoes as you entered the apartment?

'So, have we found anything from CCTV at Stockwell Gardens?'

I take their silence as an answer.

'Baylis and I were on it through the night, boss...' DC Harding pulls his laptop towards him, spins it round to face me in a deft move.

'We focussed on three particular cameras. The main camera at the entrance to Stockwell Gardens, the one in the communal lobby area and a third situated on the third floor, near the victim's apartment, which appears not to have been working.'

Baylis looks up at me, apologetically. 'I know, boss,' she sighs.

'Anyway, we've identified Milo Harrison numerous times coming and going inside Stockwell Gardens over a number of days, and he's always alone.'

'Always?'

'Every time, gov, there's no female with him, there's no one at all. We checked for anyone matching the description Tilly Ward gave us of Samantha Valentine, around five feet four inches tall, long blonde hair, bright green eyes...'

Coincidentally, Tilly Ward also has green eyes, striking enough for me to have noticed them when I met her yesterday.

'And?'

Baylis shakes her head.

'There's nothing, gov, no blonde woman either with him or without him, or anyone of that description seen going into the apartment. However...' her tone of voice lifts with promise, 'going further back some weeks,' she spins the laptop back round to face me, 'and we see this person here...'

She runs the footage, and I watch as what appears to be a female enters left of screen. I say female, though I can't be sure because the face is completely obscured by the hood of the ubiquitous black puffer-type coat they're wearing, but I sense it's a woman by the build and the way she carries herself. I watch the back of their hooded head as they press the buzzer. A moment later, Milo Harrison opens the door of his apartment before instantly shutting it again – less than a split second. The look on his face tells me that whoever this visitor is, they're not especially welcome.

'So who might this be?' I almost slosh my coffee down yesterday's shirt as I move closer to the screen to get a better look.

'Maybe the stalker that the neighbour mentioned, gov?' Davis suggests as she starts flipping through her notes. '... here we go... Mr Abdul Ahmed, lives next door, apartment 35. He claims that during a recent conversation, Milo Harrison mentioned something to him in passing about a woman he'd had a brief encounter with – a one-night stand, basically – who'd been, I quote, "bothering him". He's also the same witness who heard the raised male and female voices coming from the apartment around the time of the incident. Milo never gave Mr Ahmed a name or description of the potential stalker woman he'd mentioned to him, sadly.'

I'm holding my breath as the hooded individual presses the

buzzer again. There's no audio, but I get the impression they're speaking to him through the door. Pressing the buzzer a couple more times, they wait for another fifteen seconds or so, before finally walking away and—

'Hang on!' Something has caught my eye. 'Go back.'

Baylis rewinds the footage.

'Pause it! There! As they turn!'

At this angle – every angle in fact – the face is still completely obscured, but I see it, a nanosecond flash of white light juxtaposed against the black hood.

Blonde hair.

NINE

DAN

'Where is Detective Riley? Has Samantha turned up?' Tilly stands with a sense of urgency as Parker and Davis enter Interview Room 1. 'When can I go home?'

Her eyes dart between them, frantically searching their faces for answers. I watch from the camera link in the next room as she drags her palms down her face.

'We're doing our best to locate her, Tilly,' Davis reassures her. 'Let's sit down, take this one step at a time, OK?'

'I don't understand.' She retakes her seat on the plastic chair. 'Why hasn't she come forward? What's happened? *Where is she?*'

'It's OK, Tilly.' Parker's voice is soothing, which is partly why I've decided to place him this side of the screen, along with the more experienced Lucy. His self-effacing demeanour helps put people at ease whilst belying the dangerous weapon he conceals with him at all times – his sharp mind.

'That's why we're here, to get some answers, find out what's happened, OK?'

'Yes.' Her puffy eyes drop along with her volume. 'Of course.'

'What can you tell us about your friend, Samantha Valentine, Tilly?'

'What can I *tell* you about her?' She says it as though she doesn't specifically understand the nature of the question.

'Well, for instance, how long have you known her, where did you meet?'

'We met in the bookshop, where I work, around four months ago.' Her mouth forms a small, slightly wan smile. She has a pretty smile though, and her teeth are small and neat and white, but not so white that it's the first thing you notice.

'We're both avid readers, though Sam's more into romantic fiction, fantasy stuff and what-not, whereas I prefer biographies and historical novels.'

The duty solicitor begins scribbling in his notepad.

'Look, please, I want to say, now, on record, that I never meant to kill Milo Harrison.' Her voice is a shaky plea. 'I really didn't intend to hurt him, or anyone... I acted in self-defence!' She removes her glasses, rubs her eyes. 'He had a knife! And... I just... there was a knife on the kitchen work surface and... I can't remember exactly, but we, or she – Samantha – picked it up, and then somehow I was holding it, and then when he came at me, came at us both, I just...' She makes a single stabbing motion with her hand – her left hand.

'I just wanted to stop him from hurting her... I'm not a murderer!' She breaks down again. 'Am I going to prison for this?' I can feel her distress coming through the screen. It's uncomfortable viewing.

'Which hand were you holding the knife in, Tilly?'

She wipes her nose with the back of her sleeve. Wearing standard custody uniform of a grey shirt and sweatpants that look at least two sizes too big for her, she reminds me of a child who forgot to bring their PE kit to lesson and had to wear something from lost property.

'Sorry, can you repeat that? I... didn't catch it...' She taps her ear.

'Of course, I'm sorry,' Davis apologises. 'Which hand were you holding the knife in when you stabbed Mr Harrison?'

'My left hand.' Her voice is brittle with emotion. 'I'm left-handed.'

This tallies up with what Vic Leyton had initially surmised at the crime scene. Only Tilly Ward isn't denying that she stabbed Milo Harrison, whether it be with her left hand or right. She's admitted to inflicting the fatal wound. This is about intent – and motive.

'Samantha is left-handed too, coincidentally.'

My eyebrows instinctively rise.

'Is she?'

'We don't have much in common,' she sniffs. Her face is a melted mess of tears and mucus – someone offer the poor girl a tissue, for goodness' sake! 'But that's one thing we do share.'

Davis leans in a touch across the table.

'We've done some initial investigations, Tilly, and some of the information you have given us doesn't appear to be correct.'

She looks at once both shocked and confused.

'I'm... I'm sorry? What isn't correct?'

'The information you gave us about Samantha living at Stockwell Gardens with Milo Harrison.'

Her eyes dart between them both.

'I don't understand. Sorry, what do you mean, *"isn't correct"*?'

'No one called Samantha Valentine lives at that address, Tilly.'

'Yes, she does,' she says, with a degree of conviction beneath the confusion. 'She lives at Stockwell Gardens. I pick her up and drop her off there all the time.'

'Have you ever been inside the apartment before, Tilly, prior to yesterday, I mean?'

'Actually, no, I haven't. Usually I'll wait around the corner for her whenever I pick her up and I always drop her a little distance away so that he, Milo, won't see us. To be honest, after everything she told me about him, I was frightened of him myself.'

'But she told you that's where she lived, apartment 31, Stockwell Gardens?'

'I'm sorry, can you repeat that?' She taps the hearing aid again. 'Sometimes this thing plays up a bit.'

'It's OK, Tilly. Take your time. You say you knew Samantha lived at 31 Stockwell Gardens, that's where she told you she lived...'

'Why do you keep asking me about her address?' Her growing frustration is evident. 'I'm sorry,' she immediately apologises. 'But... doesn't she live there then? Is that what you're trying to say...?'

'Ah, there you are, Riley!'

I swing round from the computer as my boss, Superintendent Gwendoline Archer, enters the room with something of an uncharacteristic flourish.

'So, are we any closer to a charge yet?' She sidles up next to me and leans in to watch the screen. 'What's it going to be, murder, or manslaughter with diminished? She's admitted to fatally stabbing the victim, hasn't she?'

'Yes, ma'am, she has. This isn't a case of if she did it, it's *why* she did it. The account she's given us so far seems genuine, minus this all-important elusive witness, Samantha Valentine, who apparently can corroborate everything.'

'... Elusive?' Archer says without diverting her eyes.

'... Well, as yet we can't locate her, ma'am, if indeed she exists at all.'

She pulls back from me a touch.

'What do you mean, if she even exists at all? She either does or she doesn't.'

'Well, no one by that name lives or has ever lived at the address of the deceased, ma'am.'

She looks intrigued.

'No one has seen anyone fitting the description of Samantha Valentine given to us by Tilly, either in or around the apartment or with the deceased, and initial CCTV appears to back that up, though Tilly here is claiming that they're a cohabiting couple who're engaged to be married – it doesn't make sense. We've checked local hospitals and women's refuges to see if anyone by the name Samantha Valentine has turned up there, but... nothing so far. There's no contact number in Tilly's iPhone for her, and there's no photo evidence or anything from social media. The phone is with the tech team now, ma'am, but so far we haven't found one single piece of evidence that links any of these three people together in any tangible way.' I face her. 'It's quite unusual to say the least.'

'You think it's a wild goose chase?'

'I don't know yet, ma'am. I'm not sure what to make of it.'

She flashes me a wide-eyed look, as though my perplexity pleases her on some level.

'Tilly Ward's account *sounds* legit. In my opinion, she comes across authentic. And well,' I nod at the screen, 'look at her! She's a tiny, thirty-six-year-old who works in a bookshop and wears a hearing aid. She has no previous, her record is spotless, and she has no history of violence or mental health disorder. By the accounts coming in from her colleagues at Waterford's bookshop, she's a perfectly nice, unassuming, ordinary, shy type of person who seems to have got herself mixed up in something tragic...'

'... And yet?'

'And yet, what, ma'am?'

'And yet I'm sensing there's an "and yet" coming, Riley...'

Admittedly, my boss knows me pretty well.

'I think we should put an APB out on this Samantha Valentine, get the name out on social media. Let's see what, if anything, comes back from it. If she exists, then *someone* knows her, maybe knows where she is. Milo Harrison is dead, he's no longer a threat to her, if he was ever one to begin with, so why hasn't the witness come forward to back up Tilly's story, the friend who allegedly saved her life?'

'How long have we got left with her?'

'Less than nine hours, ma'am.'

There's a knock on the door and DC Mitchell pops her head around it. 'There's nothing doing on the search at Tilly Ward's address, gov, ma'am,' she says. 'Nothing that corroborates Tilly's story or evidence of a friendship with anyone named Samantha Valentine. No photos, no birthday or Christmas cards, nothing to link them together.' Her mouth is a thin, apologetic line. 'It's not a big apartment, gov, there's nothing much there but for a few clothes and some basic possessions. I'm sorry.'

I feel a tinge of sadness as I imagine Tilly Ward living alone in a small, sparsely furnished flat. I wonder what her life is really like.

'It gets worse, boss. They didn't find anything that can directly link her to the victim either, nothing to suggest they were previously known to each other, no obvious connection, and Milo Harrison's family has confirmed that he lived alone – no regular girlfriend and definitely no fiancée – they've never heard the names Tilly Ward or Samantha Valentine before.'

Archer drags her face away from the screen.

'There must be a reason why this has happened, a motive.' I look up at Archer. 'And people don't just vanish into thin air like a magician's trick. We need to find this Samantha Valentine and get some answers.'

'So you believe Tilly Ward's account that this witness is real, is that what you're saying, Riley?'

I pause, not wanting to commit myself either way.

'I don't know what our exact position should be on this just yet, ma'am. It just seems such an unlikely, fantastical story for someone like Tilly Ward to have made up in such detail. And we have intel from the neighbour to say that Milo Harrison may have been stalked or harassed by a former female sexual encounter, a blonde. According to Tilly Ward, Samantha Valentine is a blonde, and we've identified a blonde-haired person from CCTV footage outside Milo's apartment from a few weeks back. I really think we need to dig a little deeper. Try and identify her.'

'So you *do* think she exists then?'

'I'd like to exhaust every avenue proving otherwise first.' I meet her eyes. 'I've been in the game a long time now, ma'am, and I get a good sense of who is telling me the truth and who is trying to pull the wool over my eyes.'

'Ah yes, the distinguished Dan Riley's infamous intuition that all the ladies are going mad for…'

Distinguished? She's the second person to have called me this in as many days.

The just-got-out-of-bed look really must be making a comeback.

She lifts up the newspaper that I've only just now realised she's holding, and I roll my eyes. *Not her as well.*

'Oh, don't be so modest, Dan,' she smiles, wryly. 'The Press Department is exceptionally pleased with the article, as is the commissioner, so well done you!'

This is high praise indeed, coming from her.

'Things like this really do help bridge that gap between the public and ourselves, Dan. You really highlighted the difficulties and personal sacrifices we face every day in the job, as well as our dedication to solving crime. They think you came across as very likeable, very human.'

'It wasn't too difficult, ma'am, being as though I am one.'

'Yes, well, that's debatable, Riley,' she quips, 'but you seem to have been a big hit – especially with the...' she pauses, '... the female audience... a few have left some, how can I say, "favourable comments" on social media.

I feel my cheeks glow warm.

'You're winding me up, I—'

But before I can finish, something draws my eye back towards the computer screen.

Tilly Ward is on her feet, pacing the interview room. Her hands are linked together on top of her head, and her face is red. She's visibly upset.

'I want to speak to Detective Riley,' she cries. 'Please, can you ask him to come? I only want to speak to Detective Riley.'

Archer lifts a perfectly shaped eyebrow as she turns to me with a smirk.

'See what I mean?'

TEN
ERIN

Present day

'That's the last of the milk, Erin.'

Molly takes the empty carton from the fridge and places it down on the worn and grubby kitchen work surface. Like me, the years of grime it's seen are so deeply embedded that not even a little Ajax and a lot of elbow grease can shift them now.

'Don't forget to put it in the recycling bin, will you? Remember, plastics and glass in the green box and...'

'... Paper and cardboard in the black... yes, I know; don't worry, I won't forget.' Bless Molly. She really does seem to care so much about *everything*. I think she believes that even bottles and cardboard have feelings.

Molly Martin is the lady from Re-Connex, a charity that helps relocate and rehabilitate mental health patients after they've been released back into society. She wears this old, shaggy, brown furry coat and is always scratching around inside a drawer or a cupboard or a box somewhere, like a mouse. She's friendly enough, though I can never let my guard down around her. I must never forget that cute little mice can also be disease-carrying vermin.

Re-Connex has helped house me as part of the conditions of my release. I must also attend mandatory weekly therapy sessions, take daily medication, and I have to check in with an adult mental health social worker and my parole officer on the third Friday of every month for the next eighteen months, which is a drag. But at least I am 'free', in a sense at least, because while I am no longer incarcerated, I'll never be truly free. *Not until I find her.*

'Have you taken your meds today?'

I loathe the fact that she asks me this question. Doesn't she trust me? *I don't need the bloody pills anyway.* She goes into the bathroom to retrieve them from the cabinet, places them next to me on the table as she returns.

'My mother, God rest her soul, always gave me a boiled sweet after I took my medicine like a good girl. Did your mum do the same, Erin?'

'My mum's dead,' I say. That stops her in her tracks.

'Oh, Erin, I'm sorry. When did you lose her?'

'When I was thirteen. And I didn't *lose* her. She was *stolen*.'

She's silent for a moment. I can tell that she's trying to process what I might mean exactly by that statement, but decides, wisely in my opinion, not to probe any further for now.

'You know you can always talk to me.' She cocks her head. 'Some of the patients – ex-patients – find it helpful to talk about their experiences.' And by 'experiences' I think she probably means 'crimes'.

'Is your father still around?'

'Also dead,' I say. 'No family.'

She flashes me a pitiful look.

'What about friends? It's good to have a support network around you while you adjust back into normal life.'

I want to ask Molly to define what 'normal life' looks like, only I'd rather she just leave, so I try not to engage any more than necessary.

'Not really,' I reply. 'Most of them fell by the wayside after... after everything. Though to be honest with you, I prefer it that way.'

'Oh?' She seems crestfallen. 'That's a shame.'

I assume that Molly knows my history, and about Samantha. It's no doubt the *real* reason why she's asking me about my 'friends' and family, or lack of them. She doesn't appear to be scared of me though, which makes me question whether she really is familiar with my case. 'You should come along to one of Re-Connex's monthly social gatherings, meet some new people... It'll do you good! Everyone's super friendly, and it's a mix of women *and* men. You never know, you could meet the love of your life.' She grins. Molly's eyes disappear into slits whenever she smiles, which is often. Her happy disposition is sometimes a painful reminder that I used to be like her once upon a time. Now though, a darkness chases me; one I can never seem to outrun.

'The only men I like are dead ones,' I say flatly without breaking eye contact.

A look of horror registers on her face. I'm not sure why I'm trying to provoke her. I know she's only trying to be kind. 'Do you know what men fear most about women, Molly?'

She shakes her head. 'No...'

'That women will laugh at them.'

'Oh, really?' She shuffles from foot to foot a little awkwardly.

'And do you know what women fear most about men?'

'I must admit, I'm not exactly an aficionado on the subject. I've not had the greatest luck myself in that department...'

'That they'll kill them.'

'Any luck with the job-hunting yet?' Molly changes the subject as she nods at the laptop on the coffee table. She has very generously gifted it to me, ostensibly so that I can search for employment. Though who in their right mind is ever going to give *me* a job, I can't imagine. The job-hunting is merely a ruse anyway; it's not jobs I'm searching for.

'Not yet, Molly. But thanks again for the laptop.'

She stands, gives me a brief, awkward hug goodbye. *Finally.*

I watch Molly from the window as she scurries down the pathway in her big fluffy coat before turning left onto the main street. Now that she's gone, I untack the tie-dye wall-hanging and stand back and stare at the collection of cuttings and maps, and heavily scribbled-on Post-it notes I've been compiling on the wall behind it – years of covert research and study brought to the big screen at last. I break off a couple of squares of chocolate from the open bar on the table and pop them into my mouth. Chocolate helps me to concentrate. Or at least, that's what I tell myself.

How do you begin to look for someone who doesn't exist?

Perhaps the one – *the only* – 'good' thing about spending six excruciatingly long and desperate years locked away with the criminally insane, is that I had plenty of time to start finding out.

As it transpired though, I was wrong, and the police and the judges and the doctors and the lawyers – they were right all along. Samantha Valentine really *doesn't* exist, at least not technically. She was a creation of *her* own mind and not *mine*.

I know now of course that everything she ever told me was a lie. From the moment she took a breath to introduce herself, to the fatal second I stuck a knife into the heart of Bojan Radulovic, killing him stone cold dead. It was layer upon layer of them, a millefeuille of lies.

I open the fridge and take the cheap bottle of rosé from it, hastily pour myself a large measure into a chipped mug and swallow it back in three gulps.

The truth is, Samantha Valentine could be *anywhere*.

Searching for her is like looking for a ghost. It's said, however, that the best predictor of future behaviour is past behaviour, and so if it's true, then she *will* strike again. She won't be able to resist putting her head above the parapet. Her need for control and power over people and the thrill of the emotional con is just too tempting for a psychopath like her.

I can't go to the authorities for help in finding her, at least not directly. How can I possibly turn to the very people who were so complicit in my demise? Even armed with a truckload of evidence, I'm not sure they wouldn't just lock me right back up with the loonies in a bid to conceal their own incompetence. They got it wrong before; they could get it wrong again. Anyway, I don't trust the police. They don't care about truth and justice; they're corrupt.

I almost drop the mug I'm holding as the doorbell rings, startling me. *Who is that?* I'm definitely not expecting any other visitors today. Maybe Molly forgot something, though she does have a key, which she's always perfectly happy to use, announcing herself at the same time as she enters with the words, 'Only me!'

I grab the wall-hanging and hastily tack it back up.

And then the doorbell rings again.

ELEVEN

I open the door a crack, a little breathless, *a little nervous*.

'Oh! Malcolm! It's you!' I quickly wipe my mouth, in case there's any chocolate around it.

Malcolm lives across the hall, directly opposite me. I get the feeling he might actually fancy me a bit. Perhaps it's the way that whenever he smiles at me it seems to reach his sparkly eyes, and he's always making clumsy attempts at starting conversation. Actually, I'm flattering myself; he probably doesn't fancy me at all. Who would? Now, after everything, I'm as much of a ghost as she is.

'Hey, Erin, I'm sorry,' he apologises, 'is this a bad time?'

I didn't realise it had registered on my face, though I'm not disappointed to see him as such – I'm just busy.

'I was wondering if you fancied a drink?' He waggles the bottle of wine he's holding. 'Or maybe just some company?' He smiles a little awkwardly. He has a nice smile, I suppose, shy and a touch self-effacing, but I mustn't get sucked in by all of that nonsense. After all, I know from bitter experience that the devil always comes to you with a smile.

'Don't worry,' he says, as though sensing my apprehension, 'I'm not a psycho killer or anything...'

I pause for a second before taking a step back from the door. Maybe I *could* use the company. It's not much fun getting drunk on your own after all.

'That's good to know, Malcolm.' I let him in. 'But what if I told you that *I was*?' He has no idea just how close to the truth I am as he walks through into my small apartment.

'Why are you dressed as a dog?'

I feel my face flush red as I suddenly remember that I'm wearing a furry onesie, complete with a hood and ears and a tail. I picked it up at the local market last weekend because it looked warm and cosy.

'I've not intentionally dressed as a dog.' I pull at the cheap fabric, embarrassed. 'I was just trying to save on heating costs.'

'Woof-woof!' He raises a brow in tandem with the wine bottle. 'Shall we unscrew this bad boy then, or what?'

I laugh. I've forgotten how good it feels. Actually, I think I might fancy Malcolm a little bit myself. But then again, I haven't had sex for the best part of a decade. I've forgotten how that feels too.

We make small talk for a while. I'm good at small talk. It's a skill I acquired through necessity at Larksmere. Chit-chat was the language most inmates and staff understood. It was safer that way. You really didn't want to get inside the head of some of the 'people' I was locked up with – and you definitely didn't want them in yours.

Malcolm tells me he's a local landscape gardener, but that it's largely seasonal work, which is probably the reason he's drinking the same cheap wine that I am. We drink and chit-chat some more. He asks if he can play some music and downloads an old jazzy house soundtrack that I've never heard of. I quite like it.

I'm a little drunk by the time we have sex on the sofa some

hours later. It's clumsy and awkward at first, and it doesn't last very long, but admittedly, it feels wonderful to have a strong, warm body holding me. It reminds me that I'm still human – or just about. Now it's over though, the darkness returns and I want him to leave so that I can continue with my research.

'What's behind the wall-hanging?'

He nods over at it. *Shit.* The right-hand corner is flapping down – it must've come loose when I'd quickly pinned it back up.

I leap up so quickly from the sofa that I spill the last of my wine onto his naked lap.

He yelps in surprise.

'Oh, God! Malcolm! I'm sorry... that was an accident... I...'

I grab a cloth from the small kitchenette, begin dabbing his crotch with it. He watches me closely.

'So you going to tell me then?'

'Tell you what?'

'What the newspaper cuttings are that you're hiding behind that piece of fabric?'

'I'm not hiding anything,' I say, casually. 'And it's nothing that will interest you, I'm sure.'

'Shouldn't I be the judge of that?'

I get up off the sofa, throw the cloth back into the sink and pour myself the last of the wine. This is just one of the myriad reasons I don't want anyone in my life; people ask questions, *too many* questions.

'If you must know, I'm looking for someone.'

'Aren't we all?' He raises his eyebrows.

'It's a female actually.' I stifle a smile in return, let my head drop to one side.

'She missing or something?'

'Yes.'

'Oh, right... What's her name?'

I pause, reluctant to tell him. Thinking about it though,

what does it even matter if I do? It's not like Malcolm's going to know where she is, is it?

'Her name is Samantha Valentine.'

'Oh yeah! You've got onto that too, huh? Can I smoke?' He pulls his boxer shorts on as he stands.

My heartbeat rapidly quickens.

'Sorry? You too?' What do you mean by, "you've got onto that too"?'

He pulls his head through his T-shirt, begins searching for his cigarettes.

'That woman the police are looking for... I read about it, it's gone viral...'

'The police? What do you mean, *gone viral?*' My heart is now a piston in my chest, pumping painfully hard against my ribs. 'Where? When...? Where did you read this?' I snatch my phone up from the table.

He's staring at me, his brow wrinkled.

'Tell me, Malcolm! Where did you read about this?' My voice is shrill and loud and urgent, bordering on shouty. I'm trying to remain calm but my hands won't stop shaking and my phone keeps slipping from my fingers as I try and unlock it. *Damn bloody thing!*

'It was on my Insta feed this morning... the Met Police put something out about a domestic stabbing in London... they were asking her to come forward as a witness or something. I'm sure it said her name was Samantha Valentine... it stuck in my head for some reason. Why?' he asks, his brow still fixed in confusion. 'Do you *know* her?'

TWELVE
DAN

Tilly Ward's face is an eruption of fear and relief as I enter the interview room.

'Oh, Detective Riley, you're here!'

She seems a little unsteady on her feet as she gets up from her seat, like she might pass out at any moment. I grip her forearm, help her to steady herself.

'Dan, OK? Please call me Dan.'

'I have no idea what's going on, Dan, these questions they're asking me... I don't understand.' Her voice is heavy with panic. I can literally smell the distress on her. '*Please* can you tell me what's happening?'

I nod sideways at Lucy and she nods back in acknowledgement before she and Parker leave the room. I take a seat and Tilly follows suit, slumping back down onto the plastic chair. She looks shattered.

'They're talking as if Samantha doesn't actually exist and that I've made her up or something...' She exhales in short, sharp succession, in disbelief. '... But you *have* to believe me when I say that Samantha Valentine *is* a real person! I can't believe I'm actually having to say it... I... I...'

I take a few slow breaths before leaning in across the table and taking her hand. It feels small and cold in my own, like a child's.

'Look, Tilly, I know you're scared and confused.' I glance over at the duty solicitor. He's busy writing and doesn't look up. 'And I hear you, OK? I'm *here* for you.'

She looks up at me, her strikingly green eyes wide as she silently signs the words, 'Thank you' to me.

'You're welcome,' I sign back to her, clumsily, hoping I haven't messed it up and said something offensive instead. I really need more time to practise. Fiona and Pip are head and shoulders above me already and I don't want to lag too far behind.

'You understand sign language?' She says, registering surprise.

'A little,' I nod. 'I'm currently trying to learn. My son, he's...'

'... Deaf, yes, I know. You mentioned him in that newspaper article...'

'You saw that too, huh?' I'm beginning to suspect that maybe *everyone* has.

'He keeps telling me not to say any more,' she says, nodding in the solicitor's direction, 'but what possible reason would I have to lie? Everything I've said is how it was, how it happened...' She shakes her head. 'Only now they're telling me that Samantha doesn't even live at Stockwell Gardens with Milo. They're saying there's no official trace of her *at all*...?' She uses the word 'they' as if I'm not one of them.

'That's true, Tilly.' I'm careful to keep my voice soft and measured. She's fragile but her disbelief seems genuine, I sense it from her body language, her expressions and mannerisms.

'Currently we have no idea where Samantha Valentine is. She isn't officially registered to the address of the deceased, and there isn't any trace of her ever having lived there. Tilly.' I pause. 'Family and neighbours all say that Milo Harrison was a single man, he wasn't engaged to anyone, and as far as they were aware, he didn't have a steady girlfriend. They'd never seen or met or heard of anyone called Samantha Valentine, and an initial search of your phone shows no communication between you and anyone with that name.'

I train my eyes on her, release her small hand.

'We're doing our best to find her, Tilly, but you can see why we're struggling here, can't you? We can't seem to verify who Samantha Valentine is by the usual methods. She has no social media presence, we can't find any phone records registered to that name and there's nothing on the electoral register... No one with the name Samantha Valentine was born in the UK on the date of birth you gave us for her, 14/03/1989, either.'

She blinks at me, frowning.

'But that *can't* be.' She shakes her head. 'How can that possibly be?'

'I don't know, Tilly, I'm hoping you can help me understand this. Milo Harrison was a son and brother, he was close to his family, to his parents and siblings, they're devastated by his death.' She flinches, closes her eyes for a few seconds, like she's trying to distance herself from my words. 'They say they would've absolutely known if Milo and Samantha were a couple.'

'How has any of this happened?' She shrinks back into the plastic seat and starts sobbing. 'His family, they'll hate me, won't they...? But' – she's spluttering and hiccupping now – '...he had a knife... I didn't mean to kill him.'

I lean in closer, hand her another tissue. The last one is a wet ball of mucus and I discard it into the wastepaper bin.

'Listen, Tilly,' I lower my voice, 'I need you to work with me here, OK? I need you to help me understand the truth because you're absolutely right, none of it makes sense.'

She blows loudly into the tissue, sits up straight in the plastic chair.

'Can I have a piece of paper and something to write with?'

'Of course.' I nod as I hand her a chewed-up black Bic pen and pass her a sheet of A4 paper from the table. Immediately she begins scribbling.

'If there's anything you need to tell me, Tilly, anything at all, now would be a good time, and I promise,' – I place a hand over my heart, ask her to look at me, which she does – 'I give you my word, OK? Whatever this is, we can work it out, together, you and me. All I need is for you to be honest with me.'

'But I *am* being honest with you, Dan... there has to be some mistake. Samantha can't have just disappeared! Someone must've seen her, knows where she is? What about CCTV? What about other witnesses?'

'We're working on it, Tilly.'

I sit back, stay silent and let my words sink in.

She stops sketching for a moment, drops the pen.

'You don't think... Do you think it's possible that she's been *lying* to me?'

Her voice drops down to a fearful whisper. 'Perhaps Samantha *isn't* who she told me she is? Maybe she's been, I don't know, pretending to be someone else...? I can't think of another explanation for all of this.' She covers her mouth suddenly, stifling a gasp, as though it has just dawned on her that such a preposterous thought could in fact be true.

'That's what I'm trying to find out, Tilly.'

She's shaking her head.

'But... but... she told me he was beating her... that he was abusive... I saw bruises on her... no... no... I can't believe... was she... was she *lying*...?' She searches my eyes with her own. They look wide with disbelief. 'But why? Why would she... why would *anyone* do that...?' She gasps again as more reality appears to dawn upon her. '*Oh my God.* What does this mean for me, Dan? What will happen to me? Will I go to prison for murder? What will I tell my employers?' She flops forwards, over the table. Her hands are shaking so badly that I simply can't help but take hold of them again.

'I was just protecting her, protecting myself... I didn't want anyone to get hurt! I don't want to go to prison! I'm not a murderer! This can't be happening!' She stops wailing for a moment. 'What if something's happened to Sam? Maybe she's being held hostage somewhere... I don't know, there has to be some kind of explanation for all of this... Samantha's my friend, she wouldn't... Oh God, Dan, I'm *begging* you, you *have* to find her.' She slides the sheet of paper across the table back at me.

'That's her,' she says, 'that's Samantha.'

I look down at the surprisingly detailed sketch of a woman's face, a pretty, oval-shaped face with wide eyes, a thin nose and a neat, enigmatic smile. It's a good sketch. Clearly, Tilly has some artistic talent.

'You do believe me, Dan, don't you?'

THIRTEEN
ERIN

I feel terrible thinking about asking Malcolm to leave. But he's asking too many questions and it's preventing me from thinking in a straight line, so I don't see I've got much choice.

> Following a fatal stabbing on Thursday, police are appealing for a witness to come forward...

I bolt upright, barely managing to click on the link with my vibrating fingers.

> Samantha Valentine has been missing since an incident that took place at Stockwell Gardens, South West London, at approximately 6 p.m. on Thursday. A thirty-four-year-old local man was pronounced dead at the scene, and a thirty-five-year-old woman was taken into custody. Samantha Valentine is thirty-six years old, around five feet four inches, approximately 120 lbs, with long blonde hair and green eyes, and is currently believed to be in or around the South-West London area. Anyone with information should contact the Serious Crime Unit and speak to SIO, DCI Dan Riley on...

I reread the words until they start to bleed around the edges, too frightened to blink in case they disappear. *Is it possible?*

Adrenalin is flooding every crevice of my body. There's not much in the way of detail given, but the basics sound promising – a small, blonde-haired female with green eyes has fled the scene of a fatality, and another female is in custody. The MO sounds horribly familiar, and the description of the 'witness', though generic, is accurate, save for her age. Sam said she was thirty-three years old when I met her, over seven years ago. That would make her forty years old today. Though of course, how old *is* a pathological liar really?

There's more though! I gasp as my eyes hungrily try to take in what they're seeing. It's another link, *to an artist's sketch*! Oh. My. God. My heart is hammering painfully against my ribs as I click on it, holding my breath as it downloads onto my phone. Suddenly, I feel every drop of blood drain from my body, and for a moment, all I can do is sit, paralysed, on this shabby second-hand sofa, dressed only in my underwear, with Malcolm leaning over my shoulder in his boxer shorts.

It's her.

'Is that your friend, Samantha?' He stares down at the sketch. 'Actually,' – he glances at me, then back to the screen – 'she looks a little bit like you! Different hair and that, but... You sure you're not sisters?'

I'm too stunned to answer him. The Met Police post has been shared thousands of times already and people are beginning to comment on it.

Who's the woman in the sketch?

I saw her today down at my local Tesco. I thought she looked a bit shifty.

Why are police looking for her, what's she done?

> She looks pretty...
>
> I hope they find her...

It's official. Samantha Valentine is trending news. *Now everyone was looking for her.*

Over the many years of being repeatedly told that Samantha Valentine didn't and doesn't exist, it's been almost impossible at times not to doubt myself, or my sanity. I'd asked myself over and over again, what if I really *was* just a headcase? Like, do you even know if you're suffering from complex mental illness? Isn't that part of the illness itself, that you're not aware of your condition? Having lived – or rather, survived – alongside some of the UK's most dangerous and criminally insane for the duration that I did, I still don't know the answer to that question. But what if I actually *was* suffering from psychosis and delusions that had made me genuinely *think* she was real? You see, if enough people keep telling you the same thing over and over again, eventually you can't help but start to believe it. The reinforcement is real. And consistency is everything.

In hindsight, I realise now that Larksmere Hospital had in fact used very similar methods on me that a sociopathic conwoman like Samantha herself did – only not as successfully. They'd also tried to brainwash and gaslight me into accepting their narrative using, among other things, drugs and ECT, or passive-aggressive veiled threats of punishment and loss of privileges, in a bid to break me down. All those educated doctors, qualified therapists and practitioners with half the alphabet after their names that I'd been passed between at Larksmere, they could've learned a trick or two from Samantha Valentine, she was the *real* true professional among them.

This changes everything now though. This right here is my moment of truth. Malcolm is talking over my shoulder, but I don't hear his words. My head hurts with questions. Why was Samantha in London? What has she done? *Where is she?* I was right though, I always knew she would eventually turn up. After all, along with the truth, scum always floats to the surface.

Using the name Samantha Valentine this time around was risky though, and not just a little audacious. Why has she done that? Surely she knows there's a chance I could come forward to the police, screaming from the rooftops that I had 'told them so' seven years ago – if only they had listened to me! Now someone else is dead and more lives will be ruined!

I think of all the media coverage a story like mine would elicit if it all came out. Social media is an untamed beast now. Everyone's a keyboard warrior, or a podcaster and an influencer, a journalist or a social commentator of some sort. My story could go stratospheric. There would be a press feeding frenzy. All of them scrabbling to relay the shocking and sensational tale of how I'd been tricked, brainwashed and coerced by my 'best friend' into killing a man who turned out to be an innocent stranger. And of course, how the police had failed me, not to mention the man I killed. It's got Netflix written all over it.

Nobody likes betrayal or injustice, and in this story there's both, and more, by the truckload, with a trailer on the back. Who wants to think of anyone sane being locked away in a mental institution due to police failures? It's the stuff of nightmares, right? And people love nightmares, *other people's nightmares*.

Maybe there would even be a public apology, both to myself and Bojan Radulovic's family. I imagine this scene for a moment, the idea of the Chief of Police addressing TV cameras, slightly red and shamefaced, forced to admit to a catalogue of errors for not taking me seriously. It's too late for any of it now though; public apology or no, that ship sailed and sank long ago. How can I possibly ever trust the system now? How can I ever trust *anyone*? If I want any kind of justice, *I know what I have to do.*

'I'm sorry, Malcolm, but I'm going to have to ask you to leave.'

I breathe the words from my lips without taking my eyes from my phone. 'I've got things to do.'

He looks hurt when I finally glance over at him. I don't mean to intentionally offend him, but I haven't got time to waste. I've been waiting for this moment for over six years. I have meticulously prepared for it.

'What have you got to do right now, this minute, that's so important? I thought we might snuggle down on the sofa for a bit... watch a film maybe, you can choose if you like?'

I hear the rejection in his inflection and guilt pangs in my chest. I haven't got time to worry about Malcolm's feelings. He has no idea what this means to me, and I'm not about to tell him.

'I need to go somewhere,' I say, beginning to look around the room for some clothes to put on. I can't go to London dressed as a dog. That really would be *barking* mad.

'Where?' he asks. 'Is it something to do with this woman, this Samantha Valentine, whatever her name is...? Who is she? How do you know her?' He's asking questions again, and again I don't answer him.

'I'm really sorry, Malcolm.' I hurriedly start to dress, hopping on one leg as I stuff the other into my jeans and throw my arms into an old, thick sweatshirt. It'll be cold in London. He watches me with a puzzled expression as I struggle with the zip on my jeans, like I really might be crazy.

'Erin... what's happened? Why do you need to leave all of a sudden? And... hang on, are you... are you *crying*?'

'No!' I say, too loudly and sharply, causing him to widen his eyes a touch. 'No,' I lower my tone, wipe my face with the back of my sleeve. 'It's nothing, Malcolm, a touch of hay fever probably. And I just remembered that I have to be somewhere, that's all. I have to meet Molly.'

'Hay fever? In February?'

I throw his joggers and socks at him.

'You need to get dressed and go.'

He blinks at me.

'... O... OK... If that's what you want.'

I go to the broom cupboard, pull out my small holdall and start throwing items from my wardrobe haphazardly into it. I can feel Malcolm's eyes on me as he silently dresses.

'You taking a trip away somewhere?'

'I'm taking some clothes to Molly's to be washed. My machine's broken and they can't deliver a new one until next week.' It's the best excuse I can come up with in the moment.

'Oh!' he says, as though it could be a legitimate reason. 'Well, I have a perfectly good washing machine over at mine, you could always...'

'Thanks, Malcolm,' – I cut him off – 'but I said I'd take it over to Molly's. Can you close the door on your way out?'

He looks crestfallen as he stands, hovering by the sofa for a few moments before finally shuffling towards the front door.

'Right... Well, I'll be off then.' He turns, smiles, a little awkwardly, and it doesn't quite reach his sparkly eyes this time.

'OK, well, thanks for the um... the wine, Malcolm,' I say without looking up.

'I thought you were going to say something else then!' His cheeky chuckle quickly fades to nothing as he opens the door.

'Well, bye then, Erin.'

'Yeah, goodbye, Malcolm, take care of yourself.'

He's still loitering by the front door as I stuff a pair of old pumps into the holdall, like he has something to say but is undecided.

'Will... will I ever see you again, Erin?'

I zip up my bag and look over at him. He seems a little sad about this prospect and it throws me off a touch.

'Don't be silly, Malcolm, we live opposite each other.' I manage a small smile for him. I don't want to create even more suspicion in him than I know I have already. He probably thinks I'm a total Fruit Loop. When the police come, I wonder what he will say to them. 'Of course you'll see me again.'

I just hope it won't be from behind bars.

FOURTEEN

The first thing I do once I alight at King's Cross station is find a newsagent's and buy a couple of those burner phones that drug dealers use, and a king-size Snickers bar.

The 18.15 from Leeds to London was rammed to the rafters. The last time I took a train was back in 2021 and things appear to have changed during those lost years in ways I couldn't quite have predicted. The carriage was so full of commuters that you couldn't get a cigarette paper between them, and as I glanced around, I noted that *everyone* was glued, head down, to their smartphones. Scrolling has now officially replaced the art of spontaneous conversation, it seems, though this works for me. The less you talk to people, the less they can get to know you. Knowledge is power after all, and you must never give your power away.

Eventually, I managed to find a spare seat next to a hulk of a man who clearly had no concept of the term 'personal hygiene'. He grunted, grumbling as I shuffled and squeezed in next to him, unfazed by his offensive odour.

For a time at Larksmere, I'd shared a 10 x 8 'room' with a morbidly obese, double-murdering paranoid schizophrenic called Candice who claimed to have received 'messages' from the TV telling her to kill both her parents. She believed that washing yourself in anything other than holy water was a sin, often choosing instead to smear herself in her own urine and faeces. Even once she'd been forcibly sedated and cleaned up by a team of nurses, the stench would linger for days.

Once I was seated, I opened my laptop and punched the name DCI Dan Riley into the search engine and settled down to some reading...

The motion of the train must've caused me to nod off at some point though, and I had hit the ground running, straight into a nightmare. Snippets of my subconscious mind and past memories flash up in random five-second frames, like the trailer of a particularly twisted horror film. *Coming to an Odeon near you soon, rated 18!* At one point I see Bojan Radulovic's face, the stunned look of surprise and shock on it, like he can't quite believe that I just stabbed him through the heart and now he's going to die.

'Help me, Erin, come quick... he's got a knife... I think he's going to kill me!' *Samantha.* Her voice resonates like an echo chamber. My mum is there too of course – no nightmare would be complete without her. At one point in the dream, I'm a baby and she's cradling me in her arms, only somehow, I have the understanding and vocabulary of a grown adult.

'Why didn't you protect *me*, Erin? Your own mother? Didn't you love me?' She's crying, only as I look up at her face, I see that it isn't my mum's image at all – *it's Samantha's.*

I woke with a start, hyperventilating and sweating, as we slowly ground into the station, the ugly, high-pitched screeching sound of metal on metal setting my teeth on edge. Passengers were staring and I quickly dropped my head. Had I been calling out in my sleep? I pulled my bobble hat down over my forehead and sank into my coat. I don't want to be memorable, not now, not today.

With the burner phones purchased, I head towards a chemist. Mindful that I could be seen on CCTV, I wrap my scarf tightly around me and pull my hood up. I'm not a big fan of cold weather, but tonight I'm grateful for it. Making my way over to the haircare section, I begin to peruse the boxes of hair dye. There's so many of them, rows and rows with names like Liquorice Brown and Bodacious Blonde. I grab a box of peroxide, a mixing pot, a brush and some toner, and throw them into a basket along with a pair of scissors, and try not to make eye contact with anybody.

It takes me a good twenty minutes to find the Bull and Barrow pub from the station. I'm indifferent to my reflection in the windows of the posh designer shops as I hurry past them, not exactly sure where I'm headed, just another faceless person in the crowd.

King's Cross had long been a particularly unsavoury part of the capital, a grimy, industrial haunt, notorious for thieves and unfortunates. Now though, it looks like it's been given the mother of all makeovers with its sleek, high-rise trendy offices and water features, surrounded by designer boutiques, posh restaurants and art galleries. For a brief moment, it makes me believe that redemption really is possible.

The Bull and Barrow pub is tucked away down a small side street that's more of an alleyway really. It's poorly lit and refuse bags of overspilling rubbish and rotten food line the narrow pavement. Deliciously greasy cooking smells waft out from an open back exit of a fast-food restaurant, reminding me that all I've consumed in twenty-four hours is a bottle of wine and a Kit Kat. I hear the staff in the kitchen shouting to each other in a foreign language that I can't identify. One of them glances over at me as I pass by and I quickly turn away.

I check in using the name, Molly Malcolm. Not the most original perhaps, but it'll do.

'How long you staying for, Molly, one or two nights?' the

man behind the bar asks. If I'm correct, I think his name might be Pete. He has multiple piercings in almost every part of his face, and the skin on his forearms is blurred with ink, which is exactly how he was described. I imagine he thinks he's quite an imposing figure to look at, but I've seen far worse than Pete.

'A few days,' I reply. 'Maybe more...'

He gives me a bit of a hard stare, like he's sizing me up.

'London's a big city,' I say. 'Lots to see.'

He looks at me for a moment longer before breaking into a smile.

'It sure is, sister. Eight point eight million people living here today, though I reckon that's a bit of a conservative estimate myself. Anyway, I wouldn't want to count everyone, put it that way. We need a £50 deposit in case you trash the room,' he sniffs. 'You paying cash or card?'

As anticipated, the room is poky, but it's clean and perfectly adequate for my needs with a bed, a small dressing table, a chair and a tiny bathroom that's just big enough to stand up in. I plug in my laptop before I take a hot and cold shower. The thermostats in the showers at Larksmere were forever faulty. One minute they'd be scalding hot and then the next, a blast of ice-cold water would take your breath away. Eventually, through necessity, I learned the rhythm between the two temperature extremes and knew when to take a step back. Oddly, since my release, I've found myself manually doing this little dance whenever I shower, turning the tap from hot to cold, and back again. I wonder what my therapist would make of that? Not that it matters. I won't be seeing her again.

I'm thinking of Molly as I empty my medication, pill by pill, down the toilet, and then start to wash my hair. Little round, foraging, mousey Molly and her inherent need to help others so that she can reassure herself that she's a good person by doing good things. I wonder how long it will be before she realises that I've absconded? I hope she won't get into any trouble on my behalf. When all of this is over with, I hope someone will explain everything to her. Maybe Molly will understand – *maybe they all will*.

After my hot and cold shower, I towel dry my hair in front of the old, de-silvering mirror and rake a brush through it. I've read somewhere that there are two ways of spreading light: to be the candle, or the mirror that reflects it. I'm not sure which of these I am, or indeed if I am either. A mirror is little more than a belief system anyway. We only ever see what we want to see in the mirror.

I take a deep breath in as I begin to cut at my hair with the scissors. I'd inherited my thick, dark hair, along with the green eyes, from my Venezuelan father, who died when I was four years old from prostate cancer. I often wonder what my life would've been like if he'd lived. For one thing, I know my mother would still be alive today. I'll be sad to see it go – my hair is almost the last thing I have left of him.

I start off gingerly with the scissors, but after a while it begins to feel more like fun than I thought it would and so I hack away at it with abandon until it's just below my ears, in a short, and not-so-neat bob. I stand back from the mirror, admire my handiwork for a second before I begin mixing up the peroxide in the small red plastic pot. I've never dyed my hair in my whole forty years on this planet. I've never needed to, although, admittedly, a few stray greys have started slipping through. I play the YouTube video I'd found earlier as a guide and separate my hair into small sections with clips before carefully pasting the smelly blue gloop onto my head. Eventually though, I give up on the video and just slap it all on and wrap a plastic bag around it. I can feel the burn of the chemicals, harsh and hot against my scalp, almost instantly as I tear open the Snickers bar with my teeth.

There's 8.8 million people in London, though I think that's a conservative estimate... Pete's words loop around my head. Now that the police have released an artist's sketch of Samantha's face and requested the public's help in locating her, I suspect she will have gone into hiding, maybe even in plain sight.

She'll probably be using a new alias and identity, or she could even have fled the country, and yet something tells me that she's here, in this city somewhere, watching herself going viral on social media from a place of safety, relishing the notoriety. *I can feel her close.* The more I think about it, the more I'm convinced that she has used the name Samantha Valentine again deliberately. What other explanation could there be? Does she *want* to be found? Is it the thrill of the chase that she's after, by outsmarting the police and the public, *by outsmarting me?* I can't help feeling that this is all very personal somehow and that she's taunting me. *But I just don't know why?* Had she thought about me over the years, kept abreast of my case? Did she know where I was all the time I was in Larksmere? I'm convinced that she did, and that it gives her a frisson, knowing that I was convicted of killing Bojan Radulovic and subsequently sent to a mental institution for the criminally insane. It made me want to smash things up when I imagined her sense of delight at having duped me into killing for her, congratulating herself at being clever enough to pull the wool over everyone's eyes and then – pouf! – disappear without a trace. '*Where did that evil bitch go?*' I bang out the beats of the words with my fist against the small wooden dressing table.

Sometimes, like now, the rage overwhelms me. The injustice and the hatred and the vengeance, slowly choking me to death. I want it to end, but it won't until I find her. And it won't end until I know why she's done this to me. It's like a funeral without a body. I can never move on.

I finish off the Snickers bar and start on a tube of fruit pastilles that I'd forgotten I had in my handbag. I pop two into my mouth at once, not even bothering to check what colour they are. Now that her name is out there in the public domain, it's only a matter of time before the cops will link me back to her.

My crime went largely unreported at the time it was committed six years ago, and the name Samantha Valentine remained elusive to the press at large. But the police knew about it because I told them, *they* knew her name – *and did nothing*. Soon it will flag up, if they do their intel correctly, and they'll come looking for me. Only they won't find me. This time I'm one step ahead. This time I'm armed with knowledge and, unlike the police, I know exactly what and who I'm up against.

Anyway, I can't rely on those bozos, or trust them – that would be a grave mistake – but I need more information; information that only the police will have access to. It's their job to find people, and like old, pierced Pete downstairs at the bar said, *There's over 8.8 million people in the city, sister...*

The cops don't know it yet, but they are going to be the ones who lead me to her. They have the resources to find her far quicker than I could working alone. Finally, with their help, I hope to be able to right the wrongs that have been done to me, to Bojan Radulovic and his family, this time using my own kind of justice. But first I'm going to have my say, tell them my story in all its glory and gory detail. *And this time they're going to listen.*

I pick up the burner phone, switch it on and fire it up before punching in the digits.

'Hello, yes... Hi... My name is Erin Santos. I'd like to speak to Detective Chief Inspector Dan Riley, please.'

FIFTEEN

DAN

It was almost midnight and I was just about to leave the office when the call came through to the incident room. I'd just got off the phone to Fiona to tell her I was on my way home as well. Honestly, it's like a conspiracy.

We've been busy ever since we released Samantha Valentine's name and sketch to the media. Sensing there's more to the story, they're pumping us for information, and members of the public have begun calling and messaging the incident room. Already she's been sighted at a bus stop in North London, and at a petrol station in Penge. Someone rang in earlier claiming to have seen her on a beach in Broadstairs yesterday, and, roughly at the same time, in Regent's Park in London – all of which will, I suspect, come to nothing but will need to be followed up regardless. Interestingly though, no one is yet to come forward claiming to actually *know* Samantha Valentine personally, or where she might live. And, perhaps most importantly, she hasn't come forward herself.

It has of course crossed my mind that, assuming she really does exist, perhaps she doesn't want to be found, which in itself could be telling. People don't generally hide unless they have something – or someone – to hide from. My duty, first and foremost, is to make sure she's safe.

'What *do* we know? What *don't* we know? And in the middle of that, what do we *think*?' I said when addressing the team this morning, right before I'd released Tilly Ward on pre-charge bail. Her conditions are that she must relinquish her passport over to us and she has a curfew between 7 p.m. and 9 a.m. while we continue our investigation. Plus, we'll keep a close eye on her. Not that I think she will try and abscond. Tilly Ward is a vulnerable adult who appears genuinely confused and traumatised by what's happened, and by what she's done. This morning, when I asked her if she had the support of family and friends, or a neighbour she could turn to, she said, 'I don't have any family, Dan. Sam was the only close friend I really had.'

'I hope you've done the right thing, Riley,' – Archer's voice had an amber tone to it when I had debriefed her – 'releasing that name, *and* releasing our suspect at the same time. I hope you're sure about this.'

'I believe her, ma'am,' I replied. 'Something is off about this whole case. We're digging deeper into Tilly Ward's background now, but so far it seems that she's pretty much the last person who'd make up such an extraordinary story, let alone murder anyone. She's already confessed to inflicting the fatal wound – albeit in self-defence – so why lie about the rest of it? It doesn't make sense?'

'To get herself a lesser charge perhaps, Riley?' she said, tersely. 'You'll have every nutcase phoning in now, you realise that, don't you? And it'll be more time and manpower and money spent... The press are bloody loving it. That sketch that Tilly drew seems to have ignited the public's interest.'

'I thought all publicity was good publicity, ma'am?'

She looked up, sharply.

'We're going to look like idiots if it turns out this Samantha

Valentine is a non-entity and we've released a murderer. Actually,' – she pauses – '*we* won't look like idiots, Riley, *you* will.' Her comment didn't concern me. I have no problem with looking like an idiot, it comes naturally. But I *do* have a problem with not doing my job properly. And there's definitely more to all of this than first meets the eye.

'You'll have to get this sorted lively, Riley,' she snapped. 'I don't want mistakes made, not while we're under such scrutiny from your friends in the press.' She straightens the papers on her desk carefully until they're all perfectly aligned.

My friends?

'Anyway, you know as well as I do that we don't need to prove motive for a murder charge. And you had better hope that Tilly Ward doesn't run,' she'd added sagely. 'Because it'll be your ass on the line.'

My little chat with Archer had wrongfooted me. I need Samantha Valentine to come forward or be found quickly, or to somehow prove that she doesn't exist, so that Tilly Ward can be charged accordingly. Surely Archer couldn't argue that her story is such that it needs further investigation? I mean, a partially deaf, middle-aged bookseller with no previous history of violence, stabbing someone who appears to have been a stranger to death in their home doesn't happen every day, *it just doesn't*. Add to that Tilly's bizarre explanation, and I owe it to all involved – not least Milo Harrison and his family – to get to the truth, even though at this point, I have no idea what that truth might be.

It was a good omen that Davis was the one who picked up the call, not to mention timing. I was almost out the door.

'Gov! Gov... I've got a woman on the line... she says her name is Erin Santos and she's asking to speak to you personally, about Samantha Valentine.' Her eyes widen. 'She's claiming to know who she is, gov...' I take my arm out of my coat sleeve and double back on myself.

'Put her through, Lucy.' I pick up the receiver, clear my throat. 'DCI Dan Riley speaking...'

There's a slight pause.

'You sound exactly as I imagined you would,' the voice says. It's soft, with a slight Northern burr to it.

'How can I help you, er...?'

'My name is Erin Santos,' she states clearly. 'Please call me Erin.'

'OK, Erin, what can I do for you? Do you have some information for me regarding a missing person?'

'She's not missing,' she says, flatly. '*She's hiding*. Most likely in plain sight as well.'

I raise my hand to signal to the team that this could be something. I place the call on loudspeaker, start recording it.

'And before I continue, there's no point in trying to put a trace on this call, Detective Riley. I won't be on long enough, and it's a burner phone anyway.'

The room falls stone cold silent. If someone shed a hair now, I think I would hear it drop from their head.

Davis's eyes are on mine and I give her the nod to start the trace.

'Please call me Dan, Erin. And why would I want to put a trace on the call?'

'You'll find out soon enough,' she says. 'Sounds like the gang is on it already anyway. Are they any good?'

'Who – my team, you mean?'

'Yes. Or are they a bunch of incompetents who like a nice clean case to wrap up in a pretty little bow, regardless of the truth?'

I detect a slight malice in her tone for a brief second. I wonder why it's there.

'They're a good team of hard-working detectives and police officers, Erin.'

'I'll take your word for that, Dan,' she says, earnestly this time. 'You, at least, strike me as the type who believes in truth and justice.'

'My colleague tells me that you have some information for us, information on a witness we're looking for, someone called Samantha Valentine, is that right? You said she was hiding?'

'Yes.'

'Do you know where?'

She pauses.

'I know who Samantha Valentine is. Well, I know who she is to me.'

My heart starts beating hard in my chest.

'Who is she to *you*, Erin?'

'What can you tell me about the crime that took place recently? The murder that happened in Stockwell Gardens, the man that was killed...'

I look over at Davis. She's shaking her head. If she's using a burner phone without GPS, it'll be nigh on impossible to trace her.

'Only what's already been released to the press. Why? Do you know something about this crime?'

There's a pause.

'The woman who was arrested, was she a friend of Samantha's by any chance? A close friend, someone she trusted?'

OK, *now* I'm excited.

'Why are you asking me that, Erin?'

'Did Samantha tell this woman that she was being abused by the man she went on to kill? Did she engineer such a situation to happen following weeks, months even, spent grooming her, creating a credible, believable story where *she* was the victim, a story, incidentally, concocted entirely from lies? Oh, and let me guess,' she continues, almost whimsically, 'did she stab him in the chest?'

Do I answer truthfully? It's clear that whoever Erin Santos is, she knows *a lot* of detail about the crime – unreleased detail.

'Did she use a kitchen knife? Was it one single, deep and fatal puncture wound, straight to his heart, or something similar?'

My hands are shaking with adrenalin as I think about my strategy. I make a call on it.

'Yes.'

Silence.

'Erin? Are you still there?'

'I'm here.'

'How do you know all of this, Erin? How do you know Samantha Valentine? Were you also familiar with the victim?'

'I liked that article that was written about you in the paper the other day.' She changes the subject. 'I saw it on social media. You look...'

I hold my breath, hoping that she isn't going to say, 'distinguished'. I really don't think I could cope.

'... Trustworthy. I see a genuineness in your eyes. You see, my instincts are highly evolved now, Detective Riley. I've learned how to read people and situations better than most. I suspect that you're a very good judge of character yourself.'

Davis is staring back at me, unblinking.

'It can help with the job, Erin.' I keep my tone friendly and conversational. I don't want her to hang up.

'Gov!' My finger shoots up to my lips as Mitchell enters the room. She stops, tiptoes towards me, her head shaking in what looks like disbelief as she places something onto my desk.

'The woman who killed your victim...' Erin continues. 'Would you say that she's the antithesis of a murderer, looking at her? Is she a *nice* person, a bit vulnerable in some way perhaps, maybe even shy or naive, and definitely not the sort who goes around stabbing people to death?'

Now my heart stops dead in my chest.

'Do you *know* the woman arrested at the scene?'

'Ha! I'm right, aren't I? And, no, I don't know anything about her or who she is, even. But I *do* know that there are *two* victims in this crime, Dan – the deceased *and* the perpetrator of that fatal wound.'

'What do you mean by that exactly, Erin?'

The pause is long enough for me to think she may have hung up.

'Samantha Valentine is a con-woman.'

I hear her take a sudden sharp intake of breath, as though she's in pain.

'Are you OK? Erin... hello? Erin...?'

I hear movement, some shuffling in the background.

'Listen, Erin, would you prefer to talk in person? I can come and meet you...'

'You have no idea who you're dealing with, Dan,' she interjects, though it's unclear who she's referring to exactly, herself or Samantha Valentine.

'So tell me.'

She's sucking air through her teeth now – it definitely sounds like she's in some kind of discomfort.

'If your team are as good as you say they are, Dan, then my police file is probably on your desk already. Read it. It'll explain more.'

'Erin, listen, don't hang up, take my number, my private number...'

Davis's eyes widen. It's not standard procedure, I realise, to give out my personal digits – Archer would have harsh words to say about it, I'm sure – but something about this caller tells me she's legit, and I want her to trust me.

I recite it to her, though I can't tell if she's taken note of it or not.

'... I have to go now,' she says. 'I'm washing my hair. Nice talking with you, Dan. I'll be in touch soon.'

SIXTEEN
ERIN

'... *Argh...!*'

I tear at the plastic bag from my head, cursing as I rip it off. It feels like it's going to burst into flames at any moment.

Rushing into the bathroom, I grab the shower attachment, start rinsing the peroxide off in a panic, sweating and puffing as the cold water gushes onto my burning skin. Twenty minutes it had said on the box. Only ten had passed and already I couldn't take the pain anymore. Marilyn Monroe must've been hard as nails. Regrettably though, it meant I'd had no choice but to cut short my conversation with Detective Dan. Just as it was getting interesting as well.

The detective has a nice voice; it's deep, with a sort of gentle consideration to it. It matches his face somehow. I can't trust him of course – he's still a policeman – but I get the impression that he's something of a maverick by the fact that he's given me his personal phone number. Plus he's a family man, and I like that about him, envy it I suppose. He'd referenced his wife and children affectionately throughout the article I'd read on him, which makes me feel a touch regretful that I'm going to use him for my own ends, to get information from him. But all's fair in love and war – and justice, let's not forget justice.

I picture Detective Dan right now, reading through my police file. I wonder what he's thinking, and, moreover, what he's going to do about it. I wasn't lying to him when I said he has no idea who he's dealing with. *I wasn't lying full stop.*

My scalp feels tender and sore as I rub my now-much-shorter hair with a towel. Glimpsing myself in the old mirror, I drop the hairbrush, gasp.

I don't recognise myself. My short, slightly uneven hair is now a bright yellow colour and looks like the bad DIY dye job that it is. After the toner washes off and it dries though, it lifts slightly, looks a bit cooler and less brassy. Anyway, it's no Vidal Sassoon number, but it'll have to do. You see, in order to *find* Samantha Valentine, I have to *think* like Samantha Valentine. To beat her at her own game, Erin Santos has to vanish into thin air, just as she did.

I find my small cosmetics bag and begin searching through it for a red lipstick. It might work well with the blonde. I very rarely wear make-up anymore. I certainly didn't need it at Larksmere, though some of the more manageable inmates and I would make each other up from time to time, largely to relieve the monotony and to remind ourselves that we were women, women who once may even have been desirable. It's amazing what a bit of lipstick can do to lift your mood, it really is.

'Wit-woo! You look nice, Molly.' Pierced Pete raises his eyebrows in quick succession as I enter the bar from the guests' entrance. Maybe blondes really *do* have more fun. When I'd arrived at the pub earlier, I'd made sure that my long dark hair had been tucked up well inside my bobble hat so that no one would see the dramatic change when I revealed my new hair later on. 'Hope it's not on my account.' He winks at me, affords me a glimpse of two gold teeth as he grins. Perhaps it's the lipstick?

The Bull and Barrow is a typical old-school London pub with worn, burgundy velvet benches, low, orange replica Tiffany lighting, and ugly, dark wooden furnishings. Years of ingrained nicotine and grime have turned the flock wallpaper a cack-brown and I can almost still smell the stale cigarettes in the air. My eyes are drawn to a collage of sun-faded photographs on a wall featuring a timeline of people who have enjoyed a drink here – or two, given the look of some of them – over the decades. Pete, at various stages and ages, features in more or less all of them.

'We've had a fair few famous faces in here over the years, sister, let me tell you,' he says proudly, nodding at them. 'All sorts, from Hollywood legends to legendary gangsters, and everything else in between.'

I should probably say now that I've deliberately chosen the Bull and Barrow pub as my London HQ. I am not here purely by chance. Though there is a chance that what I'd heard from an inmate at Larksmere *is* a bunch of bull.

Sandra had mentioned this place, not to me directly, but I'd overheard her talking about it many times in the stories she told other inmates. Sandra ended up at Larksmere after she became involved in drugs and subsequently, criminal activity, because one very rarely exists without the other. She was diagnosed with bipolar disorder and depression as a teenager and had spent what had sounded like a truly horrible life in and out of prison and mental institutions. She claimed to have been a well-connected drug dealer for a time and, being from London, had mentioned the Bull and Barrow in King's Cross as being 'the kind of place where you could get anything, fake ID, drugs, guns, girls...' 'A proper den of iniquity,' she'd called it.

Sandra had shot, and killed, a fellow drug dealer while high on her own supply. Regrettably, the woman's five-year-old son had been caught in the crossfire and was seriously injured, though thankfully survived. Subsequently, Sandra tried to commit suicide by shooting herself in the neck, only somehow the bullet missed every vital part that could've ended her life and exited her body without doing any lasting damage, save for the visible (and invisible) scars left behind. I'd been terrified of her when I had first entered Larksmere. She had the unsettling demeanour of someone who could switch on you in a hair's breadth and was built like a barn door. Largely though, she left me alone, and I never had any trouble from her personally.

Sandra liked to tell stories, so it's still a long shot, coming here, but I had overheard her mention a heavily tattooed and pierced guy called Pete who ran this place. It has to be the same guy I'm currently looking at.

'I don't doubt it,' I say. I can't help wondering, as I stare at their faces, what they might be doing now, these people captured in these photos, smiling and happy for that brief moment in time, and what's become of them.

'You want a drink before you go off out and make someone's night tonight?'

Pete grins at me again, a touch lasciviously perhaps. Is he flirting with me? Aside from that mad moment with Malcolm earlier, which I'm still trying to process, I've been out of the game for so long that I can't tell.

'Go on, why not?' I smile, hoping I haven't got lipstick on my teeth. That's never a good look. 'I'll have a Jack Daniel's and Diet Coke.'

'A double for the lady?'

'When in Rome...'

'You're looking at the photographs there...' He starts to fix my drink. 'Were you looking for someone in particular?'

The fact that he asks me this question makes me think that I'm definitely in the right place – he's suspicious.

'Actually, I was looking for my friend, Sandra. Sandra Morton, Morty.'

His eyes widen a touch in surprise and, I'm hoping, recognition. 'I thought she might be in one of them.'

'Big Sandra, South London Sandra, you mean?'

Well, Sandra was definitely 'big' and I believe she was from Peckham, originally.

'Yeah, that's her. She spoke highly of this place, and of you. She said if ever I was in London, that I should come and see you and that you'd *look after me.*'

He grins again. It's *definitely* lascivious this time. I go along with it. I need his help.

'Did she now? Well, that was nice of her, wasn't it?' He leans in towards me suddenly, his whole demeanour instantly changing. He appears aggressive, even a touch menacing, but he's going to have to do much better than that to intimidate me.

'I was at East Sutton Park with her for a while, regrettably,' I sniff, *lie*.

East Sutton is an open women's prison in Kent. I knew Sandra had been there at some point because she had talked about that too.

'What were you inside for?' He softens a little, though a touch of wariness remains as he grabs a bottle of bourbon from behind the bar and places it down hard on the wooden surface.

'Drugs,' I say. 'My ex was a dealer. I wouldn't rat him out so they gave me eighteen months for perverting the course of justice. I made a mistake,' – I shrug – 'getting involved with him, I mean.'

He pours another large slug of dark liquid into my glass, watching me carefully. 'Cheers!'

He bangs it with his own and I swallow back half of it, relish the burn at the back of my throat.

'Well, you'll get no judgement here from me, sister. Like they say, if you're not making mistakes, then you're not doing *anything*. So,' – he pours me another shot of bourbon, his menace dissipating – 'your accent tells me you're not local, not originally at least. What brings you to the big smoke then? Aside from the weather and fair prices – and the good-looking barmen, of course?'

I let out a little breathy laugh, humour him. I really must work on perfecting different accents. Samantha was *so* good at them, a born natural.

'Oh, you know, a bit of business, here and there. A change of scenery is never a bad thing.' I smile at him. 'And it's always nice to meet new people, don't you think?'

'I'll drink to that, sister.'

After topping me up once again, he screws the lid back on the bourbon and props his elbows up onto the bar. He moves his face close to mine – too close for my general comfort, I can feel his breath against my cheek – but I don't flinch.

'So, lil sister, are you looking for a mister?'

His breath smells of bourbon with a punchy top note of gum disease. Like most men I meet, I find him repellent and am mistrustful of him, but I remind myself that I'm simply playing a game. I just have to think like Samantha would. I shrug my shoulders at him, smile a little coquettishly.

'I'll go wherever Cupid's arrow takes me.'

He grins back at me, his gold teeth illuminated in the low orange light.

'So, what else did Big Sandra say about me, then, eh?'

I glance around me. It's gone midnight and the place has emptied out a bit now; only a few shady-looking suspects remain, lurking behind in the shadows of the dark corners. I prop my elbows up onto the bar against his, shuffle in close and look him straight in his small, dark eyes.

'She said that you could get me a gun.'

SEVENTEEN

DAN

The file from West Yorkshire Police dates back to 2019, seven years earlier. A thirty-four-year-old local woman named Erin Santos was arrested for murder. The victim was a man named Bojan Radulovic, though Erin had insisted he was known to her as someone named Ari Hussain. My brow creases in confusion. *What the hell is this?*

According to one of the statements given during interview at the time – an interview that was conducted by a Detective Amanda Pritchard at Leeds Central Police Station – Erin claimed that Ari Hussain was her friend's fiancé – and that friend's name was – you guessed it – *Samantha Valentine*.

My stomach somersaults as I read.

… Santos claims that Samantha told her she was being abused by her fiancé, Ari Hussain, for many months… (Erin) has confessed to fatally stabbing Mr Radulovic, believing that her own life and the life of her friend, Samantha, were in immediate danger…

'*Good God...*' I whisper underneath my breath. 'This is almost a duplicate script of our crime, Davis.'

'*What?*'

She comes in closer, starts reading over my shoulder.

'Tilly Ward's statement, and this Erin Santos's – it's practically identical, Lucy. Both women say they were protecting someone called Samantha Valentine, and both say they believed that she was being abused by her partner before they ended up killing him in self-defence...'

My mind is glitching like a faulty radio. The same name, the same crime, practically. It *can't* be coincidence. These crimes happened six years apart, in two different cities, perpetrated by two different women who, at first glance at least, appear to be unconnected to each other. An icy chill suddenly runs right through me. What are we dealing with here? Is this Samantha Valentine some kind of a Svengali figure who befriends people and then coerces them into *murder*? Is *that* her MO? If it is, then it makes her an extremely dangerous individual indeed.

'It says here,' Davis's voice pulls me out of my thoughts, 'that Erin has a history of mental health issues and spent time on a psych ward at a place called Ashdown Hospital, a couple of years prior to her arrest...'

She hands the file back to me.

'... No trace of anyone named Samantha Valentine officially in existence...' I read the police report aloud. 'She is *not* registered at the address of the crime, there are *no* witnesses... nothing to link Erin to anyone with that name, *no* photos, *no* social media...'

I glance up at Davis again.

'Get a warrant for all the social media companies – request information on any active, inactive and deleted accounts for anyone named Samantha Valentine in the past decade.' I nod at DS Baylis. This could go way back, years even. Con artists, if that's what we're dealing with, in whatever form they may come, always leave a trail of victims in their path. You don't just wake up one morning and decide to diddle someone out of their life savings or coerce them into murder. From what I know, most con artists start honing their skills from an early age.

'Check for any connections between Erin Santos and Tilly Ward, anything that could possibly link them together. We need to rule that out straight off the bat.' I nod at Mitchell. 'And cross-reference any victims of coercion and con crimes where someone may have used a similar MO...'

I've not worked on many — strike that, *any* — cases before where someone is suspected of coercing another into killing for them. It's unusual to say the least. The only example that springs to mind is Charles Manson, the 60s cult leader who brainwashed his followers — usually very young, vulnerable women — into committing grizzly murders in an attempt to start a race war. Though he was eventually imprisoned for first-degree murder and conspiracy to commit murder, he never actually dirtied his hands by killing anyone personally. A coward no less, as well as a psychopath.

I turn to Baylis.

'I want you and Harding on the CCTV footage we have of the person in the black puffer coat, the unwanted visitor at Milo Harrison's address. I think it's a woman, and I want to know who she is *and* why he didn't want to see her. Oh, and do a search on the name Ari Hussain, find out if it's legit.'

'On it, boss.'

'If Erin Santos calls again, put her straight through and see if we can get a trace this time, OK — straight through to me directly.'

Davis is still reading the file as I collapse down onto the swivel chair behind my desk. When I glance up I see that she's staring at me.

'What? What is it, Davis?'

She places the papers carefully down onto my desk, like a

deck of cards. I don't know if Davis has ever played poker before, but something tells me she'd be good at it.

'They didn't believe her, gov.'

'Who didn't believe her – what?'

'Us, the police, they didn't believe Erin's account at the time, they didn't buy her story about Samantha Valentine.'

I sit forwards sharply, a fresh new injection of adrenalin cutting through my exhaustion. 'They thought it was all a ruse, gov, and that she made up a false witness as an alibi. It's there, in her file.' She nods to it.

'So... what happened to her? Was she convicted of the murder?' I'm really not liking the sound of this.

'She was charged with it, but it says she took a plea and got manslaughter on the grounds of diminished responsibility and was sentenced to...' – she slowly trains her eyes back on mine – '... six years in Larksmere High Security Psychiatric Hospital.'

My thoughts must instantly register on my face because Davis raises her eyes.

'Exactly, gov. No one in their "right mind" would ever want to go there.' She shoots me an apologetic smile. 'Sorry, bad joke, boss.'

'Was she though? In her right mind, I mean, when she was sent to Larksmere?'

I can only hope that Erin Santos *wasn't*, because the alternative doesn't bear thinking about. Being insane in a place like that would be hellish enough.

Larksmere Hospital's formidable reputation precedes it. As an institution that houses some of the UK's most dangerous criminally insane individuals, it's not exactly known for its five-star accommodation and refined clientele. Why didn't Yorkshire Police look into Erin's story in more detail, I wonder? Was she deemed an unreliable witness due to her past mental health issues? Was she *discriminated* against and ended up there as a result? This might explain her animosity towards the police.

Come on, Erin. Call me back, tell me what happened, tell me your story.

'Gov.'

Parker is in front of me with a satisfied look on his face.

'We've found an address for Erin Santos.'

Parker reminds me a little of my younger self in some ways, though perhaps I flatter myself. He's got a good head – and heart – on him. On the morning the news got round the building about my son's diagnosis, he bought me a bacon sandwich and a cup of tea from the canteen and left it on my desk. He never took credit for it, but I knew it was he who'd left it there – he'd forgotten to put the ketchup in.

'She's living in charity housing in Leeds after being released from Larksmere, a little over six weeks ago. She's effectively on licence for the next eighteen months.'

Davis throws me a sideways glance. *Just six weeks ago.* My mind starts buzzing like a hornet's nest. Erin Santos was released from the country's most notorious mental hospital a little over a month ago and now we have an almost identical crime to the one she committed six years ago – under influence or not – with the same name, Samantha Valentine, at the heart of it. I turn to Parker.

'Get in touch with Leeds Central and get them to send a car round to that address, now, tonight.' I have no faith in my request bearing fruit however – something tells me that Erin Santos is already long gone.

EIGHTEEN

It was 2 a.m. by the time I crept into bed and spooned into my warm, sleeping wife underneath the soft, clean sheets. I nuzzled into her, hoping to savour the feeling a moment longer before I fell asleep – but it was too late.

My son's cries woke me with a start sometime later. Fiona groaned awake as she pulled the duvet back, but I stopped her before she could throw a leg out.

'I'll go.'

I fed Jude his bottle of formula or 'milky num-nums' as his big sister, Pip, calls it, slumped on the sofa while looking through Erin Santos's police files. It made for unsettling reading. Erin's account of what had happened seven years ago was dismissed by investigating officers at the time as an 'elaborate' story, one she'd concocted to minimise her culpability. Police found no evidence to support Erin's claims that anyone called Samantha Valentine existed. They could find no trace of her, though from what I can tell, their efforts weren't exactly exhaustive. They concluded that Erin Santos was delusional and suffering from 'adverse mental health issues'. And of course, I already know where she ended up.

I read on, but each word seems to fill me with more dread. In retrospect, it doesn't make the police look good. Archer isn't going to like this one bit.

The unexpected shrill ring of my phone causes me to jolt upright. Instinctively, I glance down at Jude, but he's still sound asleep in the crook of my arm, and my heart sinks in my chest – *he can't hear the phone ringing*.

'Dan Riley.'

I hear breathing down the line. There's a pause.

'*Erin*, is that you?'

'Hello, Dan,' she says as I place the phone between my ear and shoulder and gently lay Jude down onto the cushions next to me. He snuffles but is otherwise undisturbed, bless him.

'I'm really glad you called back, Erin. I've been reading your police file.'

'I'm sorry for calling at this late hour – I know you have a young family.' She sighs. 'Must be nice, having a family to come home to. It's all I ever wanted really, you know, to have a little family of my own. Sounds corny, doesn't it?'

I hear regret, or perhaps resentment, in her voice.

'That's still possible, isn't it, Erin? And no – it doesn't.'

Turns out my earlier hunch was right. There was no answer when Leeds had sent a patrol car to do a welfare check on Erin. I sense that she's likely gone on the run, but I don't yet know why exactly, or what her connection is to Milo Harrison's murder. 'After all, you're a free woman now, Erin.'

She snorts, softly.

'Ah yes, a *free* woman! I suppose it all depends on how you interpret the word "free", doesn't it, Dan? I'm a "free" forty-year-old convicted killer who's been locked away in a secure psychiatric hospital for the past six years. I mean, come on,' she scoffs, 'would *you* swipe right?'

'Where are you now, Erin? Are you in London? Can we meet?'

'I went dizzy when I saw her name on the Met news feed. I thought I might actually pass out for a moment.' She ignores me, continues. 'You see, Dan, when I was rotting away spiritually, mentally and physically inside that medieval cesspit, Larksmere, I wasn't sure this day was ever going to come, you know? The day when Samantha Valentine resurfaces and my truth is validated and I'm vindicated at last. Only... here it is! But d'you know,' she sighs again, 'I thought I would feel better than I do, knowing there was someone else out there, another victim of that twisted psychopath and that I'm not alone... but in all honesty, Dan, I think it might have made me feel *worse*.'

Has she been drinking? I detect the gentlest slur around the edges of her words.

'I've been searching for her for the past six years of my life, all that time while I was incarcerated. *Six years* that should've been spent building a life and a home, having that family I always wanted, maybe even a career. But instead, because of her, whoever she *really* is, I became a murderer and a liar, a mentally ill danger to the public, and then I was sent to atone for it all in hell.'

The gravity of her words silences me.

'Do you know what ECT is, Dan?'

'ECT?'

'Electroconvulsive therapy, or ECT for ease. They put you under general anaesthetic for it, you know, knock you out, and then, well, God only knows what they do to you, but they dig about inside your head, have a little tinker around, shuffle things about a bit. It's supposed to change your brain chemistry or something. Like a factory reset of the mind.'

'Is that what happened at Larksmere, Erin? Did you have ECT?'

Her own silence hangs heavy down the line.

'I should never have been there,' she says quietly. '*She* put me there, and the police did nothing to stop her. Do you believe me, Dan?'

I can hear my heartbeat pulsing loudly in my ears. *Do I believe her?*

'At the time, police found no evidence to support your story that anyone named Samantha Valentine existed, Erin.'

'There is now though, isn't there, Dan – evidence, I mean? This crime you're investigating, it's the same story. She used the same MO, didn't she? *And she used the same name.* That was a gamble, don't you think? Very bold, but then,' she snorts, 'that's Samantha all over.'

'Why do you think she did that, Erin – used the same name again?'

'Oh, I'm sure she's just *loving* all the attention on social media, all the mystery surrounding her. *"Who is Samantha Valentine?"* It's what narcissists like her thrive on, after all – attention, positive or negative, it doesn't matter, it's all the same to them. Or *maaaybe*' – she elongates the word – 'it's something more personal than that.'

'More personal? Personal in what way? Did you fall out with Samantha? Did something happen between you and that's why she did this?'

I hear her take a breath to speak, but then she stops herself.

'You do realise, it's all just a game to her, Dan. She befriends people, fast. And then she love-bombs them, casts her spell upon them and puts them under it until they're completely in her control, nothing more than a grateful puppet for her to play with and manipulate. There was no fallout, no argument between us, never... she was my friend, truly, the best friend I've ever had. She seemed to understand me better than anyone else I've ever met before...' Her voice trails off into a melancholy whisper. 'One thing I *do* know is that she thinks that she's cleverer than you or me. And the maddening truth – no pun intended – is that she's probably right.'

'We sent a car to your address earlier, to do a welfare check. You weren't at home. I have to ask you this, Erin, but where were you last Thursday evening?'

Her shrill laugh jangles my nerves a touch.

'Finally! I've been waiting for you to ask this question, Dan, and the truth is, I don't have an alibi for the night of your murder, but I was at home, alone. I ate scrambled eggs on toast for dinner while watching *Grease* – one of my favourite films, incidentally – and drank a bottle of red wine. Usually, I prefer white, or sparkling, ideally, but it was on special in Spar.'

'Are you somewhere safe, Erin? Re-Connex has reported you missing.'

'Bloody hell, that was quick!' She seems surprised. 'Good old Molly... Listen, I want it on record that she's done nothing wrong. I broke her trust and I'm sorry, but I had to.'

'Who's Molly, Erin?'

'Oh, and you'll probably speak to Malcolm as well, I'm sure.'

'Who's Malcolm?' I reach for a pen on the coffee table, write the names down on the back of a gas bill.

'My neighbour from across the hall. We slept together yesterday afternoon, just so you know.'

'Oh. OK...'

'But he really doesn't know anything about me. Perhaps you can apologise to him on my behalf as well? Tell him Erin says, "I'm sorry."'

'I'm concerned for you, Erin. Part of the conditions of your release is that you have to make your parole officer aware of your movements. I don't want you to get into trouble. Why did you leave your address abruptly without telling anyone? What are you running from, Erin?'

'Not running *from*, Dan, running *to*. She'll do it again, you realise. She won't stop until someone stops her.'

'Who? Samantha?'

'Yes.'

'And you want to stop her?'

The line goes silent for a moment. At this point I have no idea if Erin Santos is somehow involved or even jointly responsible for Milo Harrison's death, but the fact that she was released from Larksmere just six weeks previously and an almost identical crime to her own has since been committed naturally rings some alarm bells, big ones.

'What are you going to do, Erin?' I get a feeling that she's planning something, and the knot in my guts seems to be telling me it's not especially good.

'Can I speak to this woman, the one you arrested, the one who claims to know Sam? It would be helpful if I could. I know what she's going through right now, what she must be feeling, I can help her...'

'I'm afraid that's not possible, Erin. Look, I understand why you might not have much faith, or trust, in the police. Reading the case file from 2019, it seems you were let down. But I want to help you, Erin, I really do.'

'*Let down...*' she repeats the words back to me. '*Let down*, yeah, that's a good one, Dan. I believe you though, when you say you want to help. It's why I chose you. I see it in your eyes – a determination, *a shared quest for truth and justice.*'

'What does justice look like to you, Erin? I can hear that you feel wronged, and reading your file would suggest you may have some cause. But you have to let me deal with this.' I'm growing increasingly concerned that her view of justice may look something more like revenge, and so it's a gentle warning.

'"Righteousness and justice are the foundation of your throne; loving kindness and truth go before you." Psalm 89:14. I learned the Bible by heart while I was in Larksmere,' she tells me, proudly. '"Give justice to the weak and the fatherless; maintain the right of the afflicted and the destitute." Psalm 82:3.' Her voice drops, hardens suddenly. '*I know what my justice looks like, Dan.*'

This is doing nothing to assuage my concerns.

'Who *is* she, Erin? Who *is* Samantha Valentine?'

She bursts into musical laughter.

'Ha! You tell me. You're the detective. What does the devil look like, Dan? I've spent every single day since I met her asking myself this very question – that together with *why?* You get a lot of time to reflect when you're locked away in a cell, zombified by the anti-psychotic drugs they pump you full of to keep you compliant and ensure you don't have a single human thought left inside your head.' She takes a breath. 'Do you know the worst part of all of this?'

'There's a worse part?'

She laughs.

'Ha, yeah, I like you, Dan, you're funny – and you're right! It's all pretty much a shit show, but the truth is...' – she pauses – '... I was never happier than when I was with Sam. Those months we spent together were some of the best of my life. Actually, maybe *the* best.'

It sounds as if she means it. 'Do you know, throughout my first year at Larksmere, even then, I was *still* hopeful that she might just somehow magically reappear and explain everything, tell the truth about what happened and that it was all a mistake – can you believe that, Dan? I was in denial – trauma bonded me to her, you see, even after I knew the truth, *even after everything*. I still missed her. I still *loved* her.' Emotion catches in her throat. 'What a sad, pathetic fool I was.'

'Why aren't there any photographs of you and Samantha together, Erin? It says in your file that you knew each other for a good few months before what happened. Surely during that time you'd have at least one or two pictures? Presumably you did stuff together, you went places together... Why couldn't you produce any? We can't find any, and Tilly—' I stop, curse myself inwardly. It was a sloppy slip-up born of sleep deprivation, but that's no excuse.

'*Ah*, so her name is *Tilly*, this new victim of hers that you've arrested? You do realise, Dan, that Tilly's no more a murderer than I am. Well, I know that technically she is, and technically I am too, but she never would've been, if she hadn't had the misfortune of meeting Samantha Valentine... If *I'd* never met Samantha Valentine... You *really* don't seem to know what you're dealing with here, do you?' She sounds a little irritated now. 'So let me tell you. I am of the belief that Samantha Valentine is a very slick, experienced con-woman; she's a trickster, a fraud, a charlatan, a scammer, a swindler, whatever you want to call her, or whatever she wants to call herself on that particular day, I should imagine. She's a chameleon, a shapeshifter, someone who, I suspect, can, in an instant, morph into anyone she chooses to become with an authenticity that you or I could never hope to imitate, even with a BA from RADA. *Because this is what she does*, Dan, she fools people, she lies about *everything*, and she's *extremely* good at it, I must warn you. She had me hooked on the line good and proper. I fell for her fictitious abuse story like a burning building. I was the perfect prey.'

She breathes deeply, as though her diatribe has taken it out of her. 'But getting back to your original question, I took *many* photos of us together, though Sam would often delete them immediately. She didn't much like herself in photographs, or so she said. I always thought she was just being self-critical and humble, because of course she was – maybe still is – very beautiful, only now of course, I know the real reason for her camera shyness. We even set up a photo-sharing library. When I was arrested, I tried to access that shared library to prove to that stone-cold bitch, Detective Pritchard, that I wasn't lying, but when I tried, the whole thing had been deleted. Pouf. Gone. Like it had never existed. Like *she* had never existed.'

'Did she ever defraud you financially? Take money from you?'

'No, though I'm sure if she'd wanted to she could've. I don't believe money was ever her objective. Not in my case at least – I didn't have much to extort – though I'm sure she has conned many men out of it in some way, shape or form over the years. She didn't have much respect for men; we were alike in that way and I mean no offence when I say that, Dan. I get the feeling you're probably the exception to the rule. I realise that not *all* men are monsters – *some women are too.*' She pauses.

'Anyway, Sam always seemed to have a lot of expendable cash. I just assumed it was "Ari's" money that she was spending. She told me that he worked in the city, that he was wealthy. It was a complete fabrication of course. Because Ari Hussain never even existed.'

'So why then, Erin, if it wasn't for money, why do you think she did this to you? What was her motive?' If what she's saying is true, then why would Samantha Valentine want either of these men killed? What was her connection to them? Had those men wronged her in some way? And why would she groom two innocent women into murdering them for her?

'I'd *really* like the answer to that myself, Dan.' Her bitterness crackles down the line. 'I don't know *why* she did it. I don't know *why* she chose me. I had very little for her to gain from me in any way. Over the years I have wracked my brains, what's left of them, to try and come up with a viable reason as to why this happened. I never had any enemies, or none I was aware of. I thought about ex-boyfriends. I'd had a few messy break-ups in the past, but nothing that would warrant the revenge of my complete destruction. I didn't go around deliberately wronging people or hurting them. Truthfully, I can think of no one who would want to destroy my life for *any* reason.'

She sighs heavily again. 'Maybe she just liked the look of me? Or *didn't* like the look of me? Or perhaps I reminded her of something, of someone from her past that triggered a bad memory? Maybe it was because there was a "y" in that particular day, or maybe it was just my rotten luck, a case of wrong place, wrong time? *You, the police,* should've been the ones who found the answers to those questions, Dan.' Her voice tightens. 'Questions that were never asked at the time because *I wasn't believed*. The scam she did on me, and, I suspect, also on this Tilly woman, was an emotional one, a psychological con. Maybe she simply targeted those men just like I suspect she targeted me and Tilly – on a whim? She knew an awful lot about Radulovic as it turned out though, so I suspected that she *was* familiar with him in some way, or was stalking him perhaps. But equally, it could all have just been a sick, twisted game, her victims targeted at random. You tell me how the mind of a psychopath works...'

She exhales through her nose. 'On some level I think it was driven by her need for power, some deep-rooted, twisted, inadequate desire to gain control of another person so completely that they no longer have an autonomous thought of their own and exist only for her and her desires. I realise now that I was just a vehicle, someone to do her bidding for her. Perhaps she wanted to see how far she could take it – how far she could exert that level of control over another human being – and what measure of her power and my loyalty could be greater than killing for her? It's the closest I've ever got to finding some way of explaining it all, of understanding it.'

Tilly Ward's terrified and confused face suddenly flashes up in my head. If all of this is somehow true, then I *have* to find this Valentine woman; I have to find her fast.

'I was a normal person once, you know, Dan.' She sounds different now; there's a desperate edge to her voice. 'OK, so I'd experienced some trauma in my childhood and that led to me making some bad decisions in my teens and twenties. I had some personal issues to work through, like many people. My mental health had deteriorated and I was depressed, I was taking drugs and eventually had a breakdown... But you have to understand, I was turning my life around when I met her, I'd turned a corner. I had started to believe that I had the chance to have a normal, happy life and move forward from the trauma of my past and start again... but instead... instead, I met *her*.'

I hear the pain in her words.

'Tell me your story, Erin,' I say. 'Tell me about Samantha Valentine. I want to know *everything*. Start from the beginning.'

NINETEEN

ERIN

July 2019, seven years ago

The air changes as she enters the room, feels different somehow, like someone important has just arrived.

I take one look at her and my heart drops down into my new shoes. *Brilliant.* I am *never* going to get this job now. She comes and takes the seat right next to me, despite there being room elsewhere, squeezes in close so that I'm forced to shuffle up a bit to accommodate her. She turns to me with a smile.

'Hi, I'm... *Oh. My. God.*' She points to my feet, at the shiny black patent high-heeled courts I'm wearing. They have this cute little bow detail on the back and I'd bought them especially for the interview. 'The shoes though! They're *adorable*! Where did you get them from?' Her bright green eyes – not unlike my own – sparkle as they search me. 'You here about the job as well? Is this your second interview? Hang on.' She touches her chest with a perfectly manicured hand. 'Yes!... I remember you! Last week, you were arriving just as I was leaving.'

'Oh!' I smile at her politely, secretly pleased. *She likes my shoes. She remembered me.* 'I'm afraid I don't remember seeing you.' I squirm. That sounded rude. 'I'm sure I would've if I had,' I add, because clearly she's someone you don't easily forget. I glance down at her shoes. She's wearing black patent red-bottomed stilettos too, only hers are fiercely high, six inches at least. She reminds me of one of those women who only seem to exist in films. Women who look expensive and effortless and cool at the same time. Suddenly, I feel like a poor relation sitting next to her in my safe beige skirt and cotton shirt combo – the frumpy sister.

'I like your perfume.' The words tumble awkwardly from my mouth, but I'm compelled to return her a compliment – and she does smell incredible. The spicy, exotic scent she's wearing conjures up images in my head of sexy fire eaters and flamenco dancers performing to live music against a Spanish sunset.

'Baccarat Rouge,' she whispers behind her hand, conspiratorially, leaning in closer, like she's sharing top secret information. 'It's a game changer, trust me. A few squirts of this bad bitch and you'll never have to buy yourself another glass of champagne ever again.' *Great*. She's funny as well. I literally don't stand a hope in hell.

I knew it was a long shot anyway, putting myself forward for a job like this, a receptionist for a trendy TV company in a hip part of town. My confidence levels are practically at zero, but I figured I can greet people, I can smile at them and be helpful, can't I? Like, how hard can it be? Anyway, maybe a job like this will force me out of my comfort zone, which isn't even all that comfortable when I think about it. Now though, as I look at her, my fantasy of working for Austin Marz Productions is rapidly evaporating before my eyes like smoke.

My first interview had gone well though, or at least I'd thought so. I'd genuinely liked Jeremy Austin, one of the company directors who had interviewed me. He was nothing like the arrogant, egotistical media mogul who was up his own backside that I had fully expected him to be. Instead, he came across as quite humble and self-effacing and had put me at ease. I'd left feeling really hopeful about my chances, and about my future.

'I'm Samantha,' she introduces herself. 'Samantha Valentine.'

'I'm Erin. It's nice to meet you.'

She grips my hand and yanks me towards her, plants a kiss on both my cheeks. I feel the residue of her lipstick, her strong perfume on my skin, as I pull away, a touch taken aback. 'And it's a pleasure, Erin.' She tugs at her silky blouse, accidentally opening another button, though she appears not to have noticed.

'Jeez, it's really hot today, isn't it? I'm not complaining though, I *love* the heat, do you? I mean, it's not the same as being in Ibiza or anything, is it, but still.' She flips her long blonde hair from her face. 'I was there a few weeks ago, in Ibiza... have you ever been?'

'No, actually, I—'

'Oh, you *must* go. Everyone should go to Ibiza at least once in their lifetime. It should be a legal requirement, you know, a rite of passage?' She laughs, displaying a set of neat white teeth, but not so white that they're the first thing you see when you look at her. 'It's a magical place, quite spiritual...' – her voice momentarily tapers off as though she's been caught in a particularly nice memory, – '... plus it's full of rich guys with big boats.' She throws her head back, laughs some more. 'Are you single, Erin?' I point at her button, open my mouth to speak. 'I got engaged in Ibiza, just a few weeks ago,' she continues. 'He proposed to me during sunset at Es Vedrà. I mean, where else?' She waggles her left hand, shows me the admittedly impressive-looking diamond ring on her finger. 'He gave me a rock, on a rock.'

'Wow. It's beautiful.' *And huge.* 'Congratulations.'

'Aww, thanks, hun.' She shimmies in her seat. 'You married?'

'No, I...'

'Kids?'

'No. No. No husband or kids. I'm single at the moment.'

'Oh nice. You live alone or with family?'

Her quick-fire stream of questions unsettles me a little. She's not the one who's supposed to be interviewing me after all.

'Sorry,' she apologises, as though sensing my discomfort, 'I don't mean to be nosy. I'm fairly new to the area, haven't got many friends... Billie-Jean no-mates, me!'

This surprises me. Looking at her, I imagined she'd be exactly the type of person who has to check their diary months in advance before making arrangements. She looks like she already has this job.

'Oh, well, I...' But then, a girl with purple hair pops her head around the door before I can continue.

'Erin Santos?'

'Um, yes! That's me.' I stand abruptly, sending my handbag – and its contents – to the floor. *Shit!* My face burns as I scrabble to scoop it all up, and Samantha bends down to help me. 'Jeremy is ready for you now.'

'Good luck, Erin,' she says, smiling as she hands me half a sticky packet of wine gums and a tampon. 'May the best girl win!'

TWENTY

I was literally biting my own fist with excitement as I left the offices of Austin Marz Productions – *my new place of employment!* I couldn't believe I'd got the job! Jeremy, my *new* boss, had to explain it to me, *twice,* before it sank in.

'Really?' I blinked at him, rapidly. 'You're *definitely* giving me the job?'

'Yes,' he laughed. He has a nice smile, it's really warm and friendly. 'We think you'll fit in very well here, Erin, and we look forward to seeing you on Monday!'

So, a take-out and a film it is then, to celebrate! I practically float out of the revolving doors onto the street. *I got the job!* I fist pump the air. *Yes!*

For the first time since forever, I felt a tiny glimmer of hope that things were changing. Life was turning a corner, and this time I was following it – a sat nav to better places. Mum would've been proud of me today, I know it.

'*Errrrrin!*'

I hear someone calling my name and spin round. She's hurrying towards me, her arms outstretched, like she's greeting an old friend she hasn't seen for ages. It's the girl I just met in the interview room, the one I was convinced would get the job on sight. Lucky for me, it turns out I was wrong. I guess I really *do* need to work on my self-confidence.

'*Erin!* Awww, congratulations, hun! I'm really pleased for you! You got the job! Well done, you!' She throws her arms around me, gives me a giant warm hug. I feel myself stiffen in her embrace. I'm not used to such public displays of affection from virtual strangers. I'm not used to affection at all.

'Thanks so much, er, Samantha, I... I'm in shock, to be honest.' I break away, her perfume lingering on my shirt. 'I really didn't think I'd get the job, especially when I saw you.'

'Ah well.' She sighs, rolls and flutters her eyes, theatrically, as she clutches her chest. 'I guess, in the end, I just wasn't his type.'

I think I should maybe laugh right about now, so I do, though a touch awkwardly.

'Oh, don't look so worried.' She gives my arm a soft, playful slap. 'There's plenty of other jobs out there! At the end of the day, the best girl won, right? Really, I'm genuinely happy for you!'

I smile at her, gratefully. I suppose she does seem it. 'One must always be gracious in defeat,' she says in a dramatic voice. 'Though one should never consider defeat as an option in the first place.' I laugh again. I have no idea who this woman is, but she's definitely different, and engaging.

'Come on,' – she links my arm in hers – 'let's go and celebrate your new job at that fancy new rooftop bar in town. It's a beautiful evening and we must toast your good news and commiserate mine by getting suitably smashed out of our skulls.' She gives me a conspiratorial sideways glance. 'Unless you have other plans of course.'

Some hours later, I find myself sitting in a fancy giant deckchair on a rooftop makeshift beach bar that boasts the most incredible view of the city I've ever seen. I'm on my third Porn

Star Martini, the DJ's playing some uplifting house music and there's impossibly cool people everywhere, drinking, dancing, and generally being gorgeous.

'Wow, it looks so stunning from up here,' I say, staring out towards the city below, '—all the lights! It's like it's covered in magic glitter.' I turn to her. 'Thanks for bringing me here, I never even knew this place existed!'

'Ah well, stick with me, kiddo, this place turns into a club after 10 p.m.' Her eyes twinkle, mischievously, like the very lights below.

'You said you'd recently moved to the area?' I ask, hoping to find out a little more about her.

'Yes, my fiancé, Ari – I moved in with him not too long ago, at the new apartments over at Pengally Court. Do you know the ones I mean?'

I do. They're in a great location, close to the city but surrounded by lush green, well-kept grounds, a private little oasis, tucked away in among the throng. Only rich people can afford to live in them.

'Wow, lucky you!'

She gives me a strange look.

'Yeah, *lucky me*.' Though the way she says it makes me think that she doesn't quite believe it. 'Ari's got a very well-paid job, basically, he's loaded,' she explains. 'Though honestly, I swear I didn't know this when we met. He kept it quiet for a while, you know, to test me, see if I was a gold digger or whatever, which I'm not by the way,' she adds from the corner of her mouth, comedically. 'I'd never dig for anything, not with these nails!' I laugh along with her. 'Anyway, I suppose what I'm saying is that I don't actually *need* to get a job. Ari is in favour of me adopting the more traditional role of stay-at-home wife, but I want something to do with myself all day while he's off out making money. I get bored and lonely, and we all know what the devil says about idle hands...'

'Of course, I understand,' I say, though I don't, not really. Everyone I know has no choice but to work to pay the bills and survive.

'Who does Ari work for, what does he do?'

'Rogan Hanley, you know, the big financiers in London? Equities or something... They have an office here in Leeds, so he goes between the two.'

'Wow,' I say again, 'you hit the big time with him then. When's the wedding?'

'Next year, in Dubai.'

'In Dubai. Wow.' It's the third time I've said 'wow' in quick succession. She probably thinks I'm a dick.

'Tell me about *your* family.' She changes the subject as she signals to the waiter for two more cocktails. 'Do they live in Leeds? Are you guys close?'

I knew this question was coming – it always does eventually – but I have to get over it. I won't ever make friends with anyone ever again unless I do. My therapist says, 'Just tell the truth, Erin. If it scares people off then they're not your tribe. What is meant for you will not go by you.'

'I don't have any family,' I say, sipping on my drink simultaneously, as though a mouthful of Porn Star Martini would make it any less true. 'Both my parents died and I have no brothers or sisters.'

She turns to me slowly then with a strange look on her face.

'Well, darling, *you do now!*'

TWENTY-ONE

We're both drunk by the time we fall out of an Uber and into my apartment, gone 3 a.m.

'Oh, don't worry about that,' I say, giggling as she hops on one foot, trying to remove her Louboutins at the door.

'Na-ah!' She wags a finger. 'We take our shoes *off*, and we place them *behind the door*, that's the rule. Ari always *insists* upon it!'

I help support her, though I'm not exactly the steadiest myself.

'Well, you're in my apartment now, I don't care if you keep them on or off.'

She places them neatly together by the front door – though it takes a couple of attempts – as I go into the small lounge and ask Alexa to play 'something fun'.

'I want a grand tour!' She instructs me, loudly, drunkenly, as she begins to pad, barefoot, through my apartment. Brazenly opening the door to my bedroom, she throws herself face down onto my bed. I giggle again, go back to the kitchen and look for the bottle of cheap Prosecco that I know is buried somewhere behind the out-of-date ready meals in my fridge. 'Summer

Nights', the song from the musical *Grease*, is playing and I start singing along to it.

'Oh my God, I *love* this song!' she shouts from the bedroom. '*Grease* is one of my favourite films of *all* time.'

'Mine too!' I call back. '*A well-a well-a well-a, ooh!*'

I pour us both a shaky glass as we sing loudly in unison and bring it to her in the bedroom. I haven't drunk this much alcohol in ages. I know I shouldn't, it's really not good for me, but whatever, I'm enjoying myself. I can't remember when I last had such a fun night out, and I really could do with a new friend – or any friend, for that matter. It's difficult to admit – even to myself – that I'm desperately lonely.

When we finally stop belting out the film soundtrack some minutes later, she props herself up on her elbow, pats the space next to her on the duvet, gestures for me to join her. I flop down onto the bed, kick my shoes off and listen out for the thud as they hit the wooden floor.

'Do you mind me asking what happened to your parents?'

The question instantly takes the edge off my happy buzz. I know there's no way around it though. 'The only way out of anything, Erin, is through it.' I hear my therapist's words again and take a breath.

'My father died when I was four years old, from prostate cancer. He was from Venezuela, originally. Sometimes I think I have memories of him, but perhaps they're just fantasies I created in my mind based on the things Mum told me about him. And my mum...' I pause. 'My mum died a week after my thirteenth birthday. She was killed by her partner.'

Her eyes widen.

'Oh, Jesus, Erin... That's some seriously heavy shit, hun.'

I laugh.

'Yeah, *no shit.*'

'Listen, we really don't have to talk about it if you don't

want to...' She taps a floppy hand against my arm, lets it rest there.

'It's fine,' I say, even though it isn't. Having to have this conversation is the miserable legacy I'm left with.

'He stabbed her through the heart in a moment of rage during one of their many arguments and she died almost instantly, right there, on the kitchen floor, in front of me.'

She looks suitably horrified.

'Oh. My. God! That's just awful... that's just so... *horrible*. Did he hurt you too?'

'No. Never. To the outside world, he appeared to be the perfect partner and stepdad. He was covert, you know, the worst kind of abuser? The kind that no one would believe it of. But there was this darkness in him, this demon that would rear its ugly head, and Mum, she was always on the receiving end of it, everything was always her fault.'

'Yes,' – she lowers her eyes and looks away – 'I understand.' But I wonder if she really does, or if anyone does, for that matter, unless they've been through something similar themselves.

'We had a barbecue the night it happened. It was a glorious summer's evening, a lot like tonight, I s'pose, balmy and warm, the air perfumed by the jasmine in our back garden, the kind of summer night you don't ever want to end, and definitely not how it did...'

Other than to my therapist, I haven't really spoken about what happened that night in detail to anyone, but I'm surprised how naturally and easily the words find me as I talk to her.

'I can't remember how the argument started between them, it was something and nothing, like it always was, I'm sure. They'd been drinking at the barbecue – he was a heavy drinker – but Mum, well, I think he – the abuse – drove her to drink more over the years.'

She's searching my face with her eyes as I speak.

'He was holding this metal spatula at the time, and he hit her with it, smacked her right round the face. The sickening sound it made, of the metal making contact with her skin, it still triggers me today.' I shudder, close my eyes in a bid to distance myself from the memory.

'She told me to go upstairs then, and that was code for she was going to get a beating and to stay out of the way. And so I went up to my room, put my headphones on. I remember at the time I was listening to the song, "Keep on Movin'" by Soul II Soul...' I start to sing it, softly, badly probably, and she nods, joins in with me for a moment. Her singing voice is much nicer than mine, melodic and pretty.

'I could still hear them going at it though, even with the headphones on and the volume cranked up. I figured they would run out of steam soon enough, like they usually did, but I felt so powerless, so helpless, *so angry*...'

She takes hold of my hand, squeezes it tightly. 'I'm sure you did...'

'The row seemed to go on for hours. I wanted to climb out of the window and go next door, ask them to phone the police, *again*. Not that *they* ever did anything, the police, I mean, useless bastards.' I snort, pushing back tears and contempt. 'They let him go *so* many times. Mum would never press charges against him anyway. She was too scared of the repercussions, and honestly...' I turn on my side to face her, our noses practically touching. 'I think, in spite of everything, she actually still *loved* him, still believed it could all just work out if she hung on in there a little longer, if she was just more of this and less of that, and vice versa. If she could just get him some help, if he could only battle through whatever his demons were, then he'd be the good man she knew he could be again.' I inhale, deeply. 'It's like those people you see playing the slot machines in Las Vegas, you know, who sit there, putting coin after coin in the slot on autopilot. Maybe the *next* coin will be the one that'll win big... And perhaps, every now and again, maybe you *do* get a win, and this gives you intermittent reinforcement that you really could hit the jackpot, *if you just keep playing*, and so it goes on, coin after coin after coin... until eventually you run out of money – or die, in my mum's case.'

She's nodding, her head cocked, her face a picture of empathy.

'After a while I couldn't take it anymore, the sound of screaming and glass smashing. And so I stomped down the stairs in a huff. I remember being a bit scared, but also angry, you know? Like, why can't we just be a normal family, and why won't he stop and why won't she stop him and...?' My guts are churning as I speak. I don't want to put myself back there, in that dreadful moment, but I can't stop now.

'I saw them through the kitchen door from the stairs – he had her on the floor. I could see her legs kicking violently back and forth and I remember thinking, *Oh God, he's strangling her! He's killing her!* I think I shouted, "Stop!" or "Mum!" or both maybe, but then Mum was up on her feet and... I didn't actually see the knife go into her. She had her back to me at the time, but I saw it, shiny, in his hand and I saw his arm come down.' I pause, close my eyes and try not to visualise. 'She fell backwards, straight, like a tree. And then... then I saw the blood.' I hear the crack of emotion in my voice, my tears imminent. 'It was... it was just so *quick*...'

'It's OK, darling.' She starts to stroke my hair, gently tucks a piece behind my ear. 'It's OK, hun... come on now...'

I really mustn't cry. It's been such a brilliant evening and I don't want to spoil it.

'He turned and he saw me then, standing on the stairs. He said something like, "Go back to your room..." But I couldn't move. I couldn't do *anything*. I was literally paralysed by shock and fear, like I'd turned to concrete. So, I did nothing. I just stood there on the stairs and did *nothing*.' I drop my chin.

'I honestly don't remember much after that, but I do remember the police coming, when they took Ray – and Mum – away. I remember the sing-song of the sirens as the ambulance pulled up outside. Ray Denis, that was his name, the man who killed my mum. He died three years into a life sentence for murder. He slashed his own wrists in his cell and bled to death. And so, that was that!' I turn to her. 'Do you want a top-up?'

She hasn't taken her eyes off me the whole time I've been talking.

'Do you know,' – she props herself up on one elbow – 'that is just about the worst story I think I've ever heard. You must be one hell of a strong woman to have dealt with the trauma of such a terrible tragedy – you're a true survivor, Erin, do you know that?'

I shake my head, scared to speak in case I dislodge the hard lump in the back of my throat. 'The guilt, it has tormented me my whole life since. I know I should've stopped him, but I... I just stood there, frozen with fear. I should've protected her that night; she was my mum. I should have done *something*.'

'You were thirteen years old, for God's sake!' she says. 'You were just a child! *You* were the one who needed protecting! It wasn't your fault, Erin, none of it.' Her brow wrinkles. 'Who was this Ray Denis piece of crap anyway?'

'I think he was originally from Australia or New Zealand or somewhere. I think he was a truck driver, one of those long-distance ones. Sometimes he had to travel, and it would be peaceful then, just me and Mum, together.'

'Did he have any family, any children of his own?'

I blow air through my lips.

'I don't know... maybe. I do remember playing with another little girl who came to visit a couple of times, but I could only have been five or six at the time and I can't remember any names. I think I heard them arguing about it once or twice maybe, though they argued about *everything*, or rather, *he* did. Though I'm sure he could've lied about that too.'

'What a vile excuse of a man,' she spits, angrily. 'I'm glad he's dead. Oh, hun, how have you coped?' She looks at me, her head tilted to the side, her green eyes wide and watery, and a little drunk.

'Well,' I sigh. 'I haven't really, that's the truth. Actually, I had a breakdown last year.' I may as well be honest and tell her everything, what have I got to lose? If it scares her off, then so be it. It means she isn't 'my tribe', or whatever crap my therapist says. 'I ended up in hospital for a few weeks. I really messed up my teens and twenties, you know, trying to deal with all the guilt, to come to terms with everything, and it all just finally came to a head. I couldn't cope with the way I was feeling anymore...'

'Oh, hun, who *didn't* mess up their teens and twenties?' She rolls her eyes.

'Yeah, well, I took far too many drugs, I drank too much...'

She raises her eyebrows. 'And I repeat...'

I manage a smile. She's being nice.

'I thought I was coping, but I was just trying to bury it all, you know – bury my pain and sadness under alcohol and drugs and dead-end relationships with men I didn't even *like*. Anyway,' – I clap my thighs with my palms – 'I'm thirty-four now. Time's running out. I just need to get back on track, make my mum proud. Maybe this new job will be the start of that. Who knows, maybe I'll meet the man of my dreams, get married and have a child of our own? That's what I really want, if I'm honest, to have the family I was denied thanks to that evil bastard, Ray Denis.'

'Yes!' she says, jubilant. 'You can do *anything* you want, Erin. Anything you put your mind to, just remember that – and I know that your mum would be proud of you. Look at you! You survived all of this on your own. I don't know how you've done it. You're a legend, you really are!' She pulls me close into an embrace, begins stroking my hair. 'You poor love. Why is it always the good people who seem to suffer?'

I shake my head but I don't speak. If I dislodge the lump in my throat it will definitely open the floodgates.

'You and I, we're the survivors of this world, Erin.' She continues to stroke my hair gently, like my mum used to when I was a child. It feels soothing. 'I will look after you – we can look after each other. What do you say, hun, yeah? We'll take 'em all on together!'

I nod and smile, though tears are now leaking from the corners of my eyes.

'Together.'

TWENTY-TWO

The next couple of months were intense. Welcome to the *Samantha Valentine Show*, folks! Boom! There she was, in my life, this beautiful powerhouse of a woman – a super-cool, vibrant, funny, stylish and intelligent woman – who wanted to be *my* friend. And can I just say how much I desperately needed one of those at this point in my life. The transient, largely drug-fuelled 'party pals' that I made throughout my twenties could no longer feature if I was to make a proper go of it. Hang out with winners and you're more likely to become one, right? It also works in reverse.

That summer, I made more memories with Sam than I'd ever made with any other girlfriend – or boyfriend, for that matter. I suppose, in some ways, it was a lot like a love affair – emotional, intense, exhilarating – just without the sex bit, although Sam would often flirt with me outrageously at times. She once told me, 'If I was a heterosexual bloke and saw you in a club, I'd fancy the pants off you.' I didn't think she was gay, but I do think she enjoyed blurring the lines. And truthfully, I found the attention intoxicating.

Sam took me to art galleries and museums that I had never

even heard of, let alone been to, quirky one-off pop-ups, and small fringe theatres showing avant-garde productions. She was passionate about all forms of culture – acting, music, fashion, books and film and art and photography and travel – all the things I loved and had an appetite for.

Sam loved life like I never knew it was possible to. She seized it by the throat and embraced it all unapologetically. Perhaps surprisingly, she wasn't pretentious, or a snob, particularly. She was just as comfortable eating cross-legged in front of the telly in pyjamas with a KFC bucket of chicken as she was wearing Prada at a Michelin three-star celebrity chef's restaurant. She could also be goofy and was often self-deprecating. Once, at a fun fair, I remember how she belted out the song 'Life is a Rollercoaster' at the top of her voice in an Irish accent while we were on the Big Dipper. She took her bra off as we did the loop-the-loop and threw it into the air as we screamed and laughed until I had snot bubbles coming out of my nose and couldn't breathe.

Shopping expos together were always epic, spraying each other with expensive designer perfume in department stores until we went nose blind, testing lipsticks and bronzers on our hands and taking advantage of the free in-store makeovers. I remember she even cut and styled my hair for me once or twice, gave me this glamorous, big, bouncy blow-dry that honestly could've passed as a professional job. Sam had an eye for beautiful and unusual things and instinctively seemed to know what would suit me, like she already knew me better than I knew myself somehow.

'You have such an incredible figure, Erin, and your hair... those eyes... you should be proud of being a beautiful, strong woman. Don't hide your light under a bushel, hun. Be yourself.'

We even started *running* together. Usually, I'd begrudge having to run for a bus, but it meant I got to spend an hour before work with my amazing new friend and keep fit at the same time. It also meant I wasn't as desperately lonely.

Sometimes, we'd meet during my lunch hour at work, grab sandwiches and sushi and still lemonade from Pret and eat them under our favourite tree in the park, a comfortable silence passing between us as we people-watched the world go by – it was a glorious summer that year, days of endless sunshine just rolling into the next. That's how it felt, being with Sam, like I was standing in eternal sunlight whenever I was around her, and as a result, I began to view the world through a different lens. Slowly, I was starting to build the confidence that I lacked and that had held me back for so long. I felt so grateful to have met her.

There was one particular night when we got dressed up and she doused me in Baccarat Rouge perfume – her ridiculously expensive signature scent. We spent the entire evening flirting outrageously with these three slick city traders in some achingly hip and expensive hotel bar in the city – something I would never have had the guts to even think of doing before I met her. I gasped out loud when they footed our champagne bill for the night – it was topping £500!

'See,' – she'd nudged me, giggling as we'd made a hasty retreat, trotting off in our heels – 'I told you that stuff is magic, didn't I?'

But even after a few intense weeks of seeing her practically every day, and as heavily invested in our friendship as I had become in that short time, I knew very little about Samantha Valentine. She was an open book and an enigma at the same time – a complete paradox, looking back on it. Intermittently, I would ask her questions about family and life, just stuff that would come up in general conversation, only she was masterful in the way she could divert and deflect any topic, quickly turning the spotlight back on to you without you even being aware she was doing it. She often used humour to distract – she would sometimes randomly just burst into song, or start speaking in a daft accent. Ah yes, *accents* – Sam was *brilliant* at them, exceptional even, better than most trained actors on the telly. She could mimic anyone from any place or region or country, even, and sound like she was born and bred there. I'd be in fits of laughter, stunned, and so impressed at how effortlessly she could seamlessly slide from Cockney to Geordie to Scouse to Scottish to Spanish to South African – like it was second nature.

'You're *ridiculously* talented!' I'd tell her, seriously. 'Honestly, you should have your own TV show!'

Now, of course, I see it for what it really was – diversion tactics. *I see everything now.* In retrospect, by showcasing her incredible interchangeable, chameleon-esque talents in a bid to distract me from asking questions, Sam was also showing me who she really was – someone who could transform into anyone at the flick of a switch, a pretender, *a fake*. Only I didn't identify it back then. I didn't recognise the red flags, even though they were waving at me like a Soviet Union protest march. I didn't even know what to look out for. I certainly couldn't have had any idea I might be in any danger. Also, and perhaps importantly, Samantha was a woman, and I had learned, been taught even, to mostly be wary of men – they were the true enemy, not beautiful, funny, kind, intelligent women, like her.

One thing I *did* know about Sam, however, was that her mum now lived in Perth, Australia – 'She remarried some alcoholic hillbilly,' or so Sam told me – and they weren't particularly close. I clearly remember her telling me that because looking back, it had felt somehow different when she'd said it, like on a subconscious level I instinctively knew she was telling me the truth, perhaps the only time, as it turned out.

'She's also an alcoholic.' She sighed. 'We don't really communicate much anymore. Sometimes I think I would like to pick up the phone, but I already know how *that* conversation would go... What do *you* think you would say to your mum now, Erin, if you could have one last conversation with her?'

I'd never had a friend like Samantha before. The time and attention she gave me during those few months was heady and seductive. Like the drugs I was doing my best to steer clear of, I lapped it up like the starving, lonely addict that I was. But I knew *something* wasn't quite right. Little things didn't add up.

TWENTY-THREE

Sam said her car – a BMW, 2018 plate – was written off in an accident she'd had some months before I met her. As a result, she was nervous about getting back behind the wheel, so I would always drop her home in my shabby old Fiat Punto that I could barely afford to run. She'd ask me to stop a little short of her apartment building, and I would watch from a distance as she disappeared, waving, through the revolving doors. I was desperate to see inside her fancy-pants apartment – and meet her fiancé, Ari – but she never once invited me up there. There always seemed to be a legitimate reason why.

'Ari's asleep and he has to get up early...' 'Ari's got a business associate over tonight, so I don't want to disturb him.' 'Ari's family are visiting...'

After six weeks, whereby we had now officially become 'besties' and I could no longer imagine or bear the thought of my life without her in it, I finally managed to pluck up the courage to mention it.

'How come I haven't met this amazing fiancé of yours yet then? Is he actually real?' I ribbed her, light-heartedly. She'd told me all about the lavish and glitzy wedding they were planning in Dubai next year, and admittedly, I was desperately hoping she would invite me. Secretly, I'd even fantasised about her asking me to be her bridesmaid, because that's what best friends do, right?

I could picture us both on her wedding day, standing together in front of a mirror, Sam looking like a celebrity, dazzling and gorgeous, in her ridiculously expensive handmade designer gown that showcased her incredible figure. I am next to her, wearing a simple yet chic silky slip dress, admiring how beautiful she looks as we toast each other with vintage pink champagne...

My greatest concern at the time though was that Sam might be embarrassed by me and that's why I had not yet met him. I was paranoid that perhaps I wasn't cool or clever enough to meet what sounded like Ari's exacting and high standards. Ari, the fancy financier in London who travelled all over the world. Educated Ari, who was loaded and hung out with CEOs and influencers I'd never heard of. The dynamic city boy who drove a brand-new soft-top Mercedes that was probably worth a small house somewhere. Sam had pointed it out to me once, in the private car park of their apartment complex. It was sleek and black as vinyl, shiny enough to fix your make-up in the reflection on the paintwork. I could just picture her in the passenger seat, next to her husband-to-be, stereo cranked up, platinum blonde hair whipping in the wind, like something from a slick social media marketing campaign. *I* wanted to do life like Samantha Valentine did life, big and bold and brave and beautiful and bombastic. I was completely in awe of her.

Some people, it would seem, have all the luck because on top of the above, Ari Hussain was also seriously fit. Dark-haired, dark-skinned and dark-eyed, he looked like some kind of AI-generated Arabian god. Or at least he did in the pictures I'd seen on her phone – pictures she showed me of them together on dates in opulent and trendy five-star hotels and restaurants, where the food looked like art and way too good to eat. There were photos on bright white beaches with crystal-clear waters in the background, Sam in a sparkly diamanté bikini, Ari, tanned and toned, his arm draped around her waist.

'You will, I promise,' she said. 'He's desperate to meet you too! He's just always so busy, working, travelling...' But I could sense something was off.

Whenever Ari returned from one of his business trips, Sam would disappear for a couple of days, though she always kept in regular contact with me on Snapchat.

It was following one of these occasions that I first noticed the bruising.

The UK summer weather was breaking records that year, someone had made the local news for frying an egg on their own doorstep, and the annual, mandatory hosepipe ban had been put in place – but that day, when she came to meet me for lunch, Sam was wearing a long-sleeved shirt. It was tipping thirty degrees outside and the humidity was uncomfortable, so it struck me as odd, though it was more a passing observation than an immediate concern.

'So, how is it, having your soon-to-be betrothed back home?' I asked her, keen to get the gossip. Everything about them as a couple seemed so perfect, I imagined the sex had to be incredible too. 'Did he have a good trip? Did he bring you back anything gorgeous, something sparkly and expensive?'

'He hasn't mentioned it much... and of course, it's wonderful to have him back.' But I could tell instantly in her voice that something was wrong. She wasn't her usual effervescent self. Her tone was flat. She was masking upset – something my mum had done regularly – I had no difficulty recognising *those* signs.

'Are you OK, Sam?'

'Yes. Sorry, I was miles away, hun.' She sipped her iced latte and brought the conversation back round to me again. 'So, how's work going? Have you managed to seduce that filthy rich, gorgeous boss of yours yet then, or what?'

Some weeks later, while we were out running together, I noticed a particularly nasty-looking, large bruise on her upper thigh. It was dark and purple, the colours of a storm.

'Ari and I were messing around in a hot tub. It's a sex injury, sweetie.' She brushed it off with a wink, but it felt disingenuous, and horrible little maggots of doubt started burrowing their way into my thoughts.

I was at work when I got the message from her asking me to meet her, urgently, at my place. Sensing an emergency, I left immediately, giving my supervisor the excuse that I'd been violently sick in the toilets with a stomach bug. She couldn't really argue with me, though it looked like she had wanted to.

Sam was waiting outside my apartment when I arrived. Her left eye was badly swollen and I could see she'd been crying.

'Oh my God! Sam, what's happened?' Though deep down, I already suspected.

That afternoon she told me everything. The perfect couple that she'd led me to believe she and Ari were didn't exist. It was all a sham.

'He hates me going out, he hates me wearing nice clothes, he hates me having friends… This is why I don't like us having our photo taken together. Photos of me with *anyone* send him into a violent, jealous rage. I can't even *call* someone without him knowing, as he put a bug on my phone… he knows my every move. And he especially hates *you*; he thinks you're trying to come between us and spoil our relationship.'

It all appeared to make sense to me then, why she'd never invited me up to her apartment and why I'd never met Ari in person. I have to admit, in hindsight, it was pretty clever, very plausible. It never once occurred to me to question anything she was telling me at the time.

'You *have* to contact the police,' I told her as I held her and let her cry it all out in my arms. I felt safe in the role of her comforter; it was a role I was familiar with. It made me feel useful and needed and fed into my co-dependency. 'You have to tell them what he's like, what he's been doing to you!' I was crying myself now. I couldn't bear to see her like she was, a shadow of her usual vibrant, vivacious self, her fat, puffy eye rapidly disappearing into her lovely face. This couldn't be happening to her, not Sam. Only I knew, more than most, that abuse doesn't discriminate. It really can happen to *anyone*.

'You said yourself that the police are useless. Every time I've called them for help in the past, they turn up and he switches into Mr Nice Guy again and makes me look like *I'm* the one who's unhinged! Last time, they threatened to arrest *me* for wasting police time – can you believe that?'

'*What?*' My heart rate shot up. This was history repeating itself – the victim-blaming, taking the side of the cunning, covert abuser and re-traumatising the victim while the abuser walks away unscathed. Acute rage burned inside my chest as my PTSD became triggered. *Why* do they *still* let this happen? Why do they always let these bastards get away with it? If only the police had taken more notice of my mum back then, if they had *really* listened to her and *believed* her, then maybe, just maybe, she'd still be alive today. Now, all these years later, they were doing the same thing to my friend Sam, to another beautiful, vibrant and innocent woman who they should be protecting. Nothing, it seemed, had changed. It enraged me.

We made a plan that afternoon, Sam and I, over many tears and as much wine.

'You know you *have* to leave him, don't you?'

She nodded, solemnly.

'He jokes that he'll kill me if I do.'

'*Jokes?* Who jokes about killing their fiancée, Sam? You *have* to take it seriously – we have to take his threats seriously. *Please*, Sam,' I begged her, 'look at what happened to my mum.'

I was genuinely scared for her. I knew how this story could end. But I could never, at this point, have known the real tragedy it would become.

Sam's situation was all too believable to me; after all, I'd been here before. At no point did I think it might not actually be *real*. The bruises I saw on her body, her swollen black eye, they were real. Her tears and emotions were real too. I *saw* them and I *felt* them. No one invents a lie like that. Why would they?

'We can do it when he's next away on business,' I said, springing into action mode. I felt powerful and determined. 'We'll take all your stuff and place it in storage. We'll do a moonlight flit. You can leave your phone at your apartment, so it looks like you're at home the whole time on the tracker. Don't worry,' – I started to chew my fingernails with anxiety – 'we'll get you a new phone, a new number if we have to. Then you come and stay with me until we figure out what's next, OK? Does Ari know my surname?'

'Nope, don't think so, I've never told him it.'

'Does he know where I live?'

She shakes her head.

'Perfect. Then he won't find us, will he?'

'He's got money, he'll hire a PI or something.'

'We'll get a non-molestation order out on him. *I'll* protect you,' I said. 'I won't let him get to you, Sam, I *promise*. If the police won't help you, then *I* will.' I seized both of her hands in mine and squeezed them tightly. I don't think I'd ever been as sincere about anything else before in my life.

'He goes away again next week,' she said.

'We'll do it then.'

'If he doesn't kill me first,' she sniffed.

'Over my dead body.'

I wasn't going to let that happen, not this time, *not again*.

TWENTY-FOUR

DAN

Molly, the lady from the housing charity, Re-Connex, is clutching her large handbag to her bosom like a protective shield, her brow furrowed in concern as she chews her bottom lip.

'I was only with her yesterday, and she never mentioned anything to me about taking a trip anywhere. She knows she needs to inform us of her movements, and she's on a curfew, so she can't stay anywhere overnight without permission. Has she done something wrong, then? Is that why you're here? Is Erin in some kind of trouble, because I'm sure whatever it is, it's all a mistake?'

'There's a few clothes missing, gov,' – Davis pops her head around the door – 'but her passport is still here, so it looks as though she hasn't left the country, or maybe gone for long.'

'OK. Check for any CCTV, Davis.'

'Gov.'

I knew Erin wouldn't be here. I know she's not here, in Leeds. But that's not ostensibly why Davis and I are.

'The laptop I recently gave her,' – Molly turns in a circle – 'I can't see it, she must've taken it with her.'

'You gave Erin a laptop?'

'Yes,' she says, biting her bottom lip again, her eyes darting between Davis and myself nervously. 'Have I done something wrong?'

'Of course not, Molly. Do you know where Erin was last Thursday, the twelfth? Did you see her that day, was she here, in the apartment, do you know?'

Her brow furrows into deep grooves along her forehead.

'Last Thursday... hmm... no... I wasn't here last Thursday. I was here on the Friday though, the thirteenth – ooh! Friday the thirteenth!' She looks spooked, starts biting her lip again. 'I do hope that's not significant.'

'Did she seem OK?'

'Perfectly.'

'Do you know if Erin has any connections to London, if she has any friends or family living there?'

'None that I know of, or that she's ever mentioned to me. I didn't think she had any family – or friends. Well, except for me.'

'Has anyone visited Erin recently, Molly, have you seen anyone here, in the apartment?'

She looks petrified now, like I'm about to cuff her and bundle her into the back of a van.

'Honestly, I really don't know. Maybe you could ask her neighbour, from across the hall, his name's Malcolm.' Her eyes disappear into slits as she smiles. 'Shall I fetch him?'

She scurries from the kitchen with purpose, returns a few moments later with a tall, slim man with messy, curly hair in tow. He looks like he's just got out of bed, but hey, who am I to judge? I assume this must be Malcolm, the neighbour Erin had candidly confessed to 'being with' the night she went AWOL. I'm still not sure why she told me about their encounter.

'They're here to ask about Erin,' Molly explains to him, touching his arm. Her eyes are twinkling as she looks at him –

uh-oh, I sense someone has a crush! 'She left here last night and now no one knows where she is.'

'When did you last see Erin, Malcolm?'

I know when Erin told me she'd last seen Malcolm, but I want to hear it from him, check their stories match up.

'Yesterday,' he replies with a hint of caution. 'I was here with her, in her apartment. Why? Is she OK? What's happened to her?' He seems genuinely concerned.

'How long did you spend time together, here in the apartment? Was it just the two of you?' Davis takes out her notebook.

'Yes, it was just us. I dunno... four, five hours maybe.'

Molly's face crumples. She looks utterly crushed.

'I didn't know you knew each other that well,' she blurts out, clearly unable to disguise her upset. Malcolm glances sideways at her. 'Are you two... *seeing* each other?' She bristles at him. 'Because, you know, Erin is a vulnerable adult, *Malcolm*, and it's *my* job to protect her, make sure no one takes advantage of her... *and she's also a convicted killer who says "the only good men are dead men".*' She mutters the last part, but it's too late, I've heard it, and judging by Malcolm's wide-eyed expression, he has too.

'Take advantage of her? She's a *what*? What are you talking about, Molly, I...'

Feeling it better we speak alone, I take him to one side.

'What's going on?' he asks. 'Where's Erin? Why are the police looking for her?'

'We don't know where she is, Malcolm. Maybe you can help us?'

He shrugs and shakes his head at the same time. 'Erin told me that you and she were... *together* the other night, is that correct, Malcolm? Are you and Erin partners?'

The question clearly blindsides him.

'Um... No, we aren't together, not yet, although we *did*...' he scratches his bed-hair, unruly curls bouncing with the momentum. '... This hasn't got anything to do with that woman, has it?'

Davis and I exchange glances.

'What woman is that, Malcolm?'

'The one that your lot are looking for, some witness or other, um... Samantha someone... yeah, that was the name, Samantha Valentine. Erin had all this stuff about her pinned on the wall, newspaper cuttings and maps and whatever, hidden behind the wall hanging...'

Davis immediately goes over to it, untacks it. There's nothing behind it, but the marks and residue on the wallpaper suggest there was recently.

'She was touchy when I asked her about it. She told me she was looking for someone she knew, someone called Samantha Valentine, and it reminded me that I'd seen something on social media that day, about a request for a witness to come forward in a murder case with that name, and well,' he snorts, 'she flipped out then, literally, jumped up and started crying, throwing clothes into a bag – she told me she was taking them to Molly's to be washed because her machine was on the blink. I said she could use mine, but she was just, I dunno, on a mission. I could tell she was spooked, like, really freaked out about something, but when I asked her about it, she told me to mind my own business, more or less. And then she asked me to leave.' He pauses. 'Did Molly just say that Erin is a convicted killer?' His brow crinkles in confusion as he turns to me and then Davis. 'Did I just hear her say that?'

I flash him a simultaneously rueful and empathetic smile.

'Nah...' He shakes his head. 'I can't believe that Erin's capable of *killing* anyone... she's...' He pauses.

'She's what, Malcolm?'

He micro-shrugs.

'I dunno, she's, you know... *nice*. I like her. I really liked her.' He sounds genuine.

'Do you know if Erin has taken her medication with her, Molly?' I turn to her. 'Where does she keep it, ordinarily?'

'In the bathroom.' She scurries off to look for it before shortly returning, a little out of puff.

'It's gone,' she says, struggling to catch her breath. 'Maybe she has it with her. I do hope so.' Concern shadows her face. 'It's dangerous to come off anti-psychotics and depressants quickly, or any drug for that matter.' She's biting her bottom lip again.

I glance at Malcolm.

'The night of the incident, last Thursday. Did you see Erin that day, or evening? Did you hear her go out, or return? Where were you that night, Malcolm?'

'In my apartment,' he says, 'where I always am, alone, most of the time anyway.' I detect a hint of regret in his voice. 'But I know Erin was home the whole day, and evening. I heard her moving around inside her apartment, the sound of the TV on. And later on that night, I saw that this film she likes was on telly, you know, *Grease*? And so I called to her through her letter box to let her know it was on.'

Grease? Wasn't that the film that was playing on the TV in Milo Harrison's apartment when I attended the crime scene? Yes, I remember switching it off. Erin didn't mention any of this when I had asked her about an alibi for the night of Milo's murder though. I suspect he's covering up for her, although I don't think his motives are sinister. He seems genuinely fond of her. I pull him to one side again.

'I've spoken to Erin, Malcolm.' I drop my voice. 'She's OK. I think she's safe, but we need to find her...'

'You *think* she's safe!? When did you speak to her? What is this all about?'

I glance over at Molly. She's talking to Davis while simultaneously very obviously looking over at us, or rather, at Malcolm.

'Erin asked me to tell you something, Malcolm, to give you a message.'

'A message, for me?' His eyes widen.
'She said to tell you she said she was "sorry".'

TWENTY-FIVE

'Glad you could make it, DI Pritchard. I'm DCI Riley and this is DS Davis – Dan and Lucy. Good to meet you.'

She shakes my hand brusquely, with an air of authority, or perhaps superiority, though I'll reserve my judgement for now. Either way though, I'm sure it has helped her move up the ranks as quickly as she has in her by-all-accounts impeccable career to date.

Detective Amanda Pritchard, or Detective *Inspector* Amanda Pritchard, as it now transpires, was the investigating officer who had interviewed Erin at length following the death of Bojan Radulovic, seven years ago. She's currently on CID at Leeds and has agreed to meet us, informally, at a nearby coffee shop.

'You're here to talk about the Erin Santos case, aren't you? About Samantha Valentine? I have to say,' she says, 'I was shocked when I saw *that* name come up again. In truth, it gave me a little chill.'

'Why's that, DI Pritchard?'

'Amanda – and listen, before you say anything more, there's something I have to say.' Her expression hardens as she leans in closer, takes a large sip of the hot, strong black filter coffee she's ordered.

'Erin Santos was – is – a dangerous woman. She's a pathological liar and a fantasist. At the time of her arrest she was suffering from delusions, from auditory hallucinations – she thought people were talking to her when they weren't, and telling her things that weren't true, seeing people who weren't really there – that kind of stuff. She was paranoid and depressed and vulnerable and needed professional help.' She blows on her coffee, takes another sip of it. 'That said, I genuinely believed that Erin *genuinely* believed that what she was telling us about Samantha Valentine was true at the time, because in her mind it *was* true. She could present as normal, but she was also cunning and manipulative.'

It's a pretty damning opening statement and it's got my attention.

'Manipulative in what way?'

'Ways plural, you mean,' she says. 'She got under your skin somehow. I know they all do in their own way – the murderers and the abusers and the kiddy-fiddlers and the rapists – but Erin really tugged hard on those heartstrings. The death of her mother at the hands of the abusive stepdad, being let down by the police, her traumatic childhood... all of that,' – her eyes are still fixed on mine – 'but it was just an act, Dan. She talked the talk, she told a good story – and she was pretty damned effective at making it sound authentic. Only it isn't – it wasn't – true, none of it.'

I hear the conviction in her voice but there's something else. She seems a little spooked perhaps.

'And you're *absolutely* sure about that, Amanda?'

She laughs, a touch derisively, though I could just be searching for it.

'Abso-freakin-lutely.' She sits back from the table. 'Did you read her file, her medical history? Erin Santos is a paranoid schizophrenic; she was nuttier than a squirrel's pocket when she killed Bojan Radulovic. The previous year, she'd spent a stint in a psych ward after a full-blown, drug-induced psychotic breakdown. She wasn't a well woman, which is why she ended up where she did – in Larksmere. No one ends up in that place of purgatory unless they need to be there, you know that.'

'But the stuff about her mother's death,' Davis interjects, 'it *was* true that she was murdered by her partner in front of Erin when she was a young teenager. And it's true that numerous 999 calls were made alleging DV assaults over a period of years, all resulting in NFA... She didn't lie about that either.'

'Maybe so,' she shrugs, 'perhaps this is what contributed to her mental health decline over the years, and maybe it's why the – very lenient, in my opinion – judge handed out the sentence to her that he did. But as for Erin's story about this supposed Samantha Valentine character? Nah,' – she shakes her head, erudite – 'I'm afraid I didn't buy it.' Her eyes dart between us. 'There was absolutely nothing, not a shred of evidence, to suggest any such person existed. This crime you're currently investigating, this murder – look at the timing of it. Erin Santos gets released from the funny farm and, oopsadaisy, there's an almost identical murder a short time after! Strange, that.' She arches her brow. 'A real coincidence, wouldn't you agree?'

Admittedly, she does have a point, and it's not like we haven't considered this. Only, when Tilly Ward claims to have first met Samantha Valentine, Erin was still a patient at Larksmere. The timing doesn't quite add up, or not at the moment. I need to get Erin Santos's mugshot in front of Tilly Ward lively, see if we get a positive ID from her.

'And why would she go missing?' she continues. 'That's also why you're here, right? Ask yourself, why would Erin Santos go on the run now if she has nothing to hide? Innocent people have nothing to hide from the police.'

'Maybe it's *because* of the police that she's hiding.' I put it out there. 'Maybe she believes history will repeat itself. Perhaps she thinks she'll be blamed or framed for this murder too.'

She looks up from her coffee, sharply.

'What do you mean, "too"? You think we bungled the original investigation, is that what you're saying, DCI Riley? You think Erin Santos is *telling you the truth?*' She has the tiniest smirk on her face now. 'Erin confessed to stabbing Radulovic, she admits to sticking a knife through his heart and killing him.'

'Actually, reading through all the statements and recordings from the interviews, she confessed to killing *Ari Hussain*, not Radulovic,' I correct her. It may sound as if I'm being pedantic, but this distinction is important.

'There's no evidence to link Santos back to our crime, currently. And our suspect has also confessed to killing our victim. But the MO is more or less the same,' I explain. 'She acted in self-defence, she was defending her friend, Samantha Valentine, against her abusive boyfriend, Milo Harrison. Besides,' I continue, 'Erin was at her address, here, in Leeds, when the incident took place. She has an alibi.' I'm not entirely sure why I tell her this when I suspect Malcolm may have lied – perhaps it's her slight arrogance. It's beginning to grate on me.

'Tell me, Dan, how does a fully grown adult female simply vanish off the face of the earth?' There's a definite facetious tone now. 'Santos claimed Valentine was at the scene of the crime when the incident happened. Here one moment and then – pouf – gone the next, never to be seen again! No record of her anywhere, no sightings, no social media, nothing that suggested she existed? I'll tell you why, shall I?' She leans forwards again. 'Because she doesn't exist – it's as simple as that.' She taps a clean, neat fingernail on the table in emphasis.

'Why wasn't it looked into properly at the time, Erin's account of what happened? Aside from basic intel, her story was largely dismissed. But I've been through the statements, Amanda.' I match her gaze. 'I've read them, word for word. If it turns out to be true, and we go on to find Samantha Valentine, then there'll be an inquiry and you'll have to explain why so many things slipped through the net, why so much of what Erin said, repeatedly, over and over in great detail, was never thoroughly investigated or followed up at the time.'

Her smirk has now dissipated into a grim, thin line. Something like this could prove to be a stain on her exemplary character if she turns out to have been wrong, and she knows it. Do I now detect a hint of doubt? Judging by her record, Amanda Pritchard *is* a good detective – no doubt there – and I'm not here to call her professional judgement into question as such, but we can all make a mistake, a bad call sometimes. We're not robots – not yet anyway.

'That artist's sketch you released to the media, it looks a lot like Santos – as soon as I saw it, I thought of her.' I feel as if she's playing this like a game of chess now, like somehow being 'right' is more important than the facts.

Personally, I've not yet met Erin Santos in the flesh, but I have seen her photograph, taken at the time of her arrest, and while I can't deny that there may be some similarities between her photo and Tilly's sketch if you look for them, I couldn't say with any kind of conviction that it was an accurate likeness at all.

'Erin had dark hair, didn't she? I thought Samantha was a blonde? Both Erin and our suspect agree that her hair is blonde.'

'*Is?*' She smirks again, her eyebrow twitching. 'I never forget a face, Dan, not least a murderer's. And I said "thought of her", not positively identified her.'

'You said "it looks a lot like Santos".'

'Well, I should imagine she's changed a bit over the years, like we all do, even if we haven't been locked away in the loony bin, but like I say, as soon as I saw the sketch, her name came into my head – and she could've dyed her hair, obviously.'

'But you're not *certain* it's her?'

She exhales, checks her watch as if this is all growing tedious and she needs an escape.

'"No" would have to be the answer to that, Dan,' she says flatly. 'I can't say for *certain*.'

'Why do you think Erin targeted Bojan Radulovic in the first place? What was her motive for killing him? No connection was ever established between the two of them. Erin says she'd never met him in the flesh until the day she killed him.'

'I think she was lying,' Pritchard says with a degree of conviction. 'I believe that she *did* know Bojan Radulovic. She probably knows your new victim too.'

'But there was no evidence of that – of her knowing Radulovic prior?'

She holds my gaze.

'No. Just a hunch.'

'I know Erin had historic mental health issues, but she also had no previous history of violence and was lucid, cognisant and communicative at the time of her arrest, wasn't she?'

'Yep,' she agrees, nodding, 'she was all of those things, and perhaps you could include articulate, amenable and recalcitrant to that list as well, if you like. Look, you can use whatever fancy words you want, but just because she wasn't barking at the moon doesn't mean she wasn't insane, or capable of committing murder and attempting to cover it up with an elaborate piece of fiction.' She fidgets, a touch agitated in her seat and knocks back some more coffee. 'The truth is, I don't know exactly why she targeted Radulovic. Of course, she told us at the time that she believed he was someone else.'

'Ari Hussain, Samantha Valentine's fiancé. Erin said she'd never met him, yet she seemed to know an awful lot about him – or the "him" she believed he was. She knew where he lived, she knew how old he was, his birthday – even his star sign – Pisces, in case you're interested.' Though judging by her expression, I suspect that she isn't. 'She correctly named his mother, the company where he worked, and she identified a car that she believed was his. There was a lot of detail in her statements, don't you think, a wealth of information?'

'Yes.' She nods. 'Like I say, she was extremely good at creating fiction, it was all just a narrative that she concocted. I don't know her exact motive, but I suspected that she was most likely stalking Radulovic. I thought that maybe they'd had some sort of tryst, a brief sexual encounter – Erin was a young, attractive woman, if I remember – and she became obsessed with him, fixated upon him. My theory is that he probably realised fairly quickly that she was a complete wacko and no doubt tried to distance himself. Her psychopathy, however, was such that she couldn't allow a rejection like that to go unpunished, so she killed him.'

I think of Milo Harrison's neighbour then, the witness who mentioned something about him being harassed by a woman he'd had a one-night encounter with, and the CCTV I saw of the hooded person I felt sure was female, that flash of blonde hair. *Could it actually have been Erin Santos?*

TWENTY-SIX

ERIN

Present day

'Now what would a pretty little thing like you want with one of those?'

Pierced Pete is looking at me with amusement, like it's a trick question.

'Same reason you're looking for a quick shag.'

'Oh yeah, and what's that then?'

'None of my business,' I shrug.

'Ha!' He shakes his head, piercings rattling. 'I'm afraid it doesn't work like that, sister.' He turns to walk away.

'How about this?' I open my large tote bag, show him a glimpse of the contents, the bundles of banknotes stacked on top of each other. 'Does it work like *this*, perhaps?'

He peers inside, gives a little whistle.

'Well, *now* you could be *sprechen Sie Deutsch*.'

Before I left for London, I withdrew a substantial amount of money from my bank account. It's money I'd inherited from Mum's apartment upon her death, the apartment I grew up in and the place where she died. After it all happened, I went to live with Mum's distant cousin, Jessie, and her family, some twenty miles or so away in Halifax, and it was Jessie who decided to sell it and then put the money into a trust for me. She also invested some of it on my behalf, wisely, as it turned out. When I turned twenty-one, I was able to purchase myself a cool apartment in town with some of the money – the only sensible thing I ever did – and spent a terrifying amount of the rest of it on partying and drugs, which of course made me feel guilty, and so the cycle would perpetuate. I just couldn't escape the guilt I felt, the remorse and regret that permanently hung around my neck like a noose, and so I did whatever I could to try and bury it, rub it out with drugs and alcohol. I was a mess, mentally, and I needed help, but at least I had a home. In the end though, I even lost that. After Samantha, I lost *everything*.

Eventually, I was forced to sell my apartment to pay for my legal fees for my court case. Again, I had no choice, but it had crushed me further still. Somehow, yet again, I felt I had let my mum down, even from beyond her all-too-early grave. I'd managed to lose it all, *even my mind*.

Some cash still remained though, which is why I'm standing here with my tote bag filled with wads of the stuff. After all, it's not like I can take it with me: *not where I'm going anyway*. As far as I'm concerned, it'll be money well spent.

'I don't care what type of gun it is, just as long as it comes with bullets and it works. And I want some new ID, a passport and a driver's licence, a National Insurance number.'

'It's all *I want, I want*, with you, isn't it, sister?' His gold teeth gleam in the light as he grins.

'I'll pay extra, obviously.'

'I'll need a deposit. Half of what's in that bag should do it.'

'I don't think so, *brother*. You get the money when I get my items – that's fair.'

His eyes are like lasers on mine for a few moments. I don't break his stare.

'Leave it with me then, sugar tits.' He sniffs back mucus, loudly, from his throat. *Euch*, he really is quite gross. I think of Malcolm then, though not because *he's* gross – the opposite perhaps. I keep seeing that look on his face – that flash of hurt – as I threw his clothes at him and told him to leave my apartment. And then, when he'd turned to me at the door and asked if we'd ever see each other again, I had lied, and I suspected he knew it too. He looked so sad and regretful. And I recognised that look because I see it every day in the mirror.

I close my large tote bag, zip it up and make to leave.

Maybe I really could find redemption in a 'normal' life with someone like Malcolm? We could buy a little place together in the countryside, overlooking a cornfield, somewhere quaint and pretty with roses growing around the door. We could start over, love each other and be happy in our perfect little bubble. It all sounds so simple, so easy when I say it to myself like that, like it really could be possible. But then I remember, *I am a killer* – a convicted killer who ended up in a mental institution, and I always will be, no matter who I am with or where I live, or how much time passes. People will find out, people always do. And then they will judge because that's also what people do, and I will be viewed with caution and contempt, maybe even fear. How could Malcolm ever fully trust me? He couldn't, not with a past like mine. How could I expect him – or anyone – to? I can never outrun it. This is who I am now, this is what she made me.

'I'll be upstairs. You know my room number?' I look up at Pete's swarthy complexion. His eyes are vacant behind his stare, like they once had life in them before bad choices knocked the crap out of every positive feeling he ever had.

'Off by heart, sister,' he grins. 'Give me twenty-four hours and I'll see what I can do.'

'Perfect.' I swipe the almost-full bottle of JD from the bar top as I leave, a gift to myself, and blow him a kiss. 'Cheers.' It's exactly the sort of thing Samantha Valentine would've done.

I take a couple of large swigs from the bottle before I close the door to my room behind me and lock it. I have to forget all about Malcolm. It's a ridiculous fantasy that I can't afford to indulge, and yet momentarily, it had felt so good. I throw myself face down onto the bed. My fleeting fantasy has only added to my misery and rage, to my sense of injustice and loss at those years and the life I can never have that she stole from me, nor at the system that failed me and allowed her to. They *all* had to be held to account. Bojan Radulovic's family deserved to know the truth of what *really* happened that day, and of what had happened to me too. I had attempted to reach out to them while I was locked up in that place of torture. But the carefully considered letters I wrote to the Radulovic family were all returned to sender, unopened, or so Larksmere told me, though I suspected they were lying. Sometimes I wonder if *anyone* tells the truth about *anything*, ever. Perhaps that's the only real truth of all.

I flip over on the bed, swig some more JD and wonder what Samantha is doing right in this moment. Who is she now? What kind of life does she have? Is she someone's wife, a mother perhaps? This idea hurts me the most, that she may be out there, right now, playing happy families with an unsuspecting brood who undoubtedly adore her. I visualise her, kissing her ridiculously handsome and equally as successful husband goodbye at the door of their impressive home of a morning, dressed in school-run uniform of crisp, fitted white shirt and tight leggings, a mandatory pair of Hunter wellies on her feet, her dark designer sunglasses perched on top of her perfectly styled Scandinavian blonde hair as she ushers little Balthazar and Alice into her brand-new Range Rover Discovery.

This particular picture of domesticity *really* kills me. That she may have gone on to have the life that I had so wanted for myself – a husband and family, and a normal, happy existence –

is too much for me to bear. It makes me want to break things. *It makes me want to kill someone.*

I can see her in my mind's eye as I swig, jaw clenching, from the bottle of JD, all flawlessly chic and efficient, head of the PTA committee at her children's posh primary school where she attends summer fetes and kids' parties decorated with balloon arches and bespoke, colourful gluten-free, vegan rainbow cupcakes. I picture her throwing summer BBQs and sipping cocktails in her well-kept garden for all her 'NCT mummy friends', sauntering down the decking in her 'haute-hippie' expensive summer dress, holding a plate of 'picky bits' with a trail of Baccarat Rouge and an army of hangers-on behind her. Samantha Valentine – always the centre of attention. I see them all, smiling and laughing with her, none of them having an inkling of the truth of who she really is and what she's capable of. I'm sure even if they did, they simply wouldn't believe it.

The telephone conversation with Dan Riley had lasted longer than I'd anticipated. But he had asked me to tell him my story from the beginning, and I had gladly obliged, giving as much detail as I could remember. My memory isn't what it used to be before I was sent to Larksmere though. The years of drugs and ECT therapy must have given me brain fog. I should never have been given those drugs, or the regular electric shock treatments that I was forced to endure so many times over that I lost count. It has to have had an adverse effect on my brain, scrambled it, maybe even killed parts of it off. I've thrown all that toxic medication down the pan now though. My pill-popping days are over. I never needed them in the first place, only now, after years of having them forced upon me, my body and mind have been tricked into believing that I do. I look down at my shaking hands, try to ignore the jittery feeling inside my belly, the tell-tale signs of withdrawal fast approaching. Maybe chocolate will help? I push the piles of money aside as I dig around in my tote bag. *'Yes!'* I strike gold – a Curly Wurly! It's slightly misshapen, but still perfectly edible. I tear it open with my teeth and think about Dan.

Detective Chief Inspector Dan Riley was the listener I thought he would be. He paused in all the right places and let me speak without interruption, which I appreciated – and he didn't ask stupid questions. I chose him well. I don't know yet if he believes me, or if he thinks my story is genuine, but I sense he has enough reasonable doubt to investigate further, to conduct a thorough investigation, properly this time. *I just need one person to believe that she's real.*

Of course, I know how it looks, my disappearing like this and breaking the rules of my parole, because I've intentionally designed it that way. Samantha Valentine has committed another crime. Running makes me look guilty of something, but they'll find no connection to me at the crime scene. I was somewhere else. The truth is, for now at least, I *want* DCI Riley to suspect me because then he will search for her – and, ideally, lead me to her. I need information from him, and the best way to get it is to give it. If I strike up a rapport with him, we could help each other on a quid pro quo basis.

Realistically, it's the only way I have even a slim chance of finding her. Unless of course, I can somehow talk to this latest victim/killer, Tilly. Talking to her could be extremely useful, not to mention cathartic.

Anyway, my name will be in the press soon, if it isn't already, and then everyone will know what Samantha did and therefore by default they'll also know what *I* did. And then I'll be hounded. I'll never escape it. If my name leaks and the press link it back to this murder, they'll combust. I don't have much time to find her before this whole thing explodes.

Dan Riley is currently in my home city, just as I had anticipated he would be. No doubt he'll have spoken to Molly already, maybe even to Malcolm too. I wonder what they told him? Moreover though, I wonder how Malcolm *feels*, knowing as he must by now, that he's slept with a murderer, albeit an unwitting one? I hope he doesn't hate me. I should've told him the truth, given him the option to walk away. I would've understood if he had. Maybe I'll ask Dan about it when I next call him. He's probably on his way to Larksmere about now, to speak to the revered Dr Wainwright. Or *Dr Lobotomy*, as I prefer to think of him. At least I know what *he'll* tell him, it'll be the same story that cold-hearted bitch Amanda Pritchard will tell him too, if she hasn't already. They'll say I'm mad. That I'm bad. *That I'm dangerous.* What's one more person to convince?

They'd be right about one thing though. I *am* dangerous, or I will be soon, hopefully. I never was, or never *wanted* to be dangerous – I wasn't born dangerous and I wasn't dangerous at the time I committed my crime, even. *I was duped.* I was tricked and fooled. I played the joker, the fall guy, the willing disciple following her leader, a leader she believed in and trusted. *A leader she loved.*

What, might you ask, should be the punishment for such deep betrayal?

In twenty-four hours, I'm hoping Pete can help me answer that one.

TWENTY-SEVEN

DAN

'Well, I don't know about you, gov, but I wouldn't want to walk through this place late at night on my own,' Davis remarks as we pull up outside Larksmere High Security Psychiatric Hospital. It's our second stop in Leeds, since we arrived this morning, hoping to find as much information as we can on Erin. Or, better still, find her in the flesh.

I don't disagree with Davis's observation as I stare up at the imposing old Victorian building with its dirty red-brick façade and two large turrets on either side. The enormous clock, set in the middle, gives it the appearance of a face somehow, the arched, dark entrance like a wide-open mouth, ready to swallow you whole.

'It's a pleasure to meet you, Detective Chief Inspector Riley, DS Davis. Please, come through to my office, take a seat.' Dr Wainwright ushers us through into quite a grand, Regency-style room with a high ceiling and fancy cornicing. A huge, arched, stained-glass window faces out onto the pleasantly green and neatly kept sprawling gardens that surround the imposing building. Even the impressive vista can't ameliorate the oppression all around me though. Larksmere isn't a happy place, you can feel it in the walls, though judging by Dr Wainwright's affable smile beneath his bushy beard, I'm sure he would beg to differ.

'Nurse Ledbury said you were here to talk about Erin Santos.' His brow creases in concern, adding, 'She's OK, isn't she?' His eyes dart between us. 'She's not long been discharged, you realise, just a month or two ago. I'd heard she's been doing well by all accounts...'

'We're investigating a murder, Dr Wainwright,' Davis says.

'Good God,' – I see the whites of his eyes as they widen – 'she's not been *murdered*, has she?'

'No, sir, she hasn't,' she reassures him. 'It's in relation to the recent homicide of a man named Milo Harrison.'

'Well, thank goodness for that at least. I mean for Erin, not this poor Milo chap.' His eyes shift focus between us once more. 'So, why exactly are you here? What does it have to do with Erin Santos?'

'Dr Wainwright. You were Erin's primary psychiatrist while she was a patient here at Larksmere, weren't you?'

'Yes, that's right, I was. Erin came to us in 2019, after she was convicted of manslaughter on the grounds of diminished responsibility.'

'And you diagnosed her yourself?'

'Of course. She was my patient.'

I look over at the wall to the left of me, spot the painting above the huge bookcase that's crammed with antique leather-bound books. It's an oil on canvas portrait of Dr Wainwright looking terribly regal, with his chin raised and his glasses perched halfway down his nose. It's in keeping with the period feel in the room and, I imagine, Dr Wainwright's opinion of himself.

'But by the time she left Larksmere, she was repentant for her crimes and, I believe, with the continued help of prescribed medication and God's love, she could be rehabilitated, hence why I was in favour of granting her recent release.' He pauses. 'These things don't happen quickly, or without much due consideration and discussion, you understand.'

'Was Erin schizophrenic, Dr Wainwright?' Davis asks.

He taps his fingertips together as he considers his answer.

'She was certainly delusional when she first arrived – she held recalcitrant beliefs that weren't based on any reality, refusing to change her mind even when presented with evidence to the contrary. She was experiencing visual and auditory hallucinations. I believe she heard voices – or at least one other than her own internal voice – and she appeared disorganised, disorientated. I remember that she was quite lethargic when she joined us initially, very out of sorts – she had anhedonia.'

'Anhed—?'

'*Onia* – anhedonia,' he explains. 'She couldn't find the joy in anything. She had a loss of interest in pleasure, in life itself.'

I should imagine most people who find themselves here would. Even the set of colourful flower paintings on the adjacent wall look somehow depressed.

'And how was Erin's behaviour throughout her stay here, was she a good patient? Was she ever aggressive or violent?'

'Violent? No, never.' He shakes his head. 'Generally she interacted well with staff and fellow patients and largely abided by the rules we have here at Larksmere, and she accepted her treatment without incident, or some of it anyway.'

'Some of it?'

'Well, Erin wasn't keen on the idea of ECT; she objected most vociferously to it initially. There were times, in the beginning, when she needed to be sedated to allow us to... *help her*. But eventually she complied.' He breaks eye contact, looks away.

'What did she tell you about Samantha Valentine? I'm

presuming you know who I'm talking about when I mention that name?'

'Yes, of course I do.' He pushes his glasses further up his long face. 'I got to know Samantha quite well over the years. Erin told me a lot about her, in great detail. Samantha was another identity, if you will, a character that enabled Erin to mentally transform between one version of herself and another.'

'And that was your belief, was it, Dr Wainwright?'

'My *belief*? Detective Chief Inspector?' His bushy ginger eyebrows start to twitch. 'It was my *professional diagnosis* that Erin was suffering from dissociative identity disorder and that she had created another identity, Samantha Valentine, in a bid to protect herself from her childhood trauma, and later, from the truth that she had killed a man. Though I suspect it was even more complex than that.'

'How's that? I'm sorry,' – I apologise, playing to his ego – 'I'm afraid I'm only a detective, not a trained psychiatrist.'

He links his fingers together on top of his antique leather desk.

'Of course.' He nods, graciously, now that he's certain I know my intellectual place. 'Erin Santos was a somewhat depressed, traumatised individual. She had BPD – that's borderline personality disorder – and she showed signs of bipolar disorder. Her mistrust of others prevented her from forming meaningful and lasting relationships throughout her life. However, this sadly perpetuated her loneliness and ability to feel socially accepted, and I believe was largely the reason why she created Samantha Valentine, a character who was dynamic and desirable and magnetic – all the things Erin herself wasn't, or didn't believe herself to be. She, Samantha, that is, was a coping mechanism.'

'Like an imaginary friend, you mean?' Davis chimes in. 'I had one of those as a kid.'

'Not quite.' He cocks his head at Davis with a condescending smile. 'Imaginary friends are not a diagnostic tool for mental illness, DS Davis, and neither are they necessarily a sign of psychosis or future mental health issues. Having an imaginary friend as a child is a perfectly normal, healthy part of a child's development, and often provides a sense of comfort, or a way in which to explore one's creativity, or emotions.

'Dissociative identity disorder, however, is almost always preceded by some kind of severe trauma as a child, be it abuse, or neglect, critical illness, or experiencing a traumatic event, such as in Erin's case, witnessing her mother being stabbed to death. I believe it was this trauma that led to her splitting, and to her creating a narrative whereby she got to be the heroine in the end this time, the one who saved her "friend" from her abusive partner, *by killing him.*'

He pauses, thoughtfully. 'She carried a terrible burden around with her, the guilt of being unable to help her mother, to save her life. And she used drugs and alcohol to self-anaesthetise, to deaden these feelings that were just too painful to live with, like so many of us do, Detective.'

I nod, pause for a moment to digest what he's told me – that Erin and Samantha are, in fact, one and the same person.

'So, is Erin Santos a psychopath, Dr Wainwright? In your *professional diagnosis?*'

He isn't blinking. I'm sure I've read somewhere that psychopaths blink less than neurotypicals do.

'A psychopath...? No... I don't believe so. She wasn't highly narcissistic, and she wasn't sadistic. Her dissociative identity disorder and the drug-induced delusions were not a good mix, however. I suspect she killed her victim in a bid to free herself on some emotional level, to absolve herself of the guilt and torment she felt about her mother. She wanted a chance to rewrite the script and change the ending, if you will. Ironically, these actions did nothing to prevent the pain of her remorse, they merely transferred it.'

'Transferred it?'

'Throughout her time here at Larksmere, Erin displayed deep regret over the death of Mr Radulovic. I believe she had a genuine conscience about her actions. But Samantha? Less so. Being Samantha allowed her to indulge in the fantasy of revenge – I suspect to get back at the men who'd wronged her, her mother's killer, for example – which of course regrettably became a reality. At the start of Erin's journey with us, she blamed Samantha Valentine, and, I feel I should say, the police, for what had happened to her.' He smiles a little apologetically. 'She never once deviated from this narrative, not until about a year or so ago anyway, incidentally, when she began to find faith.' He smiles warmly, as though this pleases him. 'We are, none of us, passive observers of reality, Detective; we are simply narrators. The brain invents stories that may well *feel* true or real, but oftentimes are based upon our cognitive biases, unhealed wounds and emotional residue.'

'So we are all of us liars? Is this what you're saying, Doctor?'

He chuckles, good-naturedly.

'No, not exactly.'

'Dr Wainwright, did you ever, at any given point during your interactions with Erin, believe she was telling the truth about Samantha Valentine? Did you ever consider that she could, in fact, be a real person and that Erin wasn't making her up?'

He sits, motionless for a moment before stroking his beard.

'I'm sorry, DCI Riley, DS Davis, but perhaps you'd be good enough to explain the *direct* purpose of your visit here today? I am, of course, most happy to assist the police in any way I can, but it would help me to understand the nature of your questions, and how to answer them correctly.'

I detect a hint of discomfort in his voice now.

'Well, a straight yes or no would be helpful, Doctor. You see, we arrested a female suspect in the murder of Milo

Harrison last Thursday night, at his apartment in South West London. He was stabbed to death in an almost identical crime to the one Erin Santos committed seven years ago, a crime which saw her end up here, in your care. Seven years later, our current female suspect says that she stabbed Milo Harrison while also protecting her friend, Samantha Valentine, in what appears to be an almost identical crime to Erin's.'

I hear his sharp intake of breath. He's still not blinking.

'And this happened last week? Does...' He clears his throat, clearly rattled by what I'm telling him. 'Does Erin have an *alibi* for the murder?'

'Of sorts. But we're waiting on forensics to tell us more.'

He brings his fingers into a praying position and presses them to his lips.

'And because of this new, similar crime, you think this means Samantha Valentine could actually be a real person? Because that's not possible, Detective Riley.' He shakes his head. 'Good God.' He stands abruptly. 'This is... this is a *disaster*... the governors... the press... Oh, Lord, we've only just released her...' He's talking to himself as he starts to pace the room – they say it's the first sign of madness.

'I'm sorry, Detective Riley—' He stops. 'But I need to make some urgent phone calls.'

'Why is it not possible for Samantha Valentine to be real, Dr Wainwright? And please, sit down, there's no need to panic about this. Erin isn't a suspect, currently. We just need to find her, talk to her.'

'Isn't she?' His calm, slightly elevated composure of moments earlier has completely vanished. 'Erin Santos *is* Samantha Valentine, Detective Riley, the two co-exist inside her mind, they're intertwined, two parts of the same person. If Samantha Valentine was at that crime scene, then so was Erin, it would be physiologically impossible for her not to be.'

The sudden sound of Davis's phone ringing cuts right through his words.

'It's forensics, gov.' She places her hand over the phone. 'There's a hit... DNA found at the scene belonging to...' She stops, looks over at us.

'Oh, dear Lord...' Dr Wainwright's voice has an edge of fear to it as Lucy slowly begins to nod her head.

TWENTY-EIGHT

DAN

There was just one last place Davis and I had needed to cross off the list before we left Leeds and headed back to London.

'Now *there's* a name from the past I haven't thought of in a while. Of course I remember her.' Jeremy Austin, one of the directors at Austin Marz Productions, had looked genuinely surprised. 'The girl who worked here on reception for a short time, you mean? The one who ended up in prison for murder?'

'Manslaughter actually,' I found myself correcting him, 'and she "ended up" in Larksmere Hospital.'

He raises his eyes – that place needs no introduction.

'Yeah, really dreadful business, that. We were all pretty shocked about it. None of us could believe it, myself especially.'

'Why was that?' I looked around his office at the ergonomic furniture, the gumball machine on his desk and the large, framed iconic movie stills on the walls – all very 90s retro hip, a bit like Jeremy himself. I found myself wondering if his friends might call him 'Jez'.

'Well, I was the one who gave her the job.'

'And why *did* you give Erin the job, do you remember?'

He ran a hand foppishly through his thick hair.

'I liked her, is the truth,' he shrugged. 'I liked Erin. She was sweet and friendly, had a nice warmth about her, even. She wasn't here for long – a couple of months at best – but she was popular with the staff and clients and she was good at her job.' He paused, seemed to drift off momentarily, somewhere in his thoughts. 'You'd just never have believed it in a million light years, looking at her, that she'd be capable of anything like that. None of us saw any signs, no red flags – *nothing*. We told the police the same thing back then as well.'

'So the police *did* interview you back in 2019?' I'd been through all of the statements and I hadn't seen any from Austin Marz in among them.

'Not me personally, but I think they spoke with HR and maybe to some of the girls who worked on the front desk at the time.'

My eyes were drawn to the platter of pastries on his trendy, kidney-shaped desk, leftovers from that morning's breakfast meeting, I imagined. It would be a travesty if they went to waste. 'It was seven years ago now though,' he said. 'And I have trouble remembering what I ate for breakfast most days.'

'If you're lucky enough to have had breakfast at all,' I quipped with a smile, glancing down at the pastries again, but the hint was lost on him. 'Did you interview anyone by the name of Samantha Valentine for the same receptionist position, on the same day you interviewed Erin?'

'Ah, well, we're back to the whole breakfast thing again,' he apologised. 'I mean, we're talking about a long time ago now, and I've probably interviewed a hundred plus people over those years...'

'Do you ever remember a blonde woman with green eyes, a striking-looking woman, wearing strong perfume perhaps?' It was a bit of a long shot, I realised, but smell is a powerful sense that can often trigger memories. Erin's recollection of Samantha's signature perfume – Baccarat Rouge – was vivid. She'd referred to it as 'exotic and intoxicating'. And that she was wearing it on the day they had met.

Perfume. When I thought of it, the redhead at the press conference was wearing a strong, exotic scent. It had lingered in my memory – perhaps I could even still smell it. Was it significant somehow?

The corners of Jeremy's mouth turned outwards.

'Can't say I do, sorry. Best thing I can do is call HR, see if they may have kept any previous applicants' résumés on file – and Zoe, Zoe Brookes, our head receptionist, has worked here for over ten years. She remembers Erin, maybe you should speak to her.'

There was nothing doing when we went upstairs to speak to the HR department though. They had neither Erin's nor any résumé belonging to anyone named Samantha Valentine on file, and Erin's employee records threw up nothing new of value. It was a dead end. I could only hope the head receptionist, Zoe, might have something for us.

'Oh yes,' she said with sage conviction as we stopped to speak to her on our way out. 'I remember Erin well. Honestly, it was such a shock when it all came to light, because Erin was just so... I dunno, ordinary, maybe even a bit unremarkable, I suppose.' She tucked a piece of her purple-highlighted hair behind a multiple-pierced ear. 'Still, you never know what people are really like behind closed doors, do you?' She looked at me, conspiratorially. 'People wear masks. And hers was a pretty good one. Erin was the last person you'd think would stab someone to death in a psychotic rage. I'm pretty sure it said in the press that she was mentally ill. She kept it well hidden though, I have to say. Gave us all the willies for some time after, it did. We had no idea we were working so closely with a psychopath at the time. I mean, she could've targeted one of us!'

'Was Erin good at her job, Zoe?'

She exhaled loudly. 'To be fair, yeah, she was, and she was

reliable, for the most part. I do remember I had to pull her up once or twice on occasion though, for leaving early without permission.' This all fits with everything Erin has told me.

'You mean she just upped and left work without explanation?' Davis had her notebook out.

'Yeah, well, sort of... I know that on one occasion she told me that there was an emergency with a friend or something, and she had to go to her immediately – and then she just shot off.'

I glanced at Davis and our eyes met.

'Do you know when this was, Zoe? Did she ever tell you who this friend was that she had to "shoot off" and see?'

'Ooh, well, now you're asking. I can't remember exact dates – it was years ago – but Erin worked here from the June or July of 2019 until the September, so it would've been during those months. And no, she never mentioned the friend's name to me. But I do remember that it had sounded urgent and that she genuinely seemed worried. The next day she turned up on time and never mentioned it again.' She began to blink rapidly at me, her purple eyeshadow – to match the hair, I assume – shimmering. 'Can I ask why you're asking about Erin now, all these years on?'

'Back in 2019, following the incident, did police speak to you? Did you give a statement regarding Erin, about her employment here, anything you might've seen or witnessed?'

She shook her head. 'I wasn't here in the office the day they came to speak to everyone – it was a rare day off for me. I know they interviewed a couple of the other receptionists who worked here back then though, and they spoke to HR, but I didn't get to talk to them in person and they never contacted me directly, or asked me to contact them. I didn't think I had much to tell them anyway, other than how shocked and freaked out I was by it all.' Suddenly, she appeared nervous. 'Erin is still in prison, isn't she?'

'Erin Santos was released from Larksmere Psychiatric

Hospital around seven weeks ago. We're conducting a murder inquiry and we'd like to speak with her.'

'Oh my God!' Her hand shot up to her mouth. 'She's not on the run, is she? She's not going to come here?'

'No, no,' Davis reassured her. 'It's really nothing to worry about, Zoe, we just need to speak to her.'

'Thank God,' she clutched her chest, exhaled.

'Did Erin ever mention the name Samantha to you, anyone called Samantha Valentine, a friend of hers?'

'I don't remember her mentioning any names, I'm sorry... but she did talk about this one friend *a lot,* if I remember rightly.'

My adrenalin started pumping furiously. For some reason, I hadn't expected her to say that. 'The blonde one, with the red lipstick and the perfume? Her, you mean?'

My heart exploded in my chest.

'You *saw* her? You met Samantha, this friend of hers?'

Her eyes widened and she took a micro step backwards, away from the front desk.

'Um... well, yeah, no, I mean, I never met her socially, if it's the same woman we're talking about. I didn't know her name, but I'm pretty sure she came here for a job interview on the same day as Erin. I don't know if they knew each other previously, or if that's how they met.'

'Would you recognise her again, this woman, if you saw her?'

Davis couldn't pull her phone from her pocket fast enough. 'Did she look something like this?' She slid the sketched image of Samantha Valentine in front of her. I held my breath as she stared at it.

'Honestly?' She looked up after a moment. 'I really can't say. I suppose it could be. She was blonde, attractive, in her early thirties, and she looked, I dunno... *expensive*. She wore a pair of Louboutins, you know, the ones with the red soles,' – she looked at Davis – 'and I distinctly remember thinking that if she could afford to buy a pair of those, then she doesn't really need this job! Wish I could afford them.' She sniffed. 'And the perfume she wore, it got up your nose a bit, do you know what I mean?'

'Yes, Zoe, I know *exactly* what you mean.'

Adrenalin was dancing inside my guts. Zoe doesn't know it, but she may be a vital witness, perhaps the *only* witness to a suspected sighting of Samantha Valentine, *a person who doesn't exist*.

'So, yeah, I think that's how they met, maybe. Anyway, I saw her a couple of times after that, once while she was waiting outside the building, across the road. I assumed she was waiting for Erin, though it could've been someone else. And then another time, I saw them coming out of Pret A Manger together, walking towards Elmo Gardens. I assumed they were going for lunch in the park. Why?' She looked at me and then at Davis. 'Erin hasn't killed her as well, has she?'

TWENTY-NINE

Hair fibres, in among Milo Harrison's blood. Together with Tilly Ward's DNA, *they found Erin's hair at the crime scene*. I don't know why I'm as surprised – nor strangely as disappointed – as I am to learn this, not after hearing what DI Pritchard and the eminent Dr Wainwright had to say. Also, there's a possible link between Erin and our latest victim, Milo Harrison, as it turns out.

'Harrison went to university in Leeds,' Mitchell had earlier informed me. 'He lived less than half a mile from Erin's home town back in the early 2000s. Maybe she knew him, gov.'

It was possible of course. Was there historic bad blood between them? Had they been in some sort of a relationship and it went bad? Had she started stalking him *way back then*? These are the questions skipping through my head, and yet despite this, and despite the DNA evidence, I find myself struggling to truly believe that Erin Santos was involved in Milo Harrison's murder. Harrison's family and friends were adamant that they've never heard of the name Erin Santos nor Samantha Valentine. They felt positive they would've known if he was, or ever had been stalked by anyone. They were a close-knit family who supported each other and were open about their problems.

Maybe I'm losing my touch and Erin's just too good at what she does – convincing people into believing her, *getting under their skin,* just as Amanda Pritchard warned me. Is that what's happened here? This is what I'm asking myself as I wait behind the door of the Met Police media suite, back in London after a long day already. I take a few deep breaths. Why do I keep coming back to the feeling that she *is* telling me the truth, at least on some level? I rub my temples with a thumb and forefinger. The cognitive dissonance is giving me a banging headache.

I can't rule out the idea that Erin is dangerous though. If all of this *is* true, then she could already be targeting her next victims, grooming them into killing on her command. Had she set her sights on Malcolm? Was it a covert heads-up she was giving me when she told me they had slept together? The idea sends a chill through me. Erin is really screwed now though. And I'm just about to explain to a room full of journalists why.

'Good afternoon, thank you all for coming. I'm Detective Chief Inspector Daniel Riley of the Metropolitan Police, Senior Investigating Officer on the homicide of Milo Harrison, thirty-two, from South West London. Further to the arrest made last week, I can confirm that a thirty-four-year-old female has been released on pre-charge conditional bail pending further inquiries.' I try not to blink in time with the camera clicks, the pops and flashes that shock my eyes shut. I don't know how these celebrities do it, day in and day out. No wonder they all wear dark glasses and look pissed off. I compose myself and hope that my tie is straight. I'll get trolled by the fashion police otherwise. People relish commenting about this kind of stuff – you know, lucky people with a lot of time on their hands and not much else to think about.

'On Thursday, we released an artist's sketch of a woman we

believe could be using the name Samantha Valentine. We have, as yet, been unable to locate this witness who, it's been alleged, left the scene of the crime.' The room is silent, save for the camera clicks. I pause. 'Following a forensic update, we are now looking for another person of interest and *potential witness*.' I choose my words deliberately. I need Erin to call me back.

'Erin Santos is a former patient of Larksmere Psychiatric Hospital with a previous conviction for the manslaughter of a man in 2019. We believe she may be in the London area and we need to speak to her in relation to our ongoing inquiries.'

'DCI Riley!' A member of the press raises a cursory hand and begins to speak at the same time. 'Is Erin Santos a suspect? Did she murder Milo Harrison?' His question sets off a chain reaction among them. Now it's like a round of bullets being fired.

'Why have you released a murder suspect, Detective Inspector? What made you let her go?'

'Mr Riley, can you give us the name of the suspect? Is Erin Santos dangerous? Should she be approached by the public? What are you doing about finding her?'

'Dan!' A slim, red-headed woman wearing glasses catches my attention. She's standing towards the back of the room. 'Dan, can you tell me how Erin Santos and Samantha Valentine might be linked? Is Samantha Valentine even real?'

I don't exactly recognise this particular journalist – she's too far away and her face is mostly obscured by the sea of fellow hacks and cameras in front of her for me to get a proper look at it – but *something* about her presence *feels* familiar somehow. And she's not too far off the money either, although it's more complicated than that if what Dr Wainwright and Amanda Pritchard say is anything to go by.

'We're following intel and leads as to her current whereabouts. We're confident we can find her. First and foremost, we want to make sure she's safe.' The cameras start to pop like fireworks as Erin's police mugshot flashes up on the screen behind me. 'Erin Santos is a forty-year-old white female, with, we believe, long dark hair, though this picture is over six years old, so it's possible she's changed her appearance and could look significantly different. She's five feet four inches, with a slim build and striking green eyes, and she speaks with a soft Yorkshire accent. If anyone knows Erin, or knows where she is, please contact the incident room on the number on screen now, below. Thank you.'

'Were the victim and Erin Santos a couple, were they in a relationship? How is she related to the case?'

The truthful answer is that I don't yet know. Currently, we've found no definitive link between Erin and Milo Harrison, aside from the fact that the victim lived close to Erin in Leeds during a two-year university degree over a decade ago. Dr Wainwright, however, had confirmed the dates that Erin had been let out on day release, prior to her being discharged from Larksmere. And one of those dates was the same date Tilly Ward claims to have first met Samantha in a bookshop in town – it tallies. There's no CCTV of course, the team has already checked. But the store owner vaguely recognised Tilly Ward's photograph when Parker and Mitchell had paid him a visit.

'I think I *may* have seen her before,' he'd told them. His answer was more definite when Parker had shown him a picture of Erin though.

'No.' He shook his head. 'I don't recognise her. Sorry.'

It's possible that Erin could've also met Milo Harrison during one of these day-release outings somehow. Maybe she never *stopped* stalking him?

'We allow the patients a few hours of unaccompanied freedom on these occasions,' Dr Wainwright had explained. 'We like to gently integrate them back into society, help them build their confidence and show them trust in a bid to assist their preparation for the big bad world outside the comfort of these walls.'

I'm not sure 'comfort' would have been the word I'd use.

'We're investigating every line of enquiry at this stage, going where the evidence takes us.' I nod at the enthusiastic young journalist whose hand is still raised high, like he knows the answer to a question in class and is desperate for the teacher to pick him. I don't tell them about the hair in Milo's blood being identified as Erin's, or the enormity of such a finding at this stage, because there'll be a public panic, and in turn Erin could panic and do something inadvisable, like kill someone, or have them killed. As it is, I'm secretly struggling with a degree of guilt already. I feel as if I'm betraying her somehow by going public, despite the evidence dictating that I must. I doubt she'll call me again after she sees this.

Anyway, behind the scenes as I speak, it's all systems go on 'Operation Verde'. Archer has thrown bodies into it. There's now a thirty-strong team, including experts and analysts and specialists. We'll be working in shifts round the clock. There'll be no stone left unturned.

'Dan...' It's the redhead again. 'At the time of Erin's arrest back in 2019, is it true that she claimed to have been conned into killing her victim by her friend, Samantha Valentine? Is there a chance you think that Erin may actually *be* Samantha Valentine?'

OK, this time, she's *definitely* on the money. I'm curious as to how she knows this information, though I know just how 'thorough' some investigative hacks can be – I'm married to one after all. Still, this isn't public information. Samantha Valentine's name was never reported in the press back in 2019.

'I'm afraid that's all I can give you right now. Except that I would like to make a direct appeal to Erin Santos.' The room falls to a hushed silence as I address the cameras. 'Erin, please call me, or you can go into any police station you choose, and I will come to you in person. I'm here to help you. Please get in touch.'

I don't know if Erin will see my personal appeal, maybe she doesn't currently have access to a TV or a smartphone? So far she's used a burner phone to communicate with me, just like she claims Samantha had used with her, an *untraceable* burner phone. She's been clever, but still I don't understand what her motives are for doing this. By re-enacting the same crime and then going on the run, she must know that she'll be caught eventually and thrown back into Larksmere. I would tag 'or worse' on the end of that sentence, but I don't think it exists. Davis and I couldn't leave that maudlin place fast enough.

Why would she do this to herself? I try to straighten it all out in my head. If I've got this right, then back in 2019, when she committed her crime, Erin believed that her 'split' self, Samantha Valentine, had coerced her into doing it. She does the time for it in a mental institution, presenting throughout the full duration of her sentence as Erin. So where exactly did 'Samantha' go during this time? Dr Wainwright told me that Erin had never once in all her years at Larksmere presented to him, or anyone else it seems, as Samantha Valentine, this supposed 'other self', though he had an explanation for this of course. I suspect Dr Wainwright probably has an explanation for *everything*.

'The drugs she was prescribed, and the treatment she underwent, they would've prevented her from manifesting into Samantha Valentine,' he told me with unwavering confidence. 'Erin felt great loss at the time for this second self though; she actually grieved for Samantha, for her friend who had suddenly abandoned and betrayed her, in her mind of course.'

I left the press conference in a hurry, ignoring Archer's call on the way out. No doubt she wanted to critique my performance. Or tell me that my tie wasn't straight. I look around briefly to see if I can spot the redhead. She's at least five people deep in front of me and I can just see her vibrant-coloured hair as it bobs towards the exit, the exotic, spicy scent of what I'm sure is her perfume, trailing behind her. It triggers something in me, but I'm not sure what or why, exactly. I push my way through the reporters in a bid to catch up with her. By the time I filter outside though, she's nowhere to be seen.

THIRTY

ERIN

I stare at the screen, too scared to blink in case I miss a second. Dan Riley is making a public appeal for me to come forward and – woop-de-do – he's mentioned that I am a convicted killer who served my sentence in a secure psychiatric hospital. *Nice one, Dan!* Now *everyone* thinks I'm a dangerous homicidal lunatic on the run. To add further insult, they've only gone and shown that hideous photo of me from seven years ago – that dreadful mugshot taken at the time of my arrest. I gasp in horror as it flashes up on screen, cover my mouth with both hands. My long, dark hair looks greasy and dishevelled, hanging lankily around my sallow-skinned face, and my eyes have practically disappeared back into my skull, with dark circles shadowing them. As far as mentally deranged killers go, even I have to admit that I look the part.

My face flushes hot with shame and injustice. Malcolm is probably watching this right now, asking himself what the hell he was thinking, sleeping with such an unattractive psycho killer. To be fair to myself, I *did* actually tell him the truth, albeit in jest. Well, I wasn't going to put him straight there and then, was I? Even if Malcolm didn't think I was a nutcase before I told him my story, he certainly would after hearing it.

I turn up the volume on my laptop; the noise of my heartbeat pounding in my ears is drowning out the sound.

'Following a recent forensic update, we are now looking for another person of interest and potential witness...'

'*Potential witness?*' What is he talking about, when he says, 'following a recent forensic update...'? They can't possibly have found anything at the crime scene that links me to it. I wasn't – I'm not – a witness. *I wasn't there.* Dan already knows this because I told him – I told him *everything*.

'Please contact me, Erin, it's not too late. We can resolve this...' I find myself smiling. There is something undeniably warm and genuine about Dan's face that I can't seem to help myself smiling at, because as it currently stands, I have very little to smile about. But what does he mean, 'not too late'? Late for what exactly? I click on the clip again, play it back from the beginning with a sinking feeling in the pit of my stomach. Now that my name and picture are in the public domain, I will need to be super vigilant. The police are looking for me, *everyone* will be looking for me.

I have to find Samantha before they find me. I can't let that happen. Not now that I'm so close.

I take a bite out of the Bounty bar that's on the table next to me, start to chew, try to think. That dreadful picture flashes up on screen again and I hit the pause button, stare at it for a moment longer before glancing at myself in the old mirror above the stained sink. Will I be recognised from this photo? I look so different now to how I did back then – it's the hair mostly, but age hasn't exactly been kind to me either. Surprisingly, there were no on-site beauty spas at Larksmere, and being stuck inside that place has put ten extra years on me at least, but is it enough?

I'll need to go to a charity shop, buy some different clothes and accessories, some glasses, hats, and scarves and—

The sudden sound of knuckles rapping on my door startles me. I freeze, stay radio silent and listen. Is it the police? Have they found me *already*? A slew of fresh panic explodes inside my belly. I press my ear to the door and listen.

'Molly... it's me... *Open the door.*'

Pete. I hesitate. Maybe Pete has seen the appeal on telly and recognises me. Maybe he's standing behind the door right now *with the police*?

'*Molly...*' he repeats, urgently, 'open the freakin' door! I've...' – he drops his voice down to a whisper – '... I've got your... *shopping delivery.*'

Shopping delivery? For a brief moment I have no idea what he's talking about, but then it comes to me. Ahh, *that* shopping delivery. My memory really isn't what it once was, no doubt, down to the draconian treatments I was forced to endure at Larksmere. My brain glitches more often now, and I experience memory blanks. It's unsettling, like dying for a few seconds before returning to life again.

The bolt is stiff, the metal sliding between my shaking, sweaty fingers, as I struggle to unlock it.

'You like to keep a man waiting, you, don't you, sister?' He pushes past me into the room and throws the black holdall he's carrying down onto the bed. The screen on my open laptop is paused on my unflattering mugshot photo and I smack it shut before he sees it. It's not that I necessarily think that Pete would dob me in to the cops if he found out who I was – after all, he's hardly on the right side of the law himself, especially if I think what is in the bag, is in the bag. But I don't know Pete's situation. I don't know Pete at all.

'You can thank me later,' he says, nodding at the holdall. 'Go on, open it then, check it, make sure it's what you're looking for.' I unzip it, cautiously. 'It's all there,' he sniffs, 'the piece, the bullets, and the ID – passport, driver's licence and a new NI number. You're good to go, cupcake.'

I perch on the edge of the bed, open the passport. My new name is Alexandra Louise Fisher. I quite like it, it sounds a bit posh. Sadly though, the picture accompanying it is anything but. I'd got the pictures taken in haste at one of those self-serve photo booths at the train station earlier. I realise that no one's passport photo is particularly flattering, but this one is a real doozy. The new blonde hair looks dry and frazzled, like a straw wig perched on top of my head, and the colour washes me out, like I've been dead for a week and dug up. I pick up the gun. I've never seen a gun up close before, let alone handled one. It's cool to the touch and heavier than I expected. I can already sense its power between my fingertips, the weight of life and death hanging in the balance at the squeeze of the trigger.

'You ever used a gun before, Molly?' Pete is watching me with vague amusement. I shake my head. 'Nah, I thought not.' He comes behind me, presses himself into the small of my back and places an arm around my waist. I try to forget it's there as I raise my hand and point the weapon at the wall.

'You're a left-hander...' he observes, 'you should've said.'

'Does it make a difference?'

'Not if you're on target,' he snorts. 'It's a semi-auto.'

'What does that mean...?'

'It means when you fire a bullet, another one will automatically load for you. BANG, BANG, BANG!'

I flinch in shock, and he laughs, clearly amused. *What an asshole.*

'Want me to load it for you?'

I reluctantly nod.

'Give it here then, cupcake.' I watch as he cocks the gun, pushes the bullets inside the barrel and flicks it shut. Clearly, one of us has done this before.

'There's a spare box of bullets in the bag.' He nods to it.

'Thanks, but really I only need two.'

He shoots me a curious glance.

'Why only *two* bullets?'

'Ask no questions and I'll tell you no lies.'

He shrugs.

'Your business, sister. Just don't be bringing whatever it is to my door, you understand? This is a respectable establishment. And blood is a real mothertrucker to get out of the sheets. And...' his voice drops down a notch, hardens slightly, 'I don't want the filth sniffing round here neither. Any feds at my front door and there'll be a bloodbath on your hands, most of it your own, you get me?'

'Yes,' – I spin round to face him, the loaded gun still raised in my hand – 'perfectly.'

'Whoa! Jesus! Easy there, blondie.' He leaps backwards, places a hand in front of him. 'That thing's loaded! You want to splash my brains all over the walls, do you?'

I think about answering him truthfully.

'No, of course not, sorry,' I say, placing it back down onto the bed.

'So...?' He looks at me. 'Do we have a deal?'

I stare down at the gun; its dark, hard metal edges gleaming, menacing.

'It's a quality weapon, that one. I could've got you a small sawn-off for one-fifty, but something tells me a girl like you might prefer to carry a bit of class, am I right?'

I go over to my tote bag, unzip it.

'I'll do the piece for seven-fifty, the ID in total comes to a *bag of sand*, so it's a round one seven-fifty in total.'

'There's two thousand pounds there,' I say, dumping the cash on the bed. 'Keep the change. You can count it if you like.'

'I trust you, sister.' He looks into my eyes and – uh-oh – I'm getting the vibe he may want to stay for a 'drink' and 'keep me company'. I'll have to let him down gently – *either that or shoot him.*

'And that's very generous of you.' He raises his eyebrows as he looks at the cash on the bed, grinning manically. 'How about I throw in a bit of scampi and chips for dinner, eh? I don't usually mix business with pleasure, but I could make an exception for you, blondie.'

'Yeah, sure. I'll meet you downstairs in a bit,' I say. 'I'll need to freshen up first and I've got a phone call to make – an important one.'

He seems pleased.

'I'll hold you to that, Molly, or should I say, *Alexandra*?' His gold teeth twinkle as he grins.

'Please,' – I force a smile – 'call me Alex.'

THIRTY-ONE

DAN

'Ahh, Dan!' Archer looks at the gift bag I'm holding, cocks her head. 'You really shouldn't have!'

'I didn't, ma'am,' I say, placing it onto her fastidiously tidy desk.

Archer is a neat freak, obsessively so in my opinion. Even her pens are colour-coordinated and in a perfectly aligned row – black, blue, green and red. It's the antithesis of my own 'organised chaos', which isn't even that organised when I think about it. She stares at it before moving it a millimetre to the left, making it more symmetrical, in line with her staple gun.

'What is it?'

'It's perfume.'

She raises her eyes.

'Bit early for Christmas shopping, isn't it?'

'I bought it in a department store in Leeds, ma'am. Don't worry, I put it on expenses.'

'I'll bet you did, Riley.' She smirks.

'It was a snip at £250.'

If she thinks I'm joking, I'm not. My heart almost stopped when the assistant had rung it up on the till: 'She's a lucky lady, whoever she is.' She'd beamed at me with a set of dazzling white teeth as I'd handed over my credit card, palms sweating.

'Erin Santos claims this is the perfume that Samantha Valentine wears, her "signature" scent.' I wonder if Archer has a signature scent, and if so, what it might be. Something a little spicy that gets up your nose, I imagine.

She snatches the box from her desk, starts to unwrap the cellophane. 'OK. What does that have to do with anything?'

'We spoke to a woman named Zoe Brookes while we were in Leeds, ma'am. She's the head receptionist at Austin Marz Productions, the film production company where Erin worked in the months leading up to her arrest. She remembers her well.'

I watch her as she struggles with the wrapping, reaches into her desk for a pair of scissors. I imagine the inside of her desk drawer is as precise as a brain surgeon's knife tray.

'She also claims to have *met* Samantha Valentine.'

She looks up at me sharply then stops what she's doing.

'Erin was seen by this colleague with a woman who fits the description both Erin and Tilly Ward have given us of Samantha Valentine – a blonde, attractive woman, memorable, in her thirties, well-dressed, wearing red-soled designer shoes... wearing *that* perfume...'

She takes the large, square red bottle from the box.

'It's Baccarat Rouge, ma'am. It's a favourite with all the celebrities, apparently. The assistant in the store told me that Rihanna wears it.'

'And this Zoe Brookes, this receptionist, she remembers all of this seven years on and hasn't said a word until now?'

'It appears she was never asked about it until now,' I reply curtly. 'How would she even have known it was important? Samantha Valentine's name was never released to the media back then and no one was looking for her. They wrote off Erin's account of what happened. They didn't believe her story.'

'But you do, Riley?'

'The people Erin worked with, they all expressed how shocked they were at the time about what happened to her; none of them knew why she did what she did. They say she was nice, she was *normal*...'

'She had mental health issues, Riley,' she cuts in. 'She'd been in a psychiatric hospital before she went on to kill Radulovic. She'd had a traumatic childhood, problems with drugs and alcohol, she no doubt wasn't in her right mind at the time. I feel sorry for the woman, really, genuinely, I do have compassion for her.' She meets my eyes. 'Don't look so surprised, Dan!'

'I didn't realise I was, ma'am.'

She sprays some of the perfume on her wrist, waves her arm around a little. I've seen women do this before and have always wondered why.

'It helps the scent to settle.' She sniffs her pulse point, as though I'd asked the question aloud. 'Hmmm... not bad...'

It hits my nose instantly, that strong, woody, musky amber-type smell, earthy, yet somehow sweet too. I'm almost certain it's the same perfume the red-headed journalist was wearing at the press conference. It's very distinctive. *Intoxicating*.

'What I'm saying, ma'am, is—'

'I know what you're saying, Riley.' She squirts herself liberally with a couple more blasts from the bottle – probably somewhere around thirty quid's worth.

'I think we should get this Zoe Brookes in to make a formal statement, ma'am, like she should've done seven years ago.'

'And she was introduced to this person as Samantha Valentine, was she? Does she have any evidence, CCTV footage, photos, witnesses, anything to support this?'

'No, ma'am, but the description alone and...'

'Did she positively identify her as Samantha Valentine from the sketch?'

'Well, she said it "could've" been her, ma'am.'

'... It *could've* been anyone, Riley,' she snaps. 'Look, Erin Santos's DNA was found at Milo Harrison's crime scene. Her hair was found on his corpse, for Christ's sake, mixed in with the poor man's blood! There were only three sets of DNA found in that apartment: the victim's, the perpetrator's and... Erin Santos's.'

'Yes, ma'am, about that...'

'Even after what DI Pritchard told you,' – she ignores me, continues – 'and what Dr Wainwright said, if you're so convinced this Samantha character exists, then how do you explain *that?*'

She's sort of got me on that one, I'll admit. But I do have a possible explanation, a possible explanation I'm pretty sure she won't want to hear.

'DNA doesn't lie, Riley, you know that. Erin Santos was there at the crime scene. Erin Santos *is* Samantha Valentine, or thinks she is, and we need to find her – fast.' She replaces the lid on the perfume bottle, smacking it shut with the palm of her hand.

'So, with your shopping expo complete, perhaps now you can get back to the job in hand of finding our suspect and bringing her in before this bloody story breaks the internet? Have you seen the insane nonsense people are coming up with on social media? No doubt Netflix will be sniffing around for the rights to turn it into a docudrama in no time at all. *The Woman Who Wasn't There*... or something,' she says with an uncharacteristic theatrical flourish.

'But what if she really *was* there, ma'am?' I know I'm pushing my luck, but I can't just ignore conflicting information, and now a potential sighting from a witness. Moreover, *I can't ignore my intuition.*

She isn't listening to me, I can tell.

'Has Erin contacted you again?'

'No, ma'am. I think my TV appearance may have put paid to any ongoing communication with her.'

'Yes, well, that's regrettable,' she sighs. 'But our duty is to protect the public – the innocent must always be our first priority, Riley.'

'What if Erin is one of the "innocents" herself in all of this, ma'am?'

'Well, then her DNA wouldn't be on the body of our victim, would it – and yet it is, Riley?' I can feel her irritation rising.

'What if it was *planted* there, ma'am?'

I'd taken a call from the forensic lab on the journey back to London and spoken with a very jovial lady by the name of Muriel Barnes-Jones. I needed to know their exact findings.

'We extracted over ten or more hair fibres from the blood at the scene and from the victim himself,' she informed me.

'Could the victim have reached out and pulled at her hair while he was trying to defend himself perhaps?'

'Well, you might automatically assume so,' she'd agreed, 'given the number of hair fibres found, but that doesn't appear to be the case. There was no hair found in, on or around the victim's hands, no DNA underneath his fingernails, as you might expect. Rather, it was largely recovered from his torso, and more were mixed in with the blood found around his chest, around the wound. The hair fibres themselves are interesting in that they're small snippets of hair, no more than a centimetre or two in length, blunt in shape, like they'd been cut.' She sounded perplexed. 'It's not what I would expect from an ordinary hair sample found at most crime scenes, one which has somehow shed or been pulled out. You would generally expect them to be longer or to have a root attached maybe, if they'd been ripped from the scalp. The pattern in which they were distributed on his body was unusual as well, like they'd been randomly sprinkled...'

This had really made my head spin.

'Planted by who exactly?' Archer is up out of her chair now. I can still smell those few squirts of perfume lingering in the air – mind you, at £250 a pop, I'd hope to.

'I haven't got time for this, Riley,' she says, shortly, 'and frankly, neither have you. While you and DS Davis were shopping in Leeds, intel has come in on Erin Santos's whereabouts.'

'Oh?'

'CCTV picked her up at Leeds Central railway station. She boarded a train and was again picked up on camera at the other end in London King's Cross. 'They've identified an address.'

THIRTY-TWO

ERIN

There is a particularly bitter irony to the fact that, having spent the past six or more years of my life being silenced, dismissed, and disbelieved, it now seems that everyone can't wait to hear my truth. Or, I suspect, more accurately, to watch me being thrown straight back inside Larksmere asylum. Seriously – it's nothing more than a modern-day witch hunt.

Dan Riley's TV appeal has sent the keyboard Karens into meltdown, and that awful photograph of me that's been plastered all over it has garnered some pretty brutal comments: 'She even *looks* like a serial killer,' one had observed, with another describing me as 'Larksmere's finest alumni'. Though maybe they have a point there... 'Why was this woman released when she's clearly mentally deranged and dangerous? She's the perfect example of a failed system.' And, my personal favourite, 'Is she *really* only forty?'

I snap Molly's laptop shut and switch it off. I can't stomach reading any more and I'm fearful of being traced. Molly could've put a tracker on it, one of those 'Find my laptop' AirTag things that everyone's using to help them find all the essential items that they must keep losing. I imagine it's just the sort of sensible, practical thing that Molly might do.

A sudden gust of wind causes the old bedroom window to rattle, startling me. I place a hand on my chest in a bid to soften the jitters dancing inside it, peer outside through the grubby net curtains onto the grimy, wet street below. Are they already watching me, the police? Are snipers currently positioned on the rooftop of the Bull and Barrow, poised to take me down at the first sign? I drop the curtain, quickly.

I need to leave this place – *now*. Judging by the reports I've read online, it'll only be a matter of time before the police come and smash the door down, no doubt fifty men strong, being as though I'm so 'deranged and dangerous', and I certainly don't want Pete's premonition of a bloodbath coming true. He has his sheets to think of.

Somehow, I have to get to Samantha Valentine before they get to me. Only, the truth is, I still have no idea where she is. I'm no closer to finding her than I was when I was caged up inside Larksmere having my brain lobotomised. And even if she is here, in this city, no doubt she'll have absconded after seeing Dan's TV appeal and all the media mayhem this story is creating, disappeared into the shadows unnoticed, a ghost once more. Perhaps I was wrong and DCI Riley *isn't* the man for the job after all. Potentially, he's scuppered my plan by publicly giving her the heads-up. If she's smart – and Samantha is nothing if she isn't that – then she's probably already on a plane out of here and I'll *never* get justice.

Frustrated, I hastily throw my clothes into my now-much-lighter tote bag, wrap the gun in an old T-shirt and bury it underneath them. Then I give the shabby room the once over with a cloth and some bleach, being careful to wipe down all touch surfaces and the old mirror – it's probably the first proper clean it's ever seen.

'Oi! Where d'you think you're sneaking off to, sister?' Pete calls out to me as I'm halfway through the pub, heading towards the exit.

I wince, roll my eyes. I was hoping to slope off without him noticing, only I get the distinct impression that Pete has other intentions for me, or, far more worryingly, *us*. 'I've got scampi and chips in a basket going cold here, blondie!'

I swing round at him with a pasted-on smile.

'I've just a couple of errands to run first,' I say, breezily. 'Keep it warm for me.' I give him my best flirtatious face, the sort that Samantha could muster up at the drop of a hat and have any man in the palm of her hand – or woman, for that matter. 'And the scampi and chips too!' I wink at him over my shoulder, my smile vanishing instantly as I turn my back on him – *creep*.

I can't risk using public transport. London is one great big closed-circuit television camera. Forget about your best side – if you're lucky enough to have one of those – with so many cameras on you day in day out, there's no side of you to hide.

I think about hiring a car while I'm rummaging through the rails of clothes in the charity shop, mindful of the CCTV cameras. I've been careful to keep most of my face covered with the thick scarf I'm wearing. I don't want it to look as if I'm trying to deliberately conceal my identity though – it's a delicate balance. Thankfully it's still pretty chilly out and there's a light drizzle in the air, so the scarf is appropriate. Now though, I'm looking for something a bit different, something to change things up a bit.

I grab a pair of smart black trousers and a fitted white shirt, choose a pair of suede boots from a collection of tatty old footwear on a shoe rack – the best of a bad bunch. I check that they're my size before taking them to the counter and purchase them along with another two scarves and a black woollen double-breasted dress coat that cinches in at the waist – Samantha would definitely have approved. I throw in a pair of reading glasses and some tarnished gold costume jewellery to finish the look off.

'That'll be £69.40.' The hippie-chick behind the counter rings them all up.

Jeez, £70 for a load of old cast-offs? Things really *have* changed since I've been locked away. 'Can I get you a bag, hun?' she says in a sing-song voice. 'It's 25p extra, but it *is* biodegradable.'

Hun. The word triggers me. 'Hun' was what Sam always used to call me. She'd tag it on the end of everything. 'You OK, *hun*? You want a drink, *hun*? Would you kill for me, *hun*?'

'No, thanks.' I wouldn't pay 25p for a plastic bag on principle alone, even if it is biodegradable. *Even if I was a millionaire*.

'Is it OK if I use the changing room?'

Hippie-chick looks up at me, her plaits wobbling as she nods and points. 'Sure, it's just through there, the curtain behind the books.'

I notice the TV screen on the wall above her is switched on to the BBC news channel. Trust me to choose a charity shop where the staff have an interest in current affairs. Why isn't she watching a music channel or something? Young hippie-chick here looks more like a *Love Island* fan to me – but then I think it's fairly safe to say that, given my past history, maybe I'm not the best judge of character.

I listen out for the news as I hurriedly strip off my old clothes and change into my new 'office chic' ensemble. I throw the thick black dress coat over the top before brushing my hair and adding a dash of red lipstick. It's as I'm standing back a little from the mirror, observing my transformation, that I hear my name mentioned.

'... Erin Santos... early forties with long dark hair and green eyes... she was last seen on CCTV at Leeds Central station, where she boarded a train to London King's Cross...' I surreptitiously pull back the curtain a touch, peer through it at the TV screen that hippie-chick is now, of course, avidly blinking up at. '... A former inmate at Larksmere High Security Psychiatric Hospital, police have advised the public not to approach Santos and if they do see her, to call them at the first opportunity.' That dreadful photo of me flashes up on the screen again.

'... *Police have advised the public not to approach Santos.*'

My face glows with anger. Sometimes I'm amazed that I still have any anger left in me. You'd think, after all these years of injustice, that particular reservoir might've run dry, and yet it is the gift that keeps on giving. The police really are a bunch of muppets. They got this all so wrong from the very beginning, and seem hell-bent on continuing with the same narrative even now, all these years later. I suppose I shouldn't have expected anything less, really. I plan to call Dan Riley again once I've hired a car and put him straight. Maybe he can do the same for me about this forensic evidence they've supposedly found at this crime scene I was never at. It's currently being suggested on social media that my DNA was discovered inside Milo Harrison's apartment. Only, I know that *can't* be right. It's probably just fake news. Still, I'm incensed they can report such lies so seemingly legitimately without evidence, or recourse. Does *anyone* care about the truth anymore?

I tear back the curtain, the metal rings singing with the momentum. *Screw them all!* What does it matter anyway, what people are saying about me? When the *real* truth is finally revealed in all its shocking glory, then I'll be a media sensation for all the right reasons, and heads will roll. I'm almost sad that I won't be around to witness it when it happens.

'Wow!' Hippie-chick remarks, wide-eyed, as I step from the changing room. 'Look at you! You look... awesome!'

I was right. *No one* tells the truth anymore. Anyway, at least it appears she hasn't recognised me from my photo that's still on the screen above us.

I flash her a fake smile. I doubt she can tell the difference. Samantha Valentine may be a cunning chameleon, able to adapt and mimic sincerity like the professional emotional fraudster she is, but six years in that hospital from hell has taught me nothing if not how to portray my emotions – real and, especially, otherwise – convincingly. Besides, I learned from the master.

In hindsight, one of the things Samantha inadvertently taught me is how to hide in plain sight, like the misplaced set of keys you've spent hours searching for only to find they were right under your nose all along.

Now though, I reckon I can give her a run for her money. When I find Samantha – and I will find her – she won't know what's hit her. Subservient little Erin, her well-trained puppet, her faithful and adoring follower, *her friend*, is no longer the person she was so effortlessly able to deceive and destroy without care or conscience. I'm different now. *I've changed*.

'Thanks,' I say, turning back to smile at hippie-chick as I strut out of the shop in my new ensemble, '*hun*.'

THIRTY-THREE

DAN

The incident room at Operation Verde the next morning is buzzing with anticipation. Intel has come up with an address in King's Cross – the Bull and Barrow, a notorious pub known for its links to criminal activity and the underworld. It's been raided more times than a dieter's fridge at midnight over the years and it's believed that Erin may be staying in one of the 'guest rooms' there. I can only imagine what the inside of one of those looks like. Is there even a minus rating on Trustpilot?

What did Erin mean that time when she told me on the phone that she wasn't running *from* something, but running *to* something? I could be wrong – and Archer seems to delight in the idea that I might be – but I think she's planning to exact some kind of revenge on Samantha Valentine for what she believes are the myriad injustices she's suffered at her hand. Only if that *is* the case – and she's both Erin Santos *and* Samantha Valentine simultaneously – then wouldn't this mean that by default she'd be taking revenge on *herself*? It could be that the sassy Samantha side of her hates these men who have somehow wronged her in her eyes – I suspect Samantha probably *was* stalking both her victims, and knew them in some form

– but that Erin's character is horrified and dismayed by her actions and furious at being made to take the rap for it – *from herself*. I have to say, this is one absurd case – and it keeps getting stranger still.

I glance at my phone on my desk. No contact from Erin. I doubt she'll call again now, not if she's seen the press conference. I wish I didn't feel as crappy about it as I do, but as Archer had rammed it home to me, I have to look at the facts and go where the evidence takes me. My first priority is getting justice for Milo Harrison and his family, and ensuring public safety. *Only, I just can't stop thinking about Erin.*

'Don't go all left field on me on this one, Dan,' Archer had warned me before I'd left her office. 'Don't keep looking for ghosts. This witness, this colleague of Santos's you spoke to in Leeds, she couldn't give you a name or a positive ID. It's all just hearsay. She's probably been reading all the nonsense on social media. Goodness only knows how people come up with some of the bullshit that's written, putting two and two together and making seven hundred and fifty-seven. It beggars belief. Too much time on their hands, if you ask me.'

Unusually, I don't disagree with her. A story like this makes clickbait gold. It also brings to the surface all the self-styled bedroom sleuths, journalists, conspiracy theorists, and perhaps above all, the haters.

'And you said yourself that Dr Wainwright confirmed that Erin was on day release on the same date Ward says she met Samantha Valentine. What's the news on Ward, by the way? Are we keeping a close eye on her?'

'Yes, ma'am,' I assured her. 'She's hardly set foot out of her apartment since we bailed her, ma'am. Once or twice to go grocery shopping, by the looks of it. The rest of the time the blinds are shut, no movement whatsoever. Surveillance did see someone leaving the address this morning though, around 11 a.m.'

'Do we know who it was?'

'A woman, apparently, boss, a redhead.'

A redhead? My stomach had clenched when Parker had briefed me on this, earlier. 'Send any images they have over to me now, Parker, ASAP.' I instructed him. Could it be the same redhead I'd seen at the press conference? The one wearing the perfume that I'm convinced is also the same as the extortionately overpriced bottle of Baccarat Rouge that we purchased in Leeds? Incidentally, it was still lingering inside my nostrils, or the memory of it anyway. If it is her, then it's safe to say that the press must've somehow got wind of Tilly Ward's identity, and that adds another layer of potential aggro. Until she's charged, I'm mindful of keeping Tilly Ward's name – and face – out of the public eye.

'I don't want her hounded, Parker. Keep an eye on her – and any press who might be sniffing around.'

'Look, Dan.' I was about to leave Archer's office, only she hadn't quite finished with me yet. At least her tone had softened slightly, sounded less irascible. 'We've all fallen foul of a psychopath or two during our career at some time or another,' she said, casting me a pitiful glance. 'They're notoriously clever, highly manipulative types – I don't need to tell you that. They'll have you twisted up in knots, thinking black is white, some of them – that's what they do, that's their MO. They try to mess with your head, gaslight you, play on your empathy, get inside your mind...' She tapped the side of her temple with a finger. 'So she had you on the hook, got you searching for someone who doesn't exist, or does, but only in her messed-up mind. I've read the files, I've seen the statements Santos gave at the time, and admittedly, she sounds convincing enough. But it's all a fantasy, Riley, a picture she painted at the time and one she's repainting now. Even seasoned senior investigating officers like you can be taken in. As I say, it can happen to the best of us. Don't beat yourself up over it.'

'I wasn't, ma'am,' I replied flatly.

I made to pick up the gift bag containing the perfume from her desk, but she stopped me with a raised hand.

'Actually, you can leave that here, with me, if you like, Riley.'

'Sorry, ma'am,' I flashed her a rueful smile as I snatched it from her desk. 'Like you said, Christmas is a long way off.'

My phone pings as Davis and I ready ourselves to head off to the Bull and Barrow. A SWAT team has been deployed, largely due to the Bull and Barrow's notorious reputation and clientele. We don't believe Erin is armed, but that's not to say the occupants will welcome us with open arms either. Some pretty nasty characters have been known to frequent that particular establishment, so the element of surprise is paramount.

Parker has sent me those images of the female seen leaving Tilly Ward's apartment yesterday morning – the redhead. Only, once again, it's tricky to get a clear view of her face. In every shot, her head is either lowered or she's turning away in the opposite direction of the camera, *almost as if she's aware of it*. You can't miss the glossy red hair though, and she's wearing the same burgundy-coloured coat that she had on when I saw her at the conference.

'We need to find out who this is, Mitchell.' I slap the image on DS Mitchell's desk in front of her. 'I saw her at the press conference, and she was seen coming out of Tilly Ward's apartment that same morning. I think she may be a journalist. Check which publications and news crews attended the appeal, see if we can identify her and then get her on the phone if you can.'

'No problem, gov. Oh, by the way, boss, I wanted to introduce you to one of our new recruits, DC Adriana Ayers.' She turns to the young-looking woman next to her.

'This is your first assignment since qualifying, isn't it, Adriana?'

She smiles up at me, a touch shyly. 'And it looks as if she may have come across something interesting already.'

The twinkle in Mitchell's eye piques my intrigue. 'Great. Well, welcome aboard, Adriana. It's all hands on the pump for this one.' Frankly, we need all the help we can get.

'Nice to meet you, sir.' She shakes my hand firmly — always a good sign. No one likes a limp handshake.

'Oh, don't bother with all that "sir" nonsense, please. It's embarrassing and it makes me sound like an old school master.' To be fair, she doesn't exactly look long out of school herself.

'You know you're getting old, son, when policemen start to look young.' I hear my dear old dad's voice in my head. Four years have passed since he died, and yet sometimes it feels like three days.

'Where were you stationed before, Adriana?'

'Nowhere, sir. I'm a graduate.' She looks a little apologetic about this admission.

'Fresh from college, aren't you?' Mitchell raises an eyebrow. 'Hasn't had to deal with the dregs.'

'Oh,' I say. She's one of *those*. 'Lucky you, then.'

These days, with a degree under your belt, you can bypass the traditional route of earning your chops in uniform and fast-track straight into a DC position — no need to pass GO. There's a shortage of detectives at the Met, you see — *though I can't imagine why that might be* — and not everyone with a desire to do the job has had to earn their stripes 'dealing with the dregs' before they reach such lofty status.

For what it's worth though, in my humble opinion, a stint in uniform stands you in good stead for a future detective role. As a uniformed officer, you have to see and deal with all sorts — especially the 'dregs'. You're the troops on the ground, the foot soldiers, and getting your hands dirty prepares you for this job more than any degree ever could. But I'm not judging Adriana as a privileged fast-tracker, at least not just yet. Especially since Mitchell says she has something interesting for me.

'I've read through all the files, sir,' she says, 'all the statements. It's quite a perplexing case.'

That's one word for it.

'You've hit the ground running with this one, my apologies.' I smile broadly at her, clap my hands together. 'So, what you got then?'

'A comment on social media.'

I decide to hear her out before I let my heart sink. We've had nothing helpful from social media so far, no real leads. Most of what's been written is either pure fiction, supposition, hate, or a cocktail of them all.

'Go on...'

'Someone made a comment on the Samantha Valentine sketch that drew my attention.'

Adriana's shyness seems to have evaporated as she flips the screen around to show me with a confident spin of the laptop. 'As you can see, there's hundreds of comments, and this one was published yesterday at 16.04 GMT.'

I start to read it.

> I had a best friend at prep school called Samantha Valentine back in the 80s, before my parents dragged me to the UK when I was eleven years old (I feel like it hasn't stopped raining in 30 years – lol!). She dumped me for a new best friend – ironically some Pom who joined our class mid-term. (sad emoji face). I don't remember her name, but I remember hating her for stealing my BFF at the time!
>
> A couple of months after I moved to the UK, I found out that Samantha had killed herself. She hanged herself from a tree, only no one really knew why. (Crying emoji face) It was such

a shock. I knew her since kindergarten and she was just eleven years old! (Another crying emoji). I remember her always being such a happy, sweet, fun-loving little girl – no one understood why she did it. This isn't her in the sketch (obvs) btw, but the name made me think of her and so I felt I had to share! Be kind, folks, you never know what others are going through!

'The location of the sender says, Subiaco, Perth, Western Australia.' She looks up at me. 'Didn't Erin claim in one of her original statements given at the time of Radulovic's murder, and, most recently, in your transcripts from your phone interactions with her, that Samantha Valentine's mother lived in Australia?'

'Yes, that's right, she did.' Clearly, Adriana wasn't lying when she said she'd read through all the statements.

A chill lightly tickles my spine.

'So,' – Adriana lowers her head, back to being self-conscious once more – 'I've sent her a DM, asking her to get in touch. And I also took the liberty of forwarding her Erin's photo, the mugshot we released of her yesterday, just in the very small chance there's a connection. I mean, it's probably nothing, sir, just a sad memory she has of a childhood friend she once knew, someone unrelated to the case, someone with that same name, but I think we should look into it at the very least.'

THIRTY-FOUR

ERIN

I hit the brake too hard, lurch forwards onto the steering wheel.

Shit. I've never driven an automatic car before and it feels strange – I keep reaching for a gear stick that isn't there through force of habit. It's been over six years since I was behind the wheel and I'm rusty to say the least.

I check my reflection in the rear-view mirror as I blow my fringe out of my eyes, try to concentrate on the road ahead. I wish now I had just bitten the bullet and gone to a professional hairdresser's instead of doing a hatchet job on myself. Aside from the astronomical prices, which I resent paying, I didn't think it wise to. Spending two hours or more staring back at someone in a mirror and there's a greater chance I'll be recognised. If I'm to complete this mission successfully, then I have to think like Samantha Valentine would think; I have to stay one step ahead of the game. Now though, my penny-pinching feels like it's coming back to bite me in the ass. I miss my long hair – the safety and protection it gave me – and I hate being blonde. Anyway, I don't know why I'm fretting so much; soon it won't matter what colour my hair is.

'Alexandra Fisher, right?' The receptionist at the car hire

firm flashed me a disingenuous smile. I could tell it wasn't a real smile because it didn't reach her eyes and had faded to nothing almost instantly. Genuine smiles leave a muscle residue that is slower to dissipate. Again, I thought of the smile that Malcolm had greeted me with when I opened the door to him the other evening, that slightly coy, stupid great grin on his face as he waggled the bottle of wine at me.

'*Shall we unscrew this bad boy then, or what?*'

'That's me.' My smile was largely for Malcolm as I handed over my fake driver's licence to her. I felt a sudden flash of panic. What if creepy Pete has sold me a dud? What if they find out it's fake and call the cops on me? I held my breath as she punched my details into the computer, stabbing the keyboard, sharply, with a long, painted fingernail.

'Yep, you're all paid up and good to go, Alexandra. Joe will take you to your vehicle.' She handed me the keys, not even bothering with the disingenuous smile this time. I knew how she felt though, stuck in a dead-end job she clearly hates with colleagues that no doubt get on her wick and a pay cheque at the end of each month that does little to reflect all her hard efforts. Really though, she had no idea how truly lucky she is. I would say that 'I'd kill' for such an un-challenging, monotonous, dead-end, *normal* job now, but that sounds like a not-so-funny joke. Even everyday, glib sayings hold a different meaning for me now.

I switch the radio on. I listened to a lot of radio while I was in Larksmere. It sometimes helped to drown out the screams at night and made me feel more attached to humanity. I always found it a more personal experience than the TV, like the actors were speaking to me directly. I often found their voices soothing. BBC4 was my favourite station to tune in to. Sheer boredom alone was enough to drive you insane in that place, if you weren't insane already – and of course, *most* people were. Sometimes I would sit in the recreation room with my fellow in-patients – we were never allowed to refer to ourselves as 'prisoners' despite it being exactly what we were – listening to *The Archers* or *Woman's Hour*. It's not that I chose to socialise with them – mental health feels contagious when you're surrounded by it – but human beings crave company and contact. Loneliness is a debilitating disease that grows if it's left untreated, but admittedly, it was kind of bizarre to find myself chuckling away alongside violent and disturbed murderers, arsonists and criminals, even if I was supposedly one myself. After a while, if you're around it for long enough, crazy really does begin to feel normal.

I switch the radio on to BBC4, let it play in the background as I head towards the Airbnb that I'd hastily booked online – a trendy-looking apartment in Battersea. I might as well spend the last of what little cash I have left on something comfortable and a bit posh, to go with the new name. I like to think that maybe I've earned it, even if I don't deserve it.

Delilah is waiting outside the property as I pull up. She comes towards me when she sees me, waving enthusiastically with a wide smile of relief. I'm ten minutes late.

'Alexandra, yah?' She stoops down as I open the electric window. 'Alexandra Fisher?'

'That's me!' Well, it is now. I switch the engine off. 'I'm sorry I'm a little late, the London traffic...'

She rolls her eyes in sympathy, as though it needs no further explanation.

'Dreadful, isn't it? Can't get around anywhere in this city anymore, too many people. Too many people who shouldn't be here,' she adds sniffily.

I smile, though I have no compunction to become embroiled in any kind of conversation with her, let alone one with racist undertones.

She stops for a moment, a slightly bemused look on her horsey face.

'Gosh, have I... have we met before?' Her brow creases.

Panic sweeps through me, but I take a deep breath, let it pass.

'I don't think so,' I reply, as I snatch up my tote bag, the gun still rolled up inside it. She's still staring at me with a perplexed expression, as though it's going to come to her any moment. 'I'm sure I would've remembered.'

'You really look like someone I know.' She crinkles her nose up. 'I just can't think who now.'

'Really?' I reply, pretending to busy myself with my small amount of luggage so as not to have to look at her directly. 'I get that a lot. I must have one of those familiar faces.'

My guts tighten. I guess I can be forgiven for the paranoia. After all, my face is currently trending on social media thanks to Dan Riley and his flying monkeys. No doubt it's the closest to being famous as I'll ever get, while I'm still breathing at least.

'Would you like me to show you around?' Delilah says in her clipped home counties accent that screams of privilege and success.

I pray I haven't just said the word 'no' out loud.

'It's all pretty straightforward, yah? There's instructions on how to use the washing machine and the cooker, and the Wi-Fi password is underneath the fish magnet on the fridge.'

'Perfect,' I say, wondering what kind of person needs instructions on how to use a cooker, or if she thinks it's just me who's the idiot.

'And there's everything else you need, a rice steamer and an air fryer, a NutriBullet, cooking utensils, pots and pans and cutlery, the whole enchilada...'

Cutlery. We weren't allowed knives and forks at Larksmere, not the real stuff anyway, for obvious reasons, I suppose. Instead, we had to eat our meals using these strange latex rubber knives and forks, which proved especially challenging on 'meat Mondays'. You needed a hacksaw to get through some of the unidentifiable chewy gristle they served up to us. Often, I gave up and used my fingers instead, like a savage. *When in Rome...*

'Is it just you who'll be staying the two nights?' Delilah flicks me a sideways glance, key poised in the door. *Why is she still here? How hard can it be to turn on a frickin' hob?*

'You really don't need to worry about showing me around,' I say, as if she needn't waste any more of her valuable time. 'I'm sure it's all pretty self-explanatory.'

'It's no bother.' She watches me closely. My paranoia is fast becoming harder to ignore – it's the way she's looking at me. 'I like to give all my guests a brief once-round, show them what's what. That way you won't need to contact me, unless it's an emergency of course, like a leak, or an explosion, or there's a dead body or something.'

A dead body? It's a strange thing to say and it stops me in my tracks for a second. Is it just an attempt at humour, or something else?

'Here we are,' she says proudly as we enter the apartment. Immediately, she begins plumping up the cushions on the huge, impressive-looking sofa. It's a thing of beauty, this sofa, large and low and L-shaped in a rich, dark aubergine-coloured velvet with sumptuous, squishy-looking cushioned seats that make you want to take a run up and throw yourself into them. *It's got Samantha Valentine written all over it.*

I check the time. It's coming on for 9 p.m., although it's been dark for a couple of hours or so now. I wonder if the police have turned up at the Bull and Barrow yet, or if they're there right now with their battering rams and taser guns and shouty loud voices. I bite my bottom lip, stifle a smile. Creepy Pete is going to curse me to hell. But I doubt he'll talk. He's the one who has provided me with a deadly weapon after all. I could murder that scampi and chips now though, pardon the inappropriate pun. I've only eaten half a family bag of M&M's all day and my stomach is making embarrassingly loud growling noises. I hope Princess Tippy-Toes here hasn't heard them.

I wander over to the hi-spec open kitchen area, run the tips of my fingers over the smooth, sparkly diamond granite work surface. Oh, to live in a place like this! Maybe I could've, *would've*, done, if I'd never met Samantha. Who knows what my life would've gone on to become if I hadn't shown up to the job interview that day, if I'd missed the bus, or got sick? *Why couldn't I have just got sick?*

They say you should never think about the coulda, shoulda, woulda in life, but for me, that's impossible. I've had my life snatched from me, my freedom and liberty, my reputation and my future – *my sanity*. The sense of this loss burns like a raging fire inside of me that can't be extinguished – at least, not until I find her.

I spot the large wooden knife block, sitting next to a shiny chrome, full barista-style coffee machine that looks like it's never been used, with the six, dark wooden handles in various sizes protruding from it. I remove the largest from the block, feel the solid wood, weighty in my hand, the curved, perfectly shiny blade, cold to the touch against my skin. For a moment I'm mesmerised by my warped reflection in the blade, stare at my misshapen image, somehow indicative of how I am now – a distorted version of myself.

He flashes up in front of me then – Bojan Radulovic. I see his handsome features as he comes towards me, the flash from the blade as I bring it down into his chest, and the whites of his eyes as they expand in horror and shock and fear.

I grip the knife tighter in my hand, will the flashback to pass. I can barely bring myself to think about that day, that pivotal moment when his life ended and mine did too, metaphorically anyway, but try as I must to lock it away in the recesses of my memory, it returns with a vengeance, each time with a touch more clarity than before. I know there's only one way to erase it for good.

'... *Annnnd...*' I realise that Delilah has been talking in the background and I haven't heard a word she's said. I quickly replace the knife before she sees me with it. 'The *pièce de résistance...* ta-da!'

The floor-to-ceiling shutters make a satisfying clicking sound as she concertinas them open. I can tell that this is her favourite part of the tour – the big reveal.

'How's that for a view?' She stands back, checks my expression eagerly. 'Phenomenal, isn't it?' She sighs. 'I never tire of it.'

I stare out at the London skyline, at the clusters of buildings that look like they're made out of mirrors, reflecting the light, even on a miserable, damp day like today. It's not a view I'm familiar with, I'm a Yorkshire lass, more accustomed to rolling hills and countryside, *and padded cells*. Admittedly, it's impressive nonetheless.

'That's the old power station over there,' she points. 'They regenerated it some years ago and there's a great shopping centre inside, some cool bars and bistros... everything you need, yah?'

I nod. What I *need* is for her to leave now. 'Well,' she says, placing the set of keys on the table with a loud clank that I'm sure wasn't intended. 'Enjoy your stay, Alexandra.'

'Thanks so much, Delilah – and, don't worry,' – I smile at her, sweetly – 'I'll be sure to let you know if any dead bodies turn up.'

THIRTY-FIVE

DAN

'You gonna pay for that damage then or what?' The landlord at the Bull and Barrow jabs his finger in the direction of the broken door, his eyes bulging, clearly vexed. The door is off the hinge, the wood split in too many places to ever be salvageable. It's the direct result of the 'element of surprise'. And boy, is he unhappy about it.

'You lot think you can just steam in here, mob-handed and smash the gaff up, don't you?' he spits, angrily. 'Damaging my property *and* my reputation?'

'Well, at least you can restore the door,' Davis remarks, poker-faced.

He turns to her sharply. 'Funny.' He growls. 'Where's your warrant, eh?'

Pete Samson, the renowned landlord of the notorious Bull and Barrow public house, isn't a small man. Somewhere around six foot four with a thick, heavy-set build, he has a slight stoop from his shoulders and looks like he snacks on small children for breakfast. Lucky for Davis and me, he's outnumbered today. And speaking of small children, at some point, I'd really like to get home to see my own. I've been on the go for the past seventy-two hours practically straight.

'We don't need one, Pete – I can call you Pete, can I? My name's Detective Chief...'

'I don't give a rat's arse what your name is, sunshine—' he booms, 'get out of my pub, go on, all of you, piss off. You've got no business here, no business preventing me from running *my business*.' The veins in his neck are purple and protruding. 'Everything's legit, my taxes are up to date, you'll find nothing you're looking for here. And no, you can't bleedin' well call me Pete.' A fleck of spittle lands on my cheek as he angrily projects. 'This is persecution, this is, police harassment... it's criminal damage is what it is...'

I wipe his spittle off my face with the back of my hand. I could be wrong, but something tells me that the offer of a free drink might be off the table.

'Do you know the reason we're here, Mr Samson? We can always talk about it down at the station if you prefer. You can make a complaint there if you like.' I flash him a rictus grin.

'Don't worry,' he says, teeth clenched, 'I fully intend to.' He nudges the broken door with the tip of his boot. 'That's going to cost me money, that is. I can't rent the room out now, can I? Have you any idea what it'll cost to replace? Course you ain't, don't bleedin' well care either, do you? Next time, try asking nicely before you send the thugs in.' He glowers as the last of the SWAT team retreat. 'Bunch of muppets,' he grumbles underneath his breath as they make their way downstairs to search the rest of the property.

'Where is she, Mr Samson?'

'Where's who? Seriously, you think I'm a mind-reader on top of everything else, do you?' His small, dark eyes settle on mine. 'Whatever – whoever – you're looking for, they ain't here, are they? You got eyes, look,' – he points – 'the room, it's empty.'

I can't argue with him. There's no sign of Erin inside the

grotty single guest room, or of her ever having been there. It's neat and clean – a bit too clean perhaps, judging by the overall standard of the place, and the overpowering smell of bleach.

'We have reason to believe that a suspect wanted in connection with a recent murder has been staying here, at this address, in Room 7. Her name is Erin Santos. She's a former inmate at Larksmere, convicted of manslaughter back in 2019.'

He glances up at me then. I could be mistaken, but I think I see a flicker of surprise in his eyes.

'Did you check her in, Mr Samson?

'The blonde, you mean? She wrote her name down in the guest book, paid cash, and I gave her a key, if that's what you mean by "checked her in".'

'Can we see this guest register, Mr Samson?' Davis asks, with a saccharine smile.

'No, you can't. You can piss off!' He stomps down the stairs, back to the bar. Davis and I follow behind him.

'The woman staying in Room 7, Mr Samson,' I continue, 'I'm right in saying that it was a woman who was staying here?'

He releases a long breath.

'Man, woman, whatever you want to call yourself these days,' – he shrugs – 'I don't pay too much notice, if you know what I mean, keep myself to myself. I spend most of my time here, behind the bar.' He stops, pauses, lets out a breath.

'Look, this is King's Cross, right? Thousands of visitors come here every day, 365 days a year. I probably wouldn't recognise any of the guests who've ever stayed here if you lined them all up next to each other.'

'They'd recognise *you* though, wouldn't they, Mr Samson?' Davis raises an eyebrow. She's on form today.

He smirks. 'Yeah, well, some things are worth remembering, ain't they, sweetheart?' He rakes his eyes over her, roughly shoves the guest book across the bar towards me. 'There was this little blonde bird. Can't remember her name, nor much about her. She was staying in Room 7, but she checked out last night, and when I say "checked out", I mean she left the key behind and I ain't seen her since. Pity really, I was looking forward to having that scampi and chips...'

He appears to have a moment of reverie.

'Scampi and chips?'

He snaps himself out of it as Davis flips open the guest book, which is basically a tatty, thumb-worn, old lined exercise book that you can buy in any newsagent's.

'All mod cons here, eh, Mr Samson?' I remark, nodding at it.

He curls his lip at me. It makes him look even more menacing than his resting face already is.

'You know, you two ought to do stand-up together,' he says, 'something to fall back on if the day jobs don't work out, or maybe I should say, *when* they don't. And I trust technology even less than I trust you feds,' he sniffs, 'which is saying something.'

I start flicking through the pages.

'In case you hadn't noticed, we ain't the Dorchester. Here, people come and people go. I don't ask questions and I stay out of other people's business, something your lot should try doing once in a while. Anyway, the blonde. I think she said her name was Milly – Milly or Molly maybe.'

Davis and I exchange glances.

'Ah, yes. Here she is.' The name and date are roughly scribbled down in almost illegible handwriting. 'Molly... *Malcolm.*'

Incidentally, I'd taken a surprise phone call from Malcolm while I was on the way here to the Bull and Barrow. I was hoping he had something useful to tell me, but as it was, he simply wanted to ask me to pass on a message. *Like I haven't got enough to do.*

'Have you found her yet, Mr Riley? Have you found Erin?' His voice sounded sad and urgent. I feel as if somehow, in amongst all of this mess, these two people – Malcolm and Erin –

genuinely seem to have connected with each other. I feel a bit choked when I think about it, about what might've been if things were different. Maybe I'm going soft in my old age.

'Not yet, Malcolm, but we're working on it. Have *you* heard from Erin? Has she tried to contact you, or Molly perhaps?'

'No.' The disappointment hung heavy in his voice. 'Nothing. And I don't know about Molly, for some reason she isn't speaking to me at the moment. I've no idea why, or what I've done wrong.'

I did. Blatantly, Molly has a crush on Malcolm. The poor girl practically turned to blancmange in his company. And the look on her face when Malcolm said that he and Erin spent the afternoon together, in her apartment! I couldn't make my mind up who I felt more sorry for in that moment, her or him.

'Anyway, I'm sure Molly would've said something if she had. We're all really worried about Erin, *I'm* really worried about Erin.'

He sounded miserable and I felt a pang of empathy for him. I guess you can't help who you fall in love with, but it's my duty to warn him.

'Erin suffers from various mental health issues,' I say it as gently as possible. 'She could be a danger, Malcolm, to you and to herself. So if she does contact you, or tries to meet with you or—'

'Mr Riley... Detective Riley,' he butts in, 'if you see Erin, *when* you see Erin, will you give her a message back from me, *please*?'

'OK, Malcolm.' I let out a small sigh. 'What's the message?'

'Can you tell her I said, "You don't need to be"?'

Looking here at Mr Samson's 'guest book', 'Molly Malcolm' checked in two days ago, but the information on when she checked out is blank.

'Did you speak to Molly during her stay, Mr Samson? Did you chat together?'

'Only the basics, when she arrived, like "Hello, please sign in, no smoking in the rooms..."'

'She didn't come down to the bar to get a drink, or something to eat?'

'Maybe. Can't really remember. I serve dozens of people every day. After a while, their faces seem to blur into one, know what I mean?' He pours himself a neat Scotch and throws it back in one.

'I take it you have CCTV on the premises that we can check?' Davis says. 'It's one of the conditions of your licence here, isn't it, Mr Samson, that you must have working CCTV in operation to retain your licence?'

He gives Davis a hard stare from behind the bar.

'It got damaged, a few days ago. Stopped working.' He loudly sniffs back mucus from his nose and throat. 'I've called an engineer out, but they ain't got no one till next Tuesday.'

'Great, well, we'll see you next Tuesday then!' Davis smiles.

He exhales, laughs as he shakes his head. 'I quite like you, sister, you got balls,' he smirks, 'probably literally.'

Davis flashes him a hard stare in return, unimpressed.

'Why does the room smell so strongly of bleach, Mr Samson?'

'It's a crime to keep the place clean, now is it? Seriously? It smells of bleach because it's been *cleaned*, ready for the next guest.' He rolls his eyes, clearly exasperated.

'Was *this* the woman who was staying with you?' I place Erin's mugshot in front of him. 'You may have already seen her picture on the news, on social media.'

'Don't watch the news. Life's miserable enough, ain't it? And I only use one website – OnlyFans.' He grins at Davis, displaying two gold teeth.

'Quite the charmer you, aren't you, Mr Samson?'

Davis can barely disguise the disgust on her face.

'How much do they pay you lot to do this shit, eh?' He

gestures around him at the empty bar, most of the guests having made a hasty exit upon our arrival. 'Not enough, I'll say. An attractive woman like you could make a good little earner out of OnlyFans as a sideline – you should give it some thought.'

'That's enough, Mr Samson – the photo.' I tap a hard finger on it, for him to look. 'Is *this* the woman who was staying here, is this 'Molly Malcolm'?'

Reluctantly, he glances down at it.

'No.' He shakes his head, and for the first time since we arrived, it seems genuine. 'You got the wrong girl, mate. All that effort, all that damage for nothing...' He tuts, shakes his head ruefully. 'The girl that was here was a blonde, attractive, yeah, she was... really pretty...' He seems a little contemplative for a moment. 'Actually, I quite fancied her.'

Blimey, there really must be something in the air tonight.

'She looked nothing like this minger here.' He nods at Erin's photo with a curled lip. 'Never seen her before in my life.'

THIRTY-SIX

ERIN

There's a diner, somewhere in the USA, where you can actually order the very same last meal that infamous serial killers on death row requested to eat before they were put to death. I'm not kidding. You can choose, among other delights on the menu, John Wayne Gacy's final meal of chicken, twelve fried shrimp, French fries, and a pound of strawberries, or, if you prefer, Ted Bundy's medium-rare steak, eggs over easy, hash browns and toast with butter and jam, all while being surrounded by artefacts and trophies of their heinous and grizzly crimes. Only in America, *right?*

Tonight though, I've opted for a double cheeseburger with all the trimmings, some French fries, a portion of chicken goujons, fried onion rings, a large Coke and a side of mac 'n' cheese. Dessert is a tub of Ben & Jerry's cookie dough ice cream, if I'm not in a coma by then, though I'm willing to put the effort in. I've a hunger on me tonight, like my body knows something is about to happen and is preparing itself for what's coming.

'Thanks.' The delivery driver had looked down at his hand through his helmet visor, clearly underwhelmed by the three pound coins I placed in it, my gratitude for *his* efforts – this is an important meal after all. Ordinarily, I would've been more generous to him, only I've worked in restaurants and bars before – back when I was the younger me, when I was someone else – and as anyone who's ever worked in the service industry knows, you *always* remember the big tippers.

I take a few loud slurps of the ice-cold Coke through the straw and arrange the food neatly on the table, placing the gun down next to it. Observing the strange juxtaposition of the weapon next to a side order of mac 'n' cheese, I stab at the hot and salty French fries with a fork and stuff them into my mouth. After a couple more attempts, I abandon the fork and use my fingers instead.

Once I've worked my way through this feast, I'll take a hot and cold shower in Delilah's painfully trendy, Scandi-chic bathroom that's frankly too nice to even think about defecating in. It's filled with palm plants and gorgeous-smelling designer wash products, which I fully intend to make use of. The cheap, harsh shower gel I had to use at Larksmere always used to give me thrush.

After, I'll play some music and drink some wine, but not too much. I have to drive.

The only way I have even the slimmest hope of getting close to Samantha and finding the answers I need and the justice I am searching for is by getting close to Dan Riley. I find Dan, then maybe I have half a chance of finding her. I'm going to call him once I've digested this lot and freshened up a bit. I don't want to be all gassy when I speak to him. That wouldn't be polite.

Aside from an explanation as to how my DNA could've possibly been found at Milo Harrison's crime scene – if indeed what's been reported is even true – what I want from Dan Riley is access to this Tilly woman, the woman who stabbed him, just as I stabbed Bojan. I like to think that by now, I'm able to be on first-name terms with my victim. After all, I took his life, even if I didn't mean to.

And I *really* didn't mean to, just as I don't suppose Tilly ever meant to kill Milo Harrison either. I wonder why Samantha chose Milo as a target in the first place. Was it for the same reasons she chose Bojan? What had he done to secure a place on her hit list? What had *either* of them done that she would want to groom innocent people, like Tilly and I, into ending their lives on her behalf?

Dan, who I am also on first-name terms with, has no idea how much I *need* to speak to Tilly Ward. Right now, Tilly is the only other person on this planet that I know of who knows that Samantha Valentine actually exists. And this makes her very special to me indeed. I want to meet her, in the flesh, *to know it's really real*. I want to hear her story and I want to tell her mine. I want to know if it was the same tragic tale for her as it was for me. Did *she* fall in love with Samantha too? Did Sam drill down so hard and far into her soul that, even now, *even now* Tilly *knows* that she's been betrayed and deceived by her in the worst ways imaginable, she *still* loves her? Misses her? Wishes they could still be friends?

I realise, suddenly, *ridiculously*, that I'm crying. Tears, hot and salty, like the French fries, are sliding down my cheeks. I watch them, motionless, as they drip down onto the table and splash onto the gun, before I brush them away. I feel cross with myself, *stupid*. Since when have tears ever helped me? I cried a river of them while I was locked up in Larksmere. Not a day passed by during my first year inside when I didn't shed a few, *or many*. I would try to cry in private – though there wasn't such a thing as privacy in Larksmere. I couldn't even have my period without *someone* knowing about it. The moment I set foot inside that place, every part of me belonged to the doctors and nurses and therapists. Nothing was sacred, not even my thoughts, in fact, *especially* not my thoughts. They even tried to take those away from me too. Sometimes, when my brain judders and I have split-second memory blackouts, I think they were successful.

I know that it will bring me some comfort to know that I am not Samantha's only victim; no doubt it would bring some for this poor Tilly woman too. After all, there's safety in numbers, right? Tilly and I are honorary members of 'The Samantha Valentine Survivors' Club', a club that everyone wants to be a member of, *said no one ever*. But here we both are.

I know Dan won't *allow* me to see her, but maybe he can lead me to her directly. That would be a start.

I flip open Molly's laptop. I need to delete some old accounts before the feds find them, if they haven't already. Everything's traceable these days, *everything except Samantha Valentine*.

I log in to my old email account, one that pre-dates Samantha. I'd forgotten I even had it, to be honest. Prisoners – sorry, *patients* – at Larksmere weren't allowed to send or receive emails directly of course, but sometimes staff brought round printed correspondence that had been sent from family, friends and loved ones. I never once received one of those sought-after printouts from loved ones or friends because I never had any of those.

I scan my eyes down the inbox, it's all just junk anyway, sales and marketing crap, most of it and… hang on!

I jolt backwards in my seat, so hard that it hurts the small of my back.

DoYouKnowWhoSamanthaValentineIs@gmail.com

The subject matter says: My name is Tilly Ward…

Oh. My. God. My heart starts pounding, knocking hard against my ribs. It's pulsing loudly in my ears as I touch my chest, take a breath before I click on it.

My name is Tilly Ward. You don't know me. But I think we may have someone in common. Her name is Samantha Valentine.

THIRTY-SEVEN
DAN

'She wrote to me.'

'*Erin!*'

I was at home – I know, I could barely believe it myself – in the middle of a sign-language tuition session with Fiona and the kids, when she called.

I have to say, her timing was as lousy as ever.

'I'm so sorry,' I give Leanne – the interpreter – and, perhaps more importantly, my wife, the best apologetic, overburdened, somebody-help-me-I'm-drowning-type face that I can muster as I stand, 'but I really *do* have to take this call.'

'Tilly Ward. She sent me an email.'

'When?'

I head into the kitchen, hear my daughter, Juno, shouting out to me in the background in her adorable helium baby voice.

'Come back, Pop-Pop...'

'In a minute, Pip, Pop-Pop won't be long.'

I close the door behind me, immediately start pacing up and down with all the excess adrenalin that's trying to push through my skin.

'Is this another bad time?' she says. 'Because I can always—'

'There's no such thing as a good time, Erin. I've got three kids, remember?'

'Yes. I do. Tell me, Dan, what are their names? What's your baby son's name? I imagine you gave him a strong title, something classic that won't date, something like George or Charles or William – am I right?'

'I'm not going to tell you my children's names, Erin...'

'Why not?' She sounds offended. 'I was just trying to make conversation, only I can hear that maybe you don't really want one of those right now, so I'll just hang up and...'

'... His name is Jude,' I say quickly.

'Hmmm, *Juuuude*.' She rolls my son's name from her tongue. 'It's a bit different, I suppose, a little *obscure* even. Was that the reason you gave him the name, after Thomas Hardy's *Jude the Obscure*?'

'My wife chose it,' I say, not wanting to admit that it had nothing to do with any literary genius and everything to do with Fiona's crush on the actor Jude Law.

I'm not exactly keen on being blackmailed into giving over my son's name, but I have to try to get her to trust me again somehow – and more importantly, to keep her talking. But how does she know Tilly's surname? Has it been leaked to the press? Did Tilly tell Erin herself?

I've no idea what Tilly's playing at by contacting Erin. Has she not yet seen her photo on social media, recognised who Erin is? Did she send the message before Erin's photo was made public? She must've done. When I think about it though, if Erin really *is* Samantha Valentine, then wouldn't she already know Tilly's surname anyway? Sweet Jesus, my head feels bent out of shape. Is she just screwing with me, is this all just some crazy-making game? I rub my temples with my spare thumb and forefinger, try to focus.

'What did Tilly say in the message, Erin?'

I've got to keep her talking long enough to alert the incident room that she's on the line. I'd given Erin my own personal phone number to use, but I have another, my force-issued phone. I hold my breath as I fire a text off to Davis from it.

She's on the line.

'I'm appreciating the most beautiful view right now, Dan,' she says. 'It feels like I'm on top of the world, looking down at it, or maybe not down, that makes me sound like a real Negative Nelly, doesn't it? Maybe looking "out" is better. Anyway, you live in an incredible city.'

'So you *are* in London?'

'Not for much longer, Dan.'

I sit down at our kitchen table, on top of Custard, Jude's soft cloth cat. He squeaks as I pull him out from underneath me and throw him on the floor.

Sorry, Custard.

'So, then, tell me, Erin, what's the plan?'

I try to keep my voice level and chatty, towards upbeat. I don't want her to hear the anxiety that's tightening my larynx and making my throat feel dry. I take a sip of juice from one of the kids' beakers on the table. There's only a mouthful left, and the second I swallow it, I need more.

'We had a conversation over email. It was very cathartic, I think, for both of us. She sounds so nice, so innocent, so *ordinary* – Samantha's dream victim, I should imagine.' There's a pause. 'Tilly told me that she's hard of hearing, and it made me think of you, Dan, of your son. Surely you can see that Samantha chose her because she's vulnerable, just like I was, albeit in a different way perhaps...' Her voice trails off. 'What Samantha does, what she *did*, to both Tilly and me...' I hear the crack of emotion in her inflection. '... She *has* to be stopped, Dan, before she destroys another living soul.'

'How did Tilly get your email address, Erin? Did you think to ask her, maybe?'

'Ha!' She snorts softly. 'You're the detective, Detective. The message was sent to a very old account. One I'd forgotten I even had. I'm sure, after your TV appearance yesterday, it probably wasn't that hard to find. You threw me under the bus, Dan. You went public with my identity, told everyone about my conviction' – her voice drops behind her teeth – 'and you showed everyone that *hideous* photograph of me. *Why'd ya do it, Dan?*' Suddenly, she switches into this strange, southern US accent, which is a little unexpected – and freaky. '*Why'd ya have ta tell all, ta y'all?* I've been practising,' she explains.

'Practising what?'

'Different accents.'

'Why?'

She pauses.

'*Just for fun, yah?*' Her attempt at London, however, definitely needs work. I suspect she's stopped taking her medication. I really need to think hard on how best to play this.

'Your DNA was found, Erin. It was found at Milo Harrison's address, at the scene where he was murdered. Forensics found hairs on his body, on his chest, mixed in with his blood – your hairs, Erin.'

She doesn't respond.

'Did you know that Milo Harrison went to university in Leeds back in the early 2000s?'

'Really?' Her voice registers surprise. 'No. I didn't know that.'

'Apparently, he lived less than half a mile from your old address during that time. Did the two of you ever meet, Erin, back then?'

She sighs. 'Leeds is a big city, maybe not as big as London, but I wouldn't want to do a head count, would you?'

'So it's just a coincidence then?'

She takes a breath.

'As it would seem, yes. People come from all over the world

to go to university there, over 40,000 people at any given time – only I wasn't ever one of them. I flunked my GCSEs and I've never even been on the campus grounds. Besides, I spent most of that time of my life off my face on drugs and alcohol or house-ridden with agoraphobia and depression.'

'But you did have relationships with men back then? Boyfriends, partners? Friends with benefits?'

'I may have been a substance abuser, Dan, but I think I'd remember if I'd had *any* kind of relationship with your dead man. Look,' she says, the frustration rising in her voice, '*I don't know him!* What is it with you lot? Why are you so determined to try and make me fit the role of perpetrator? It's history repeating itself again and again... when will it *end*, Dan? When will you believe me?'

She's clearly agitated.

'My job is to protect the public,' I continue, 'and to help bring people to justice, and to ensure they are neither a danger to themselves nor to others – which one are you, Erin, or are you both?'

More silence. I've overstepped the mark.

'Erin? Please don't hang up.' I clench my fists and teeth simultaneously, raise my eyes to the ceiling and silently beg her not to cut the call. 'We can talk, just between us. My job is to help you, and protect you too, Erin. I just want to—'

'Were the hairs short?'

I stop talking. Why would she ask that?

'The hairs found at the crime scene, on the body, were they more like clippings, perhaps?'

Forensics *had* said that the hairs were shorter than you'd expect to see if they had been pulled out from the head, or naturally shed. These were more like 'snippets', the lady from the lab had said. How would Erin Santos know that? Is it because she put them there? Why would she place her own hair at a murder scene?' I'm not sure why I'm expecting things to make sense anymore. Nothing in this case has made sense from the beginning.

'Yes, they were short hairs, Erin. Your short hairs.'

'I believe you, Dan.' Her voice sounds level and calm. 'Only I didn't put them there. Samantha did.'

THIRTY-EIGHT

Is she really still running with this? I have to remind myself that Erin's unwell, and that, according to Dr Wainwright, her psychopathy is such that she really does believe that she and Samantha are genuinely two separate people. I'll run with it too, if it keeps her talking on the line.

'Don't you see, Dan, she's setting me up! She's doing it all over again! Oh my God...' Her breathing suddenly increases, as though it's just dawned on her. 'My hair! She cut my hair once, do you remember, Dan, I told you about it!'

Is she trying to gaslight me, manipulate me into believing that somehow Samantha Valentine conveniently has kept strands of her hair all this time?

And yet, now I think of it, I do vaguely recall her mentioning it.

'During those months I spent with her, Sam trimmed my hair on a couple of occasions, you know, like when *friends* give each other a makeover? She must've kept some of it – kept hold of some of my hair! And she's planted it at a crime scene that I was never at, that I had nothing to do with. *Oh. My. God.*' She lets out a succession of short breaths. '*Why* is she doing this to me, Dan? What did I ever do to her? What does she *want* from me?'

The anguish in her voice is uncomfortable to listen to. She sounds so tormented. She needs help.

'That bitch planted my hair on him after *she* killed him.'

'Did something happen between you? Did you have a sexual encounter with Milo? Did he ghost you afterwards and you felt used and worthless? Were you upset by his callous treatment of you? Is that why you killed him, Erin?'

She pauses.

'I didn't kill him.' Her voice is level and calm. *Why does it sound as if she's telling the truth?* What does the truth even sound like? I don't know, but I know when I hear it because I *feel* it – we all do.

'*She* killed him. I don't know why she killed him. But who knows, maybe you're right, maybe she was stalking him...'

'Who said anything about stalking him?'

She snorts.

'Don't try and trip me up, Dan. It doesn't become you and you're better than that. Besides, we both know that's exactly what she was probably doing. Though I'd say she *targeted* people more than *stalked* them. Stalkers tend to want to be close to their object of obsession. I think Samantha just wanted to destroy hers – like some kind of sick power game. She's more like an assassin in that respect.'

'Well, I guess you know her best.' I pause. 'Why don't I come to you, Erin? Just me, alone, no one else. Please? We can talk, face-to-face. Just two people, meeting up for a coffee and a chat.'

'What, so that you can lure me in and then lock me back up in the booby hatch again?' She scoffs. 'I think I'll have to politely decline your invitation on this occasion, Dan – much as I'd like to meet you in the flesh. Tell me, was there any other DNA found at the crime scene? Was it just mine and

Tilly's and the victim's, or was there someone else's, because—'

'We paid the Bull and Barrow a visit,' I interject. 'You did a good clean-up job, Erin. Why don't we save ourselves some time here and meet up? It'll make it so much easier for both of us. No bells and whistles, no drama – just me. I promise I'll do my best by you, Erin, you have my word on that.'

'Your best!' Her laugh is derisive. 'D'you know, I actually really did trust you, Dan. I thought that maybe you believed me, that you were the one who had the ability to see past the lies and prejudices and would conduct a proper investigation, do what should've been done from the beginning, only it seems you're just the same underneath as the rest of them. Worse perhaps, because I'd been willing to put that trust in you. Oh, whatever,' – she lets out a protracted sigh – 'I really should be used to being let down by now, shouldn't I? But at least it shows one thing.'

'What's that, Erin?'

'That even after everything that's happened to me, I'm still capable of putting my trust in someone.' She laughs. 'Good God, I really am doomed!'

'Malcolm is concerned about you, Erin.' I pull out my ace card. I need her to stay on the line – we need that trace. 'He's genuinely concerned about your well-being. Actually, he asked me to give you a message.'

My work phone flashes.

Attempting trace now, gov.

'Would you like to hear it, Erin?'

She pauses long enough to have me worried that she may have hung up again.

'Go on then,' she says, quietly. 'For what it's worth.'

'He said to tell you, "There's no need to be." I think it was in response to your message, which I duly relayed to him, by the way. I am a man of my word, Erin. I know you think that you can't trust me, but you can.'

She blows air through her lips.

'Now you see, this is where you let yourself down, Dan. Surely you must know by now that you shouldn't really trust *anyone*, not a hundred per cent, not even yourself, in fact, sometimes *especially* not yourself! Trust is a precious, fragile gift that takes a lifetime to build, and yet only the most ephemeral moment – a brief second – to shatter and destroy.'

'There's a whole task force out there searching for you, Erin. Your face is all over the news and social media.'

'Thanks to you!'

'Let's put an end to this now, eh? Call it a day?'

'Yes, Dan, *let's*,' she says before she hiccups loudly. 'Whoops, please excuse me,' she apologises. 'Where are my manners? I'm afraid I'm suffering from a touch of indigestion after eating a rather large supper tonight. Funny,' she says, 'but while I was eating, I thought of that picture in Dr Wainwright's office.'

'The painting of himself, the portrait, you mean?'

'You saw that one too, huh? Like, just *how* much does Dr Wainwright think of himself, right?' she snorts. 'That great fancy tribute to himself on the wall that he looks at and admires every day – what a narcissist. No, I meant the painting next to the crucifix on the wall.'

I cast my mind back. 'The biblical one – the Last Supper, you mean?'

I wonder what the relevance is and why she's mentioned it. Is she trying to tell me that she's just eaten *her* last supper?

My stomach clenches as another message from Davis flashes up.

Possible alibi for Erin on NOM just come through! CCTV from street cam in Leeds, date & time match. Not 100 per cent but pretty sure it is Santos.

I have to read it twice. You have *got* to be kidding me! So, Erin *wasn't* there at the crime scene on the night of Harrison's murder, then? Which is it, because it sure as hell can't be *both*?

'You're spending all your resources looking for the wrong person, as usual,' she grumbles. 'Samantha's out there now, laughing her head off at all of us – at me, at the police, at Tilly Ward, *at you*, Dan. I was hopeful that you'd help me, that we could join forces in finding her, but you know what they say,' – she lets out another heavy, protracted sigh – 'if you want a job done properly, then you have to do it yourself.'

'And that's what you're going to do, is it, Erin? You're going to find Samantha yourself?'

'Well, yes!' she says, as if it's an absurd question. 'Of course. I *have* to. I have to know. I have to understand why any of this happened, and why it happened to me. I need answers. *I need closure, Dan.*' She's slipped into another US accent now, New York this time, I'd guess. It makes her sound unstable.

'What would you say to Samantha if you saw her again, Erin?'

I glance down at my work phone. It's flashing again.

Starting trace now, gov.

There's a pause on the line.

'"Vengeance is mine, and recompense; Their foot shall slip in due time; For the day of their calamity is at hand, and the things to come hasten upon them." Deuteronomy 32:35.'

'And that's what you'd say to her, is it, if you met Samantha, face-to-face?'

'Yes—' she says, 'right before I kill her.'

THIRTY-NINE

Erin had killed the call before we were able to get a trace on it, and before I could tell her about the probable alibi, about the street cam footage in Leeds.

'Damn it!' I bang my fist on my desk, which I find myself back behind just a few hours after half a night's fitful attempt at sleep. 'Where *is* she?'

Lucy is accustomed to my occasional outbursts of frustration, but poor Adriana, the new college recruit here, looks a bit rattled.

'Erin said something about a view of the city, during the call...' Lucy glances at me.

'Well, that narrows it down, doesn't it?'

Lucy's also used to my facetiousness. Actually, I think she secretly enjoys it sometimes. 'London *is* one big bloody view.'

'Yes, but only if you're up high, looking down, gov.'

'Come on, Lucy,' I whine, 'there's a million high-rise buildings in London. Apartment blocks, office towers, hotels, restaurants, the London Eye... she could be in any one of them, looking down, or out, for that matter. Damn it,' I say again, softer this time, 'we really needed that trace!'

So the day was starting off well.

'Maybe you're out of your depth on this one, Dan,' Fiona had said to me as we'd finally fallen into bed together the night before, though I knew I wouldn't manage much sleep anyway, not after my conversation with Erin. I was too pumped up, too wired to nod off.

'Thanks for the vote of confidence.'

My heart sank. Even my biggest champion had lost faith in me it seemed.

'Erin Santos is clearly a woman with serious mental health issues... Why don't you let the NCA get involved? You know, she really could be dangerous, Dan.'

'No.' I spun over in bed to face her, tickled her waist. *'I'm "Dangerous Dan", remember?'*

She giggled, touched the tip of my nose with a finger.

'Seriously, I'm worried about you, Danny.' My wife never calls me 'Danny' unless she's genuinely concerned. 'This case has really got under your skin, I can tell.'

I didn't want Fiona to stress about me – she's got enough to worry about – but she's not wrong. Just when I start to believe one thing, a new piece of conflicting information comes along to smash it to pieces and flip it on its backside.

'She'll have you going round in circles, Dan. Tie you up in knots.' I hear DI Amanda Pritchard's slightly sanctimonious voice in my head, swiftly followed by Archer's, *'It happens to the best of us, Dan. Don't beat yourself up over it.'*

'How could Erin's hair be found at a crime scene and yet we now have a very possible positive ID for her on CCTV that places her in a *different city* at the time? She couldn't have been at a crime scene some hundreds of miles away. No one can be in two different places at once.'

'Not even me,' Fiona said dryly, closing her eyes.

'Not unless they're a ghost. The only other explanation can be the one Erin gave me – the hair was planted there.'

'Maybe she really *is* two people and it's some kind of spooky supernatural thing. Wooooo!' She was clearly teasing me now. 'You don't really *believe* her story, do you?'

I stayed silent. The truth is, I'm unsure exactly what I believe anymore.

'Seriously?' She opened her dark, almond-shaped eyes then, and I was reminded just how beautiful they are as they shone back at me in the dark. I rolled over, exhaled loudly, let my arms flop beside me. 'She probably planted it there herself, when she was being the Samantha Valentine part of her character, the part that seems to want to sabotage Erin, and hence, sabotage herself. And maybe it's just someone who looks like her on the CCTV footage?' My wife always managed to summarise things so succinctly. I suppose it's the journalist in her.

'Well, *someone* is pulling my chain, I know that much. Tonight, Erin said that she'd *kill* Samantha Valentine if she ever saw her again face-to-face. And I believed her. I heard it in her voice, Fi, all that anger and resentment... all that loss and sadness. It's difficult to fake that level of emotion convincingly. But if Erin has this dissociative-whatsit disorder, this split personality, then effectively, she'd be killing herself, wouldn't she? In killing Samantha, she'd have to murder *herself.*'

'And that's what you're worried about, is it, that she may try and kill herself?'

'Yes, no. I don't know, maybe. Only I get the impression that the Erin part of her character doesn't want to die.' I thought of the budding relationship between her and Malcolm then, the connection I'd sensed – another thing that's difficult to fake.

As crazy as it sounds, if I can just save one of them – Erin or Samantha – then by default I save Erin from herself.

FORTY

'This is going to cheer you up, boss.' DS Mitchell's eyes are wide and hopeful, more hopeful than I'm currently feeling anyway. Even a hot sausage sandwich and a cup of tea hasn't done the usual job of lifting my mood. 'Tell him what you've got, Adriana.' Mitchell nods at her, encouragingly.

'Well,' – Adriana takes a breath as I bite into my sandwich – 'I managed to trace the sender of that message, the one who left the comment underneath Tilly's sketch of Samantha Valentine. Her name is Katy Russell and she lives in Subiaco, a suburb in Perth, Western Australia. We spoke on the phone – I have to say, she was a bit freaked out at first, being contacted by the British police out of the blue about a random comment she made on social media – but she soon came on board. She readily told me the story about her best friend at school, Samantha Valentine, and how she took her own life when she was eleven years old. She hanged herself from a tree at the bottom of the family garden, apparently.' My eyes widen. 'I know,' Adriana says, 'it sounded like a real tragedy. Anyway, she talked about this other girl too, a third girl who joined their class mid-term at prep school, an English girl, who went on to steal her best friend, Samantha, from her, so to speak... you know, like it is with kids that age, all the friendship dramas...'

I really hope this is going somewhere good, for Adriana's sake as much as anyone's. I take another bite of my sandwich.

'And?'

'*Annnnd...*' – she elongates the word – 'on the off chance I sent her Erin Santos's photograph, and Katy Russell has positively identified Erin as being the English girl who joined their prep school mid-term and stole her best friend, Samantha Valentine.'

I stop mid-bite, try to let that just sink in for a moment.

'*What?* So, this Katy Russell is saying that *Erin* was living in Australia as a young girl, and that they both knew Samantha Valentine, a girl from their class who went on to kill herself?'

'Uh-huh.' Mitchell is nodding and smiling. 'She says it's the *same* person.'

'And Katy Russell has positively identified Erin Santos as being this old classmate of hers, *in Australia*?' I blink at Mitchell, shaking my head. 'But we've checked Erin out – she's never lived in Australia. She was born in Leeds and has lived there most of her life, when she wasn't locked up in Larksmere anyway. This Katy woman must've got it wrong.'

Mitchell shrugs.

'It's what she says, boss. Obviously, Erin looks older in the photo, but Katy says she *recognises* her, gov. She sounded pretty certain that the photo Adriana sent her of Erin was someone she knew back then as Julie Edwards.'

'Julie Edwards?'

So now Erin Santos is *three* different people? I'm struggling to cope with this idea already. Maybe Fiona *is* right and I should stand back and let the big boys take over.

'So,' – Adriana picks up where Mitchell has left off – 'after doing the calculations from the dates Katy Russell provided, I found a Julie Edwards from the BMD records in Western

Australia, born in the right area *and* in the right year.' Her blue eyes twinkle as she speaks. 'I also found a phone number for an Edwards family listed in the local directory, along with an address. I rang it but no one picked up. It let me leave a voice message though. So I gave them the incident room number – asked them to give us a call.'

She checks my expression. How is it possible for Erin Santos and Julie Edwards to be the same person? My heartbeat starts to pulse in my ears – *how can that be?*

'We've also found Samantha Valentine's family details. They still live in the area, by the looks of it. Shona and Ned Valentine, her parents. We've got a number, gov.' She checks her watch. 'It's around 8 p.m. in Perth. Now might be a good time to call.'

'OK, see if you can get them on the phone – and great work, both of you.'

My head is buzzing as I make my way into my office. Maybe Katy Russell is mistaken? She *has* to be. After all, it was thirty-odd years ago now and some people change much more than others over the years. We'll need more than that to go on to justify us digging around Down Under. Maybe this Katy has some old school photographs she can give us that would help clarify Erin's identity? That said, when my old mate from back in the day, Tony Wentworth, had strong-armed me into attending an old school reunion with him a couple of years back, aside from the bald heads, weight gain, wrinkles and even tooth loss in ol' Jason Redfoot's case (he was the school heartthrob, once upon a time), I recognised more or less everyone from class 5G of Newton Comp on sight. They all looked the same really, just older and more jaded.

I'm about to pick the phone up when Archer bursts into the room.

'Someone found a wig.'

I'd like to think that today couldn't get any more bizarre, but I'm mindful of tempting fate.

'Found *a what*? Where?'

'Stuffed in a ladies' sanitary bin inside a toilet at the media communications centre – a *red* wig. A cleaner found it and handed it in. Anyway, you should've told me you were looking for a redhead.' She flutters her eyes at me, mock-flirtatiously. I try not to look as horrified as it makes me feel, even in jest.

Superintendent Archer has red hair, though it's not as vibrant as the woman's from the press conference, hair that now transpires was most likely a wig.

'Seems she just waltzed right into the building, past security, without anyone noticing her, while *also* somehow managing to avoid the CCTV cameras.'

Archer seems to be enjoying watching me squirm. *How the hell had that happened?*

'I've asked Lucy to get it sent off to the lab, see if they can get any DNA from it, find out who it belongs to.' She shakes her head at me and tuts. 'Your fans will be disappointed in you, Riley. You do realise that if we don't find Erin Santos soon, you'll be *cancelled* on social media. The keyboard Karens and wannabe Miss Marples can turn on you in a flash, you know...'

My phone rings.

Saved by the bell.

'I've got a Mrs Shona Valentine on the line, gov, Samantha Valentine's mum in Australia. Hopefully she can shed some light on this, clear up any confusion about who her daughter was, and about this Julie Edwards girl.' I hear the hopeful anticipation in Adriana's voice.

'Put her straight through.'

FORTY-ONE
ERIN

Dan Riley didn't know it, but I was sitting outside his house – or apartment building, as it is – looking up at a lit window – his lit window – throughout the entire duration of our last phone conversation, which I'd ended abruptly right after I'd told him that I'd kill Samantha if I ever saw her again. He could tell it wasn't a lie; I sensed it from him. And so if Dan can tell when I'm not lying, then by default he also knows when I'm telling the truth, right?

It was really much easier than I'd thought it would be to find Dan's private home address, which is kind of worrying when you think about who he is and what he does for a living. Once I had the name of his son though, it was pretty much a straight line from there. In his newspaper interview, Dan mentions both his children's ages, so it wasn't difficult to do a search on babies registered in that month and year with his name. His address is right there on Jude Joseph Riley's birth certificate, written in black, florid ink, along with his parents' names and occupations, which were stated as journalist and police officer, respectively. Dan's so humble, he didn't even state his full rank on his own son's birth certificate. I wish I liked him less than I do.

During my stay at Larksmere – which hilariously makes it sound like a grand country spa hotel when I say it like that – I'd honed my research skills down to an art form, eventually anyway, once they started to let me use the library and gave me limited internet access. With a bit of hard graft, I can discover where someone lives and who they live with, how many kids they have and where they work. I can find out where they went to school, or if they have a mortgage, or whether they shop at Waitrose or prefer to bulk-buy in Costco. I can even find out how much money they have in the bank or if they've ever ordered a sex toy online – it's all there if you look hard enough, you've just got to be prepared to put the effort in. In a long list of ironies, I have more of a criminal mind now than I ever did before I set foot inside the prison system.

It's still sinking in, the conversation I've just had with Dan, but it would seem that Samantha has, once again, set me up. That psycho bitch has deliberately planted my hair at Milo Harrison's murder scene to make it look like I was there and that I was somehow involved. Only she didn't bank on Tilly Ward finding my email address and sending me a message, did she? *No. She. Did. Not.*

Tilly Ward, God bless her, is my get-out-of-jail-free card, *literally*. I have been so hung up on finding Samantha, so distracted, that I almost missed the fact that she is the key to this. She can confirm that I am *not* Samantha Valentine. One look at me and she can tell the police that *I'm not* the woman who befriended her and took up residence inside her head, subsequently coercing and controlling her into ending Milo Harrison's life. Together, we can *prove* that it's all just an elaborate set-up, nothing but a con. This is just one more piece of evidence that supports the claims I have made all along, *claims no one listened to.* Samantha is the one who should be sitting where I'm sitting now, fresh out of the funny farm, a convicted criminal on the run, with the police and the media on her tail. Yet again, she has managed to flip the script and place the spotlight firmly back on me. There's a touch of Machiavellian genius to it, I'll admit.

'Can you forward me the email exchanges between you and Tilly Ward, Erin? It would be good to have them on file, for our reference, and it may help with your defence.' Dan's soft voice had a sage edge, as though he was trying to convince me that it would be in my best interest if I did.

'Sorry, Dan – they're private, just between us. And I won't need any help with my defence. I don't need one anymore. Anyway, I'm done defending myself. It's all I've been doing since the day this shitshow started. I know that eventually it will all come out because the truth always does, Dan – years, sometimes decades, even centuries later. Only I'm not waiting around that long for justice.'

It turns my blood to ice when I think that Samantha has kept my hair for all these years. She retained a piece of me with her, part of my DNA, like a trophy. I shudder.

'You have the most beautiful hair I think God ever gave a woman, do you know that, hun?'

Sam liked my hair. And I liked her liking it. I wanted her to like everything about me, as much as I liked everything about her. Sometimes she would brush it for me until it shone, just as I had told her my mum used to do when I was a child.

'Keep still!' she would chide me as she roughly raked a brush through it. My mum was always much gentler. 'I need to get all the knots out.'

Aside from it giving me the creeps, the idea that Samantha had purposefully collected and kept my hair shows me just how calculated she really is, how premeditated all of this must've been from the beginning. She had been plotting, and pre-empting, and planning all of this *way back then*. She even had the foresight to keep something she could potentially use as a future weapon against me down the line – my hair – just in case. Why had she done that? What had I done to her to make her hate me that much that she would want to destroy my life like she has? All the while I was being this faithful, caring, doting friend, she was covertly and purposefully plotting my complete destruction. Sometimes, when I was at Larksmere, I thought the not-knowing why any of this happened might actually kill me, along with the guilt I felt about Bojan's death. Both of these things haunted me daily and continuously, the nagging question, 'Why?' following me everywhere, whispering torturously in my ear until I wanted to bash my own brains in.

Another thought has just struck me, one that is equally as sickening, or perhaps more so. Had Samantha *deliberately* plotted and orchestrated Milo Harrison's murder *just* to enable her to frame me for it and have me sent back to the booby hatch? Was it all just for my benefit? A small part of me feels secretly pleased that it even could be. It means that Samantha considers me a real threat, *just as she should*, because I'm the only person who knows that she really exists, you see. Until Tilly Ward popped up.

'Did you speak to Tilly on the phone, Erin?' Dan sounded worried. He's probably pissed at her for reaching out to me – she's on bail after all. But as it turned out, she had wanted to speak to me as much as I wanted to speak to her – and *she* found *me*.

Can we meet face-to-face, Erin? PLEASE? Tilly had typed the word in bold upper case in her email. Clearly, she was desperate, craving comfort and solidarity too, only I couldn't rule out the idea that Dan may be using her as a double bluff in a bid to get me to open up, to let my whereabouts slip, or arrange to meet her somewhere so that they could ambush me. It could very well be a trap. I had to play it safe.

I'm so scared, Erin. I don't know what's going to happen.

What if the police don't believe me, like they didn't believe you? Will they put me in prison? Her fear and confusion felt so much like my own that my eyes instantly welled up with tears. Truthfully, I'm amazed I still have any left.

You won't have to worry about any of that soon, I wrote back.

There was so much I wanted to say to her, so much I wanted to ask and to know about her own experience of being under Samantha Valentine's spell, but I was paranoid of being watched, or traced, or set up. I had to keep it short. *Soon it will all be over. I promise.*

Why do you think she chose you, Erin? Why, out of everyone, do you think Samantha chose you to be her victim? I stared at the words on screen.

I thought I'd know exactly how best to respond to Tilly's question; after all, I've spent seven long years asking myself the very same thing. But when it came to my reply, I struggled, my fingers hovering over the keyboard as I tried to find the right words. *A reason for everything, and everything for a reason, right?*

There's this belief that all of life's events – even negative ones, or perhaps especially those – have purpose or meaning behind them. Often 'the reason' is attributed to a higher power, or a deterministic view of the universe, kind of on par with that other irritating phrase, 'it was meant to be'. I think it's a whole heap of crap, myself. Imagine saying something like that to a mother who has just lost her child to cancer, or in a fatal car accident, *or murder...* 'Hey, chin up, everything happens for a reason – it was all meant to be!'

I wanted to tell Tilly that I thought perhaps Samantha had chosen me because of my deep childhood trauma – witnessing the brutal death of my mum – or the fact I was a recovering addict who'd suffered a psychotic break as a result. Maybe it was because I was unstable, or overly suggestible, or that I was vulnerable and considered *weak*. In the end though, I settled for just three words: '*I was lonely.*'

A small black-and-white cat suddenly runs out into the road, triggering a neighbour's security light. The bright white light arches above me, illuminating the entrance to the apartment block, and I slide a little further down into the driver's seat, pulling my scarf up over my face until the light times out.

It's a smart-looking apartment complex, I suppose – the Rileys have not done too badly for themselves – tucked back and away from the main road, although if you listen carefully you can still hear the faint sound of the ever-present traffic, humming in the distance. Like New York, London is a city that never sleeps. Not that I care especially, because neither do I much anymore. Once upon a time though, I used to love nothing more than a leisurely, long and lazy lie-in of a weekend. I've never been good on little or no sleep – who is? Previous boyfriends have even been known to comment on how grumpy I could be of a morning if I wasn't well rested enough. Jason Willis – more of a friend-with-benefits than a proper boyfriend at the time – used to refer to me as 'crotchety', which I always thought made it sound like I had a personal hygiene problem. At Larksmere though, I learned how to get by on just a few hours a night. Sometimes, I was frightened to shut my eyes, fearful that I might never get to open them again.

I stare at the glove compartment and think about the gun that's inside it – the gun I placed there. It had felt so heavy and so powerful in my hand, like I was holding the very tangible embodiment of life or death right there in it. I have to admit, despite my general, overall pacifistic nature and 'be kind' philosophy, it gave me a tiny electric thrill knowing that now, at last, I would be the one yielding that power.

FORTY-TWO
DAN

'I have to say,' – she takes a few sharp breaths – 'I'm... I'm sorry, but it's my heart... jeez, it's going like the clappers... It's not every day you get a call out of the blue from the British police, asking about your daughter who died over thirty years ago! I was just about heading up the wooden hills as well... *Ned!* Hang on, sorry, ... *Nedddd!*' I hear the sound of heavy footsteps on stairs, the low grumbling of a male voice in the background. 'It's the British police on the phone, they're calling from *London...*'

'British police? What the blazes do *those bastards* want?' His Australian accent is notably more pronounced than hers.

'*Ned!*' she hisses. 'I'm sorry, I apologise on my husband's behalf. He's fallen off the wagon *again* and is a bit upset with himself, a bit grumpy. My mother always said that I married beneath me.' She laughs, though I sense there may be a ring of truth to it.

'I can only apologise if I'm keeping you from your bed, Mrs Valentine. And I'm really sorry for any distress this may cause you. Did my colleagues give you the heads-up on why we contacted you?'

'... They didn't really say much... just that you wanted to

speak to me about my daughter, about Samantha, something about a message on social media?' I hear the click at the back of her throat as she swallows, dryly, no doubt apprehensive about what could be coming next. 'It's been thirty years now. My Sammie will have been dead for thirty-one years this November. Though sometimes it feels like it only happened yesterday.' Her voice sinks. 'You never get over losing a child, trust me, *never*.'

'I believe you, Mrs Valentine.'

'Shona, please.'

'Shona, do you remember a girl who was friends with your daughter back in prep school, a girl named Katy Russell?'

'Katy! God, yeah! Of course,' she says. 'Jeez, I haven't heard that name in a while. I knew Katy well, back then anyway. Thick as thieves they were, her and my Sammie, BFFs as they say now. They were always off out somewhere together, roller-skating in the park, swimming at the beach, riding their bikes... all that kind of kids' stuff, and if Katy wasn't over at our house, then Sammie was hanging out at hers... Yeah, they were close at one time, those two girls, like sisters. Ahhhh,' – she sighs as she reminisces – 'I've not seen Katy in years. I don't know if she'd even recognise me now, from all that time ago – probably not. Ned says he doesn't recognise me anymore either.' She laughs again, though it has a melancholy tinge to it. 'She's married now, I think, Katy, got kiddies probably. I never heard anything about her moving to the UK though?' She pauses. 'Nothing's happened to her, has it? What's this got to do with our Sammie?'

'It's complicated, Shona,' I say, which is an understatement. 'We're currently conducting a homicide investigation—'

'What! No!' She gasps.

'Don't worry!' I quickly interject. 'It's not Katy, Katy's alive and well, and, I believe, still living in Australia... It was something that she mentioned, a comment she made on social media about a girl named Julie Edwards – someone both she and your daughter, Samantha, knew back in school, is that right?'

There's a moment's pause.

'Oh. Her.' Her voice tightens. 'What about Julie Edwards?'

'So you knew her?'

'Yeah. And I never liked her,' she says bluntly. 'She was that posh little Pommy girl who turned up mid-term during the last year of prep school and broke up their friendship. She set her sights on being Sammie's new best friend and pushed Katy out – three's a crowd and all of that. It caused a real stink at the time,' she says. 'I remember there were a lot of tears, and I had to have a heart-to-heart with Katy's mum, Christie, about it all. Katy was so hurt. Even I was cross with Sammie; I thought it was cruel to just dump her friend like that, and I told her off for being disloyal – she'd known Katy since kindergarten. But this Julie Edwards girl, she seemed to just come out of nowhere, and then...'

'You met this little girl, this Julie Edwards?'

'Oh sure, yeah, a few times. And like I said, I didn't like her much. Bit of a perfect princess, you know what I mean?'

I suppose I did. My own little 'perfect princess', my Pip, loves to dress up in a tutu that she wears with these glittery purple wellies. 'Make a *swish*, Pop-Pop!' she says, waving her little magic star wand about, and then granting it to me with a bash on the head. She thinks it's *hilarious*.

'Why didn't you like her much?'

She pauses.

'I didn't like the hold she had over my daughter, or the fact that she'd pushed poor Katy out of the picture. Sammie was always a big softie, a real sweetheart. She hated the idea of upsetting anyone. But she would never hear a bad word spoken about that Julie Edwards girl. We'd get into a fight if I ever brought up any misgivings I had. She seemed to look up to her in a way she never had anyone else before, followed her like a shadow.'

'And what was this Julie like, do you remember?'

'She always seemed like a perfectly sweet, polite little thing whenever I met her. And she was a real stunner too, all long, ice-cream-blonde hair, with these really big, dazzling green eyes – like an angel.'

Blonde hair. *Green eyes*. My heart jumps in my chest.

'But there was just something about her...'

'What was that, Shona?'

She lets out a breath.

'Oh, I don't know. Just something not quite right, wasn't it, Ned?' I hear that low grumbling voice again in the background. 'I don't know, maybe it was just a mother's intuition. All I know is that within six months of meeting that girl, my Sammie, my beautiful baby girl, was dead. She was only eleven years old.'

Her words haunt the painful silence that follows.

'It was Sammie's older brother, Nicholas, who found her. He came home from soccer practice one evening, and there she was at the bottom of our garden, hanging from the apple tree, near the swing Ned had made for her with a bit of rope and an old truck tyre. Poor Nicholas...' Her voice drops. 'He never got over it, finding his little sister like that. He gets flashbacks to this day, and he's in his fifties now.'

'It must've been dreadful, Shona.'

'Do you know, that tree never once bore fruit again after it happened. Since the day we moved into this place, almost half a century ago now, that tree produced a ton of apples each year, without fail; great big, fat, juicy green apples, so many that we couldn't even give them away in the end, could we, Ned? But after that, after our Sammie died – nothing ever again.'

'Did you find out why it happened, Shona? *How* it happened?'

She blows air loudly through her lips.

'Well, that's just it.' I hear the strain in her voice and feel guilty that I'm having to be the one who makes her recall such a devastating tragedy. 'There was nothing, no signs, no depression, no previous self-harm, no mental health issues. We've spent a lifetime since wondering if we missed the red flags, but... The shock was... well it was...' She struggles to find the right words. 'It was too much. It *shattered* our family, tore our lives apart, literally like a bomb had detonated in the middle of us.' Her voice is hoarse with emotion. 'We were never the same again. How could anyone be after that? Samantha was always such a perfectly normal, happy little girl, let me tell you. *She was*. I remember that year – the year she died – she was especially looking forward to Christmas because Ned and I had talked about getting her a pony, you know, a little old nag she could trot about on and take care of, and she was so stoked about it.'

'My God, Shona, I'm so sorry.' My paltry apology is scant compensation, I'm sure. 'Did the police ever look into Samantha's death? Was there a coroner's report?'

'Accidental death.' She sniffs. 'But they suspected suicide because of the way...' She clears her throat. '... because of the way the rope had been tied, or something. They said she would've had to have done it deliberately, herself. But with no note, and no previous concerns from us or from the school, they couldn't say conclusively either way.'

'And what did you and Ned think?'

'How could I, as a mother, bring myself to believe that my happy-go-lucky little ray of sunshine, my beautiful eleven-year-old daughter, had deliberately hung herself? I just couldn't. Never. Still can't. It had to have been an accident somehow. Just a terrible, dreadful, fluke accident...'

Why do I sense there's a 'but' coming?

'I've never really told anyone this before, only Ned and I have spoken about it over the years, but deep down inside me

I've always suspected that she had something to do with it somehow – that little angelic, blonde-haired, butter-wouldn't-melt Julie Edwards.' Her voice sounds brittle now, simmering with resentment. 'I had no proof or evidence or anything of that sort, and Julie was away on a family vacation when Sammie died, but it was just *here*,' – I hear the thudding sound her fist makes as it connects with her breastbone – 'right here inside my chest, my intuition – a mother's instinct. I felt it so strongly, Detective Riley. Do you know what I mean?'

She has no idea.

'I just thought that if my Sammie... well, if she did kill herself, then somehow Julie Edwards had something to do with it, told her to do it maybe, oh, I don't know... maybe I'm just talking shit. Maybe I'm still in denial, all these years later. Ned's therapist says he still is, and that's why he's become a pisshead!' She whispers the last part down the phone, but there's no malice in her voice. She sounds fond of him still. I try not to think about what it would do to a family, a tragedy like that.

'Do you think you'd recognise Julie Edwards if you saw a photo of her, Shona?'

'Heck, yes! I can even see her face in my mind right now, as we speak.'

'Even thirty-odd years later?'

'Well, I mean, I can't say for certain, but yes, I'd like to think so.'

'Shona, I'm going to send you over a link, right now, to this phone, and I want you to stay on the line and click on the link. Can you do that for me?'

'What the hell, send it. Ned... *Ned*, get your arse up over here and have a look at this...'

'I want you to tell me if you recognise the person in the photograph I'm about to send you, and if you do, then tell me her name, OK?'

I pull up Erin's mugshot on my phone, click send. After a

few seconds' delay, I hear the ping of it arrive at her phone, and hold my breath.

'No. That's not her,' she says, instantly. 'That's not Julie Edwards... I'm pretty certain it's not her, is it, Ned?'

I hear him grumbling in the background again. *Is he muzzled?* 'Nah... Ned doesn't think so either. This woman doesn't look at all familiar to me. I suppose... I suppose the eye colour is similar, the green eyes... but Julie Edwards had this ice-white blonde hair, and the shape of her face, her nose... yeah... no... it's not her.'

'And you're absolutely sure about that, Shona?'

She sucks in a breath. *'Definitely.'*

FORTY-THREE

Tilly Ward lifts her head up from the photograph of Erin Santos that I've placed in front of her on the table and fixes her eyes on me.

'Oh my God!' Her hand shoots up to her mouth. 'That's *definitely* her – yes, that's Samantha!'

'And you're sure about that? You're absolutely one hundred per cent sure that *this* woman in *this* photograph is the person you know as Samantha Valentine?'

She meets my eyes once more. *'It's her.'*

I nod, drag my hand down my face. *This is insane.*

Immediately, I send Davis a text message.

Positive photo ID on Erin Santos from Tilly Ward.

But I couldn't quite get my head around it *still*. Katy Russell had identified Erin Santos as being a girl named Julie Edwards, who she went to school with, only when I sent Shona Valentine the same photo of Erin, she swore blind to me that it *wasn't* her. So who's right and who's wrong? Both? Neither? *Which the hell is it?*

'I've got a whole heap of old photo albums from her school days,' Shona had told me. 'And Julie Edwards is in some of them, though not many. For some reason, I didn't want to have to look at her face whenever I went back through them. Like I said, Detective, there was just something about that kid that I didn't like, *didn't trust.*'

She'd promised to dig a photo out and send it to me.

Tilly had looked pleased to see me as she'd opened the door to her apartment.

'It's nice to see you, Dan,' she signed to me. Or at least I think she did.

'Hello, Tilly,' I signed back, a little awkwardly. 'How are you?'

'Wow,' she said, her eyes widening, 'I'm impressed. Have you been taking lessons?'

I shrugged. 'Not as many as I would like, Tilly. Can I come in?'

'Yes, of course, please.' She stood back from the door and I stepped inside, wiped my feet on the doormat.

'Um,'– she looked down at them – 'would you mind...'

'My shoes? Oh, yes of course.' Professionally, I'm not obligated to take them off, but I choose to comply. She watches as I remove them and place them next to her own, positioned neatly by the front door, which makes me think of something Erin might have told me during our phone conversations, *something about shoes being by the door...*

'I thought perhaps you had already seen the photograph that we released to the press.'

'No,' she says, visibly upset. 'I haven't switched the TV on in days, or looked at my phone. I've been completely alone. I don't want to read the news. I'm too frightened to go out of the house, even. I'm jumpy, loud noises scare me... well, they sound loud to me, even though they're probably not loud to you!' She tucks a piece of her hair behind her left ear, and I catch a glimpse of her hearing aid. 'I can't sleep, can't eat...' Admittedly, she looks pale and drawn in the face, like a ghost, and her green eyes are sunken and a little bloodshot. There's something different about her to the last time we met though. I'm not sure what it is yet, can't quite put my finger on it, but it's definitely *something*.

'I must look like such a fright,' she apologises. 'I'm glad my colleagues can't see me now.'

'I'm sorry, Tilly,' I say. 'I'm sorry any of this has happened to you. Is this from your colleagues?'

I nod at the greeting card on the table, one that says 'You will be missed' on the front. She nods solemnly.

'The whole team signed it,' she says. 'I'm really going to miss them too. I can't go back now, can I, even if they'd have me? Are you here to charge me, Dan?' She blinks up at me, her eyes widening. 'Is that why you're here?'

'No, no...' I soften my voice, reassure her. 'Just to talk. Let's sit down, yeah, try to relax. I know it's not easy with everything you're dealing with right now.'

She slides into the seat at the kitchen table.

'That is *not* a good photo of Samantha.' She looks down at it. 'She won't like that one bit when she sees it. She's much prettier in the flesh. When was it taken?'

'When she was arrested, Tilly, in 2019, for the murder of a man named Bojan Radulovic. And her name is not Samantha Valentine, it's Erin Santos.'

'Erin Santos... Er-in San-tos...' She lets the name roll off her tongue. 'So who is she then? Why is she pretending to be someone called Samantha Valentine? What will this mean for me, Dan? Will you find her? *Have* you found her?'

'Not yet, no. But we will.' I nod.

'I just can't believe any of it.' She lets her hands fall onto the table with a slap. 'Was it *all* lies? Was there really no abusive boyfriend? Did I kill an innocent man because I believed, because she *made* me believe, that we were in danger, that he was going to kill us? Why would she *do* such a thing? Why would anyone?' She covers her face with her hands, shuts her eyes. She's painted her fingernails red – I'm sure they were natural when I last saw her. Seems a bit out of context somehow.

'Tilly, have you had any contact with Erin Santos?'

'What?' Her brow wrinkles.

'Did you send Erin Santos an email?'

'No! Why would I do that? I've never even *heard* the name Erin Santos until you just told me. The woman in the photo is Samantha... *my friend...*' her voice trails off. 'Or I thought she was. I'm sorry,' she drops her head, 'this is all so much to take in, to process...'

I reach across the table, place my hand on top of hers. It feels soft and cold to touch.

'I know, Tilly.' I pat it. 'But you're sure you have never contacted Erin Santos by email, or otherwise?'

'I *swear* to you,' – she pulls her hand away, starts to cry – 'I have no idea who Erin Santos is, let alone have an email address for her. I don't even own a laptop anymore – it's with the police, and you can check my phone if you like.' She pushes it across the table towards me. 'Will I go to prison?' Her bottom lip quivers. 'I didn't mean to kill him. I didn't mean to kill Milo Harrison. She told lies, *so many* lies...'

'I know she did, Tilly.' I take a packet of tissues from my inside pocket and give them to her.

'Father of three,' – she holds them up – 'always prepared, right!'

I smile. She remembered.

She takes a tissue from the packet and blows her nose, hard, into it.

I glance around her small, sparse apartment. It's neat and

tidy, but not what I'd call homely. I stare at a lone cup and a single used plate on the kitchen work surface.

'It's tricky to explain it all to you, Tilly, but you're wrong in some ways.'

'I don't follow.' Her green eyes are glassy with tears.

'Samantha Valentine was, is, real, but only in Erin Santos's mind. It would seem that she's suffering from something called dissociative identity disorder, you may know it better as split personality. In effect, she's two people in one mind, two very separate people.'

'Oh God.' She covers her mouth with a hand. 'How do you know this?'

'Erin is a former patient at Larksmere High Security Psychiatric Hospital.' Her eyes widen. 'She killed a man in what's almost an identical crime to your own, citing the same defence, the same story... that Samantha Valentine had coerced her into it, that she'd controlled her, and brainwashed her into believing that abuse was taking place and...' – I take a breath – '... well, it's one hell of a messed-up story, Tilly. I'm only sorry you ever had to be involved in it.'

Seems I'm nothing if not the king of the understatements right now.

I sigh. 'There's no escaping a charge, Tilly, I won't lie to you. Right now I'd say you're looking at manslaughter, possibly with diminished responsibility, given the exceptional circumstances.'

'So I *am* going to prison then?' she says in her flat monotone that's sometimes less flat and monotone than it is at others.

'I'm not a judge, Tilly,' I say, not wanting to give her any false hope, 'I can't say what the outcome will be, but given your exemplary background, given the fact that that I hope, by then, Erin Santos will be safe in custody, it could well be that a judge looks leniently upon you and understands the complexities of this unprecedented case. Maybe you'll be given a suspended sentence? I don't know. Let's hope so, eh?' I give her arm a little reassuring squeeze.

'Why do you think she chose *me*, Dan? Why do you think Samantha, or Erin, or whatever her name is, chose me to do this to?'

I shake my head, let out a long breath.

'I don't know, Tilly.' Though it's fairly obvious why, looking at her.

'Is it because of my hearing aid, do you think? Maybe she saw me as more vulnerable than most people, easier to manipulate?'

I drop my head slightly to the side. 'Maybe.'

She nods, pulls her tatty beige cardigan around her small frame, like she has a sudden chill.

'I was lonely,' she says, 'I think she saw how lonely I was, how lonely *I am*.'

I keep my hand on her arm.

'I hope it's not the same for your son, Dan. Being deaf, being hard of hearing, it makes you different, and people... well, people look at you differently, treat you differently, view you as somehow lesser than them. They can't even help it most of the time, it's not their fault, it's just... *instinct*.'

I have to look away. It pains me too much to think that this could be true and that my son may experience similar discrimination in his life because of his condition.

'May I use your bathroom, Tilly?' I need to excuse myself.

'Of course, just through the door, to the left.'

I make my way into the bathroom, close the door behind me. I take a few deep breaths and try to compose myself, stare at myself in the cabinet mirror before I open it. I know I'm being nosy, but it's almost instinctive. *Doesn't everyone do it?*

As I peruse the bottles of shampoo and soap, the toothpaste and sanitary products, I see it, hiding behind a box of old-fashioned bath salts, that large, red, square bottle of perfume.

Baccarat Rouge. A rush of adrenalin bolts through me as I take it from the cabinet and squirt a tiny amount onto my wrist, wave it around a bit, like I'd seen Archer do that time in her office. It seems odd and out of place, this exorbitantly expensive designer perfume, sat alongside all her other basic, cheap toiletries. I know it's the same perfume that Samantha Valentine/Erin Santos wears – and the redhead. *The redhead*, that reminds me!

'A woman was seen leaving this address the day before yesterday, sometime in the morning. A red-haired lady in a purple coat.' I walk back into the small kitchen. 'Do you know who I'm talking about, Tilly?'

She's silent for a moment.

'Have you been watching me, Dan?' I think I see a tiny flicker of surprise on her face.

'Just keeping an eye out for you, Tilly.'

'She's a journalist, I think. She must've got my name and address somehow. She doorstepped me, just turned up out of the blue. I told her she'd got the wrong house, the wrong person, and she went away again.'

I hold her gaze for a moment.

'She didn't give you her name, the name of who she was working for, she didn't say which publication?'

'No. And I didn't ask. I just wanted her to leave.'

I nod. 'OK, well, be prepared for this story to break, Tilly.'

I'm not going to sugarcoat it for her, that wouldn't be fair of me. She needs the heads-up. 'There'll be a swarm of "redheads" when it does, trust me. You want my advice? Have your say when *you* decide to have it. And just tell the truth.'

'Yes,' she agrees with me, perking up a bit. 'I always do.'

FORTY-FOUR

ERIN

The sound of life outside wakes me with a start. *People*. The noise they're making brings me abruptly out of my sleep. I rub my eyes, burp – I'm still feeling a touch gassy after all the food I ate last night – and check the time. It's 5.47 a.m., early, and yet the pavement is already buzzing with *so many people*. People running, people walking, people with coffee cups, people with prams, people walking their dogs, people on bikes, people waiting for buses, delivery people... I realise there's people everywhere of course, but in London it's something else. You can't escape them. And the noise is *deafening*. I think about Dan's young son. He's deaf. I read it in that newspaper article on him, that PR exercise I imagine he was cajoled into doing by his domineering boss. I could tell that he wasn't comfortable talking about his son. I had sensed such sadness too, like somehow he thought it was his fault he was deaf. But I know it isn't. It was just chance, the way the cookie crumbles, the wrong side of luck. It was just *life*.

A woman in fancy running gear turns her head to look at me through the car window as she jogs past. I turn away, flip the visor down and check myself in the mirror. I rub the rims of my eyes with a licked finger. My mascara has run – teach me for buying the cheap stuff – and the red lipstick has all but vanished, but otherwise, I'll do.

I sit up, bring the seat back to an upright position and glance over at Dan Riley's apartment. His car's still here, but, oh... hang on, it's him! He's making his way out of the front entrance now, and he's getting into his car! How's that for timing?

I scrabble around for my car keys. *Shit, shit, shit.* He's on the move. I start up the engine, wait for him to pull out of the complex. I don't want to follow him too closely. I can't afford to arouse his suspicion.

I can barely see through my sleepy eyes as I indicate left, keeping a safe distance behind him as I follow him through the traffic lights, down the unfamiliar streets. My heart is thudding painfully against my ribs. It's too early for this. And I haven't even had breakfast. I take a breath, switch the radio on, press a few of the buttons in quick succession.

'... and on this gloriously *cloudy* morning as well! Next up, it's our Kimberley with the London news...'

'Thanks, Douggie.' The husky female voice rings out through the stereo. 'Met Police are still searching for a missing former mental health patient in London following her disappearance last week. Erin Santos, forty-one, originally from Leeds...'

'Forty-one?' I shout at the radio. 'I'm forty! Jesus!'

I throw a hand up in the air. They're trying to put years on me! As if I haven't lost enough of them already! They had better get it right in my obituary, not that I'll ever get one of those, I suppose. Who's going to write anything about *my* death, aside from all the journalists and keyboard warriors commenting on how it couldn't come too soon? And of course, they'll show that awful photo of me, won't they? The one that makes me look like a deranged child killer who's never heard of concealer. I'm sure, when they go on to make the documentary about this case, about me and my madness and my 'crimes', they'll wheel out Dr Wainwright to have his say. *He* would never miss such an opportunity to be in front of the camera, the centre of attention. I can just see him now, sitting there in his office, that portrait of him in the background as he talks in that slightly condescending way that he does, a make-up lady pressing powder onto his sensitive skin. I'd noticed, over the years, that Dr Wainwright's skin was sometimes quite red and inflamed across his cheeks. I asked him about it once, during one of our sessions, and what looked like a particularly angry flare-up. I could tell he didn't like the fact that I'd mentioned it. He tried to disguise it, but I knew that secretly he was seething that I, this mad, murdering degenerate who was so far beneath him, would have the audacity to point out what could even be considered as a flaw in his otherwise perfect image of himself. He said it was a rare skin condition that he'd inherited on his father's side.

I say it was karma.

Don't get me wrong, I don't *hate* Dr Wainwright, it isn't that. He isn't that different, or special, to most people really. He's just so busy looking into the flaws of others that he's blind to his own.

'You can't park up here, love.' An old man taps on my window and I jump. My hand shoots up to my chest. 'Restrictions... roadworks,' – he rolls his watery grey eyes – 'all up this bleeding road they are. You'd think they were digging for treasure! Best to take a different route.'

I nod and wave politely.

'Yah... thanks for the heads-up!' Or that's how I think Alexandra Fisher would say it, anyway.

I shiver as I close the window. It's a damp, chilly morning and I turn the heating on, gasp as the cool, stale air hits me. I wish I'd brought my onesie with me now.

'*Why are you dressed as a dog?*' Malcolm's voice speaks to me, *again*. I really *must* stop doing that. I have to build a firewall around my thoughts. I can't allow them to wander, or distract me. But it was just the *way* that he'd asked me the question, as if it was perfectly normal for me to answer the door dressed as a dog, and he was just curious. I realise I'm smiling as I swing another left. Dan is two cars ahead. I mustn't take my eyes off him, not for a second. My adrenalin levels are peaking. I can feel it, sense it like rain. Something is coming. *My day of reckoning is nigh.*

He's gone *to work.*

I feel my dopamine levels crash and burn as I watch him pull into the underground car park at the police station. I pull over. I'll have to hang back. Wait. Watch. See where he goes next.

My stomach growls as I recline my seat once again. I need coffee. Why didn't I think to get a coffee? A pain au chocolat too? I look out of the window, try to distract my thoughts away from food.

'*And put a knife to your throat if you are given to gluttony. Proverbs 23:2.*'

I must try to exercise more self-control. *A knife to your throat... Boom!* The flashback hits me hard as Bojan Radulovic comes marching out of the apartment complex, his brow all wrinkled up as he powers towards me with purpose.

'He's got a knife, Erin!' Samantha grips my arm in fear. 'He's going to kill me!' I can feel it in my hand, the smoothness of the handle against my skin, the cool blade glinting as she hands it to me... only now when I look down at Bojan's hand, it's not a knife that he's holding.

I didn't much like her, that Detective Pritchard, but she'd told me the same thing at the time, when she'd interviewed me.

'It wasn't a knife he had in his hand, Erin, it was his mobile phone.'

Only I didn't believe her. I truly believed at the time that I had seen the knife for myself, in his hand as he'd approached, only it had all been the power of suggestion, hadn't it? I *thought* it was a knife because *she* told me it *was* a knife. And seeing him there with it in his hand, it all fitted into place, because, why *wouldn't* he have a knife? For months, Samantha had been telling me that he was violent, that he was abusing her and had threatened to kill her, just like Ray Denis killed my mum. She tapped into my trauma so completely that in that moment, I would've done anything she said, anything to save her from him.

A fresh rush of anger fires up inside me, but hang on... Dan's back on the go again... He's alone as he steps out of the police station, his sidekick's not with him, the one he referred to in his article as his 'work wife'. He turns left out of the station, and I quickly indicate, pull out. I stay close, but not too close, behind him.

After about five minutes, he turns right off the main road and right again, down a side one. I slow down behind him, pull in behind a cluster of parked cars. I watch as he exits his vehicle, hear the 'beep, beep' of his alarm as he locks the car and begins to make his way towards a set of apartments, only he's coming *this* way. I snatch my phone up, look down at it, pretend to read something. He doesn't even turn to look as he walks straight past my window, and I let out a breath of relief. He hasn't seen me. My eyes follow him, watching as he presses the intercom buzzer. I crane my neck, see if I can get a clearer view, but I'm way too far away to see which number it is and... My phone slips from my grip and falls straight between the driver and passenger seats. Why *does* that always happen? I curse, slide my hand in between them, try to grip it with the tips of my fingers. When I look back up, Dan is no longer there.

'*Brilliant!*' I bash the steering wheel with the palm of my hand. 'Bloody brilliant.'

Thirty minutes later, I'm just about ready to give up and go back to the Battersea apartment. I'm cold and I'm hungry – but above all, *I'm tired*. Tired of feeling the way I do, wracked with these toxic feelings of resentment, of retribution *and rage*. I can't live like this anymore. I really *will* go mad. Perhaps today is not my day of reckoning. Maybe my day will *never* come and I'll just have to skip the revenge part and go straight onto —

Oh, he's coming back out of the apartment complex! I sit up straight, switch to high alert. He's standing on the doorstep, he's with... he's with a woman! I can't quite make her face out from this distance though. I'll have to move down a bit if I want a closer look. *Rats!* I wince at the throaty sound of the engine as it turns over, hoping I haven't drawn attention to myself as I slowly begin to move the car forwards towards them.

Then I switch it back off, turn, and look.

FORTY-FIVE

DAN

Tilly had come all the way down the stairs and up to the front doors of the apartment building to see me off.

'It's the furthest I've got in the last day or so,' she said. 'I don't feel safe in the outside world anymore. I almost had a panic attack in Tesco's when I went shopping for a few essentials yesterday. Maybe I'll do it online from now on...'

'All this terrible mess, eh?' I said as I touched her shoulder, gently. I can tell that she doesn't want me to leave. 'I'll be back to see you soon, Tilly. Don't leave the country, eh?' I don't know why I said it, the poor wretched woman can't even leave her own home.

'Will you, Dan?' She suddenly threw her arms around my neck. 'Thank you,' she signed to me as she pulled away. 'Thank you for everything you've done.'

'You're welcome, Tilly.'

'Mmm,' she said, with a strange look on her face as she stood back from me. 'You smell... *lovely.*'

It must've been that tiny squirt of Baccarat Rouge I'd give myself in the bathroom, though I wasn't going to tell her that.

That would be giving the game away that I'd been poking around her personal things.

'It reminds me of something Samantha used to wear,' she says, leaning in closer – a little *too* close perhaps. '... Or I suppose I should now say, Erin.'

Davis has her feet up on one of the desks in the incident room as I enter.

'Come with me.' I knock them off, stoop down to whisper in her ear as I pass.

'Boss?' She jumps up in surprise, follows.

'I've just been to see Tilly Ward,' I say as she closes the door behind her.

'I know. You said she's identified Santos as Samantha Valentine in the mugshot photo.'

I chew at my thumbnail, nibble at a tiny piece of loose skin at the quick.

'Yes, yes, she did. But there was something off, Lucy, something not quite right about her.'

'About Tilly Ward?'

'Yes. Something different.' I chew some more.

'Such as...?'

'I can't put my finger on it.'

'No, and you won't be able to put your thumb on it either if you keep gnawing at it like that.'

I drop my hand down into my lap.

'I'm going to go through all the tapes again... the interviews we did with Tilly...'

'Now, boss? But that'll take ages.'

'Pull up a chair, then,' I say, 'get comfortable. I need to know what it is that was different about her, because I know it's *something*.'

Davis sighs. 'Okaaaay...'

'Any news from Down Under yet – has Shona Valentine sent in those school photos?'

'It's only been a few hours, boss. Why?' She's eyeing me suspiciously.

'Would it be strange,' – I turn to look at her – 'if you were Tilly Ward, I mean, and if you were going through what she's going through, and if you'd done what she's done, to paint your fingernails scarlet red just a few days later?'

It sounds a bit ridiculous when I say it out loud, judgemental even. Only it's my job to be judgy sometimes. And it's not so much a judgement in of itself, more a kind of moral question, a question of character, I suppose. 'Imagine. You've just killed a man, in self-defence or otherwise. You're out on police bail. You've lost your job, your life, *your mind*, most probably... with all of that going on, would you think to give yourself a manicure?'

Davis shrugs.

'Maybe she just wanted to cheer herself up, boss, take her mind off everything. People do strange things in shock and trauma. I shouldn't read too much into it.'

'Yes, you're probably right, Lucy... but she had that perfume in her bathroom cabinet, a brand-new bottle by the look of it, hardly used.' The perfume is bugging me. Along with the red nails, it somehow seemed so out of context. Why would Tilly have a bottle of that exact same perfume, *expensive* perfume, that Samantha supposedly wears?

'You searched her bathroom cabinet, boss?' She gives me a look.

'What? Don't tell me you wouldn't have done the same, Davis, because I won't believe you.'

She opens her mouth to object, but, knowing I'm right, thinks better of it.

'So, you found a bottle of Baccarat Rouge in her bathroom cabinet?'

'Yes. Tucked away behind all these other basic, unbranded, cheap products – just sitting there, like a jewel.'

'Maybe it was a present from someone. Maybe *Samantha* gave it to her?'

'Maybe...' I say. 'Roll the footage, Davis.'

We're about twenty minutes into the recording when the first thing catches my attention. And as I suspected, it had something to do with shoes.

'... and so we take our shoes *off*! And then we place them behind the *door*.' It was the way Tilly had said it, or rather, sung it during the interview – melodic, and on the beat, like a song lyric, the way you might tell a child to help them learn.

I stop the footage, rewind it and listen again.

Those were the exact words, spoken – or sung – in the *same* way that Erin had described Samantha's words to her on the night they met.

'*No, no, no... Ari says, we take our shoes off! And then we place them behind the door!*'

Was it just a coincidence? It's not like people *don't* take their shoes off before they enter theirs, or other people's homes – most people do. It's just that most people don't say that exact same phrase, in that exact same sing-song voice, when they do it.

To be fair, I'd picked up on the whole shoe thing right at the start, when I first walked into the crime scene – those boots sitting neatly by the front door. I had thought it odd then, that anyone would stop to remove their shoes in the middle of an emergency.

'Maybe Tilly didn't realise the seriousness of the situation when she first walked into the scene. Maybe she didn't know how bad it was...' Davis was right to play devil's advocate. Tilly's boots by the door and her sing-song paraphrasing are not evidence of anything. Only I need to tell my intuition that, because it's setting off bells inside me – *the alarm kind.*

I let the footage roll on for a while longer, watch and listen as a tearful and traumatised Tilly recounts her story to Davis and Parker and, later, to me. It's during the interview that I conducted with her that I suddenly spot it.

'There!' I jump up from my seat. My sudden movement causes Davis to do the same. I rewind the footage, pause it on Tilly's face.

Davis blinks at the screen.

'What am I supposed to be looking for, gov?'

'There. Behind her left ear...'

She moves in for a closer look. 'The hearing aid, you mean?' She turns to me blankly.

I nod. 'OK, *now* look...'

I roll the footage onto the interview that was recorded the following day. I hit the pause button again, look up at Lucy. 'Here, it's behind her *right* ear.'

Her eyes widen.

'Now what do you make of *that*, Davis?'

FORTY-SIX
ERIN

I clasp my hand tightly over my mouth, but it's no good. I can't stop it from coming.

Groaning, I open the car door, lean out, and empty my guts out all over the pavement below – *whoosh!*

My eyes water as I retch, my whole body violently spasming and heaving and sweating as it expels the contents of my stomach – around £120 worth of contents, last night's overindulgent supper, *including* ice cream. My head starts spinning as I begin to hyperventilate, struggling to catch my breath between intermittent bursts of vomiting.

'Hey, you OK?' A woman stops as she's walking past, her brow crinkled in concern. She makes to come towards me but, seeing the mess I've made over the side of the road, takes a step back.

'Mm-hm' is about all I can manage in response. 'Stomach bug...' I croak, doubled over.

'Yeah, there's a lot of it about at the moment.' She gives me a sympathetic, lopsided smile, hands me a bottle of water, stretching her arm out as far as it can go to avoid getting too close.

'You don't look well. You should go home to your bed.'

'Yes... thanks.' I nod gratefully. 'I will.'

But there's no chance of that happening. Not after what I've just seen.

At first, I thought my mind was playing tricks on me and that it was a mirage as I watched them both, saying their goodbyes by the door, like someone stranded in the burning heat of a vast desert sees a stream in the distance. I thought that perhaps I was just seeing what I *wanted* to see. Only there was no mistaking it was her.

I recognised her *immediately*, even though she looks so different, a far cry from the glamorous blonde bombshell I remember her being. Her hair is now mousey brown and hangs in lank curtains around her noticeably thinner face, and she's dressed in the most *awful* clothes – a shapeless grey cardigan and baggy leggings – clothes that ordinarily she would never be seen dead in – though today just may well be the exception to that rule.

Samantha Valentine.

I gulp back some water with a shaking hand, spilling it down my front as I swallow greedily.

I've been dreaming and fantasising about this moment for seven years now, the moment when I would finally see her again. And yet now it's here, now this day really has actually materialised, I feel paralysed, unable to move, *unable to think*.

I watched them as they'd embraced at the door, watched as Dan had made his way down the pathway towards his car. As he was about to step inside, he stopped, turned and waved at her, like an old friend.

'I'll see you soon, Tilly!'

Tilly?

Oh. My. God. It hits me hard, like a hammer to the back of my skull. *Tilly Ward?* I feel sick again. 'Oh *no*...' I clutch my mouth, willing the nausea to pass. I don't want to throw up in the hire car – they'll charge me.

Samantha Valentine is Tilly Ward.

I sit in the driver's seat, motionless for a moment as I try to let it sink in.

'My God!' I breathe the words aloud. Yet again, she's fooled everyone, including me, *including Dan Riley*. By default though, he has at least fulfilled the role I had hoped he would, and led me to her. I take it back – I was right to choose him all along. I glance at the burner phone in my tote bag and, bizarrely, think about calling him. Instinctively, I want to give him the heads-up, tell him who Tilly Ward *really* is and how she's tricked him, how she's deceived and manipulated him into believing her cock-and-bull story, just as she did me. In a sudden burst of rage, I bang the steering wheel with my hand, over and over until it hurts so much that I scream. *That evil bitch!*

It was all becoming clear now, horribly so. It *had* been deliberate, all of it, planned and plotted and executed with aplomb. She had killed Milo Harrison and blamed Samantha Valentine, my supposed fictitious friend, my 'other self'. She must have known that I had been released from Larksmere and wanted to make sure I could never come after her with the truth, never try to expose her, by framing me for a murder she deliberately committed to silence me. I was right; she had to have planted my hair at the crime scene, to try to incriminate me, turn the spotlight onto me, mad Erin Santos, the crazy woman who was a pathological liar. In what is perhaps the most twisted part of all though, in a bid to ensure that I'd be held accountable and thrown back in the nuthouse, she'd committed her own crime *on herself*. She was playing both the victim *and* the perpetrator.

I take a breath, scrabble around in my tote bag for my lipstick and a hairbrush.

'You can do this, Erin.' My voice sounds oddly detached as I talk to myself out loud – maybe I really *am* going mad. Laughter suddenly bubbles up out of me. If that psycho bitch wants to see madness, then I'll damn well give it to her!

Finish this, Erin, you can finish this once and for all.

As I start to rake the brush through my frazzled hair, I'm thinking of all those years I have spent holed up in that hospital – a place that makes a mockery of the word itself – hospitals are supposed to be safe places after all, places of nurture and care and comfort. Larksmere was none of these things. It was a cold, desperate, lonely place of pain and despair, the antithesis of care. No one cared about you in that hell pit. Frankly, I hope it burns to the ground.

I redo my make-up, add a touch of mascara and a fresh coat of vibrant red lipstick. Then I take the bottle of Baccarat Rouge from my bag – I'd picked up a bottle from Space NK at the train station after my charity shop run – and spray it liberally all over myself, until I start to cough and choke. Opening the window a touch, I check myself out in the mirror. I want to look good, no, I want to look *better* than good, when I face my nemesis. I want her to know, *to see*, that she hasn't broken me, *right before I put a bullet through her messed-up head.*

I reach over, open the glove compartment and retrieve the gun. The pockets on my charity shop coat purchase are thankfully deep and roomy, perfect for concealing a weapon. I place it inside before throwing on a pair of reading glasses, check myself in the rear-view mirror. Ideally, I don't want her to instantly recognise me like I recognised her. She mustn't. I need a few seconds at least, the element of surprise, to give me time to push my way through the door.

The din of the outside world hits me and I wince as I step out of the car and make my way towards the front entrance of the drab apartment block. The Samantha I knew would never live in such shabby-looking accommodation. She really must be slumming it. Though it's all part of the convincing disguise of course, the act. To be fair to her, I suppose she's nothing if not dedicated to her craft.

Luck must be on my side today because an older gentleman is in front of me as I reach the entrance, punching the code into the main doors.

'After you.' He graciously gestures to me, smiling as he invites me to go before him.

'That's so sweet.' I smile back at him. 'Thank you. Um...' I turn to him. 'You don't happen to know which apartment my friend lives in, do you?' I clutch my chest, flashing him a smile as I flutter my eyes. 'I've only been here once before and I've clean forgotten it. Her name's Tilly, Tilly Ward. She's got brown hair and green eyes, and she...'

'The deaf girl? Number 66, two floors above.' He points upwards. 'I'm the floor below, thankfully.' He places a shaky hand on his knee. 'These ain't what they used to be – and that lift is always on the blink. Bloody disgrace really, what with the service charges they want out of you...'

'Oh, I know, appalling, isn't it? Just pure greed at the end of the day. It's one of the seven deadly sins, you know.'

He gives me a slightly surprised look before he turns away.

'Yeah, well, God bless you on your way.' He smiles at me once again.

'God bless you too.'

I take the stairs. I'm not fond of lifts. And I don't want to run the risk of seeing too many people. Not that it matters now. I'm already on camera. The final act in this horror story will be caught on film for everyone to see. *Coming to an Odeon near you now, rated 18!*

But this is what happens, you see, when justice is denied. Sometimes people are forced to take matters into their own hands. And this way, in what is, I realise, one crazy-assed, messed-up, ugly and tragic story, *I* get to write the ending, the final chapter. This is where I get the answers I need to reclaim my sanity, to take back the power and the control that she stole from me seven years ago and right the wrongs. Every dog has its day, right? And today it's mine.

Perhaps I really should've worn my onesie.

I stand outside the door of apartment 66. Huh. All it needs is another six at the end and that would be about right. I take a breath. I take two. And then I knock on the door. It really can't be good for my heart to be beating at the rate it currently is. It feels like it might actually burst, explode inside my chest and kill me. My hand goes up to it as she opens the door.

At first I see the anticipated flicker of surprise, quickly followed by a smattering of confusion, but then, boom! There it is, right there! *Recognition*. I watch as her expression clouds over and darkens, like a black veil falling over her face.

I give her my best smile.

'*Hello, hun.*'

FORTY-SEVEN

DAN

'But we've checked Tilly Ward out,' Davis says. 'We would've found something by now surely? And there's no connection between her and Erin Santos.

'You said yourself that she's a vulnerable character, you know.' She points to her ear rather than mention the word 'deaf' or 'hard of hearing'. 'No rap sheet, no prior, no history of—'

The door to my office swings open and Archer pokes her head around it.

'Briefing, twenty-five minutes. Be ready, Riley, Davis...'

We nod in unison.

'Ma'am.'

She pauses. 'Are there any new leads? Has Santos called you again?'

'No, ma'am,' I answer her on autopilot, my thoughts elsewhere.

'The boss here thinks that maybe Til—' Davis starts to speak.

'Yes, ma'am!' I cut in loudly. Loudly enough for Archer to glare at me in surprise. I definitely do not want Davis to tell

Archer what I think Davis thinks I'm currently thinking about Tilly Ward. Not right yet. I need more proof first.

'We'll be right down, ma'am.'

Archer narrows her eyes at me suspiciously. 'Don't be late.' They're still fixed on me as she closes the door behind her.

'Go and gather the troops together, Lucy,' I say. 'I just need a moment to think.'

'Well, don't leave it too long, boss,' – she nods behind her – 'you've seen what kind of mood she's in...'

They say a watched kettle never boils, but maybe the same rule doesn't apply to mobile phones because the moment I look down at mine, it rings. Hallelujah, please let it be Erin.

'Dan Riley speaking.'

'What the blazes has she done now, eh?' the gruff voice on the other end says. It's an Australian voice, the accent is thick and strong and unmistakable.

'Sorry, who is this, who am I speaking to?'

'The name's Edwards, Ken Edwards,' he booms.

Edwards? As in Julie Edwards?

'There was a message on our answer machine. Some sheila-woman left a message saying you wanted to speak to us about Julie. As soon as I heard that name... well, like I say, what's the little bastard gone and done now?'

'Is Julie your daughter?'

'No, thank Christ,' he says quickly. 'She was my brother Ray's girl, my niece. Haven't seen her in many years now though. Why d'you wanna know about Jools? Has she been up to her old tricks again?'

'What old tricks are they, Mr Edwards?'

'Ken. Well, like I say, I haven't seen the girl in years, but I remember her back when she was a kid. "Troubled" is the kindest way of puttin' it.'

'Troubled?'

'Yeah, she was one strange little girl was Julie. The wife

never liked her much, thought there was something off about her. He married a Pom – Vanessa. A few years after they had Julie, he brought them both out to Oz with him, She lived over with her mother, my brother's ex-wife, in a prefab in Subby. I s'pose I felt a bit sorry for the little girl really, having those two for parents. He was a wrong 'un, my brother, used to beat the livin' daylights out of her mother, he did, the brute. Julie must've witnessed a lot of things she shouldn't have as a kid. I think it turned her funny.'

'Turned her funny?'

'Yeah... as she got older, after her dad buggered off back to the UK and left them, she began to get herself into trouble, got herself known to the law, ended up in some naughty girls' school for a while. I know that her mother struggled to keep her in check. A "chip off the old block", she called her, just like her dad. She was close to her dad. I dunno what it was that she did exactly that got her sent away, conned a friend and her family out of some money, or something like that.'

I hold my breath.

'Anyway, a stint in a naughty school didn't do much to put her on the right path, Vanessa reckoned it made her worse if anything. After that she just carried right on doing whatever she wanted. She started stealing people's identities so she could take out loans and buy stuff in their names. I guess Vanessa was right and that the apple didn't fall far from the tree because he was a shyster himself, was old Ray, changed his own name a few times – though it caught up with him eventually, like it always does.'

He pauses, releases a breath.

'Julie was a bit of a bunny-boiler type, she stalked people and all of that bullshit... I think she had a restraining order out on her at one time, I remember her mother telling me. Some poor fella she got fixated on... She was a very pretty girl though, all the boys liked her, and she was smart, like she could pick things up in an instant,'– he clicks his fingers down the line, in demonstration, – 'languages, accents, computers... that girl learned to play the piano in just one weekend! Can you believe it? She just taught herself the notes one day, and the next, she was playing like she'd been practicing for years. I suppose she was quite gifted really. Shame she was a total psycho.' He pauses again. 'Ya can't choose yer family, can you, mate?'

'When you say psycho...?'

'No conscience, that's what her mother told me and the wife. Julie could do really shitty things to people and she just didn't care. She seemed to enjoy it, get a kick out of it even – or that's how Vanessa told it anyway. I think secretly she was glad when she went AWOL around the age of seventeen. One day she just upped and vanished. Pouf! Gone! Her mother never saw her again.'

'Do you know the name Samantha Valentine, Ken? Have you heard that name before?'

He thinks for a moment.

'The kid who hanged herself, you mean? Yeah, the wife always thought that Julie had something to do with it – they were friends, her and that little local girl who topped herself. Sandra reckoned there was something evil about Julie, but then again, she's a sheila and we all know they're prone to a bit of drama, don't we, mate?' He laughs. 'Jools could be very persuasive, quite manipulative, but she was only a child herself at the time, so what could we do? It was Ray's girl, wasn't it, my own niece. But me and Sandra, the wife, we had our own thoughts on why that tragedy happened...'

'I don't suppose you have any old family photos you can send over, Ken? Any pictures you may have with Julie in them?' If I can just get a positive ID...

'I'm afraid not, mate.' He sighs in apology, 'Well, all except the one. I wasn't that close to my brother in the end. Like I say, Ray was a monumental arsehole. He ended up where he deserved, in prison – where he topped himself too, as it went, stupid, selfish bastard...' His voice trails off a little. 'No idea what happened to Vanessa in the end, probably drank herself to death, poor bitch... I can send it over if you like, though I don't know if it'll be any good to you? I dug it out after you left that message, got me thinking about it all again.' He sighs. 'It was taken the day that Julie was born. I'd been with my brother that afternoon, wetting the baby's head in advance.' He chuckles.

'Please, Ken, I'd like to see it.'

'So, you gonna tell me what this is all about? Has Julie been causing trouble over the pond? She done someone else out of their life savings, is that it?'

I'm not sure I'd know where to even begin to tell him.

'We're just making some initial enquiries, Ken,' – I condense it – 'find out some background. It may be that Julie has been using a false identity.'

He snorts.

'Yeah, well, like I say, she was good at that, pretending to be someone else. I dunno, mate, you never know what you're gonna get, do ya, when you have kids? You try to do right by 'em but some of them... well, some people are just born bad, I think.'

I'm gathering my stuff – and my thoughts – together for the briefing when Mitchell knocks on the door. Adriana, the new recruit, is behind her, looking sheepish, her eyes red and swollen, like she may have been crying.

'Can we have a quick word, gov?'

'Yeah, but the key word there is "quick", Mitchell. The briefing starts in five minutes and Archer's on the warpath...'

'Um... Adriana here may have made a bit of a mistake, boss.'

Mitchell nods at Adriana encouragingly. 'Go on... tell him.'

'I... I'm really sorry, sir,' – her voice sounds shaky – 'sorry, sir, I mean, boss, I... well, I...'

'Come on, Adriana,' – I cajole her – 'spit it out. Whatever it is, it can't be *that* bad.'

Only judging by her expression, I'm not so sure.

'I don't know how it happened, boss. I must've just got confused, didn't check properly.'

'She's new to the game.' Mitchell gives me a look that says, 'Go easy on her.'

'What didn't you check properly, Adriana?'

She brushes some hair out of her puffy eyes.

'Katy Russell. The one who commented on Samantha Valentine's sketch on social media, the one who was friends with a girl at prep school with the same name.'

'What about her?'

'Well, umm, she also told us about a girl named Julie Edwards... an English girl who joined the school mid-term, and broke up her friendship with Samantha—'

'Yes... yes...' I roll my hand. 'I've just been speaking to her uncle. What about her?' It comes to me suddenly then. *Ray*. Ken has just told me that his brother's name was Ray. Didn't Erin tell me that Ray was her stepdad's name? Ray Denis, the man who killed her mother, and subsequently himself, while he was in prison?

'I sent Katy the photo of Erin Santos...' Adriana continues telling me what I already know. I need her to get to the point. 'And she identified Erin as being this Julie Edwards girl, I know...'

'I suppose it was a fairly easy mistake to make, gov,' Mitchell chimes in.

My phone beeps. Ken has sent the photo.

'What's an easy mistake to make?' I'm only half listening as I click on it.

'I-sent-the-*wrong*-photo.' Adriana blurts out, as though saying it quickly might make it less true. 'Somehow, instead of sending *Erin's* mugshot over to Katy, which I thought I had done, I sent *Tilly Ward's*.'

OK, *now* I look up.

'*What?*'

'I know, sir, boss, I'm really sorry...' Poor Adriana looks devastated, biting her bottom lip. 'Katy identified the wrong person, because *I* messed up and sent her the *wrong* photo.'

I blink at her. But if that's right, then that would mean...

I look down at the image Ken's just sent over. You can tell it's old by the faded tones and the style of clothes they're wearing. The woman in the middle, Vanessa, I assume, is in a hospital bed, holding a newborn wrapped in a white receiving blanket, looking down at her precious gift with a worn-out smile. Two men stand either side of her, one of them – Ray, I assume – is half sitting on the bed with her, leaning over to peer inside the blanket at his new arrival, while Uncle Ken beams proudly next to them, a can of lager raised in his hand. *And then I see it.*

'... And so I've contacted Katy Russell again, to apologise, and sent her Erin's photo this time, like I should've done in the first place, and...'

Adriana is still explaining away in the background, but I've stopped listening.

There, in the photograph Ken has just sent me, just visible in the left-hand corner, is a plaque that reads, 'Maternity Department', and underneath it is another sign, a smaller one that reads 'Matilda Ward'.

I almost leap over my desk.

'You, Adriana,' – I seize her by her forearms – 'are a genius!' It's all I can do to stop myself from picking her up and giving her a twirl. Matilda Ward – Tilly Ward. She's used the name of the ward she was born on. How had she done that so successfully? Had she taken the identity of a dead person named Matilda Ward, someone who had passed away young, and assumed it as her own? She had to have done because her ID had all checked out, it was all legit, British birth certificate, National Insurance number... all the dates added up. I pause for a moment, stunned. *Wow.* What a clever girl she really is.

Adriana glances at Mitchell, eyes wide in shock.

'So, you're not mad then, boss?' Mitchell's brow is crinkled in confusion.

'Define "mad", Mitchell!' I say. 'I have to go somewhere.'

'But I thought... the briefing boss... what shall I tell Archer?'

I grab my car keys and the phone from my desk and throw my coat on.

'Tell her I've gone Christmas shopping – I won't be long.'

FORTY-EIGHT

ERIN

Her face is a picture – shock, surprise, confusion, disbelief, *horror* – it's all right there, in front of me. I only wish I had a camera to hand so that I could capture this moment and keep it forever.

'How are you, Samantha?' I feel light-headed with adrenalin, but strangely calm. 'It's been quite a while.'

She takes a few steps back as I make my way towards her, forcing her deeper into the apartment. 'I don't suppose you were expecting to see *me*, were you, *hun?*'

'I'm sorry, who... who are you?' Her eyes are like moons, but there's no mistaking them, that dazzling emerald green... 'I think you may have the wrong person... My name isn't Samantha, I'm Tilly – my name's Tilly Ward. Why are you here?' She glances left to right, quickly, as though searching for a potential means of escape. That's when I see the hearing aid, behind her right ear. 'Are you a journalist? Because if you are, then I don't want to talk to you... The police have advised me not to. Please can you just leave? I'll have to call them if you don't.' She clutches her heaving chest with a hand as she cowers away from me.

For a brief moment, I suddenly doubt myself, wonder if

maybe I have got it wrong and that she actually really *is* Tilly Ward, the same Tilly Ward who emailed me only yesterday, looking for solidarity and words of comfort in our shared experience and victimhood. It makes me sick to think that even till the bitter end she's been messing with my head. I pull the gun out of my left pocket in one deft move, point it at her. Her hands fly up to her mouth, but it doesn't prevent the gasp escaping from it. *Ha! She wasn't expecting that!*

'Calling the police wouldn't be advisable,' I say. 'Sit down, Samantha.' I wave the gun in the direction of the table.

Her whole demeanour changes then. She sheds the scared, vulnerable victim façade like a second skin, replacing it with a different vibe altogether, bolder and more confident. Ah, there she is – *Samantha*.

'Erin,' she says my name as she stares at the gun. 'Erin Santos... My, my, don't *you* look different.'

'I could say the same to you,' I reply, glancing her up and down, my nostrils flaring in contempt. 'How the mighty have fallen.'

A small, thin smile creeps across her face.

'The blonde really suits you, hun. It lifts the green in your eyes, really makes them pop! I'm not sure about the length though.' She taps her lip with a finger. 'Why are you pointing a gun at me?' Her nose wrinkles, the way it always did when she found something distasteful. I used to find it quite endearing. Now though, it makes me feel like pulling the trigger.

'Put your hands on the table, where I can see them.' She raises an eyebrow, but does what I ask. 'That's right, Samantha.' I nod, admittedly enjoying myself now, enjoying finally being the one in the driver's seat, the one, *literally* holding all the power. Could anyone really blame me?

'I can still call you Samantha, can't I – being as though we both know it isn't your real name? In fact,' I say, 'let's start with that first, shall we? What *is* your real name?'

Seven years I have waited. Seven long, soul-destroying, life-changing years. I just want to hear her say it out loud.

'I don't know what you're talking about.' She blinks at me, nonplussed. 'I think maybe you're confused. Maybe you need to be in *hospital*.'

I grip the gun tightly, feel my finger twitch against the trigger. She watches me carefully. She's trying to anticipate my next move. I can almost hear the cogs turning inside her twisted mind.

'You're right,' she says after a moment, 'I'll admit, it's a bit of a shock to see you, Erin, especially after all this time, turning up out of the blue like this. And you haven't even taken your shoes off!' She glances down at my feet, but I don't follow suit. If I look away, she'll attempt to wrestle the gun from me. She's going to have to do better than that.

'Ah yes, I remember. How did it go? "We take our shoes *off*, and we place them *behind the door!*"' She joins in with me as we sing-say the words in unison.

'That's right!' She laughs, and it's still as infectious as ever.

'I apologise,' I say, ruefully, 'how ill-mannered of me, and I would've paid you a visit sooner, only I've spent the last six years of my life a prisoner in an asylum for the criminally insane. But don't worry, *hun*,' – I grimace – 'not a day has gone by when I haven't thought of you.'

'Hasn't it, really?' She looks touched. If I didn't know better, I'd even say it was genuine. 'Ahhh, that's so sweet of you. You always were a big old softie.'

I nod slowly. 'Wasn't I just?'

'So, what are you planning to do with that gun, hun? Surely you're not going to *shoot* me with it, are you?' A look of incredulity and mild hurt flashes across her features. Admittedly, she's still beautiful, even as she is now, with her lank, greasy curtain hair and the tatty old clothes.

'I've really missed you, Erin. I miss those times we had

together – you remember that summer we met, don't you? All the things we did, the places we went, all the champagne we drank? We were such good friends – you still *are* my friend, Erin.'

'A friend who'd kill for you, you mean? One you could coerce and manipulate and brainwash into believing a fictitious story, a complete pack of lies?'

The gun is shaking in my hand. I can feel the emotion rise up inside me, threatening to spill out. 'Why did you do it? Why did you do it to *me*, Sam?'

I hear the whine in my voice and I hate myself for it. Why do I still care? What does it even matter *why* anymore? The answer won't change anything – none of it.

I know I should just pull the trigger. It's what I've come here to do after all, to enact my revenge and get justice for myself and for Bojan Radulovic and Milo Harrison, justice that I've been denied all these years. I have to finish this neverending nightmare. But first, I just *need* to know.

'Who was Bojan Radulovic? Who was he to you? Why did you make me kill him?'

'*Make* you kill him? Oh no, no, hun.' She shakes her head, tuts. Tilly Ward is now nowhere to be seen. 'I didn't make you *do* anything. You really weren't well at the time, don't you remember? You were having some sort of psychotic break when it all happened. You thought he was abusing me. You believed his name was Ari Hussain and that we were engaged or something... You were delusional, Erin, just as you seem to be now, pointing that thing at me. Trying to scare the devil out of me.'

'Interesting choice of words, Sam. But I wasn't delusional, was I? I saw photos of you together, photos *you* showed me of the two of you —'

'Look, I was always your friend, hun.' Her voice is soft now, like I remember it. 'I tried to *help* you, Erin... I did everything I could to help you, but I'm not a doctor and...'

She's doing it again, trying to get me to doubt myself, to question everything. I can almost feel her words slipping like poison beneath my skin.

'Tell me the truth or I'll blow your head off.'

She has no idea how much I have wanted to say these words to her, how long I have waited.

She holds her hands up, sighs heavily.

'OK, OK... so I doctored the photos. It's not difficult to superimpose someone's face onto an image, Erin. You just need the tools. Anyway, he was nobody. Just some loser I had a fling with who thought he could ghost me afterwards, thought he could just use me and then discard me after promising me the sun, moon and stars.'

I stare at her, dumbfounded.

'*That* was the reason why?'

'Good enough reason if you ask me, hun. These men, they think they can just take what they want and then throw you away like garbage.'

'So why didn't you kill him *yourself*? Why did you make *me* believe that he was abusing you? Why lie and convince me that you were in danger? You knew, didn't you, that I'd have done anything to protect you? You knew because of my past trauma that I wouldn't let that happen to you.'

'Well, I wasn't actually *planning* to kill him,' she says from the side of her mouth, as though we're a pair of old colleagues, chewing the fat about a bit of office gossip. 'Not really. But once you came along, it just seemed like a fun idea. And it all sort of fell into place somehow. Serendipity, if you will.' She smiles at me, warmly, flashes me those dazzling green eyes. 'The police are searching for you, Erin. I have to admit, I'm a teensy bit jealous, all that attention you're getting on social media! Mind you, that photograph.' She pulls a face. 'I felt for you when I saw it. I wouldn't want to see *that* flashing up on screen every time they mentioned *me* in the press. You're really so much prettier in the flesh, hun, even with this new look you're going with. I have to say,' – her eyes sweep over me – 'though I don't dislike it, it's definitely giving Myra Hindley vibes.'

I really should just pull the trigger.

'The police won't find me, Sam. And by the time they find *your* body, I'll be long gone. Just like you were on the night I killed your fictitious fiancé, six years ago.

'How did you do it, Sam? That day, outside the apartments. You were there one moment, and the next... How did you vanish without a trace?'

She smiles, mock-bashfully, still desperate to keep the control she craves by denying me the truth.

'I can't give away trade secrets, sweetie, even to my bestie. Anyway, you already know the answer, Erin – it was in much the same way you're about to do yourself. It's not that hard, is it, to disappear, to change your identity, become someone else? Sometimes, if you're super smart, you can be many different people at once, though you need to be organised for that, have a very methodical approach, as admittedly, it can get a little confusing at times. Anyway, killing *me* won't exonerate *you*. Then no one will know the truth, will they, and you'll be a murderer.'

'I'm already one of those, thanks to you.'

She sighs. 'Don't be like that, hun. No one *forced* you to stab the stupid bastard in the heart, did they? You did that of your own free will.'

'The free will you manipulated and sabotaged, you mean, like some kind of Svengali cult leader?'

She laughs. 'Oh, but you give me too much credit, Erin. I suppose I should really be flattered. But you're not so different to me underneath it all. You've a killer instinct in you, Erin Santos. That night you saw your mother killed by your stepdad, you couldn't find it then, could you, that instinct that's buried within you, within us all? I just helped you to dig deep. And you felt better for it, didn't you? Once you'd plunged that knife into him and stopped his heart from beating, you felt *relief* for what you didn't do all those years ago, I *know* you did.'

I swallow dryly. I can't let her into my head. She mustn't get inside my head!

'You don't know anything about me anymore.' I point the gun at her as I stand, finger poised on the trigger. 'Tell me your real name.'

But then, would you believe, the doorbell rings.

FORTY-NINE

'Aren't you going to answer that?' Her eyes move in the direction of the door. 'It's probably the police.'

'Stay where you are,' I growl at her as I make my way over to the window, the gun still trained on her. 'You're right, Samantha, I *am* a killer. I'm exactly what you made me, and I *will* pull this trigger if you move.' I peer through the curtain.

Oh crap. It's Dan. Dan Riley is here. Again. *Why has he come back?*

'Hello! Tilly...?' I hear him call through the letter box. 'Are you there?'

I drop the curtain.

'You planted my hair at a crime scene, didn't you?' She shrugs, stares at me blankly. '*Didn't you?*' I bring my other hand up to the gun.

'OK! So I kept a bit of your DNA, in here.' She pulls a silver locket from around her neck, from underneath her sloppy old T-shirt. 'I like carrying a part of you around with me, Erin. We're BFFs, kindred spirits, we're *soul sisters...*'

I shudder. 'You were going to pin that crime on me, weren't

you?' I glance behind me towards the door. Is it just Dan out there, or are there more police with him?

Just pull the damn trigger, Erin, do it now!

'Was that why you killed Milo Harrison? Just so that you could frame me and have me sent back to the nuthouse? Did you take another man's life just to make sure I stayed silent? *Why*, Samantha? Why would you want to do that to me, to destroy my life, what did I ever do to you? *Just tell me why?*'

'Tilly!' Dan calls through the letter box. 'Is everything OK in there? I can hear voices. Can you open the door, please? I'm concerned. Can you hear me, Tilly? It's DCI Dan Riley...'

I could try and style this out. Will Dan recognise me? We've only ever spoken on the phone, and I look so different now to that dreadful photograph of me that's currently circulating. Even Samantha says so. And I have new ID on me, Alexandra Fisher's ID. I'll show him that if he asks.

'If you do or say anything, I'll put a bullet through you.' I look directly at her. 'I'll shoot you dead right in front of him, in a second, boom, over, bang, bang, you're dead! You get the picture I'm painting here, Sam?'

She gives a micro nod of her head.

I direct her with the gun. 'Answer the door.'

She walks towards it, effortlessly slipping back into being Tilly again, like a chameleon changing colour. I watch as she shrinks into herself somehow, makes herself appear smaller. Her posture changes, sags a touch, even her gait is different. It's quite incredible – and chilling – to witness such a transformation up close.

'I'm so sorry, Dan.' Her voice is a flat apology as he follows her into the kitchen, where I'm sitting, my fingers still on the gun in my left pocket. 'We were just having a little chat in the kitchen, me and the lady here, from the Women in Prison support group.'

Quick thinking, Sam. I glance at her. *Nice job*. But then I wouldn't have expected anything less, I suppose. She's good at what she does – the best.

'Hello there.' I stand, take my hand out of my pocket, offer it to him. 'Nice to meet you – Alexandra, Alex Fisher.' I do my best to disguise the Yorkshire lilt in my voice by lengthening my ordinarily shorter vowels. Dan'll surely recognise it if I don't put on a fake accent. 'Tilly and I were just discussing what might happen if she were to be handed down a custodial sentence when it comes to her trial, or if there even is a trial. There's a lot of information, a lot to take in...' I throw him a sage, well-meaning glance as I give him my best attempt at 'southern posh'. They say what's meant for you will not go by you, and so the fact that I am finally meeting Dan in the flesh like this, albeit unplanned, or even as myself, makes me think that it was meant to be. His hand feels warm as I shake it, and try as I do not to, I can't help meeting his eyes with my own.

He's even more handsome in the flesh than he is in the photograph I saw in that newspaper article. Handsome yet also approachable. What you might call husband-handsome. I would've liked to have married a man much like him, I think. He radiates strength and warmth and integrity somehow. *And I bet he's good in bed.* I can only hope he doesn't recognise me. I *definitely* don't want to have to kill Dan as well. Besides, I only have two bullets loaded in the gun, so this could be a problem. *Why did he have to come back?*

I see no trace of alarm in his face as he smiles at me though. He doesn't appear to have recognised me. I think I may have got away with it.

'Women in Prison, you say?'

'Yes,' I swallow. 'What with Tilly being a vulnerable adult...' I glance over at her, sitting down at the table. I briefly meet her eyes, let her know I'm still watching her. 'It's important to reassure her that there's support here for her, whatever may have happened, *whatever she may or may not have done.*'

'That's very admirable, um... Alexandra, was it?'

'Alex,' I smile, avoid his eyes as I will him to leave. *Can't there be an emergency for him to attend somewhere?* 'Tilly told me that you were here earlier?' The words come out of my mouth before I can think to stop them.

'Oh, did she?' Is that suspicion I detect? No. I'm being paranoid. Why did I even say it? He definitely hasn't recognised me. He would have arrested me on the spot by now, wouldn't he? *Oh please, Dan, please don't recognise me.*

'I'm sorry for interrupting you.' He nods at Tilly. 'Are you OK, Tilly?'

She nods feebly. 'Yes, Dan, I'm fine, thank you. Did you forget something?'

He glances over at me. Is it just me, or does he keep looking over in my direction?

'No... er, yes, actually, there was something. The sketch you drew, the one of Samantha Valentine, of Erin Santos.' I get a shiver as he says my name. 'I was hoping you might be able to do another – one with even more detail this time.'

Why would he be asking her to do that? They already have a photograph of me circulating, *that* photo. And did he say, *Tilly's* sketch? So the sketch she had drawn, the one that looked like me, the one *she had drawn* to look like me, had been released to the media by the police. I almost feel sorry for Dan and his team. She's been playing them all like fiddles. And the whole hearing aid ploy, complete bullshit, of course, but a cunning move nonetheless. Samantha knew about Dan Riley's son's diagnosis because he'd opened up about it briefly in that article. And true to form, she had used it to her advantage, as a means to manipulate. Dead people, deaf people? No one was off limits.

'We'll provide you with the supplies, the paper and pencils or charcoal or whatever you prefer... the sketch really does seem to have sparked the imagination of the public. We think it may help if we release another one.'

'If you think so, Dan, then of course.' She says it so sweetly that I want to throw up again, despite there being nothing left in my hollow stomach.

There's a pause.

'I was hoping you might come to the station with me *now*, so we can get it done and out of the way.'

'Oh, well, um...' She glances up at me. 'Of course, yes, I...' She makes to stand.

'I'm sorry, er, Dan, did you say?'

'Yes, Dan. Detective Chief Inspector Dan Riley.'

He really is rather cute.

'I certainly don't want to step on the police's toes,' – I clear my throat – 'only I've just driven here all the way from Kent. I'm based in East Sutton Park, you see – the women's open prison.' It's a decent name drop and I'm glad I thought of it. It sounds authentic. 'If I could just have half an hour with Sa— with *Tilly*.' I take a breath. 'I can bring her over to the station myself afterwards, if that suits?'

'Great,' he says, looking over at her. 'That OK for you, Tilly?'

She nods, shrugs. 'Of course.'

'Thanks, Alex.' Dan turns to me. 'Um, I hope you're not offended by my asking, but do you have any ID on you, a business card or something?'

'Yes, no problem ... hang on... I open my handbag, flash him my fake driver's licence. 'I'm afraid I don't have any cards on me, but you're welcome to check with the admin team at East Sutton.'

'Thanks. OK. Right, well, I'll see you down at the station shortly then.'

'I'll see you out, Dan.' Tilly suddenly stands, forcing me to do the same.

'No bother, Tilly.' I glare at her. 'I'll see Detective Riley out.'

Snide bitch really was going to try to pull a fast one.

'Well, it was nice to meet you, Dan. It really was.'

He trains his eyes on me as we shake hands again. For some reason I don't feel like letting go.

'Yes, you too, Alex. And thanks for offering to go out of your way to drive Tilly back to the station. You don't have to do that.'

'It's nothing.' I wave a hand dismissively. 'It's on the way anyway.'

He turns to leave, then stops. 'That perfume you're wearing...'

I'd forgotten about that. *Crap*. I think I'd overdone it a bit in the car earlier with the Baccarat Rouge. 'It smells familiar...'

'Really? Maybe your wife wears it?' I make sure to glance down at his wedding ring.

'No... I don't think so. Anyway,' – he smiles jovially – 'it's nice, I like it.'

'Oh, thanks,' I say, admittedly a little pleased. 'It's only the cheap stuff.'

FIFTY
DAN

The plan was to race back over to Tilly's apartment with a cock-and-bull story of my own, get her to come down to the station with me of her own volition, on the pretext of asking for her help. If she gets any inkling that I'm on to her, she may try to abscond, and there's every chance she could be successful too, if past behaviour is a good indicator. And I cannot let that happen. Once she's safe down at the station, we can then re-interview her, present her with this new information that's come to light, and ideally get a confession from her.

What I wasn't expecting to see when I arrived at the apartment for the second time that day was that Tilly had company. And what I wasn't expecting, even *more* than that, was for that company to be Erin Santos. I suppose in terms of a professionally successful outcome, this was the double whammy, only I was unprepared, and unsure, at first.

I hadn't recognised Erin instantly. She looks very different now to what she did six years ago. Her hair is much shorter and bright blonde and she was wearing make-up and smart clothes. Her cover about being a representative from Women in Prison was highly plausible, as was the ID she briefly showed me.

Only, she'd offered me her *left* hand when I'd gone to shake it, and if that wasn't enough to arouse my suspicions, those arresting green eyes – not unlike Tilly's, or Samantha's, or Julie's – were unmistakable as they briefly met with mine. Still, I wasn't a hundred per cent sure it was her though.

I stood on the doorstep as 'Alex' closed the door behind me, leaving me standing there with little more than a very bad feeling and a waft of her perfume. That's what did it. *It was that same perfume...*

Immediately, I realise that I shouldn't have left them alone together. During our last phone conversation, Erin had told me she would *kill* Samantha Valentine if she saw her again, and I believed her. Perhaps I would kill her too if I were her. As it was, I felt sick enough already knowing that Julie Edwards had pulled the wool over my eyes – over everyone's, it appears. But moreover, that one of the ways she garnered my sympathy was through her supposed 'condition'. She knew that my son was deaf. We'd even communicated in sign language together. She was good at it too. I feel embarrassed, angry with myself, violated, I suppose, that I'd been taken in and allowed my personal feelings, my emotions, to get in the way of my professional judgement. But I'll deal with that later. Right now, I need to call for back-up and somehow get back inside that apartment. Erin could be armed. And I don't want her to do anything stupid, even though that's how *I* feel right now – *stupid*.

I ring the buzzer of Flat 68, next door.

A woman in a dressing gown with a towel wrapped round her hair answers. She looks me up and down.

'Yes?'

I flash her my badge and an apologetic smile as she steps back in surprise. 'I'm sorry, but I need access to your apartment. Do you have a balcony?'

I'm not the greatest fan of heights, so I take an extra breath as I climb from next door's balcony onto Tilly's, and don't look down. I press my back up against the glass doors. The curtains are almost fully drawn, but thankfully not quite, and I'm able to look inside with a more or less clear view of the small kitchen/dining area. Tilly's seated at the table, and Erin has her back to me. Only, the way that she's standing, her stance, concerns me. If I didn't know better – and at this point, I don't – I'd say that she was pointing a gun at her, though I can't see clearly from here. I should call for back-up right now. We could have a potential Code Zero on our hands.

I pull my phone from my pocket, make to place the call, but at the last second, I think better of it. A terrible thought flashes into my head then. *If Erin Santos is going to shoot Julie Edwards, then let her.* Frankly, the world would be a better, safer, kinder place without her in it, and admittedly, I feel angry that she's duped me. But it's not my job to play judge and jury, no matter what she's done or who to. My job is to make sure no one gets hurt and bring any culprits to justice, just like what should've happened seven years ago. It comes to me again then, something that Ken Edwards had said on the phone. He said that his brother's name was Ray and that he'd taken his own life. Didn't Erin tell me that Ray was also her stepdad's name? Ray Denis, the man who killed her mother, and subsequently himself, while he was in prison serving time for it? Ken said he sometimes changed his name. It's got to be the same person. *Oh sweet Jesus, no...*

I pull my phone from my pocket again, but then Erin suddenly spins round, like she senses there's someone behind her, watching her. I pull back against the wall, hold my breath for a moment, too scared to move in case she comes to investigate.

'That was a pretty darn good performance, Erin.' Tilly is speaking, I can hear her through the glass. I strain to listen. 'I'm quite impressed. You've come on in leaps and bounds, hun, you really have! If I was to give you one piece of advice though, going forward, I'd say to work on your accent. You still sound like a thick Northerner.'

'Well, I learned from the master, didn't I? And *you* still sound like a liar.'

'Anyway, accents aside, I think he recognised you.'

I edge towards the window, peer through a tiny crack.

Tilly is smirking. 'Dan Riley *recognised* you, Erin. And now there'll be an army of them knocking down the door at any moment, ready to cuff you and take you back to Larksmere. Tatty-bye, my old friend! It was nice seeing you again.'

'Tell me your name, Samantha. I just want to hear you say it before I paint the walls with your brains.'

Yep, she's got a gun! I see it then as she turns slightly to the right, the black metal object in her hand is unmistakable.

'*Don't do it, Erin,*' I whisper the words into the cold air like smoke, my fingers shaking as I reach for my phone – *and then it slips through them,* smashes as it hits the concrete below me. My heart immediately follows suit. Suddenly, Erin is at the window. She's heard it. *They've seen me.*

I say a silent prayer as she slides the double doors open.

'*Dan?*' Her eyes are wide open in shock. 'Detective Riley? What are you doing *out here?*' Tilly's right though, she really needs to work on her London accent.

I know exactly how I'm going to play this out – but it's not going to be easy, and it will need an unspoken understanding between myself and Erin to pull it off, a silent understanding that I can only hope we have if I've a snowball's chance in hell of getting everyone out of this situation alive and unharmed.

'Journalists,' I say, wiping my wet hands down my coat as I step inside. 'I saw one of them on the balcony up here just now, sniffing around, bloody parasites.'

'Oh!' She sticks her head out of the double doors, looks left and right.

'I think they may have gone now – when they saw me,' I add.

I look at Erin, try to communicate my thoughts to her through my eyes. She holds my gaze for a few seconds. Is the small smile she gives me one of understanding? I can't be entirely sure. I'm pretty convinced the gun is in her left pocket though, and I need to make sure it stays there.

'Good job you were here to stop them, Detective Riley. Those rodents get everywhere.'

'Indeed.'

The biggest problem I now face is how do I alert the team of my situation and call for back-up? My phone is currently in bits on the concrete floor of the balcony. If this all goes south, then Archer's going to have my head on the chopping block. If I'm not in the morgue already by then.

Tilly suddenly leaps up from her seat as I enter the room.

'She's got a gun, Dan!' She signs the words to me silently, and again I wonder just how she has become so proficient in sign linguistics, being as though she isn't deaf, or even hard of hearing, as it turns out. Had she studied it and become more or less proficient in one weekend, like she did the piano? *Such wasted talents.*

'It's OK, Tilly,' I say aloud. 'I know she has.'

Erin turns then, and pulls the weapon from her pocket, but she doesn't point it at me.

'She thinks *I'm* Samantha Valentine.' I hear faux incredulity in Tilly's voice. To the untrained ear, admittedly, it would sound convincing. 'She thinks that I've set her up. That I'm the woman who tricked her into killing that man all those years ago... she blames me for what happened to her. She's completely mad, Dan.' She grips hold of my arm, tries to use me as a human shield as she shuffles behind me.

'I know she is, Tilly. Just stay calm, OK. My colleagues are on the way.'

I widen my eyes at Erin, like you do when you're trying to tell someone not to say something out loud without actually saying it out loud yourself. I can only hope she's caught on. And that she's on my side.

'Just tell me your name,' Erin says. 'That's all I really want, to hear you say your real name.'

'But you *know* my real name, Samantha,' Tilly says. 'You know who I am. We were friends, remember? Please, Sam, don't do this. Dan here can help you, we can both help you, can't we, Dan?'

'I hope you're not still buying into this bullshit, Dan.' Erin turns her head to me. 'She's been playing you too of course. The whole hard-of-hearing act...' She walks towards us then, and Tilly grips my arm so tightly I can feel her fingernails digging into my skin through my thick coat.

'Take it off,' she says, 'the bogus hearing aid, *take it off*!' Tilly does as she says without moving her eyes away from the gun. Erin whips it from her grasp, holds it up in her right hand. 'Look!' she says. 'It doesn't even work! It's just a piece of old plastic, a decoy, she probably bought it off eBay.' She throws it to the floor, stamps on it. I hear the crushing sound as it breaks beneath her foot.

'It's a fake, just like everything else about her.' Erin trains her eyes over to me again. 'None of this would be happening if it wasn't for the police's ineptitude all those years ago. If they'd only listened to me then, if they'd just believed me, then maybe Milo Harrison would be alive now, and I would be at home, with my husband and kids, living the life I should've had if I'd never met this sick, twisted psychopath here.' She waggles the gun at her. 'Do you know, Dan, she told me that it was because Milo Harrison ghosted her that she signed that poor man's death warrant. She had a fling with him, and he didn't want to know her afterwards... but that ego of hers, that gigantic, narcissistic ego, simply couldn't allow him to get away with such a heinous crime... and so she decided no less than death would be his punishment. It was the same story with Bojan Radulovic. She was fixated upon him too, weren't you?' She thrusts the gun forwards in Tilly's direction. 'You couldn't accept his rejection, so you stalked him, harassed him, you became obsessed with him and wanted him to pay with his life. Only you thought it would be much more 'fun' – that was the word she used, Dan,' – Erin glances quickly at me – "fun' to have me kill him for her. To play a sick, elaborate game of control built on wicked lies.'

'Put the gun down, Erin,' I say gently. 'This isn't the way to have your voice heard. This will only ensure that things are even worse for you.'

'Even worse?' She laughs then, hard. 'How could things *be* any worse, Dan? Anyway,' – she catches her breath – 'soon it won't matter.'

'What do you mean by that, Erin?'

'There's two bullets in this gun. You *know* what I mean, Dan.'

I think I do. Erin's plan is to kill Samantha Valentine, and then to kill herself. Only, I can't let her do either of those things. I want her to get the justice she finally deserves. I want her to see Tilly Ward get what's rightfully coming to her. A sentence behind bars, or most likely, behind the walls of Larksmere Hospital.

'If you shoot her, Erin, then you'll go back to prison, to that hospital. And I *know* you don't want that. I don't want that for you either, Erin. Killing her makes you exactly what she wants you to be, a murderer, just like her.'

'But I already *am* a murderer,' she says, '*because* of her.' The sound of the gun as she cocks it causes me to take a step forwards. 'You were never a cold-blooded murderer. I know what she did, Erin.'

I squeeze Tilly's arm behind me, surreptitiously, try to reassure her, convince her that I'm simply going along with it for Erin's sake, *for safety's sake.*

'I know what she's done to you... how she befriended you, how she got inside your head and exploited your trauma, your insecurities, your loneliness, *your pain*. She took advantage of you. But it's not too late, Erin. You have the rest of your life, as a free woman, to rebuild, to put this all behind you.'

The gun is vibrating in her hand; it's shaking so much that I'm concerned it'll go off. If I can get the timing right, if I can edge a little closer to her, then I may just be able to snatch it from her fragile grip. But I can feel Tilly moving from behind me now, like she's about to make a break for it and...

'"Vengeance is mine, I will repay," says the Lord! Romans 12:19!' Erin's voice is a loud and slightly manic projection, as she turns and points the gun at Tilly. 'And today, *I* am the Lord.'

Then she pulls the trigger.

FIFTY-ONE

The sound of the firearm discharging is, ironically, deafening. Instinctively, I place my hands over my ears, crouch down on the floor for cover. Tilly Ward is down. She's been hit. But she's still alive. I hear her moaning, where she's fallen, next to the sofa. I turn myself towards her, I can smell the blood and sulphur in the air.

'Is she alive?'

Erin is standing in the same position as she was, pointing the gun at Tilly's body on the floor. Her face looks pale with fear now though, like she can't quite believe what she's done. *This is a disaster.*

'Please, Erin.' I look up at her, implore her, 'Not like this.' I don't believe that she plans to kill me, or even harm me in any way. It's not me she's after. It never was. But now I seem to have got in the way. 'Put the gun down. Just... just put the gun down and we can talk, Erin.'

'It's too late for talking now, Dan,' she says. 'Seven years too late. Anyway, there's nothing more to be said. It's over.'

Tilly is groaning underneath me. The blood is starting to

disperse in a river along the cheap laminate flooring. I think she's slipping in and out of consciousness.

'Help me, Dan. She's crazy... she tried to kill me... I'm d... *dying...*'

'Goddamn it.' Erin steps forwards to look at her. '*Did I miss?*'

'Stay back, Erin.' I hold my hand up. 'Don't come any closer.'

She sighs heavily, goes to the table and takes a seat. She's still holding the weapon.

I stay still. No sudden moves.

'I was always a terrible aim,' she says miserably. 'Though maybe with a bit of luck, she'll bleed to death.'

I check Tilly's pulse. It's slowing down, but it's there. She's alive. *The devil really does look after its own.*

'We need to call an ambulance, Erin.'

'Who *is* she, Dan? Who *is* she really?' She drops the gun onto the table then and buries her head into her hands. I sit up against the sofa, bring my knees up to my chest. Tilly's blood is all over my shirt and trousers, I can feel it, wet against my skin as it soaks through the fabric, turning it crimson. I see the coat then, a burgundy red coat, hanging up behind the front door. It looks just like the coat the redhead was wearing at the press conference. The one posing as a journalist who was seen coming out of Tilly's apartment. *My God.* It was her! She had been there, right in front of me, asking me questions! Taunting me.

'Her name is Julie Edwards.'

Erin's hands slide from her face. '*Julie... who?*'

'Edwards,' I repeat. 'Julie Edwards.'

'Noooo!' she says, her brow wrinkling. 'That sounds like a boring name, very... average.' She snorts. 'Huh, no wonder she preferred Samantha Valentine. Julie Edwards,' she repeats, in a childish, silly high-pitched voice. 'It makes her sound like she wears a tabard and works in Greggs.'

'Samantha Valentine was the name of an old school friend of hers, from Perth, in Australia,' I tell her. 'Someone she knew as a child. Samantha hanged herself, when she was eleven years old, thirty years ago. No one knew why. I spoke to her mother on the phone. She told me that Samantha was a loving, happy little girl until she met Julie Edwards. Within a few months of them becoming friends, Samantha was dead. I suspect that's why she used the name. In some kind of homage to her friend, her first victim maybe?'

Erin's eyes are transfixed upon my own.

'Nothing was proven, but it seems that there was suspicion, even back then, of coercive control, psychopathy even...'

'Good God,' she says. 'Eleven years old.' Her whole body visibly sags.

I can see that Tilly's been hit in the left leg. Instinctively, I place my hand on the wound, try to stem the blood that's flowing from it.

'Her father was Ray Denis, Erin. The man who killed your mother.'

It's a dangerous call, whether to impart this piece of information to her or not, though deep down I'm certain it's true. It could cause her to want to finish the job off properly, but I make that call anyway. 'That little girl you told me you weren't sure if you remembered, the one from your childhood, when you were just five or six years old, the one who came to stay over at your house, with you and your mum and Ray, once or twice...'

Now she looks stunned, confused. She blinks at me, her brow fixed in disbelief.

'Ray Denis's *daughter*?'

I nod, the adrenalin rushing through me is restricting my larynx, making it harder for me to talk, to breathe.

'I don't believe it.' Erin is shaking her head adamantly.

'Every damn word that comes out of that maniac's mouth is a lie.'

'It's not a lie, Erin.' I meet her eyes with my own. 'I'm not lying to you, I promise.'

She exhales in quick succession. 'So, so... it *was* all personal then? This was to do with *my* mother? *Her* father?'

I can feel Tilly squirming underneath me as I apply more pressure on the wound. She's trying to say something.

'She... she took my... job.' Her voice is a low rasp as she struggles to expel the words from her discolouring lips. 'She... she took my father, and then she took my job...'

'Her *job?*' Erin scoffs. 'The job at Austin Marz, you mean, the receptionist job? Jesus, how much of a psychopath are you, *Julie?* A *job!*'

'If my dad had never met your whore of a mother...' Tilly's trying to sit up now, but I won't let her. I place a firm hand on her shoulder.

'Just stay where you are,' I say, 'help's on the way.'

'Your mother, that... bitch... she ruined his life, ruined mine. If he hadn't gone to prison...' – she coughs, her breathing sounds laboured – '... he'd never have killed himself and my mother would never have become an alcoholic... And *I'd* never have spent my childhood in and out of care homes... I was abused, thrown away like trash.'

Erin starts clapping her hands together in a slow round of applause.

'Bravo, Samantha, sorry I mean, *Julie*... a consummate professional to the end! You've got to admit,'– she turns to me, dips her head as though appraising a particularly good performance – 'she's pretty great, isn't she? So very *convincing.*'

I can hear the unmistakable sound of sirens screaming in the distance and only hope, pray, they're heading this way. Erin hears them too, because she stands. Picks up the gun.

'Listen, Erin. I really don't want you to do anything stupid.'

Which sounds stupid itself, given the immediate circumstances we find ourselves in. 'I don't want you to harm anyone else, and above all, I *really* don't want you to harm yourself. Promise me you won't do that, Erin.'

Her lovely green eyes are heavy with sadness as they rest upon me, like she's touched that anyone even cares.

'Despite everything, Dan, in spite of the circumstances of how we have come to meet, I'm so very glad that we did, and that we have.' She smiles back at me, genuinely. 'You're even nicer in the flesh than I'd expected.'

'Don't let Malcolm hear you say that,' I reply, with a gentle smile of my own. 'Look, it doesn't have to be like this, Erin. I can help you sort through all of this mess. I'll tell everyone the truth, I'll make them understand. Just put the gun away and...'

Tilly is attempting to drag herself along the floor, towards the door. I reach out, try to pull her back by her legs. If she keeps moving, then at this rate, she'll bleed out, if Erin doesn't finish her off first.

'Let me get something to stem the flow. Stay where you are, Dan. I'm going to go to the bathroom to get a towel. Please,' she says, 'don't try anything stupid yourself, just sit here until I come back, OK, don't move.'

I look at the gun, still in her hand and nod. Maybe she doesn't want her dead after all.

'OK, Erin.'

The second she leaves the room, I frantically scan the apartment for a phone. The sirens are getting louder now, closer. They're almost here, literally less than a minute away. My trained ear tells me so.

'Just hang on in there,' I say to Julie as she continues to groan and worm away from me, the blood that's pumping from her wound leaving a heavy burgundy paint trail on the laminate floor beneath her.

'Hello! Hello! Is everything OK in there?' Suddenly, I hear

an unfamiliar voice, it's coming from behind the front door. 'It's Yinka, your neighbour from Number 68... the police are on their way. Is everyone OK? *What's going on?*'

Seconds later, I hear another voice, one I have no trouble instantly recognising.

She walks through into the apartment, her mouth falling open with each step she takes.

'*What the*... Oh. My. God!'

Davis.

She surveys the scene through wide eyes, her hand over her mouth.

'Boss! What the hell's happened?' She looks down at Julie Edwards, bleeding out on the floor. 'Oh my God, Archer's going to flip out.'

Within seconds, the room is filling up with emergency services, uniformed police and paramedics.

'Is she alive?' Davis asks.

'Just about,' I say, as the paramedics get to work on her. 'How did you know I was here?'

She pulls her chin into her neck, gives me one of her looks. As if I had to ask.

'Mitchell and Adriana told me about the photo, about Ken Edwards and...'

'Have they got her?' I say. 'She's in the bathroom – and she's armed, Davis.'

'Got who, boss?' She shakes her head, confused.

My stomach lurches. *Erin.*

'Oh no...' I run to the bathroom, but the door's open and it's empty.

I sprint to the front door. There's at least a handful of police officers standing outside now, and some inquisitive onlookers have started to gather. I look left and right. It's only been a few seconds, less than a minute – she can't have gone far. I call out to a couple of the young officers.

'Suspect on foot,' I say as they jump to attention. 'Check the stairs.'

'Yes, sir.'

I lean over the balcony, look down and around. Nothing.

I catch sight of the neighbour then, the woman from Number 68. She's still in her dressing gown, with a towel wrapped round her head, and she's talking, animated, to one of the female officers, an expression of shocked bewilderment on her face.

She shrieks in alarm as I seize her by the arm.

'The woman!' I say. 'The one with the blonde hair and red lipstick. She had to have gone past you, while you were knocking on the door, did you see her? Where did she go?'

She looks at me in horror, backs away from me as I gently try to shake it out of her.

'Woman? *What woman?*'

FIFTY-TWO

DAN

Three weeks later

We sit in the waiting room at the hospital, Fiona and I.

I'm not a fan of waiting rooms. They're transient places. Nothing ever happens in them except for... waiting. It's our Jude's first of what I know will be many assessments today, for what we hope will eventually become surgery to fit him with a cochlear implant. And then maybe he will be able to hear when his mother gets cross with him, like she is with me right now.

'Why do you *always* take such stupid risks, Dan? If you knew Tilly Ward was Samantha Valentine—' We were still talking about the case. *Everyone* is still talking about the case. It's dominated the news, just as I'd expected it to. Erin Santos is more famous than the Kardashians right now. If she'd played it differently, perhaps she could've made herself a very rich woman. Only I don't think it was that kind of compensation she was after.

I'm sure Erin will be pleased to know that thanks to her image captured on CCTV in a charity shop in King's Cross, where she had undergone a makeover, it has largely replaced the one from six years ago. She'd *really* hated that photo.

I suppose I could sympathise. I'm still living down my own photo from that article, almost a month on.

'You mean Julie Edwards,' I correct her.

'You know what I mean, Dan. If you knew that, then why did you go alone, back to her apartment? You also knew that Erin Santos was on the run, *and* out for revenge.'

'Yes, but I had no idea she was going to be there at that time – or that she was armed.'

'You knew she wanted to kill her. And frankly, I'd like to have killed her myself.'

I touch her knee with my hand. 'Using your own son, *our* son, as a means to pull at your heartstrings. You've already got enough of those to pull as it is, a whole bloody orchestra of the things!' I squeeze it. 'Every parent is protective of their children, Dan, but when your child is born with a... difference, it's another level. I just want to wrap him up in cotton wool and never let anything or anyone harm him.'

'I know, Fi,' I say. 'So do I.'

I'd been dreading it, having to face Archer during the debrief. Julie Edwards is still in hospital, recovering well from her injuries. The physical ones, anyway. Once the doctors see fit, she'll be moved to a psychiatric ward where she'll be assessed, all while under arrest of course. Apparently, she has all the nurses on the ward eating out of her hand already. I wish I could say that I'm surprised.

It gives me no pleasure to say that Julie Edwards is a dangerous psychopath. Or that there's a room at Larksmere Hospital waiting for her. I would've loved to have seen Dr Wainwright's face when he no doubt heard it all on the news. Davis had subsequently spoken to him on the phone, but he was adamant that his original diagnosis of Erin still stood – that she was, is, two different people. Sometimes, the ego simply won't allow people to accept the facts, or that they could be wrong. What is truth if it's not just a belief system anyway?

Erin.

Somehow, that day, she had managed to walk right out of Tilly's apartment, past an entire group of emergency workers, neighbours and onlookers, armed with a gun, without *anyone* seeing her. I'm not kidding. It was as if she'd turned into a *ghost*. Just like Samantha Valentine.

We recovered the gun a couple of days later. She'd thrown it into the Thames. I was pleased to see that there was still a single bullet left in the chamber. One of *two*.

'I don't really want to *have* to talk to you, Riley,' Archer had said as I'd sat up straight before her, hands in my lap. 'Just tell me the facts. Is Erin Santos still missing?'

She was.

'And you have no idea where she may have gone. Or who she might be with? If she's using a new identity?'

'No,' I lied. On all counts.

'I don't quite yet know how to get you out of this one, Riley.' She'd sighed, without looking up at me. She was too busy rearranging her pens.

'I do, ma'am.' I said, placing the bottle of Baccarat Rouge on her desk.

I'd remembered the name, you see, the name on the driver's licence, *Alexandra Fisher*. Erin had flashed it before me in a split second, but still, it had somehow gone in. I suspect that she's using that name now, and that she and Malcolm are in a different country somewhere. Together. Maybe that one-night stand they had might've produced a pregnancy, who knows – it happened to me and Fiona with our Pip after all!

Honestly though, it's what I hope for her: *redemption*.

'He just disappeared,' Molly said miserably, when I had

called her to find out where Malcolm was. I'd been trying to contact him after the incident, but with no reply, I had gone to Molly for answers instead.

'I've been knocking and calling for the last couple of days,' she said, the anxiety heavy in her voice. 'In the end, I let myself into his apartment. It looks as if he's taken some possessions with him, some clothes and his aftershave he wears...' She sounded bereft, and I felt sorry for her. Unrequited love is the worst kind. 'Maybe he's gone away, on holiday somewhere!' she said, hopeful. 'You don't think he's with *her*, do you... with *Erin?*'

'I'm sure he'll be back soon, Molly,' I said.

Some lies really are for the best.

A LETTER FROM ANNA-LOU

My dearest reader,

I'm truly honoured and grateful that you chose *She Made Me Do It* to be on your reading list, thank you so much! I have enjoyed writing this book immensely, and all the time you continue to enjoy reading about DCI Dan Riley and the complex psychological cases he helps solve, then I'll keep writing them.

If you'd like to keep up to date with all my latest and former releases, please sign up at the following link. Just so you know, we'll never share your email address with anyone and you can unsubscribe at any time.

www.bookouture.com/anna-lou-weatherley

I really hope you enjoyed *She Made Me Do It* as much as I loved writing it. If you did, it would be truly wonderful if you could spare the time to leave a review. I absolutely love hearing what you think about all my titles and it really helps other readers to discover my books for the first time.

I am always so touched by the messages I receive and I will always do my best to respond personally – I love hearing from you.

You can get in touch with me on social media or through my website, anytime.

With much love,

Anna-Lou

        www.annalouweatherley.com

- instagram.com/annalouwrites
- facebook.com/annalouweatherleyauthor
- x.com/annaloulondon

ACKNOWLEDGEMENTS

Thank you to all my incredible publishing team at the inimitable powerhouse that is Bookouture, and especially to my editor, Harriet Wade, who has been such a joy to work with on this – thank you for all your invaluable help and support, I'm so grateful and I've loved it.

To my truly wonderful agent, Darley Anderson – the best in the business – and special thanks, notably to the simply brilliant, Rebeka Finch! I really can't thank you enough for all you do and have done for me and for your faith, advice and support. I'm so very proud to be part of the DA family.

A very special thanks to fellow author and all-round lovely person, Casey Kelleher, and to all the fabulous ladies at The Plot Twist book club – it was such a joy to meet you all in person. I hope you'll continue to enjoy my books and enjoy Dan! Also, thanks to Emma Robinson.

My dearest friends, Qefs, Kelly, and Sue, and John and Sam too. My PW crew, Krasi, Marike, Emma, Greta, Stacey, and Tom. I want to thank my boys, Lz and Phil-Joe, Hazza and Amz – respect for teaching me how to concentrate among the chaos. Thanks also to Brigit and Bob, Amanda and Daisy, and Jan and Lawrie. Thanks also to my sister, Lisa. Mummy, once again, I have to credit you with all the love and support and encouragement that you give so unconditionally, no matter what. You're my everything! Also, to my incredible new friend, Marie and the G-Man! And lastly, but by no means least, to all the

Penneys – SP, my Stevie Wonder. Thank you for everything. It's 'astonishing' what you can do if you're prepared to put the effort in. One four three. X

PUBLISHING TEAM

Turning a manuscript into a book requires the efforts of many people. The publishing team at Bookouture would like to acknowledge everyone who contributed to this publication.

Commercial
Lauren Morrissette
Hannah Richmond
Imogen Allport

Contracts
Peta Nightingale

Data and analysis
Mark Alder
Mohamed Bussuri

Editorial
Harriet Wade
Hannah Wilson

Copyeditor
Jon Appleton

Proofreader
Lynne Walker

Marketing
Alex Crow
Melanie Price
Occy Carr
Cíara Rosney
Martyna Młynarska

Operations and distribution
Marina Valles
Joe Morris

Production
Hannah Snetsinger
Mandy Kullar
Nadia Michael
Charlotte Hegley

Publicity
Kim Nash
Noelle Holten
Jess Readett
Sarah Hardy

RAISING READERS
Books Build Bright Futures

Dear Reader,

We'd love your attention for one more page to tell you about the crisis in children's reading, and what we can all do.

Studies have shown that reading for fun is the **single biggest predictor of a child's future life chances** – more than family circumstance, parents' educational background or income. It improves academic results, mental health, wealth, communication skills, ambition and happiness.

The number of children reading for fun is in rapid decline. Young people have a lot of competition for their time, and a worryingly high number do not have a single book at home.

Hachette works extensively with schools, libraries and literacy charities, but here are some ways we can all raise more readers:

- Reading to children for just 10 minutes a day makes a difference
- Don't give up if children aren't regular readers – there will be books for them!

- Visit bookshops and libraries to get recommendations
- Encourage them to listen to audiobooks
- Support school libraries
- Give books as gifts

There's a lot more information about how to encourage children to read on our websites: **www.RaisingReaders.co.uk** and **www.JoinRaisingReaders.com**.

Thank you for reading.

www.ingramcontent.com/pod-product-compliance
Lightning Source LLC
LaVergne TN
LVHW041620060526
838200LV00040B/1363